Escapade

Books by Kasey Michaels

Indiscreet
Escapade

Callie shook her head, dismissing his words even as she rejected the recurring and increasingly unsettling thought that Simon might be rethinking his plans for her. "You're deliberately not understanding me, aren't you, Simon? I suppose I shall just have to say this baldly. I want you to teach me how to attract a man, how to capture a man like Noel Kinsey. Is that so difficult to understand? Or do you want your mother to instruct me?"

Simon held up his hands in front of him, signaling surrender. "All right, all right, I'll do it. Dear God, help me. I'll do it."

"Good!" Callie exclaimed, feeling supremely satisfied. "When shall we begin?"

Simon sighed, looking at her as she rather childishly wriggled where she sat, smiling triumphantly, wonderfully, alluringly unaware of her exceedingly formidable beauty. "I think we already have, brat," he said dully, so that she frowned in confusion. "For my sins, I think we already have."

∽◌∾

"Kasey Michaels creates characters who stick with you long after her wonderful stories are told. Her books are always on my nightstand."

—**Kay Hooper**, bestselling author of *After Caroline*

Please turn the page for more raves for Kasey Michaels and her previous romance, Indiscreet...

Escapade

KASEY MICHAELS

WARNER BOOKS

A Time Warner Company

WARNER BOOKS EDITION

Copyright © 1999 by Kasey Michaels
All rights reserved.

Cover design by Diane Luger
Cover illustration by Franco Accornero
Handlettering by David Gatti

Warner Books, Inc.
1271 Avenue of the Americas
New York, NY 10020

Visit our Web site at
www.warnerbooks.com

W A Time Warner Company

Printed in the United States of America

First Printing: August 1999

10 9 8 7 6 5 4 3 2 1

To Mary McBride, whose spirit soars free
as the eagle's;

To Leslie LaFoy, whose X-ray vision slices
through steel walls;

To Kay Hooper, who can leap obstacles in
a single bound;

And to Fayrene Preston, whose loving heart
sees the Superman in us all.

For what do we live,
but to make sport for our neighbours,
and laugh at them in our turn?

—Jane Austen

Escapade

Book One
A Dainty
Entertainment . . .

Tweedledum and Tweedledee
Agreed to have a battle;
For Tweedledum said Tweedledee
Had spoilt his nice new rattle.

—Charles Lutwidge Dodgson

He was a handsome, well-shaped man:
very good company, and of a very
ready and pleasant smooth wit.

—John Aubrey

Chapter One

Simon Roxbury, Viscount Brockton, put his hat upon his head and gave it a smart tap, setting it at its usual rakish angle, and stood on the deserted flagway, surveying his surroundings. He took a deep breath of the damp, dripping London air that promised a heavy rain before morning, lifting his head so that his face was revealed by the flambeaux on either side of the door to the gaming hell he'd quit a moment earlier.

Physically, His Lordship was a tall man who cast a long shadow. Strong, well built, and devilishly handsome into the bargain. His proud mother could boast of her only son's remarkable sherry-colored eyes and his flattering mane of darkest brown hair that had a simply delectable way of waving about his forehead and neck. His sideburns were the private envy of many of his acquaintance.

Added to his physical attributes was his wit—his rather sardonic wit—his generous fortune, his impeccable lineage and breeding. In short, the man could safely be termed as nearly perfect. Or he would be, according to a majority of the debutantes and their ambitious mamas who frequented the London Season, if only he were more interested in the wondrous institution of marriage. Which he most assuredly was not, and didn't plan to be so for many years to come.

Still, even considering his stubborn reluctance to make some simpering miss the happiest creature in the world, Viscount Brockton remained a prime physical specimen as he stood waiting for his coach to pull up to the curb. It had only just gone three, and he'd left his two good friends behind him to gamble the night away. For himself, he had been more than ready to quit the hell, his objective for the evening accomplished. While his mission could be begun in an evening, it couldn't be settled in that same short time span.

But that didn't matter. He was in no hurry.

This was another of Simon Roxbury's commendable attributes. He was a patient man. So patient, in fact, that he only smiled as his coachman pulled to the curb and the groom jumped down to help His Lordship with the door, apologizing for not having arrived sooner. There had been a small problem with the brake of the coach, the groom told him.

"A little bit of mizzle won't melt me," the viscount assured the sleepy-eyed groom, then mounted the steps the man had pulled down and launched himself forward, into the interior of his coach . . . where he abruptly found himself face-to-face with a loaded pistol.

"Sit down, sir, and tell your coachman to drive on," the dark shape behind the pistol ordered in a gruff but still unmistakably female whisper.

Simon turned his head, looking back out the door to where

the groom stood not five feet away, oblivious to his predicament.

"Don't do it, I warn you, or I'll blow a hole straight through your head and laugh as your brains splatter all over this coach."

"What an unpalatable image," Simon remarked quietly, his mind already dismissing the possibility of being shot in order to concentrate on *not* being shot.

He could probably let go of his two-handed grip on either side of the doorway to the coach, propelling himself backward onto the flagway as the bullet went whizzing harmlessly over his head and straight into the door of the gaming hell he had so recently vacated. Probably. But, as the pistol was rather heavy, and its owner noticeably nervous as she struggled to hold it with both hands, he could also end up being shot dead before he hit the ground.

"Very well," he said quietly, so that the groom would not hear him and investigate. "I'll sit down now, if you'll withdraw that evil-looking toy a bit, madam?"

"It's not a toy, and I would prefer you did not call me madam, for I am no woman, sir," his captor responded, as he levered himself into his seat across from her and the door closed behind him, locking them together in the darkness. "Now, order your coachman to drive on."

"Of course you're not a woman," Simon agreed as affably as possible. It was always best, he believed, to humor lunatics—at least until they were disarmed. "How could I be so blind? You're a regular brute of a fellow, aren't you, at least in your heart and spirit? Pity that you've been cursed with so much of the feminine sex about you. And the voice and language of a well-bred female to boot. Yes, a man might be forgiven for believing you to be a female, although I don't believe I, myself, can remember too many proper young misses with a penchant for pistols. Such a shame. If you're a penniless second son embarked on a life of crime, I imagine being constantly mistaken for a female must prove no end of sorrow to you."

"Your death would give me no sorrow at all," she said, even as he noticed that his assailant's clog-clad feet did not quite touch the floor of the coach.

Cheeky little brat! he thought, longing to reach across the space dividing them, snatch up the pistol, and then tan the infant's backside with it. He could disarm her in an instant, less than an instant. All he had to do was remain passive, keep his smile intact, and then he could—*click*.

Simon's smile never wavered, even as his plan changed the moment he heard the pistol being cocked. "Oh, dear, you're going to be fractious, aren't you? Isn't it time all incorrigible young children were home and tucked up in their cots?"

"I said," his captor repeated, ignoring his insult, "order your coachman to drive on. And wipe that odious, condescending grin off your face, if you please. This is a serious business."

"Oh, yes, quite. I can certainly see that," Simon agreed. He weighed the possibility that he was about to have a rather large hole blown in him by a perfect stranger against the curiosity he felt concerning the reason behind this assault. Curiosity, which had been leading from the moment this little adventure had left the gate, won by several lengths. "Very well, my fine young brigand, I'll do as you ask. But only because I am amused—for the moment."

He leaned forward, causing the "young brigand" to shift quickly to the corner of her seat—the pistol still cocked and pointing in his direction—and opened the small door giving access to the coaching box. "Hardwick," he called out sharply, "you and I will be having words on the morrow concerning the depth of the devotion in which you hold your esteemed employer. I believe, you must understand, that a certain lack of vigilance on your part may have served to land that employer in an exceedingly undesirable position."

"Beggin' yer pardon, m'lord?" Hardwick asked, his florid face appearing in the small boxy opening in the roof of the coach. "Oi don't know wot yer talkin' about, m'lord, by the 'oly, I don't. Oi've jist been sittin' 'ere as it was comin' on ter mizzle, waitin' on yer, loik always. Oh, and fixin' the brake, o'course."

"That's reassuring, Hardwick," His Lordship responded genially, slanting a look toward his captor, who was now no more than three almost effortlessly breached feet away from him. The pistol, a mere two. And easily grabbed—if he was still so inclined. He was not. The pistol was cocked, and the chances of one of the pair of them being shot quite dead were high. Daring was one thing, redbrick stupid was quite another. "Otherwise, Hardwick, my good man," he continued after a pregnant pause, "I might be forced to believe you to be disloyal."

"Would you stop prosing on like some vacant-headed ninny and just *tell* him!" the intruder whispered fiercely, waving her pistol, rather wildly Simon thought.

"Patience, my dear, patience. I thought you might wish to listen to Hardwick talk. You hear how he drops his 'aitches'? You might want to practice that, yes, if you plan to make a habit out of holding up coaches?" As his captor growled low in her throat, he again mentally measured the distance between himself and the barrel of the pistol. No. It really was too much of a gamble. "Oh, very well. I was just trying to help. No need to get your back up. Now, do you have a particular destination in mind, or will I be forced to bother dear, obtuse Hardwick a second time?"

"Order him to drive toward Hampstead Heath. There's an inn there, the Green Man. Do you know it?"

"Hampstead Heath? Or, as Hardwick would say, 'ampstead 'eath? The aitches again, remember? That I do, and the Green Man as well. Know where they both are, I mean. And green I would be, indeed, to venture anywhere near that den of thieves after dark. Can't you think of some place closer to town?" Simon sighed theatrically. "Ah—there you go, waving that pistol again. Oh, very well. Hardwick—" he called out, "to the Green Man, my good fellow. And make haste. I've a sudden urge to be relieved of any worldly possessions I might have upon my person."

He then sat back against the squabs once more, crossed one leg over the other and both hands across his chest as the coach moved off over the cobblestones. He grinned, feeling rather wicked. " 'appy now, my dear?"

"Immensely so, my lord, if you must know," his kidnapper replied in a rather appealingly husky yet wonderfully feminine voice, one that was much more interesting than her purposely gruff whisper. Had he met her somewhere in Society? Danced with her? Supped with her? Insulted her in some way? He thought not. That voice was much too singular to have been forgotten. "Now, just sit there and be good," she ordered tightly, then said nothing more for a long time—until Hardwick had driven them free of the city, as a matter of fact.

Simon also kept his own counsel, although his mind was far from quiet. He was wondering, as it happened, how on earth he would ever live down being robbed by a mere girl if the news were ever to become public knowledge. A gentleman did, after all, have his reputation to consider.

Besides, it was late, and he was mightily fatigued, and possibly even bored. No, he was most definitely bored. This realization of his rather incomprehensible reaction to the grave danger he might be in was enough to keep him awake for a little while. But, after a bit, surprised at himself as he was, the gentle movement of his well-sprung coach actually lulled him into a light slumber.

He may even have snored.

"Aren't you in the least interested in why I have abducted you?" she asked at last, chagrin evident in her tone, anger more than evident in the force behind her hard kick to his shin.

"Truth be told, not particularly," the viscount answered honestly, yawning widely as he pushed himself up from the comfortable slouch he had slid into during his nap. He had been gambling and drinking rather deep for several hours, and now yearned more for his bed than he did for information. "But I rest easy in the knowledge that you will tell me everything I need to know in your own good time. That will be soon, won't it? I'm for bed, you understand, scintillating as your company has been this past half hour or more."

"God, but you're insufferable!" She directed another kick at him. "I should shoot you now, just on general principles."

Simon resisted the impulse to rub at his now twice-insulted shin, for clogs were a considerable weapon. But the girl was beginning to wear on his nerves. "I'd be more comfortable if yours was a unique statement," he said, always at his most excruciatingly polite when he was most vexed. "However, since it is not, I suppose I should spend the next few days in deep reflection, considering how I have so abused my fellow man—and woman—as to have been termed insufferable so often, by so many. Is there perhaps an organized group of you? Do you hold meetings? Keep minutes of all that is discussed? I could peruse them, learn to pinpoint my more gross failings—if I am not shot dead before sunrise, of course?"

"Oh, just *shut . . . up!*"

"So sorry," he apologized insincerely, now wondering how much longer the young woman could hold on to the cocked pistol without it going off. "Consider me a monk, sworn to a vow of silence."

"If I believed that, I'd believe anything, and I don't believe I believe that," his captor shot back with what he had to admit was complicated candor. A candor that made the potentially dangerous brat all the more interesting to him.

The whole time he had spoken and, indeed, for much of the time he'd spent in the coach, Simon had been cursing the darkness that kept his captor's face and form hidden from him. He had, however, at least been able to deduce that she was not at all tall, fairly slim—and that she smelled of lavender water and horse. Not an entirely unpleasant combination. Her accent was cultured, educated. She had only a hint of the country miss about her—one blessed with any number of brothers who had taught her manners, words, and expressions she should not know. This also confused him. Not being in the habit of seducing innocent country maids, he could think of no innocent young woman who would wish him injury or death.

Which left him with the notion, not too odd, that he was being driven into the countryside to be handed over to yet more kidnappers who would then solicit a ransom from his sure to be appalled mother, the Viscountess Brockton. His mother would be horrified, frightened, and as dependably scatterbrained as was her custom. This, unfortunately, would probably also mean that he would be at the mercy of his captors for at least a week before the viscountess recalled the location of the Roxbury family solicitors and gained access to the funds required to free him.

Of course, that also meant he would miss Lady Bessingham's bound-to-be crushingly boring rout scheduled for the next evening, which couldn't be considered entirely a bad thing.

His captor pushed aside a corner of the leather curtain and peeked out into the countryside, just now beginning to grow light with the coming of yet another damp English dawn. She let the shade fall back into place. "We're nearly at our destination, so I suppose it is time I got on with this."

"Got on with this?" Simon repeated, a small part of him at last beginning to take the evening's adventure seriously. "Would that mean that you're going to hand me over to more kidnappers, or that you are simply going to shoot me and run off with my coach? Be gentle with Hardwick and the groom, I beg you. They may put up a slight protest in concern for their master, and I wouldn't wish them injured in any way."

"Kidnappers?" The girl's tone was incredulous, and Simon exercised his jaw muscles, wishing he had exercised them less a moment earlier. Clearly the girl had not considered kidnapping, or ransom. Had he now put that idea into her head? And was that idea better or worse than the one that had instigated his abduction? "Good God, man, I wouldn't want you in my company above another ten minutes. Why on earth would I want to hold you for ransom?"

"Then you do plan to shoot me," Simon said, his relaxed pose belying the fact that he was fully prepared to wrench the pistol from her bound-to-be-tired grasp. "But you hadn't planned to do that just on general principles, if I remember correctly. Which means you have a definite reason for this small travesty. Would it be too much if I were to ask you to explain yourself?"

The pistol remained steadily pointed at his chest, perhaps even a bit more steadily than it had this past thirty minutes or more. "At last you're interested? I had begun to think you hadn't a brain in your handsome skull for anything more than how best to fuzz a card!"

Simon grinned, relaxing once more. Clearly the chit wanted to talk much more than she wished to shoot. "My handsome skull? Oh, you do flatter me, madam. Please go on. But what's this about fuzzing cards? I assure you, madam, that Viscount Brockton is known for many vices, but cheating at cards is not amongst them."

He watched as the pistol drooped slightly, then was righted. "Viscount Brockton? What the devil are you talking about? Who is Viscount Brockton?"

"Uh-oh," Simon said, smiling as the dawn broke over his predicament, if not the world at large—and definitely not over his companion's confused head. "Do I detect a small problem here, young lady? A trifling complication, perhaps? Yes, I believe so. Please allow me to introduce myself."

He held out his hand, not for a moment believing he was about to have the pistol placed in it. "I am Simon Roxbury, Viscount Brockton, of Sussex and Portland Place—and various and sundry other places in between which I will not bore you with at the moment. Now, your turn. Who did you think I was?"

But his captor didn't appear to be listening. Instead, she was muttering something that sounded much like, "Of all the cork-brained, numskulled, *idiotic*—how could I have been so wrong? The crest was his, I could have sworn it!"

"The crest?" Simon interrupted, preferring the young lady more focused on the moment at hand, and the pistol in her hand. One never knew what could happen to an untended firearm, after all. "Are you perhaps referring to the decoration on the doors of my coach? It cost me a pretty penny, to tell you the truth, but if you're going to ride about town allowing your equipage to brag of your consequence, it wouldn't do to have shoddy paintwork, don't you agree?"

He sighed deeply, wishing his friends Bones and Armand could be with him, just to watch the fun, and then pushed on, more than happy to drive his captor to further distress. "It's wretchedly expensive, you understand, this business of impressing one's acquaintance with such ostentatious fripperies, but it must be done. My mother insisted upon it."

"I don't see how I . . . how could I have—*what?* Are you talking to me? *Why* are you talking to me? God's teeth, but you talk too much! Can't you see I'm having a problem here?"

"Indeed, yes. You are having a problem. *We* are having a problem as a matter of fact. Both of us. But force yourself to concentrate for a moment, my dear brigand, if you can," Simon said affably, unable to withhold a smile at the brat's plight. "Or, as I believe I understand what has transpired here this night, you might allow me to explain our predicament?"

She remained dumb, and distracted, and Simon leapt into the breach. "Certainly," he said, pushing on just as if she had asked him to, "I'd be delighted. You came to Curzon Street this evening in search of someone—some awful, terrible person who has done you or one you love a considerable injury, possibly pertaining to card-playing?—and then crawled into entirely the wrong coach. I can understand that, what with the dark, and the rain and all. Do I have the series of events correct so far? Although I still believe I'll be having a small talk with Hardwick, who has proven to be a weak link in the impenetrable defense I incorrectly assumed I had built against being brought face-to-face with an infant brandishing a loaded pistol. And just think of the wear and tear on my horses, being forced on this journey so late at night! Why, I do believe I should be much angrier than I am. Oh, yes. Yes, indeed. I really should be angry. Perhaps even incensed. Am I dressed correctly for incensed, do you think? Perhaps if I were all in black—"

"Would you *stop*! God's teeth, but you're making my head ache!" The pistol sagged again, now being supported by just a single small hand, as the other was involved in rubbing at the young woman's temples. "I planned, and planned, and screwed my courage up to the sticking point—and for what? To end up being talked to death by this idiot? Oh, *now* what do I do?"

Simon leaned forward, only slightly, just enough to be faintly intimate, not enough to be threatening. "If I could brook a suggestion," he said kindly, "I would say you might begin by lowering your weapon?"

The cocked pistol was once more held between both hands, once more directed at his heart. "I don't think so, my lord," the young woman said cuttingly—and still in that so strangely appealing husky voice that hinted of darkened bedrooms and earthly delights, even while speaking of blood and mayhem. And why would he be thinking of such things at a moment like this? He really would have to examine his character, for it must surely be flawed. Either that, or he had developed a sense of the ridiculous that he hadn't known he possessed. Either way, he was, frankly, enjoying himself very much.

But the brat was speaking again. "I definitely will not give you my pistol. I've no great desire to end this night hauled away to the gaolhouse and clapped up in irons."

"Clapped in irons? Oh, foul, foul! As if a gentleman would do such a thing!" Moving very carefully, Simon reached to his right and dropped the shade, letting in the first light of dawn so that it could reveal the earnestness of his expression. "There has been no crime committed, I assure you. Why, I often end my evenings by ordering my coachman to take me for a relaxing drive into the countryside. Truly."

"Don't be nice to me," his captor shot back angrily. "I don't like you even a little bit, and I certainly don't trust you. You're too jolly by half, and, besides, I think you're making fun of me."

Simon's chuckle was deep, coming from low in his throat. "Making fun of you, my dear? Why, of course I am. Bloody hell, madam, what else is there for me to do—except this!"

The pistol was in his hand a moment later, probably before his former captor could even register his intent—a happy surprise of concentration and calculated movement that surely would give Simon reason to compliment himself later, once he was shed of the girl.

"Now," he said as the young woman cowered against the squabs, doubtless in fear for her life—so that he considerately uncocked and pocketed the pistol—"perhaps you'll allow me to have a slight verbal exchange with Hardwick concerning our destination. Yes? I thought so."

He leaned forward and opened the small door, all the while keeping his interested gaze on the young woman's face. As he ordered Hardwick to turn the coach around, he conducted a cursory inventory. Figure, small and slim beneath a too-large cape and atrocious leggings and crude clogs. Face, unidentifiable beneath the slouch hat and dramatic black-silk cloth tied around the mouth and nose. Eyes—the only part truly visible—a lovely, wide, rather frightened green.

He'd always had a weakness for green eyes.

"Ah, that's better," Simon said once he had done speaking with his coachman, who had muttered a few none-too-inspiring words about lordships who drink too deep before calling the horses to a halt, then beginning to turn the coach. "Now, to pass the time on our ride back to London, perhaps you'll be so kind as to tell me a small story?"

She pulled the silk scarf higher on her face, clearly wishing to hide her eyes, and failing. She was unable to do so and still see him, or to keep him from noticing that her brows, although dark, hinted of a hair color no deeper than chestnut—which went quite well with her remarkably clear, milky skin. "There's nothing to tell, my lord," she said, her tone grudging, and not a little angry. "I thought you were someone else. Either let me go or turn me over to the Watch when we get back to the city. I owe you no explanations."

"I hesitate to bring this to your attention, but anyone would think you were still holding the pistol, love. But let's be pleasant, shall we?" Simon opened a small door at the side of the coach and revealed a space that held a silver decanter and a half dozen small glasses. "Would you care for some brandy? There's always an unwelcome chill at dawn, don't you agree?"

When she refused to speak, Simon shrugged, uncapped the decanter and poured three fingers of brandy into one of the glasses. He then threw it back, allowing his eyes to close for a moment as the liquid heat ran down his throat, warmed his belly. No wonder his mother so favored the drink, although he, himself, usually shunned it in favor of his beloved champagne. "Ah, superb. A name, fair lady," he said quickly, skewering her with his eyes. "Just give me a name, and we'll call quits to this entire affair. No Watch, no magistrates, no gaol. Just a name—and your freedom. Whisper it, if you wish."

The small figure grew a full inch as her back went stiff and straight against the squabs. "I would die before I gave you my name, sir!"

"Good God, girl, what would I do with *your* name?" Simon asked, enjoying the young woman's daring high dudgeon in the face of total ruin. It would be easy enough to ferret out that information later—as he didn't plan on allowing her to disappear from his life quite yet. But, for the moment, another name interested him more. "I want the identity of the man for whom you planned a murder most foul this evening. After all, I might wish to warn him. Then again, if he really is a cardsharper, I might just wish to stand back and enjoy the show. I'm a well-loved man, and with a reasonably good heart, or so I'm told, but I am not without my small vices."

She spread her hands as if in surrender, saying, "If it will shut you up, I'll be more than happy to tell you. His name is Noel Kinsey, the Earl of Filton, and a more odious, horrible, heartless—"

"Vile, despicable, *dangerous* man would be difficult to find," Simon interrupted, shocked to his toes although he would not allow this young girl to know it. "Are you out of your infinitesimal mind? I could have had your weapon anytime I wanted. Filton would have not only had it, he would have used it on you in a heartbeat. I begin to think you'd be safer if I turned you over to the Watch, truly I do. Or I could order Hardwick to drive us past Bethlehem Hospital and we could have you fitted with your very own strait-waistcoat. You are most definitely quite mad."

"Your opinion means less than nothing to me, my lord," the infuriating girl announced even as—showing herself to be much more resourceful than he had given her credit for being—she pulled a second pistol from beneath that damned cape. The small sound that followed told him that the pistol had been cocked. "Now, my lord, if you'll consider my apology already rendered, I believe it is time we said good night."

And then, perhaps simply to reinforce his rueful conclusion that he had been outmaneuvered, perhaps because she seriously wished to do him an injury without having to resort to actually pulling the trigger of her pistol, she kicked out with one leg, sharp and hard, sending a damnable heavy clog winging straight at his head.

Chaos instantly reigned supreme inside the coach.

Simon, acting more from a sudden anger than any attack of common sense, caught the clog before it could do any harm and made a move toward the girl as she reached over to open the off door of the coach. The cocked pistol fired as she struggled to depress the handle, nearly taking his left ear as the ball whizzed past him and plowed into the rear of the coach. Hardwick gave a shout and yanked on the reins, causing the tired, already–slow-moving team to halt even as the young woman threw open the door and launched herself out of the coach.

His ears ringing from the report of the pistol, his throat clogged with blue smoke and the stench of gunpowder, Simon reacted a full second slower than usual. He bounded out of the coach only in time to observe the young woman, now minus both clogs, effortlessly vaulting onto the back of one of two horses that obviously had been following close behind the coach. With a yell to the person holding the reins to "follow me!" she was gone.

As exits went, this one was fairly dramatic, even if Simon did not consider the fact that the damned, stocking-clad female had mounted the horse without bothering to use the stirrups, landing astride on its back, and all with a fluid grace many of his male acquaintance would envy.

As it was, all he could do was watch as the two horses wheeled and sped away. He then approached his groom, who was still wiping sleep from his eyes as he cowered in the boot, and sweetly inquired of him if he hadn't thought it bloody odd that a man riding one bloody horse and leading another had been bloody following the bloody coach ever since they'd left *bloody London*?

The clogs, that had somehow ended up in Simon's hands, had gone winging into the trees lining the roadway, one following closely after the other during the course of his questioning of the footman, both shoes flung away in some heat, and with impressive force.

"Milord?" the groom exclaimed, visibly wilting under Simon's rare physical exertion, his even rarer verbal attack. "Oi thought they wuz yours, milord."

Simon pushed himself back under control. He even smiled. "Mine? Mine. Oh, I see now. *Mine*. Of course you did. Forgive me for not realizing that, seeing as how I often have two rented nags tagging along behind my coach, in the slim chance I might wish to take a ride between Curzon Street and Portland Place." He turned back to the coach. "Take me home, Hardwick, if you please," he ordered wearily, knowing that he had probably seen the last of the mysterious young woman.

It was only the discovery of a small, crumpled white handkerchief on the floor of the coach that served to cheer Viscount Brockton at all. A small white handkerchief embroidered—fairly clumsily—with the letter "C." He raised it to his nostrils to find that it smelt of lavender and horse—and bread and butter.

Still holding the handkerchief, Simon drew down all the shades and began searching the coach. He soon espied a stale crust of buttered bread wedged into a fold of the velvet squabs. He picked it up, gingerly holding it between thumb and index finger, eyeing it owlishly.

And then he smiled again, a slow, lazy smile that grew to all but split his face. He even, much to the surprise and consternation of both Hardwick and the groom, laughed aloud. Aloud, and long, and hard.

"What cheek! I've *got* to find her," he said at last, talking to himself. "She spent the time waiting to shoot me by having herself a bloody picnic." He shook his head even as he sighed contentedly, then stretched out his long legs on the facing seat and crossed them at the ankle, a gentleman once more feeling fully at his ease.

"God, now I have to find her," he mused aloud, chuckling low in his throat as he drew the handkerchief beneath his fine, aristocratic nose once more. "Armand will positively adore the chit!"

*There is a Spanish proverb, which says
justly, tell me whom you live with,
and I will tell you who you are.*

—Earl of Chesterfield

Chapter Two

Portland Place was located in a most advantageous area of London and populated by some of the *ton*'s most interesting and powerful personages. Admiral Lord Radstock resided at Number Ten and Sir Ralph Milbanke, father of the woman who had married and then cast off George Gordon, Lord Byron, resided at Number Sixty-three. And then there was, of course, Simon Roxbury, the Viscount Brockton, who, along with his widowed mother, made the elegant mansion at Number Forty-nine his principal place of residence during the Season.

There were certain drawbacks to Portland Place at the moment, thanks to the Prince Regent's penchant for building, and also thanks to the prodigiously intricate dreams of his personal architect. John Nash had taken over the construction of Park Crescent, a project to the north of Portland Place that had been begun and then abandoned when its original builder had broken ground, then promptly gone bankrupt.

For nearly a half dozen years the view to the north had been one of mounds of dirt and rubble bordered by a lovely expanse of open land. But now the area had been ambitiously renamed Regent's Park and, if Prinny had his way, the entire area would soon cast Hyde Park into shame.

Soon. Anytime now. Except that "anytime now" had stretched into months, into years, and the view to the north of Portland Place remained less than heartening. But the address was still impressive, the massive private residences definitely so. The Brockton mansion was its jewel.

This was a rather insular world. The pampered ladies and gentlemen who lived in Portland Place would scarcely ever be found more than a few blocks from the area of London known as Mayfair. They drove out to Hyde Park and Bond Street and to visit other fashionable folk at their equally fashionable residences. In other words, although he had most definitely *seen* Westminster Bridge from a distance, Lord Brockton had seldom found reason actually to cross over the thing to the other side of the Thames.

If he had, he might have driven his fine team along Westminster Bridge Road, and eastward, to Horsemonger Lane, home of Horsemonger Lane Gaol. He would find the area a fine place to visit if he was of a mind to view a hanging or see residences that someone such as he would not deem fit for stables.

It was there, in one of those tumbledown houses only a scant few miles and yet a world away from the gleaming palace Simon Roxbury called home, that one Miss Caledonia Johnston could be found. She paced the bare boards of what the landlord had laughingly called the "drawing room." She paced, and she cursed her own stupidity as her friend and coconspirator, Lester Plum, variously watched her progress and munched on a street vendor's hot cross bun.

"You did your possible, Callie. Nobody could ask more, not that anyone asked in the first place, mind you," Lester said now, sucking on one finger after another, trying to get the last of the sweet icing into his mouth. "We'll just toddle off home now, that's what we'll do. My papa says a week in this Solomon says Good-morrow city is more than enough to damn a delicate person forever."

"That would be Sodom and Gomorrah, Lester, I believe," Callie corrected automatically, used to her friend's butchering of terms unfamiliar to him.

"Whatever. Papa also warned that it's enough to corrupt any man, yet alone a callow boy like me. And if he was to get wind that the school chum I'm visiting is actually you? That I let you talk me into tagging along with you to this pen of inquiry? Well, then there'd be the devil and all to pay and that's the truth."

"Give it up? Is that what you're saying? The devil I will, Lester Plum, no matter if you turn tail and run! And that's *den of iniquity*, you lovable idiot. London is not any of those things. It's prodigiously fine, as a matter of fact, and I shall miss it when we leave. If only we had time to go to the theater, see a play, and maybe take a look-in at one of those boxing saloons Justyn told me about, or even inspect the horses at Tatt's—"

"Now, Callie," Lester said reasonably, taking up the second bun, seeing as how his good friend showed no intention of eating. Wasting food was a sin for which Saint Peter would never be able to condemn Lester Plum! "We can't do any of that, for we have neither the time nor the blunt. This was a mad scheme from the beginning, and you know it. Coming all the way to London just to shoot a man in the leg—"

"In the *knee*, Lester," Callie interrupted heatedly. "In the knee. So that he can suffer the tortures of the damned for the rest of his miserable life, each time it's damp, each time he goes all stiff and sore and can no longer spend his evenings on the dance floor or with his legs cramped under a gaming table. I want Noel Kinsey to *suffer*, Lester. Suffer! And every time it rains, each day it is cold and damp, I want to think of him and his misery, and be glad for it!"

"You're a heartless creature, Caledonia Johnston," Lester said, looking at her in obvious adoration. "And mean to the marrow, I think. I can't tell you how much I admire that in a woman. Marry me, will you?"

Callie threw back her head and laughed, as Lester had always been able to make her laugh, from the time they had been children together in Dorset. Older than she by a good three years, she was nevertheless the senior in their friendship, having found leading Lester by the nose to be as simple as doing a fine somersault downhill on a grassy slope. He was her friend, her companion, her earnest assistant and, on occasion, her willing dupe—but she loved him dearly. She really loved him, as she loved her brother, Justyn.

Blond as a summer morning, with eyes the color of the spring sky, Lester was a good half foot taller than Callie and weighed half again as much thanks to his love of good food, mediocre food, even victuals as poor as those two buns he had just downed as if they had been drizzled with the finest ambrosia. He was without guile, without selfishness, and possessed such a fine, giving heart. He was her puppy dog, her pet pig, the soft, comforting blanket she'd carried well into her fifth year, the friend of a lifetime.

So why did she long to box his ears?

"Lester," she began carefully, as if explaining sums to a toddler, "we went to the trouble to successfully lie to your father, to lie to my father—a lamentably easy thing to do with both the former and the latter, but still necessary. We saved for months to pay for our lodgings in this hovel. We rode as outside passengers on the stage for three days and two nights— which was jolly good fun until it began to rain. We found Noel Kinsey, followed him from his residence. Everything was working just as we'd planned."

"Until you crawled into entirely the wrong coach," Lester pointed out brightly if not too brilliantly, once more licking his fingers, then wiping them on his neckcloth. Lester never wasted food, but he did leave evidence of all he ate on his clothing.

Callie spread her hands wide, reluctantly nodding her agreement with her friend's last statement. "All right, all right. So we made *one* small miscalculation."

"*We* made one small miscalculation? Oh, I don't think so, Callie. I think I had nothing whatsoever to do with that one small miscalculation."

Callie smiled graciously, elaborately bowing to her coconspirator. "La, Mr. Plum, how very right you are, and how like me, such a poor, inferior female, to try to shift the blame onto your broad shoulders. Please, sir, do forgive me."

"Whoops, I don't like the sound of that, God's truth, I don't. You're going to hurt me now, aren't you?" Lester asked in some apprehension, pulling up one of his legs protectively and crossing his hands over his head. "I just said we'd had a bit of a problem, that's all."

"Yes, Lester. Yes, we did. We've had a bit of a problem. A single small hitch after a string of sterling successes. Is that any reason to abandon our plan? Would you shy at the first fence? Would I? I think not, Lester. I think not. And stop cowering like that, for heaven's sake—anyone would think I was going to throw this awful statue at you or something."

Lester looked at her levelly, slowly lowering his arms, coming out of his protective crouch as he regained his good humor, and his teasing air. "You just want to keep wearing those breeches, that's all," he said, then smiled brightly to prove that he was only funning. It was either that, or prepare to duck out of the way when she picked up that revolting statue perched on the table beside her and winged it at his head.

Callie didn't bother to hide her smile as she turned to look at her reflection in the cracked, dingy mirror that stood to one side of the doorway. She tilted her head to the right as she took in the sight of the tight-fitting inexpressibles Lester had eaten himself out of a half dozen years previously. So comfortable they were, so *freeing*, as were her borrowed hose and the high-top boots that made such a satisfying *click-click* against the flagway. How she adored striding long-leggedly down the streets of Solomon says Good-morrow as a man would, swinging her cane, tipping her curly-brimmed beaver to the ladies. Why, she could even spit into the gutter if the spirit took her.

She raised a hand to her throat, touching two fingers to her snowy neckcloth, then running those same fingers down over her buff waistcoat before smoothing the fold of the collar of her dark blue jacket. Lord, but she was fine! Too bad she had to suffer the indignity of binding her breasts. How unfortunate that she'd had to cut off most of her hair in order to cement her appearance as a young schoolboy off on a lark. And yet, all in all, she still would have said that there was nothing, simply nothing she'd like better than to dress in such freedom, such comfort, for the rest of her natural-born days.

She wheeled about smartly on her heels, one fist jammed onto her hip, striking a pose. "I do look famously fashionable, don't I? All the crack, that's Mr. Caleb Johnson, fit to rival Mr. Beau Brummell himself!" she pronounced, her smile pushing a single dimple into her left cheek.

"Well, you're as purse-pinched as Brummell is reported to be, I suppose, but that's the only resemblance I can see." Lester pulled a licorice whip from his pocket and drew it beneath his nose, savoring the smell as another man would the aroma of a fine cigar. "Your eyelashes are too long, you don't have the whisper of a beard, you're inches too short, and you're too round by half—at least in some places, you are," he pointed out reasonably.

"Well, thank you, Lester," Callie said, surprised to feel complimented by his words.

"Hah! Only you would think I was saying something nice, you know that? And how are you going to explain that mop on your head to your papa? Tell me that, will you? I have no idea how, seeing as how you told him I was taking you to your Aunt Mary Louise's for a week. Even your papa won't believe your Aunt Mary Louise would have had you shorn like a sheep. But, as long as we've come this far, and you've whacked off your hair and all of that, I suppose we can give putting a hole in the man one more try. What did you have in mind?"

Callie launched herself at Lester, squealing and falling on his neck, nearly causing him to lose his grip on the licorice whip, so that he cried out in protest. "Oh, you're the best of good friends!" she told him, kissing him on both cheeks, then settled in next to him on the lumpy couch. "Now, the way I see it is, if we followed him once, we can follow him again. Yes? But this time we might be well to do our hunting in the daylight, so as to not repeat last night's mistake."

Lester took a bite of licorice and spoke around it. "Wasn't *my* mistake, like I've been trying to tell you. *Take the horses and wait around the corner, Lester.* Did that. *Follow the coach I crawl into, Lester. It'll be easy as tumbling off a log, Lester.* Believed that, too, for m'sins. And then I damned near wet myself when the coach turned around when we weren't halfway to the Green Man, and I heard the bark of that pistol! We're just lucky you didn't kill the fellow."

"I should have." Callie muttered the words into her neck-cloth as she crossed her arms over her midsection. "I vow to you, Lester, Viscount Brockton is the most condescending, maddening, *talkative* creature it has ever been my misfortune to kidnap. And he had the gall to *laugh* at me, you know. That was the worst of it."

"Well, if it makes you feel at all better, I doubt he laughed much when you kicked that heavy clog at him, then shot him."

"I did *not* shoot him, Lester," Callie gritted out from between clenched teeth. "If I had shot him, he wouldn't have been able to hop out of the coach so quickly. I swear I can still feel his hot breath on the back of my neck, even now that we are safely here again."

"But he knows you're a woman."

Callie shifted her green gaze to the window as if expecting to see that huge black coach bearing the Roxbury crest appearing on the street outside, then deliberately banished the notion from her brain. "He put forth that suspicion, yes. But he can't know for sure, now can he?"

"And he knows you're hell-bent to put a hole in Noel Kinsey."

Callie shot a look at Lester from beneath her slitted eyelids, deciding that her friend was being entirely too astute this morning for a man who had admitted from his own mouth that he had nearly wet himself not six hours earlier. "So? You are trying to make a point, aren't you? Go on."

Lester tied a precise knot in what was left of the licorice whip, then twirled it back and forth between his fingertips. "All right, Callie," he said after a moment. "I've been thinking on this for a while. If this Viscount Brockton were to have taken umbrage at being kidnapped, at being shot at, say, he might just want to come looking for the person who kidnapped him and shot at him. Isn't that possible?"

Callie wet her suddenly dry lips with the tip of her tongue, remembering her last sight of Simon Roxbury, her last glimpse of his handsome face wiped of its lazy, superior smile. "Yes. It's entirely possible that he might want to find that person, perhaps even punish that person. However, as he's not so much as seen my face, and since I won't be making the same mistake twice and putting myself within a mile of His Obnoxious Lordship, I can't see as he presents a problem."

Lester held up a finger as if about to point out the flaw in that logic, then did. "And that's just the thing, Callie," he announced, squirming on the lumpy cushions, turning sideways so that he could look at her more closely as he spoke. "If *I* were the Viscount Brockton, and I wanted to find someone who said they wanted to shoot Noel Kinsey—well, I'd just keep myself close as sticking plaster to that same Noel Kinsey and wait for a too-short, too-female-looking gentleman and her likewise male companion to appear."

He sat back against the cushions once more, crossing his legs at the ankle, and popped the knot of licorice into his mouth. "That's what I'd do, Callie."

"Damn," Callie breathed out quietly. "Damn, damn, *damn*."

"I'm right, aren't I?" Lester sounded entirely too pleased with himself to suit Callie, who hopped to her feet and began pacing once again. "Oh, yes. I'm right. I can tell, Callie, because I think I can see smoke coming out your ears. Well, isn't this the day! I've actually thought of something you haven't. And Papa says you lead me around by the nose. Ha—a fine lot *he* knows!"

Callie ignored Lester as her mind turned over this new problem, the unlooked-for complication brought to her courtesy of the insufferably smug and arrogant Simon Roxbury. She hadn't liked the man from the first moment he'd climbed into the coach and looked at her as if she, and her pistol, were nothing more than an immense joke that amused him at first, then quickly bored him to flinders.

Now he was throwing a spanner into the finer workings of her plan to punish that miserable cad, Noel Kinsey. Wasn't that just like the man?

"We won't have to worry about him recognizing the horses we've hired for the week," she said at last, thinking out loud. "It was too dark for him to see either of them clearly, or you for that matter, except to know that you were, as you said, a man. I could go back to being a girl to throw him off the scent, I suppose, except that we have little money, I've brought none of my wardrobe here with me from Dorset, and he'll probably be looking for a small, thin female, or for two gentlemen. So, as there's nothing else for it, I'll keep on being a green-as-grass youth here from the country for his first visit to the Metropolis, and not the clog-clad servant I was last night. We'll carry guidebooks, saunter up and down the streets of Mayfair, and keep an eye open for Kinsey. We will have to make *one* small alteration to our appearance, however, to put him entirely off the scent. That will be easy enough once I explain it to you, dearest Lester. But we've only got three days left to us. We'll have to work quickly."

"You're getting too wild, Callie," Lester pointed out reasonably. "We can't just shoot the man as he struts down Bond Street."

Callie waved away his protests. "We won't have to. I've already decided what we'll do when we find him. Trust me, Lester, we'll have the job done and be back on the stagecoach and on our way home before the week is out, leaving Viscount Brockton to hunt mare's nests for the next fortnight. I promise you!" She grinned at her friend. "Well, Lester? What do you have to add to that?"

"I don't know, Callie," he answered honestly. "A prayer, perhaps?"

The statue shattered against the wall a good six inches above his head. Lester Plum was getting very good at ducking, and Callie's heart hadn't really been in the throw. Within ten minutes, however, after Callie had explained that "one small alteration" in her hastily reworked plan to take to the flagways of Mayfair in broad daylight in search of Kinsey, Lester Plum was wishing he'd just let the dratted thing hit him. At least then he would have been put out of his misery.

"Are you going to eat that honey bun, Simon, or simply allow it to grow stale sitting there?"

Simon lowered his newspaper, peered down the long table at the woman occupying the seat at the opposite end. He then looked to the honey bun in front of him and, with a quick, rearranging shake of the pages, lifted the newspaper in front of his face once more. "You can't have it, Mother. You made me promise, remember?"

"Oh, if that doesn't beat the Dutch! You would have forgotten my birthday last year if I hadn't pinned a note to Silsby so that you'd see it when he shaved you. You forgot you'd been invited to your Great-aunt Alice's for dinner a fortnight ago. I had to spend a dashed-dull quarter hour listening to her tell me that she believed I had murdered you, seeing as how none of our relatives has laid eyes on you in ages and ages. But say one stupid thing to you, utter a single meaningless phrase in a moment of weakness, and *that* you have embroidered on your brain. I've nursed a snake at my bosom, I vow I have."

Simon sighed and lowered the paper once more, this time placing it on the table, so that Roberts, the footman in attendance, scurried forward quickly and neatly refolded it for his master. "I may be a snake, Mother, but it was not your bosom that nursed me. You never would have taken time away from your horses and the card table for such domestic chores," Simon said coolly, then waited for the explosion.

It wasn't long in coming. The Viscountess Brockton pushed back her chair and rose to her considerably intimidating height of nearly six feet and gave out with a trumpeting *"Harrumph!"* She then charged down the length of the table, her striped lavender and blushing pink dressing gown billowing out behind her substantial body like a man-o'-war in full sail, and nearly succeeded in grabbing up the honey bun before Simon had time to swing it, plate and all, out of her reach.

"Ungrateful wretch!" she sputtered, collapsing into the quickly pulled-out chair to Simon's right. The Brockton footmen were all very light on their feet, which was a necessity of employment in this rather unique household, and Roberts was far and away the best of the lot. She plopped her plump elbows on the table and her double chin in her hands as she smiled somewhat sloppily at her dear son, her only child, her most perfect production. "Explain to me again, dear boy, why on earth I am forced to sit at quite the opposite end of this ridiculously long table."

Simon leaned over and kissed his mother's forehead. "So that I don't starve to death, Mother," he reminded her, then gave in and placed the plate in front of her. "Just remember tonight as Kathleen has her far-from-dainty foot shoved against your spine, trying to stuff you into your corset, that this wasn't my idea."

"Ummm . . . still warm," the viscountess fairly purred around her first bite of sweet honey bun. "If I didn't have to marry, I would toss away all my corsets and never look at another slice of dry toast, I vow it!"

Simon looked appealingly to Roberts, making a "V" of his index and middle finger. The servant quickly stepped to the sideboard and opened the airtight case holding a selection of the Viscount's finest cigars. Plucking one out and cutting off the tip with a small scissors, Roberts then positioned the cigar on a silver platter and carried it to the table, placing it in front of his employer.

After sticking the cigar in the corner of his mouth, then allowing Roberts to light it for him, Simon blew out a fine, thin stream of smoke, and said, "That's it, Mother. Turn me into a cur. Marry before the Season is out, or it's the dower house for you, woman!"

"Don't be funning me, young man," Imogene Roxbury said, plucking the cigar from between her son's fingers and taking a healthy—or unhealthy—puff on the thing. "You'll be marrying any day now, and I refuse to be the Dowager Viscountess. Dowager—what a disgusting, *aging* term. If you had any consideration for me, any true love, you would take a vow of bachelorhood."

"I have," Simon pointed out as he retrieved his cigar. "Repeatedly. You simply don't believe me."

"As I'd have to be feather-witted to do," she answered with a sniff, looking longingly at the cigar as Simon puffed on it once more. "You're rich, handsome, titled—of course you wish to be married. It's just as Miss Austen said in her lovely novel, *Pride and Prejudice.* 'It is a truth universally acknowledged, that a single man in possession of a good fortune, must be in want of a wife.' I've never been so upset as I have been since reading that silly book this past winter! You may be fighting it, but you may as well try to shout down the wind. Marry you will, marry you must, but I'll be demmed if I'll be a dowager. I'm thinking countess, at the moment, if I can find myself an earl who's willing. Countess. That has a nice ring to it, yes?"

She snatched the cigar from her son and took another satisfying puff, watching the smoke rise to the ceiling as she blew it out again. "Pity there's such a sad paucity of the bastards these days."

Simon did not bother to repress his appreciative chuckle. "Mother, you're as crude as a coachie. I'm only surprised you haven't filed your two front teeth into points, the better to whistle. Haven't you noticed that finer manners are more the thing in London Society now? The rough-and-tumble behavior of your heyday has taken a backseat to notions such as polite speech and, horror of horrors, women not drinking gin, or crossing their legs, or blowing a cloud after breakfast."

The viscountess pulled a face, even as she uncrossed her legs beneath the table. "I could kill your father for dying on me," she said, sighing. "Going through the marriage mart once was almost more than I could bear. Now, as I'm nearing fifty, and with all these namby-pamby rules at Almack's and the like, it's enough to turn me bilious. Why, in *my* day, we went to balls in our riding clothes, and thought nothing of dancing with the same man all the night long. Now—ah!—now you can't look at a man for more than three seconds without being linked with him romantically. Soon we'll be putting skirts on table legs, so as not to offend the *ladies*."

Simon looked at his mother for a long, dispassionate moment, then said, "Nearing fifty, Mother? Really. From which side, pray tell, do you approach it? Will I soon have to acknowledge you as my sister, or will we be informing the world that you carried me while you were still in leading strings yourself?"

"Ha!" Imogene exploded, leaning forward to give her son a quick, smart clap on his back. "Do you see what I mean? Say something like that to a woman of today—a *ninny* of today—and she'd fall into a swoon. Either that, or she'd descend into a sad decline it would take a diamond necklace and a trip to the Continent to cure. I'll settle for that nice fat slice of ham you've been hoarding and never planning to eat."

Simon pushed his plate toward his mother, then sat back and watched as she cut into it. His dear mother; how he loved her. Every outrageous bone in her too-tall, too-large, too-forward-by-half body. Even when she was being silly. Especially when she was being silly. Like now, having gotten it into her head that, after six years as a carefree widow, being happy as a lark in Sussex with her horses and her dogs, she felt it necessary to haul herself up to London for the Season and go husband-hunting.

She had chosen to do it by coloring her once-brown, now-graying hair a vivid blond—an unfortunate choice—and by starving herself to regain a girlish figure she'd never possessed in the first place. If she'd had her druthers, she would have simply walked up to the first man she found suitable, knocked him to the ground with one swing of her balled fist, flung him up and over her shoulder, and carried him off to the nearest church.

Simon wished she'd give up this silly notion of marriage, make a bonfire of her corsets—fed by the bottles of hair dye her maid Kathleen had been sent out to purchase on the sly—and go back to enjoying herself.

But Imogene was determined, and nothing Simon had thus far said to her had been able to convince her that she was in no fear of becoming the Dowager Viscountess, a title that seemed to be considered as several shades worse than death to the woman. What was he, a loving son, to do? Perhaps if he told her he had lately found himself quite irresistibly and romantically drawn to Armand?

"What are you smiling about?" Imogene asked, interrupting Simon's private amusement. "And why were you in so late last evening—or this morning, as is closer to being accurate? I thought you told me you and your rakish chums had planned to make an early night of it."

Simon's good mood disappeared upon hearing his mother's words. "I was, um, unavoidably detained," he said, then quickly latched on to the first thought that came into his mind. That thought had a lot to do with his last sight of his kidnapper last night as she rode away from him. "Mother—do you still ride astride when at home?"

She nodded, chewing up the last bite of sweet country ham. "Only way truly to control a spirited mount," she told him, pointing the fork at his nose. "You try riding in a skirt, Simon, with both your legs flung over the same side of the horse. To protect our femininity, you men say. Stuff and nonsense! To keep us from outshining you on the hunting field, that's why—and to keep us atop broken-in-the-wind slugs that wouldn't know a fine gallop from a gallon jug. Thank the good Lord your father didn't want to see me get my neck broken to keep my long-forgotten and never-lamented chastity intact, which is the other reason men put out for having us riding all but with our arses facing the wrong end of the horse."

She grinned widely, showing nearly all of her fine white teeth, then winked. "Now would you look at that, Simon? Roberts over there is blushing like a faint-hearted miss. Didn't think the man had ears, for all he stands there stone-faced three times each day whilst we feed our bellies."

Simon sneaked a look at the servant who, as his mother had pointed out, had turned beet red from the collar of his shirt to the roots of his shock of flaming red hair. "Another raise in your quarterly wage is in order, Roberts, I assume?"

"Yes, m'lord, if you wish it. Just until the good dear lady takes herself off home is all. If you don't mind. Makes me powerful nervous she does, sir, and that's a fact."

"You coddle the servants, Simon, even when, if you actually read those newspapers you hide behind every day, there are up to ten thousand livery servants without a place at the moment," the viscountess said, but she smiled even as she scolded him. "Well, we'll leave discussing the sad state of

England's economy since the end of the war to another time."
She then winked at her son, which caused him to roll his eyes
toward the ceiling, knowing what was coming next.

"I'm off!" Imogene announced abruptly, which caused
Roberts to leap forward quickly to catch her tumbling chair as
she stood up. It was a small competition she indulged herself
in against the footman, seeing who of the pair of them could
move the fastest. So far, the nervous Roberts was holding up
admirably, but it was still early days in their contest, and she'd
catch him napping yet.

"What do you have planned for this evening, son?" she
asked as she turned to leave the room. "That insipid party at
Lady Bessingham's, I suppose? Gad, but the woman is a dull
sort, prattling on and on about her demmed posies. I'll probably be nodding off in the middle of dinner, falling nose first
into the pudding. I wouldn't mind a relaxing drive in the
Promenade beforehand, I think, if you dare to be seen with
your outrageous mama."

Simon, who had risen along with his mother—reacting
well, although a good full beat behind Roberts—kissed her
cheek. "I would be honored, ma'am," he told her sincerely.
"My equipage and I will be outside, at your service, promptly
at five."

"And until then?" she asked, eyeing him carefully, almost
slyly. "You have the look of a man with a purpose in mind for
this afternoon, Simon. Could it be you'll be shopping for new
material for your coach seats? Pistol balls play the very devil
with velvet, or so I'm told."

"*Now* who has been overly generous with the servants,
Mother?" Simon asked, certain either Hardwick or the groom
had been speaking out of turn, and well paid for every word.

Imogene shrugged her rather impressive shoulders. "I'm a

mother. You're my only chick. I do what I must do, Simon. And I did try to get you to speak on your own, but you stubbornly refused to pick up the bait. Now, who shot at you, and why in blazes did you let him?"

Simon held out his arm to his mother and ushered her from the morning room, into the hallway, much, undoubtedly, to the relief of Roberts, who immediately collapsed in a heap against the sideboard. "You tell me what you know, and I'll supply the rest. All right?"

She nodded her agreement. "Fair enough, I suppose, as I had thought I'd have to squeeze every last bit of information out of you. I know that someone hid himself inside your coach last night while you were frequenting some low gaming hell. You lost, by the bye, not enough to hurt you but enough to be remarked upon. Halfway to the Green Man, and how I do not know, you convinced your captor to allow you to have the coach turned around, at which time there was a short scuffle, a single shot, and the brigand got away clean."

"Not quite cleanly away, Mother. I managed to gain possession of the pistol."

"As if that signifies! And don't interrupt, if you please. The miscreant bounded into the saddle of a waiting mount with the grace and artistry of a performer at Astley's Circus—although I believe I am cleaning up the language used by my informant more than a little. Shame on you, Simon. Were you foxed? Anything less than being falling-down drunk cannot be seen as an excuse for allowing a mere footpad to get the best of you."

"She kicked a clog at my head," Simon muttered angrily, then instantly wished back his words as his mother dragged him to a halt halfway down the length of the black-and-white-tile foyer and spun around to face him.

"*She?*" His mother's eyes, a startling blue that had not yet begun to fade with the years, were opened wide, her expression a ludicrous mix of incredulity and downright horror. "What sort of new playmate is this, Simon? Female brigands? My God—I wish I'd thought of it in my day. What a lark!"

"You probably would have thought of it eventually, Mother, had m'father not tamed you, then carried you off to the altar at the tender age of twelve. You see, I do remember that coming on to fifty remark. But it's not to worry. The chit was after someone else entirely, as it fell out, and apologized quite prettily for the inconvenience before she tried to brain me with her clog. She won't be bothering me again, as she's some country miss, fairly gently bred, if her speech is to be considered. She's probably halfway home by now, thanking her lucky stars she wasn't caught, and regretting the entire incident."

"After someone else entirely? Then this was not a random fit of violence, of robbery? Are you telling me that this girl—this desperate creature—was on some sort of *mission* last night?"

Simon began walking once more, which meant that his mother had to move as well, as he guided her closer to the stairs, and his freedom to get on with his plans for the afternoon. "It would appear so. And she impressed me as a young woman possessed of more than her share of determination. Rather like you, Mother, actually. Outrageous, a trifle profane, and yet oddly appealing if one was of a mind to enjoy being made a target of her rather volatile temper. And don't look at me that way. I already know I'm only teasing myself if I believe she's on her way back to Sussex or wherever, her mission not accomplished."

"You're going to chase after her, aren't you? Hunt her down? Save her from herself?" his mother asked as she ascended the first step, then turned to look down on her son, the goddess Juno in a too-ornate dressing gown.

Simon sighed. "Now, Mother—"

"Don't you 'Now, Mother' me. You're going to go after her—aren't you?"

"With a vengeance, sweet lady," he told her emphatically as the butler handed him his hat and cane. "Thank you, Emery," he said, tapping the hat down onto his head and giving his cane a quick twirl before tucking it beneath his arm. "I'm going to hunt her down with a vengeance, ma'am," he repeated from between his clenched-teeth smile, "that amazes even me. There. Are you happy now?"

"I'm not sure. And when you locate her?" Imogene pressed him, her expression now quite entirely serious, as if she had just seen something in her son that she'd always suspected and secretly feared. "What then, Simon?"

"Why, truth to tell, I haven't the foggiest notion," Simon told her in all honesty.

"I do," the viscountess murmured quietly, so quietly her son couldn't quite catch her words. "She's young, she's interesting, she talks well enough. Exasperated as he tries to be, his eyes smile even as he condemns and dismisses her. She's probably of an at least half-decently acceptable family. Damn that bun, that ham. I'm going to have to starve myself the remainder of the day, the remainder of the week. I'm running out of time now, and I know it."

"Mother, what is it?" Simon inquired with some concern as he laid a hand on her shoulder, for it wasn't like his booming, rollicking mama to be so solemn. Having the woman whisper was as unusual as would be seeing a duck fly backwards across the Serpentine. "What on earth are you mumbling about?"

Imogene tipped her head, pressing her cheek against the back of Simon's hand. "You love me, don't you, Simon? Love my outlandish ways, my somewhat daring manner, my plain speech, how I insist upon riding astride—as I'm convinced your brigand did last night?"

"I adore you and you know it—" Simon began, just to have her cut him off.

"You adore me," the viscountess repeated, sighing as if he had just disappointed her to the very depths of her soul. "Just as all those milk-and-water pusses who mince and flirt and giggle at you from behind their fans bore you past all patience. Oh, Simon, don't you see?"

Simon withdrew his hand, standing very straight. "Those stays are keeping the blood from your brain, Mother," he pronounced tightly. "I want to find this girl, this *idiot*, to save her from herself before she can get into worse trouble. She'll be hanged otherwise, and I can't have that on my conscience. That is my reason, Mother, and nothing more. If anything, I had a brief thought that I might introduce her to Armand. But that's all."

"Of course it is, Simon," Imogene agreed, her bottom lip beginning to quiver. "I'm going to lie down for a while now I think, dear, and will see you later." She turned and began slowly mounting the stairs, leaning her hand rather heavily against the smooth mahogany railing and looking almost small and frail—which was a considerable feat for one of her robust size and good health. "Perhaps Kathleen will bring me a vinaigrette, or some burnt feathers."

"Or your bottle of gin," Simon called after her angrily before whirling on his heels and leaving the house as Emery stood at attention, holding the door open for his master. "Women!" he complained to the longtime family retainer, who only nodded and said, "Absolutely, sir. Always."

A man must make his opportunity,
as oft as find it.

—Francis Bacon

Chapter Three

Simon sauntered into White's shortly before two, slowly making his way through the tables, pausing to speak to friends who called out to him. He was smooth, polite, but never wavered in his determination to end up at his usual table in front of the bow window, a happy place of prominence lately made considerably sadder by the frequent absence of Mr. Beau Brummell.

As a matter of fact, there were more than a few empty chairs at White's lately, which was unusual considering the fact that the Season had been under way for a good while, but not at all unimaginable, considering the state of the economy.

Simon knew that his mother's remark on the staggering rate of unemployment in the servant classes had a lot to do with the fact that many of his peers had been feeling the pinch that had followed hard on the heels of the final victory over Napoleon. The economy had not been helped by the past two seasons, one of the worst winters and wettest springs in more than a decade.

Spring lambs had stupidly stood in the fields with their even more ignorant mothers and died under the onslaught of spring hail, which had also ruined many a crop. Manufacturers were closing their doors, trade both into and out of England was falling at a rapid pace, and Parliament was run by fools and jabbed at by idiots.

And through it all, Prinny kept building, and the dandies, out of their desperation, kept parading and gambling too deep. The ladies of the *ton* kept up their lavish entertainments, the radicals kept haranguing, and the poor became poorer, angrier. All that was needed, in Simon's opinion, was a fiddler and a fat fellow named Nero to pound out the tune while the country burned down around all their ears.

For himself, Simon had done his possible with his estates in Sussex: cutting rents, installing the best stewards he could, and staying in almost daily contact with his people while he worked behind the scenes in London. He had quietly set up and now supported a half dozen charities. He had taken up his place in government, argued for some semblance of sanity both publicly and privately, employed as many servants as he could, and gave his lavish custom to shopkeepers, haberdashers, and vintners who were badly in need of paying patrons.

It wasn't enough, but it was all he could do. As much as he detested the degree of waste and the spendthrift ways of the London Season, he was aware that the fits and follies of London society also provided the sole support of thousands of people, from the chimney sweep to the carriage maker to the umbrella sellers in small shops along the side streets of the Metropolis.

Simon liked his friends Bartholomew Boothe and Armand Gauthier for many reasons, but uppermost in value was that they shared his concerns over the hell-bent-for-leather rush to perdition that many of their acquaintance were pursuing. Brummell, for one, was soon going to be forced out of England entirely, because of personal economic reverses brought on by reckless gaming, and because the man had a mouth that was much too glib for someone of mediocre birth and limited funds. Next to go, Simon felt sure, would be Richard Brinsley Sheridan, three parts genius, one part glorious fool, who continued to spend money long after his pockets had been emptied.

And then there was George, Simon's own dear Lord Byron, who doggedly held to his belief that the people of England, if not the *ton*, would never abandon him, even as scandal upon scandal rocked his former glory, driving him deeply into debt, pushing him headlong toward personal disaster.

It was for that reason, and to discuss both Brummell and Sheridan, that Simon was originally to have come to White's today, to sip wine with Bartholomew and Armand and consider possible ways of rescuing their friends from their own follies.

As Simon approached the table it was to see both Bones and Armand already there. He paused a moment to observe his friends without their knowledge, as they hadn't seen him as yet, and were deep in some argument.

Bartholomew Boothe was a most intriguing man to look upon, if one was of a mind to investigate the intricacies of the human skeletal structure without having to go to the bother of performing an actual autopsy: rail skinny, bony, and with a skin that was rather thin both physically and in attitude.

Of only medium height, with pale hazel eyes and unfortunately stringy brown hair, he had nothing much to show the world, and he believed that the world had even less to show him. But he was a good enough egg for all of that, Simon knew, loyal and true, if a bit of a dark cloud. He kept his friends centered, unable to go off on a potentially injurious lark without first considering all the dire consequences Bartholomew Boothe could see lurking behind every silver lining. Simon and Armand considered his bare-bones attitude and opinions much in keeping with his physical appearance, which was the reason behind his rather strange nickname.

An opposite to Bartholomew in every way, Armand Gauthier was tall, devastatingly handsome, and of a sunny disposition that made him popular with both sexes—although the gentler gender saw possibilities in his startling blue eyes, dramatic, long black hair, and impressive physique that went miles beyond the appreciation of his male friends. And, to most of the world, he was an enigma, which made Simon doubly flattered to have Armand see him not only as a valued friend, but as a confidant as well.

It was Armand who saw Simon first. Probably sensed his presence. Armand was like that. Deep. Faintly mysterious. "Simon's here, Bones," he said as Simon pulled out a chair and sat down. "Tell him what you've just been telling me."

Bones shuddered, only once, as he was an economical man in all things, then declared flatly and without preamble: "Rains every day in London, I was telling Armand. Every day. Every night. Rain's a curse."

"And there you have it, Simon," Armand Gauthier said, "the definitive answer to the question *what is rain?*—as delivered by our own good Barebones himself. It's a curse. I will only dare to speak for myself, of course, but I know that

I, for one, shall rest easier having had that explained to me. Rain's a curse."

Simon only smiled and shook his head. "Don't tease him, Armand. The poor fellow probably had a hard night of it. First the gaming hell, and a few losses, if what I saw before I left was any indication of how the fellow's luck was running. And then a ride home at dawn through yet another pouring-down rain. Is that right, Bones? You're disgruntled, and rightly so. Poor Bones. Should we fear you'll be fading into a sad decline?"

"Of the pair of you," Bones shot back, "I consider you to be far and away the worst, Simon. Armand teases openly. You grin pleasantly enough, say all the right things, then wait until I'm feeling mellow to sink your knife in to the hilt. *Yes*, I lost last night. I lost, lost, *lost*! Happy now?"

"I will confess to being rapturous, Bones, if you wish it," Simon answered calmly enough. "However, I will also remind you that I warned the pair of you against playing too deep last night. Personal amusement or profit were not the motives for the evening's entertainment, if you'll recall."

"Although you seemed to do worst of all of us, Simon, which I presume was your point," Armand put in, then looked to the still-frowning Bartholomew. "Bones—do you mean to blame your losses on our erstwhile friend?"

"Not erstwhile. I'm not that fickle. He's still m'friend," Bartholomew corrected. "Although friendship's a curse, too, if you were going to ask, Armand. Friendship, rain—they both run down the back of your neck in cold dribbles at times."

Armand shot Simon a blighting smile. "Isn't our good friend delightful? There are times I simply long to wrap him up in cotton wool to keep him safe from the world's travails.

I would then take him out from time to time, and perch him on my mantel, show him off to company when they call. Oh—and you might want to buy his dinner tonight, Simon. Mine, too, come to think of it. I actually believe I'm down a good hundred pounds thanks to your notion of what constitutes a profitable evening. I only hope you don't plan to make gaming in such private hells an ongoing custom, as I have found that I much prefer our own more civilized clubs, and cards dealt from somewhere closer to the *top* of the deck."

"From the top of the—I *knew* it!" Bones exclaimed, slapping a hand against his forehead. "There was fuzzing going on, wasn't there? Well? Wasn't there? Stap me if I'm going back there, no matter how much you beg me, Simon."

"Well?" Armand prompted when Simon didn't answer Bones. "Are we to become inveterate gamblers at all the low dives, with bailiffs living in our drawing rooms, ready to pick our bones for bills owing—they won't have much luck with you, dear Barebones, will they now?—or are we done with such evil places? You know Bones and I won't allow you to frequent such hellish places unaccompanied."

Simon made a great business out of tracing a small cross on his chest. "Upon my word, my friends, I will not darken the door of any gaming hell in this city again. I shan't have to, now that the bait has been dangled. From now on, the game will be played in more familiar and decidedly friendlier waters."

"You're that certain the fish will bite? I believe that's a tad arrogant, Simon."

"Fish do bite," Bartholomew announced solemnly. "So do sharks. They take big bites out of your pockets and leave you bloody. Ripped. Torn. Not a pretty sight. Next thing you know, you're lost in misery and hanging yourself from a lamppost just off Bond Street. It happened to my Great-uncle Theodore." He then frowned, looking pained. "We don't talk about it much—upsets m'mother."

Simon eyed Bartholomew consideringly, his affection for the man keeping him from laughing aloud at his doom-and-gloom remarks. "Sharks? Is that so, Bones? Well then, perhaps I should consider using a larger hook?"

"A stout cudgel would be more the thing," Bartholomew opined earnestly, obviously having given the notion some serious contemplation at one time or another. "Knock the shark senseless, firmly on the snout; it's the best way."

"I'll give that some thought as well," Simon promised as, with a sweep of his hand, he indicated the empty chairs at the table. "Am I late, or too early? Or is it worse than that?"

"Considerably worse," Armand told him, even as a servant placed a glass of Simon's preferred champagne in front of him. "Your latest appeals to Prinny have fallen on deaf ears, I'm afraid. Sheridan's gone to ground to avoid prison for debt. So many friends our dear Richard had, and every last one of them currently unable to remember his name, let alone his great deeds or brilliant wit. He's ill, Simon, gravely ill, and has probably gone off to die of a broken spirit, if you don't mind a modicum of melodrama. Although Dickie, knowing the man, would doubtless prefer to play the thing as a farce."

"Damn, I was afraid of that!" Simon exploded, tossing back his first measure of champagne as if it were water, then thanking the servant who quickly poured him another glassful. "Where are the others?"

Bartholomew pulled two scraps of paper from his coat pocket and read them one after the other: " 'Are you mad, man? One of the clock? In the *afternoon?*' Afternoon is underlined, three times. And this one: 'I never was much the one for pity. Pity.' Can you guess which is which, Simon?"

Simon pushed a hand through his hair, dislodging its former neatness, allowing it to fall into its more natural waves, which gave him a casual, youthful appearance his valet deplored and his mother adored. "The first from Beau, the second courtesy of George," he mumbled, then looked to Armand. "And the pair of them roundly insulted by our gesture, I suppose?"

Armand, who was lounging very much at his ease in his chair, stretched forth one long, fashionably covered arm and took up his wineglass. *"Certainement.* As I tried to warn you. Just as you would have turned away from all overtures of assistance had any of them offered it to you. However, you are not alone in your ambitions to help Byron, at least. Knowing you don't look at your invitations until we press you to do so, you may not yet have noticed that there will be a large party next week at Almack's, hosted by a dozen or so well-meaning but ill-advised ladies hoping to bring our poor George back into favor. It will be a dismal failure, of course, especially as dear Augusta Leigh is also known to be on the guest list."

"Not at Almack's, surely. And they've invited Augusta—George's sister?"

"Half sister, Simon," Bartholomew corrected, gnawing on his knuckle. "Half sister, friend, compatriot—*chérie amour?"*

"Christ on a crutch!" Simon groaned, slapping his palm against the tabletop, which earned him more than a few interested glances from other occupants of the room. "What the devil do they think that will accomplish, other than George's utter destruction? He won't attend, will he?"

"With rings on his fingers and bells on his toes. At least the scribblings in the betting book here are leaning heavily that he will, and that, to a man, everyone will turn their backs the moment he enters the room," Armand said, nodding his head as if in full agreement with the outcome the wagerers were backing.

"We have to stop him, talk some sense into him," Simon declared feelingly.

"You can't save him from his own folly, Simon, no matter how hard you try, any more than we can continue to bail Beau out of the River Tick now that Prinny's so set against him. It would only be throwing good money after bad, is the saying, I believe. That said, would you care for a stroll down Bond Street, as we'll accomplish nothing by sitting here, displaying ourselves for the edification of the masses, as it were. There's this neckcloth I've been fancying—"

Simon waved Armand back into his chair. "I was abducted at gunpoint after leaving you last night," he said baldly, having decided he needed his friends' full attention. Other than to start himself on fire, this statement seemed the quickest way of getting it.

"What? Never say so!" Bartholomew sputtered, then frowned, looking closely at Simon. "When? Where? After you left us? Well, that's what comes of frequenting low gaming hells, or so I say. Probably served you right."

"Why, thank you for asking, Bones. I'm quite fine, completely uninjured after my harrowing experience. I must say, the concern and comfort of my friends at times such as these is all that sustains me," Simon purred, lifting his glass once more. "Armand? Have you nothing to say?"

"No, I don't think so," he answered, then reconsidered. "Why, yes, perhaps I do have something to say. I believe Bones here to be dashed happy he chose to ride home with me last night. Do I have that right, Bones?"

Bartholomew nodded his agreement. "Tell us," he mumbled around a mouthful of knuckle. "What all happened, and why aren't you dead? Most people would be dead, you know."

"Sorry to disappoint you, Bones." Not one to waste valuable time in hurt feelings, however, Simon simply motioned for his friends to lean closer across the tabletop, then quickly went over the events that had transpired after he'd left them behind at the gaming tables. Also not one to flatter himself with nonsense meant to make him appear in a better light, he left out none of his humiliation at the hands of the mysterious Miss C.

"Vaulted onto the horse without assistance?" Bartholomew questioned him as Simon's story ran down to its fairly embarrassing conclusion. "But I thought you said it was a girl? No female could do that."

"Bones," Armand put in, "our friend here might not always recognize the nuances dividing a Waterfall draped neckcloth and the Mathematical knot, but I have it on good authority that he is a positive genius at deducing the subtle differences between males and females. I tend to believe him, and only wish that I could have been with him, to witness this grand sight."

"You wouldn't have thought that at the time, with a clog winging toward your head, although I do remember myself reflecting later that you might have been tickled," Simon said, draining the contents of his glass. "But I also believe both of you are missing the point. This girl, this Miss C, is bent on shooting Noel Kinsey. I can't let that happen."

Bartholomew frowned, his thin lips drawing up in a distasteful pucker. "You're going to warn him, aren't you? Why? It's not as if we like the man. Does it really matter who brings him down?"

"You truly don't understand, do you, Bones?" Armand commiserated, patting his friend's hand. "Even after spending half of last night watching Simon here lose hand after hand to the fellow. For very good reasons, our own Simon-pure here has decided to bring the dear earl of Filton low. Now, how would it look if some little milk-and-water country chit with big green eyes was to beat him to it? Why, he might never get over the ignominy of it."

Simon smiled without humor. "Exactly. I don't know what our young lady's motives may be, and I really don't care. Mine take precedence."

"You've got a *reason* to be going after Kinsey? You really do? You're not funning with me? You have something deep in mind? Why didn't I know this? Don't I listen? I'm sure I listen. You just don't talk. That's not nice, Simon. Does Armand know? Yes, I'm sure he does, even if no one bothered to tell me. I simply thought you'd scrambled your brains at Gentleman Jackson's Boxing Saloon yesterday afternoon, sparring with Armand here," he admitted sheepishly. "I mean, why else would we go to a gaming hell, when we can lose much more comfortably here at White's? I never before saw you have such a plaguey run of bad luck, Simon. Oh, and did I say I'm sorry you were kidnapped and all that? I should have said that, shouldn't I? Sorry."

Simon chuckled, amused by his friend's rambling confusion. "That's all right, Bones, I forgive you. And, yes, I am most definitely after the earl. I'll tell you about it, but at some other time, in a more private place, all right? Filton's been playing most often in gaming hells, finding the pickings easier there, where no one cavils overmuch at the slight fuzzing of a few cards—or even *knows* they're being fuzzed. I don't like him, but I must say the man is an accomplished cheat, so that it took someone with Armand's vast and varied experience, and now mine, to spot him at it. I mean to draw Filton out into the open, back to the clubs, so that I—hoping to be proved a worthy student of Armand's expertise—can then fleece him very publicly, which he roundly deserves. I do not, however, wish the man dead. Merely dead broke, and on his way to the Continent with many of the others who have had to flee their creditors."

Armand shook his head. "Which is why we'll be seeing much more of Noel Kinsey than we have the stomach for until the deed is done, I presume? It will be delicate work, Simon, if you mean to ruin him, not just relieve him of some of his money, and do it honestly at that. You can't empty his pockets too quickly, or he'll become suspicious and bolt back to his favorite haunts. If little Miss Green Eyes doesn't put a hole in him first, of course."

Simon sighed, fingering his champagne glass. "It's strange. I never thought I'd be trying to save a man like him from having a hole blown through him. It's lowering, that's what it is. Although I will admit that the possibility of an encounter with the inventive Miss C tickles my fancy. We will find her soon enough, I'm sure of it, skulking about, doing her possible to get Filton in her sights and then shooting him like a dog. She struck me as a very determined sort."

Armand closed his eyes for a moment, then looked across the table at his friend. "Oh, what a lovely picture has just formed in my mind, one you won't care for at all, so I won't mention it. After all, you've already assured us your interest in Miss Green Eyes is purely protective. Still, Simon, once we have found her—what on earth shall you *do* with her?"

"Ship her off home? Turn her over to the Watch? Spank her and send her to bed without her supper? You did say she's just a child, right? No hardened murderess?"

Simon looked at Bartholomew, who had offered these three equally unpalatable alternatives. His friend's suggestions reminded him that he hadn't had an answer to the question when it had first been put to him, by his mother. He didn't have an answer now. "I haven't the slightest idea what I'm going to do with her, Armand. I certainly believe I owe her some sort of punishment. Actually, Bones," he mused, smiling, "spanking her might not be completely unreasonable. Or locating and knocking down her father, for having so carelessly let her off her leash."

"Uh-oh, here comes Filton," Bones said, trying to look across the room and at the floor both at one and the same time, so that he ended up appearing as if he was flirting with the man just now making his way in their direction. "Can't sit here," he continued half under his breath. "Beau never invited him. Don't he know that? Encroaching mushroom, that's what he is. Probably should have let the girl shoot him, Simon. That really was wrong of you, to stop her."

"She was about to shoot *me*, Bones, and as I was just going to suggest that we go in search of the man, I consider him extremely agreeable to have saved us the trouble," Simon pointed out reasonably. He rose and turned to extend the hand of greeting to Noel Kinsey, his bright smile hiding the fact that he longed for nothing more than to knock the greedy, unscrupulous creature on his rounded rump, then step on him. "Filton! How good to see you again. Certainly scorched me last night, you did. Have you come to offer me the opportunity to win back some of my blunt? You're such a gentleman!"

Noel Kinsey smiled ingratiatingly, his gray eyes narrowed to intelligent, assessing slits, his blond hair perfection itself, as was the impeccably tailored suit of clothes that graced his tall, only slightly beefy frame. "I'm into you for less than five hundred pounds, Brockton, barely enough to produce a whisper of smoke from your deep pocketbook. However, if you've a mind for another meeting, I suppose I'm game. But not for a few weeks, I'm afraid. I've been called to the sickbed of my dearest great-aunt, and must hie off into the country for a space. With any luck she'd be tucked up with a shovel within a fortnight, and I and her lovely money will be back in Mayfair in short order. I only wanted you to know that I am not the sort to take a man's money and then not give him a chance to recoup it."

"As I've said, Filton, a gentleman to the backbone," Simon drawled, tugging his hand free of the earl's, hard-pressed not to wipe his hand on his pant leg, to clean it of the taint. "I'll be looking forward to sitting down with you again, I assure you. Never have I had such a run of curst bad luck, and I appreciate the chance to redeem myself. But here at White's or one of the other clubs, yes? No more gaming hells for me, if you don't mind. I didn't care to be surrounded by so many Johnny Raws fresh from the country. The smell of hay emanating from them was almost overpowering. So, you'll be leaving for the country today?"

"Tomorrow morning. There's no great rush," Filton supplied absently, then added, "I, alas, already have plans for this evening, if that's what you were trying to ask. A young gentleman just up from Surrey who longs to gift me with his considerable quarterly allowance. But don't champ at the bit so, Brockton. I'll relieve you of your fortune in good time, I promise. Gentlemen," he ended, perfunctorily bowing to

Bartholomew and Armand in turn, then sauntering off to sit himself down at a table well away from the coveted bow window.

Simon's lips were tight, his determination fixed, his deepest reasons still his own. "Oh, yes, my friends. Filton's mine. Mine to set up, mine to bring down. I won't brook any interference."

"You won't get any from me, Simon. Should have tripped him, knocked him to the floor," Bartholomew said as Simon took up his seat once more. "I don't like the man. Don't like him at all, and that's the truth. And that way he has of speaking, like each word was a pearl? '*Quart*-ter-ley *allow*-ance.' Hoo! Much too impressed with himself, I say, by half and half again!"

"So much for Bones's opinion of Filton. And our good friend the earl, by the by, thinks *you're* dumb as houses, Simon," Armand put in, not at all helpfully. "He cheated almost blatantly toward the end last night, and you never called him on it. I believe he sees himself as owning your entire fortune before the end of the month—if his dear great-aunt is so considerate as to cock up her toes with dispatch. If just this once, Bones is right. You should have knocked him down."

"For what?" Simon said, having drained yet another glassful of champagne in an effort to get the bad taste out of his mouth, put there by the nonsense he had been forced to utter to keep the supercilious Filton interested. "You can't just knock a man down, you know. There has to be a reason, and there will be if he dares to cheat too openly here at White's. Besides, I'm not eager for a duel when there's an easier way, and Filton's money will go a long distance with the charities."

"True enough, I suppose," Armand agreed, although he was

more the sort for a direct attack. "That's our Simon, always with an eye out to helping the less fortunate."

Silence fell over the table for some moments, until Bartholomew tapped his forefinger on the center of the table, calling his companions to attention. "You know what I'm thinking? I'm thinking, Simon, that your Miss C already has a good reason to shoot Filton," he said, smiling broadly and obviously deciding he had just said something brilliant. "She wouldn't be chasing after him with a pistol otherwise, right? If we find her, and get her to tell us her story, then one of us can call him out, to protect this poor female victim or some such rot. Simon?"

"You think he impugned her honor, Bones? Bedded her, then left her?" Simon asked, not liking the direction his thoughts were leading him. "No. She hardly seemed the sort to be taken in, romantically or otherwise, by someone of Filton's ilk."

"Hoo, now, Bones," Armand said, laughing. "Will you listen to that? Simon here has decided that his personal abductor is a woman of some virtue. Why, she probably feeds the poor, nurses the sick, and routinely robs the wealthy to give to the oppressed. Give the man a moment, Bones, and he'll have the little minx nominated for sainthood—and all because she wants to shoot Filton. Simon—are you quite sure that clog didn't hit its target? Bones, would you care to join me in examining our friend's head for any unusual bumps?"

"Oh, cut line, Armand," Simon said, smiling in spite of himself. "I have no idea as to what this girl is or isn't. I just know she wants Noel Kinsey dead, which seems to be an admirable aspiration, all in all. Look—Filton's leaving. Now, as I'm convinced our mysterious Miss C is even now somewhere outside, lurking about waiting for our unwary earl to reappear on the street, I suggest we adjourn this meeting and begin our saunter along St. James's in the hopes of finding her before she does something stupid."

"Not nice to call the girl stupid, Simon," Bartholomew pointed out, rising and following after his friends. "She might shoot you yet."

"How true, how true. And how good of you to point that out," Simon agreed with a pained smile. Then he gave Bartholomew a friendly clap on his back that nearly sent him sprawling on the floor.

"And to think m'father had so wanted a daughter," Lester grumbled, then winced as his undergarments pinched at him.

"Stop that, Lester!" Callie hissed under her breath as she smiled, nodded, and tipped her hat to a superior-looking matron and her maid who were passing by them on the flagway. Both women were eyeing Lester in some alarm as he struggled to scratch behind himself. "Ladies don't touch themselves there in public. Or in private either, as a matter of fact."

Lester stopped dead on the flagway and gaped at Callie. "They don't? How in blazes do they manage that, I wonder? Don't females ever get an itch on their backsides?"

Callie rolled her eyes, then spoke out of the corner of her mouth. "If they do, they don't acknowledge it," she explained tersely.

"Really? What about their noses? Do they get itches on their noses?"

"They might, but they don't scratch at their noses in public either. Or pick at them, if you were about to ask that next."

"Amazing! Such fortitude!" Clearly Lester was entranced with the ability of females to suppress most human functions and reactions, which he proved with his next eager questions.

"How about the hiccups, Callie? Do ladies get the hiccups? Oh—here's another one. Answer me this. Do they belch? No, I guess not. What do they do with all that air then? Do they save it up the whole night long, then go home and explode?"

"You're an idiot, Lester," Callie informed him, trying not to laugh aloud. "And stop pulling at your ribbons before your bonnet comes off. Honestly, Lester, were you raised in a stables?"

"I wasn't raised in any pink-and-white nursery, let me tell you that!" he spat with some heat. "And why I let you talk me into dressing myself up in these clothes let alone parading myself around the city streets, is something I will never understand. Why did I have to be a dowdy old maid at her last prayers? And a poor relation at that. I don't believe I look quite the thing in pink, for one, and the cuffs on this gown must have been turned twice. Why couldn't I at least have been a young lady?"

"Because we couldn't afford anything better at the bow-wow shop where we shopped for cast-off clothing, that's why," Callie patiently explained for what felt like the tenth time. "If we could have dressed me up, that would have been all well and good, but we couldn't find anything to fit. But it's better this way, actually. Brockton is probably looking for a small female. Granted, he also could be looking for two men—one small and thin, one rather better fed. Or not looking for us at all. But he'd never be looking for a young man and his, um, pleasingly *plump* aunt. Besides," she said, trying not to giggle, "I think you underestimate your charms."

"I'll get you back for this someday, Callie Johnston, I swear I will," Lester growled, nearly coming to grief over a slight rise in the flagway. Women's shoes were the very devil, he'd decided at least three long London blocks and a half hour earlier. Their shoes, their laces and ribbons, their straw bonnets that were worse than blinders on a horse.

Callie patted Lester's arm. "Now, now, Aunt Leslie, you'll have a fit of the vapors if you keep running on like this. And wasn't it you who said you wished to walk every step of Mayfair, and see all the wonderful sights? Such as the one just now tripping down the front steps of that building up ahead, for instance."

"It's Filton? Where?" Lester asked in his normal voice, then quickly pitched it a full octave higher. "I mean—*where, my dear?*" he asked before lowering his voice to a whisper. "Oh—all right. I see him now. Remember, don't hurt me."

"Of course not. At least, no more than I have to," Callie assured him, winking.

And then they were off, heading down the flagway arm in arm, pretending to be two visitors from the hinterlands taking in the sights—all the while keeping one eye on Noel Kinsey. He was already on his way across the wide flagway, heading for, in Callie's mind, a simply smacking, bang-up to the echo, high-perch phaeton. She wondered just whose money had paid for such a fine conveyance, and for the unfortunately flashy team in the traces. Certainly not His Lordship's own money, that was for sure. Her heart once more hardened against the man.

Callie's plan was simple. So simple, yet so extraordinarily brilliant and delicious that she was only disappointed she hadn't thought of it sooner. She went on the move, tugging at Lester's arm to urge him into jogging along more quickly—he really didn't have the faintest notion of how to navigate in lady's shoes, poor dear.

She made quick work of closing the distance between herself and Noel Kinsey, who was fully occupied in dressing down his groom for some infraction or another. His Lordship's back was turned, his attention diverted, from anyone passing along the flagway.

In short, Kinsey could not have been more cooperative, which didn't make Callie love him, but only gave her a wonderfully stationary target. She launched Lester forward . . . so that her friend cannoned into the earl with all his weight just as if he had stumbled over a loose stone, which he had . . . and lost his balance which, thanks to the force of Callie's shove, he did . . . succeeding in roughly knocking Noel Kinsey to the ground . . . and holding him there by the simple expedient of pretending to faint dead away on top of the badly crumpled peer—which was above everything beautiful!

"Aunt Leslie, are you all right?" Callie called out, doing her best to appear alarmed even as she quickly tugged down the hem of Lester's gown, which had risen to show just a smidgen too much of plump, hairy calf. Lester was being simply splendid—lying on his back, his arms and legs splayed out in an ungainly manner that effectively pinned Kinsey in place, his eyes shut as he feigned a very passable swoon.

"Aunt Leslie, Aunt Leslie!" Callie pleaded, bending down to gently slap at Lester's cheeks. "Speak to me, Aunt Leslie! Have you hit your head? Sir? Sir, I beg you—release my poor aunt!"

Noel Kinsey, who was sprawled facedown on the flagway, a deadweight on his back, turned his head to one side and did his best to look up at Callie. "Re-re-*lease* her? Why, you insolent pup—the ungainly lump is *crushing* me!"

"Oh, now that's not nice," Callie scolded as a small crowd gathered around them, two gentlemen already taking hold of Lester by either arm and gently raising him up. Lester was soon settled in a sitting position as he stirred, moaned, and bounced his rump a time or two on Noel Kinsey's already-abused back before being completely hauled to his feet. "See? My aunt is looking much better, no thanks to you. Now, sir, may I assist you to rise? Perhaps help you to your carriage?"

"It's a phaeton, you twit, not a carriage, and I wouldn't ask your bumbling, cowhanded help if I were on fire," the earl grumbled meanly.

Callie ignored him, positioning a hand on his elbow and lifting him up—even as she placed her other hand on the pistol in her pocket. With Lester keeping any onlookers occupied with his loud, hysterical shrieks and threats to swoon yet again, it would be a simple matter to press the barrel of the pistol against Filton's side and, in a low whisper, convince him of the reasonableness of offering both Callie and her injured "aunt" a ride back to their lodgings.

Once she had him in his stylish phaeton, and on the roadway, she would only have to get him to drive out of the city. Once free of onlookers, she could shoot him in the knee—his right knee, she had decided—and leave him near the Green Man in the care of his groom, about a half mile from where she and Lester had hidden their rented hacks.

Callie's fingers had already slipped around the pistol as she stood just to the left and slightly behind Kinsey. She was about to push the barrel—still hidden inside the large pocket of her coat—into his ribs.

And that's when it happened. Her right arm was suddenly halted in its movement, clamped in a vise-hard grip.

"I don't think so, brat, although I do admire your pluck, and your resourcefulness," a familiar, and hated, voice drawled beside her ear. "Release him. Release him now, and let him be on his way. Understood?"

Callie went stiff as a board as Noel Kinsey erupted in a

flood of complaints. "I've never been so insulted!" the earl was saying as he tugged his arm free of Callie's nerveless fingers. He bent to retrieve his ruined hat, using it to brush his person free of some of the dust it had collected while kissing the flagway. "There should be a law against bumpkins—and fat women! Fat, clumsy, *stupid* women—and their slack-jawed, bovine, Johnny Raw relatives!"

Kinsey's groom had been fully occupied in attempting to wipe what appeared to be an appreciative grin off his face ever since his employer had pitched forward to the ground. Now he belatedly raced forward to lend his assistance, helping the insulted earl climb onto the high seat of his phaeton.

"Oh, I say, Filton," an almost unhealthily thin man dressed in the latest fashions called out as he persevered in his attempts to keep Lester upright, which seemed to almost take more strength than the man possessed. "Aren't you even going to ask how the lady is faring? That's rather rude, don't you think? Perhaps you should be offering to take the poor thing up and off to a doctor?"

"Mind your own demmed business, Boothe," Noel Kinsey spat, then grinned. "Careful now, Boothe—if she topples again, she'll be the death of you." And then the earl was off in a flick of reins and the snap of a whip, never to know how close he had come to disaster.

Which was all the fault of one Simon Roxbury, Viscount Brockton, and general royal pain in Callie Johnston's unscratchable backside.

I shall be an autocrat: that's my trade.
And the good Lord will forgive me: that's his.
                    —Empress Catherine the Great

Chapter Four

"Tell me again."

Simon pulled at his left ear, a sign that he was both angry and bored. More angry than bored, as his mother very well knew from experience. Her smile widened as she jiggled in her chair like a young child being offered a treat and repeated her demand.

"Mother, don't push," he warned, then shook his head in resignation as Bartholomew Boothe succumbed to the viscountess's plea.

"I've got it pretty much figured out, ma'am. It was a ploy, see," Bartholomew began, then looked to Armand Gauthier. "That's right, isn't it, Armand? A ploy? Is that the right word?"

Armand, who had been sitting at his ease in the Roxbury drawing room, nursing a snifter of brandy he'd warmed between his palms, smiled and nodded. "You've got it, Bones. A ploy. A device, a diversion, a gambit, a bit of mischief. A ruse. A scheme, perhaps even a stratagem—if I may give our Miss C that much credit without bringing a rain of curses down on my head from our friend here."

"And brilliant!" Imogene broke in after throwing back the single glass of sherry her overcautious son allowed her before dinner, and serious drinking, could begin. "So simple, so elegant in its own way. Abducting the man in the middle of the street, in the middle of the day, with half of London watching and not knowing. The gel's got backbone, I'll hand her that, and the heart of a Trojan."

"While also possessing the brain and self-preservation instincts of a demented dormouse." Simon rubbed a hand across his mouth, considering—not for the first time—the wisdom of bringing the brilliant Miss C to his home, and to his mother. "She could have been caught out as easily as she might have succeeded, you know, and even now be incarcerated, awaiting trial. And a swift hanging. The Crown doesn't look kindly on those attempting to murder titled gentlemen. Or hasn't that occurred to any of you?"

"I thought about it," Bartholomew admitted, frowning, then brightened again. "But she wasn't caught. She nor her aunt—who is rather appealing, don't you think? No, they weren't suspected at all, not by any of us. Except by you, of course, Simon, which is why they're both locked up in one of your guest chambers now that you've hauled them here against their will. Is that a hanging offense—hauling people into your house when they don't want to be there? I think it might be. Yes. It might just be! And have you figured out yet what you're going to do with them? I mean, you can't keep them tied and jailed. Not forever, anyway. They have to eat, for one thing."

Armand rose and walked over to look down at Bartholomew, then grinned at Simon. "Isn't he darling, old friend? He still thinks the stout one is a female. Should we have him fitted with spectacles, do you suppose, or should we allow him his illusion and watch, enthralled, as he begins to court her? It could prove amusing."

Bartholomew shot to his feet in one quick motion, his thin cheeks blazing red. "What the devil are you talking about? Of course the aunt is a woman. If not, she'd be Miss C's uncle, which she ain't. Aunts are women, always were, always will be. Any dolt knows that!"

The viscountess eyed Bartholomew owlishly. "Straight as an arrow, and thick as a plank, aren't you, Bones? Poor boy." Then she held out her empty glass to her son, who decided she might be allowed a second glass, just this one time. After all, the circumstances were rather extraordinary. "Leaving Mr. Boothe's potential foray into romance for the moment, son," she said as she accepted the refilled glass, "let us get back to the reason you brought the girl dressed like a young man— and the young man tarted up like a woman—to Portland Place, shall we? After all, it's not my birthday, although I must tell you I do consider the pair of them a smashing gift. Even if I doubt either of them would make docile pets."

"She tried to bite Simon as he loaded her into his carriage," Bartholomew put in, seating himself once more. "Almost shot him last night, brained him with her clog, and now she's biting." He shook his head. "Such women are dangerous," he pronounced. "I believe I'll rethink my infatuation, seeing as the aunt's one of her relations."

"Not a word, Armand," Simon warned his friend, who had already opened his mouth, surely to say something designed to befuddle poor Barebones more than he already was—if such were possible. "Look, Mother," he went on quickly, "we've brought Miss C and her"—he looked to Bartholomew—"um, her *companion* here to you because, frankly, there seemed to be no other choice open to us. Dressed as a young gentleman or not, our pistol-wielding miscreant is obviously a young woman. A young woman with the manners of a wild Indian, but the speech of a gently bred young girl, if her vocabulary is too broad for refined company. She wouldn't open her mouth, wouldn't utter a word after I relieved her of her pistol—of both her pistols. Wouldn't tell us her name, wouldn't give up her address. I had no choice. If I had let her go, she'd only run after Filton and try to blow a hole in him again."

"From what I know of the fellow, she might be knighted for such an act," Imogene said, hungrily eyeing the dish of sugarplums she had heard calling her name this last half hour. If only her stays weren't digging at her so . . . but, no, she had to resist. "And the aunt isn't talking, either?"

"I think he'd rather be boiled in oil than admit to his name, or his gender." Armand waggled his eyebrows at Bartholomew, who looked as if he were beginning to realize he'd made a mistake that would haunt him in the form of cutting jokes for a good fortnight or more. "Besides, it's clear our Miss C is in charge there. The poor dupe seems to be placed in the position of following behind her, a ring through his nose, doing her bidding. Is that how you see it, Simon?"

Simon nodded, suddenly too weary to speak. He'd had quite a start, walking out of White's to see Filton falling to the ground, half-buried beneath a heap of skirts and flailing limbs. Amusement at the man's predicament quickly evaporated, however, as he'd heard the husky, badly disguised female voice of the brat who had kidnapped him the previous evening. His every nerve had instantly gone on the alert, so that he had deduced the preposterously daring Miss C's intent even before she could slip her hand into her bulging pocket.

From that point until now, events would probably always remain a bit hazy in his mind. Filton had made good his exit, still obnoxious, still in one piece, and blissfully oblivious to his near disaster. The "aunt" had continued his caterwauling, the intensity of the wails increasing as Filton drove off and he got a glimpse of Miss C being held, quite securely, in Brockton's grip.

Waiting until the passersby had lost interest in the small drama and walked off, Simon had then motioned for Armand to grab hold of the now-whimpering "aunt." Together, they'd hustled the odd pair around the corner, to where his carriage waited.

And now they were all in Portland Place: Simon, Bartholomew, Armand, the viscountess, Miss C, and the "aunt." Four of them in the drawing room, pondering what would happen next, two of them locked away upstairs, their mouths tightly shut and their motives still unknown.

"Let's get them down here, shall we?" Simon suggested, walking to the doorway. With a lack of elegance that betrayed his agitation, he bellowed his intention up the stairs to Emery, then dispatched the hovering Roberts to assist the butler in herding the prisoners down to the first floor.

"I am *not* being childish!" Lester declared hotly, throwing out his bottom lip in an angry pout.

"Are so," Callie answered calmly as she lay propped on the brocade coverlet, Lester's bonnet perched on the tip of one booted foot as she lounged at her ease, her arms crossed behind her head. All in all, her disposition was strangely sunny.

"You're being childish, and sulky, and—much as it pains me to say this—you're right, pink don't become you. Not a whit."

Lester's china blue eyes narrowed dangerously, causing him to resemble an infuriated cherub—a comparison that did nothing for his consequence. "I really do hate you sometimes, Callie. I swear I do."

Callie yawned prodigiously (without bothering to cover her mouth—men could do that) and looked down the length of the bed at her dear friend. He really did look silly, now that she considered the thing: dressed all in pink, his blond hair hanging in damp ringlets around his moon face, his cheeks flushed as he paced back and forth in long strides that caused his fairly snug gown to bunch up closer and closer to his full waist. She felt a pang of guilt, knowing she had been the one to land them in this particular bramble patch. Not that she wasn't *always* the one who continually thought up adventures that oftimes ended with them in the briars. "You could don the bonnet again, I suppose. Maybe then they won't figure out that you're a Lester, and not a Leslie?" she offered by way of assurance.

Lester stopped pacing to shove his fists against his waist as he glared at her. "Well, of course I'm going to keep pretending to be a woman," he said testily. "I may even have to plead my belly to keep me from the hangman." He turned to one side and cupped his hands around his rather round abdomen. "So? Do you think I could get away with it?"

"Oh, certainly. Until your beard began to grow out, I suppose," Callie returned solemnly.

"Oh, God," Lester groaned, rubbing at his already-fuzzy chin before plopping himself down on the floor in an inelegant heap. "We're going to die. I just know it. We're just going to die. I can't even abide a tight collar—how will I survive the hangman's noose?"

Callie howled with mirth, unable to control her giggles as she looked at Lester through tear-wet lashes. "You're not . . . not *supposed* to survive the noose," she got out between gales of laughter. "I believe . . . I believe that's the entire point of the exercise."

Lester remained sitting cross-legged on the floor as he reached into the pocket of his gown and pulled out his sole remaining licorice whip. "That's it, Callie," he said dully. "Keep on laughing. Laugh until your eyes cross. That way, you'll just end up in Bedlam, chained to a wall and being pissed on by the other madmen. I've seen etchings, so I know. Horrible place!"

She jackknifed to a sitting position, dangling her legs over the edge of the bed. "You know, Lester, that might not be an entirely terrible idea. We could pretend to be lunatics. You could keep to your assertion that you're a woman, and I could . . . I could . . . Lester? What could I do?"

Her partner in contemplated crime sniffed derisively. "Just keep on doing as you've been, Callie. Heaven knows that's lunatic enough for any three people. Why, they might feel so sorry for the pair of us that they'll just let us go. Give us alms and tea, perhaps, and send us on our way."

"Alms and tea?" Callie considered this for a moment. "Oh, you mean *amnesty*." She nodded. "Yes, that might work. We certainly look pitiful enough. But we can't give them our right names, Lester. You do know that."

He frowned, clearly confused. "We can't? But you know how forgetful I am about names. I'll never remember. I know!" he then exclaimed, clambering to his feet, and nearly tripping over the hem of his gown. He employed the licorice whip as a pointer, first aiming it at her and then at himself. "I'll be you and you can be me—that way I won't have anything new to remember."

Callie rolled her eyes heavenward and addressed her Creator through the stuccoed ceiling. "Do you see? Do you see what I have to put up with?" She sighed, then explained patiently, "No, Lester, that won't fadge. The viscount will simply apply to both our parents, who will then come to London to fetch us. Can you imagine your papa's surprise when he spies you out in your gown? They have to be *different* names, Lester. Names we've made up out of whole cloth. *Lies*, Lester. We must tell lies. Surely you can do that?"

"Can I?" Lester asked around a mouthful of licorice as he retrieved his bonnet and knotted the strings to the left of his second chin. "Do you remember that time we were caught out changing signposts?"

Callie blew out her breath in short bursts, her mind conjuring up a memory of that particular ill-fated adventure meant to direct the London mail coach along entirely the wrong road. Callie's new governess had been aboard the coach, and she'd already decided that, at nearly fourteen, she was done with learning the proper way to curtsy to a duke, considering she had no reason to believe she'd ever be within spitting distance of one.

She shook her head. "All you had to say was that we'd accidentally knocked the post down and were putting it back in place, as I recall. What you did, Lester, was drop to your knees and plead, 'Please, Papa, don't kill me—Callie made me do it!'" She sighed again, also remembering her punishment for having lured Lester into mischief yet again. Why, she'd had to sit on a pillow for nearly a week! "So you're right, Lester, subterfuge won't work. Not with your faint heart."

"So?" the impervious-to-insult Lester asked, then took another bite of his favorite confection. He was enjoying it so much that Callie refrained from telling him that he was turning his lips and tongue a decidedly unappealing shade of black—or that the bonnet did nothing to improve his appearance. "What does that leave us?"

Callie shrugged. "The truth?" She shivered. "Oh, how very lowering. I never tell the truth if I can help it."

"We'll toss ourselves at the viscount's mercury?"

"Throw ourselves on his mercy, yes," Callie agreed distractedly, now beginning to pace the carpeting, her insides jangling at the thought of being so bereft of inspiration as to have run out of workable fibs. "There's nothing else for it, actually," she ended, automatically reaching up her hands to straighten her neckcloth as she heard a key turning in the lock. "Just keep chewing, Lester, and let me handle the bulk of the explanations, all right?"

Lester obediently stuffed the last, long length of licorice into his mouth as the door opened, admitting a pair of Brockton servants. One carried a sword, and the other lagged behind, hesitant and bug-eyed, looking for all the world as if he expected Callie and Lester to turn into bats, fly across the room, and nest in his hair.

Callie immediately decided on her course of action. She would be haughty. Haughty was entirely possible, as her last governess—who had not been lost due to a misdirecting signpost—had been the epitome of haughty. The second daughter of an impoverished baron forced to earn her own way in life, the woman could have given lessons in pride to a peacock.

So thinking, and feeling none too shabby in her inexpressibles and top boots, Callie tipped up her chin, looked down her nose, and said, "Well? Have you been turned to stone, or have you something to say? Come, come. Speak up, man! Don't dawdle!"

The butler rather reluctantly came to attention, accustomed to responding to the voice of authority even when it was directed toward him by a scrap of a girl dressed up in men's clothing. "I—that is, we . . . no! The viscount . . . His Lordship—"

"Not stone," Callie cut in imperiously, warming to her role, "but rather a puddle of mumbles. Well? Get on with it, man! Is our presence required in the drawing room? And what's your name, man? My father would have had you flogged, were you in his regiment!"

"Emery, sir . . . um, ma'am . . . um, that's Emery!" the butler stammered, clearly impressed. "And the Viscount Brockton and his mother, the viscountess, desire the pleasure of your company, and that of your, um, your *companion*, in the drawing room. If it pleases you," he ended, his voice trailing off as his gaze sought the carpet.

His reaction pleased Callie so that she had to beat down the urge to grin—and perhaps do a small jig. But this was only the beginning. The viscount would not be quite so easy to intimidate, and she knew it. "Very good, Emery," she pronounced, holding out an arm so that Lester, still caught between genders, took it rather than wrapping it protectively in his own. "That was quite clear. There may be hope for you yet."

She took a single step forward, then halted. "Did you say the viscountess? Brockton is married, then?" Why this piece of information took some of the wind out of her newly inflated sails she had no idea.

"No, sir . . . um, ma'am. That would be His Lordship's mother, you see, and a rare one she is, if you don't mind my saying so," the second servant piped up, stepping forward. "I'd tread careful around her, as she's sharp as a tack, if you take my meaning. Oh—and I'm Roberts, footman, and a pleasure it is to be of assistance, sir." He looked to Lester. "Um, I mean, ma'am."

Emery shot the fellow a killing glance meant to freeze him in place and stop up his mouth.

"Well?" Roberts fired back verbally, obviously feeling he had something to say and not averse to saying it. "Sir, ma'am —what's the difference? Between the pair of them, I've got to be right."

Callie decided that she liked Roberts. Definitely much better than she did Emery, who was once more looking at her down the length of his thin nose as if she and Lester had lately crawled out from beneath some nasty, musty stone. "Shall we be on with it, please?" she interjected before the two servants could come to blows, aiming Lester and herself straight at the doorway. The two men parted like the Red Sea, allowing them through.

Her heart pounding, her knees considerably less than steady for all her show of bravado, Callie grabbed on to the dark mahogany railing and rapidly, jauntily, began her descent to the drawing room. She did her best to ignore Lester's licorice-garbled entreaties to "slow down, for God's sake!" as he held up his skirts and skipped along beside her.

Her bootheels clicking smartly against the black-and-white tiles of the first-floor foyer, she stopped midway between the staircase and the double doors that, she presumed, led to the drawing room, waiting for Emery to announce her. She thought it ought to be a fairly neat trick if he could pull it off, as the man was still most obviously stumbling over matters of gender just as Lester was still tripping over his hem.

It was, however, a confusion the butler seemed to have reduced in his mind. After gifting her with a slight inclination of his head, he threw open the double doors, took a single step onto the Aubusson carpet, cleared his throat and announced in typical high-nosed, butlerlike stentorian tones, "The riffraff, my lord, my lady." He then bowed himself out.

"*Touché*," Callie whispered appreciatively as he went by her.

Emery bowed to her again, this time relaxing enough to bend from the waist. "A word of warning, if I might? Her Ladyship is the viscountess, not the dowager viscountess. If you value your life, that is."

"Why, thank you, Emery," Callie said, her smile brilliant, thus beginning an unlikely friendship she had no reason to believe would last beyond the next uncomfortable hour.

With a last squeeze of Lester's faintly clammy paw, Callie took a deep breath, aimed her chin at the ornately decorated ceiling, and sauntered into the room. She began by chirping out, "How lovely to be out and about again after my recent, unfortunate incarceration. The bread and butter was lovely, by the way, thank you so much for sending it up to us. If some one of you would be kind enough to return my hat, we'll be on our way now."

"What cheek!" a deep, female voice exclaimed in high good humor from somewhere to the left of her. Callie turned her head and upper body in that direction—all the best dandies employed that small gambit, partly to impress, partly because their ears could otherwise come to grief on their high, starched shirt points.

What she saw was, undoubtedly, the viscountess. The woman was ensconced in a large, wing-back chair, her slippered toes propped on top of a brocade ottoman. She appeared, even seated, to be a very large woman, taller than most, and with an imposingly well-packed, sturdy body rather than a soft, aging one running to fat. Her eyes were a bright, lively blue, her hair a vivid, truly atrocious yellow, and her smile was one that warned of a razor tongue that she would not hesitate to employ in slicing any opponent into very small, bloody pieces. In short, this was a formidable woman. In fact, Callie took to her immediately.

"My lady," Callie said with all deference, bowing in her direction. "It is my considered opinion that you might give good lessons in *cheek*. Your son, I also believe, must have studied at your knee and then, realizing he did not possess half your wit, succumbed to rough-and-tumble bullying instead—when he does not attempt to destroy an adversary by *talking* her to death. You are, of course, aware that he has just lately abducted my companion and myself straight off the street?"

The viscountess popped a sugarplum into the pink cavern of her mouth, the three—no, four—bracelets on her arm jingling as she then brushed bits of sugar from the front of her deep purple gown. "Abducted, you say? I believe my son saw it more in the way of a rescue. But I shall investigate just the same. Simon? Would you care to answer the young lady's charges? Oh, and by the by, I once wore breeches. Demmed comfortable, aren't they, gel?" She frowned, sighing deeply. "Although yours fit much better than mine ever did. Either that," she ended with a wink, "or my mirror was wider."

"If you're quite done corrupting the already thoroughly corrupted, Mother," Simon began, stepping forward from his place in front of the mantel and into Callie's line of sight, "I think I'd like to handle the interview from here. If it pleases you, of course."

The viscountess winked, then wrinkled her nose at Callie. "Stiff-backed, just like his father. But he'll come around. Lord knows I have, and I've only had since this morning to get used to the notion. Give him time, my dear, and you'll have him right and tight, curled close round your pretty thumb just as I did with his father. But you will wait until I snag an earl, won't you? There's a love."

Thoroughly confused, but aware that his mother's words had served to put a dark scowl on her son's face—which pleased Callie mightily—she only acknowledged the viscountess's words with a small nod before turning to glare at Simon Roxbury, Viscount Brockton and King of All Interfering Monsters. "My lord?" she offered, falling back on bravado once more and giving him the opening to speak she was sure he would have taken without her permission. "May I presume that you are about to make the introductions?"

"That might be difficult, brat," he said, stepping close to her so that he could speak without being overheard, "as I don't have the faintest notion who in bloody blazes you and Miss Muffet here are!"

"Oh, I say, Callie," Lester protested, for he *was* standing close enough to hear, "that wasn't very nice. Called you a brat, he did. Only your papa and Justyn do that."

"Go sit on your tuffet, why don't you?" Simon urged, not all that kindly, then returned his searching concentration to Callie. Lester, never difficult to overpower, promptly did as he was told.

"You really are a beast, aren't you?" Callie whispered, casting her gaze around the room and seeing the two gentlemen who had supported Lester on the flagway standing together in the far corner, sipping from glasses and silently watching her. "I imagine I can only thank you that you didn't have those two men torture my companion on our way here. Not that you probably didn't think of it."

"I didn't, as a matter of fact," Simon shot back. "I did, however, consider spanking *you*. Callie, is it?"

Callie raised her chin again. Really, she was getting quite weary of lifting her chin. She couldn't imagine how her starchy governess had managed it hour after hour. And looking down her nose was beginning to make her dizzy. "All right," she said, sighing, "I suppose I may as well attack this fence head-on. I'm Caledonia Johnston, and my friend is Lester Plum. Are you happy now, my lord?"

"Happy? Oh, I'm much more than that, Miss Johnston. I am rapidly approaching euphoric," he answered affably enough, which made Callie long to see him hung on a hook against the nearest wall so that she could throw darts at him with something more lethal than her eyes. "Have you told Mr. Plum that, although at least one of our number found him to be quite fetching, pink may have been an unfortunate choice?"

Covering her mouth with her hand, so that he couldn't see the appreciative upturning of her lips, Callie gave a deliberate cough, then inclined her head toward the two still-nameless gentleman. "You were about to make the introductions, my lord?" she prompted.

The viscount, good to his word, and quite clearly not at Callie's instigation, made short work of introducing everyone to everyone else.

"The aunt *is* an uncle!" the painfully thin man who had been introduced as one Bartholomew Boothe exclaimed, first paling, then coloring a deep, embarrassed puce as he squinted in Lester's direction. "Good God, he is! I'm really going to have to consider spectacles. How embarrassing. Armand, I swear, if you breathe a word of this—"

The gentleman introduced as Armand Gauthier—and a handsome enough specimen, Callie had to admit—only laughed at his companion, then slowly walked across the floor with an ease and grace that she immediately envied. He took up her hand as it hung slackly at her side and pressed a kiss against her skin. "Enchanted, Miss Johnston," he drawled, then turned to Simon Roxbury and grinned. "This just gets better and better, doesn't it, old fellow? I can't thank you enough for including Bones and myself in your amusement."

"Why else would one have friends, if not to delight them, Armand?" Simon purred back at the man, so that Callie felt a trickle of apprehension skip down her spine. The viscount had—for reasons Callie certainly did not understand—just warned his friend "off." Gauthier must also have felt the new coolness in the room, and only inclined his head to her once more before returning to his friend and his snifter of brandy.

"If you'll sit?" the viscount said then, his tone letting her know his was not a question, but a command.

Once Callie had taken up a seat beside Lester, who seemed to be suffering a chill, he was shaking that badly, Simon Roxbury stepped to the middle of the room so that his back was turned to no one, and began to speak. "Now, if I have everyone's attention, I should like to begin at the beginning and see if we can sort our way out of this. Armand? You might want to call for pen and paper so that you can take down notes. This should make a tolerable farce, and our good friend Sheridan badly needs a new theatrical success."

"Don't be insufferable, Simon," his mother warned. "For one thing, it won't do you a spot of good. How and why Miss

Johnston got here is of no real concern—all that matters is that she *is* here. This gel's the one, and I'll have to keep these stays on a while longer if I'm to beat you to the altar. I can feel it, I'm convinced of it. Strangely, I'm not at all put out by the notion, which just goes to show I have your happiness foremost in my heart, Simon. I'm such a good mother. Ride astride, don't you, gel? Never mind. Of course you do."

"Mother—" Simon began warningly, then snapped his jaws shut, as interrupting the viscountess was about as thankless a task as trying to empty the Atlantic Ocean with a teacup.

"And you know, Simon," she continued, undaunted, "this will mean shedding yourself of that cat, Sheila Lloyd, which I can only consider a bonus, don't you? Yes, I'm quite pleased, all in all. Quite pleased. Bones—ring for Roberts, will you? My dish is empty."

Simon's low curse was nearly drowned out by Armand Gauthier's burst of laughter and Bartholomew Boothe's fit of coughing, but Callie was beginning to sense the viscountess's meaning. The meaning of several things she had said since Callie's entrance into the drawing room. She shot to her feet, her cheeks burning with indignation. "If you people think to kidnap me off the street, then set me up as some sort of *mistress* to this insufferable prig, why, I—"

It was now the viscountess's turn to choke. She did so quite stupendously, turning a ghastly purple before a sharp slap between her shoulder blades—delivered by Lester Plum, who might not have been the sharpest arrow in the quiver but who had considerable experience saving his beloved father from the man's piggish gulping of any food within sight—dislodged a nearly whole sugarplum from her gullet. "A—a *mistress*!" the older woman got out at last, using the sleeve of her gown to wipe at her streaming eyes. "God, gel, he already has one of those. It's a *wife* I'm talking about!"

Wife? Callie mouthed the word silently as her rump hit the chair cushion with a thump, her legs having all but collapsed under her. "Pretend I'm insane, Lester said," she muttered to herself. "And it's a good thing I didn't do that—for no one in this madhouse would have noticed!"

A sudden thought strikes me,
let us swear an eternal friendship.

—George Canning

Chapter Five

A firm believer in the adage that, theatrically speaking, no more than three characters should have lines in any scene, Simon took advantage of the chaos that reigned in the Portland Place drawing room to motion with a dismissive shake of his head that the presence of his two friends was no longer required.

"Only because of the great love we bear you," Armand murmured silkily as he and Bartholomew exited the room. "And only because we expect a full recounting of every word and gesture tonight at Lady Bessingham's."

That left Simon's mother—who Simon knew could not have been boosted from the room if he'd sent for a regiment of dragoons to oust her—the two mischief-makers, and himself. That was still two more than he could have wished for but, as he didn't think Lester Plum would have much to say for himself, he decided to let the man stay.

Once assured that his mother had recovered from her fit of choking, and after signaling to Lester that he return to his former seat, Simon—after fortifying himself with a deep drink from his wineglass—began once more.

"Shall we agree that we have matters to discuss, Miss Johnston?"

Caledonia Johnston looked to the ceiling, then to her right and left, her pursed lips also rather comically shifting left to right as if she was swishing her answer around inside her mouth for a few moments, tasting it, before offering, "I suppose you think I should apologize for almost shooting you last night. If you insist."

"Oh, I do, Miss Johnston, I absolutely do insist," Simon countered, admiring her courage even as he longed to throttle her. "I also insist you then forget the entire incident ever occurred. The interlude does neither of us much credit."

"If you say so, although it's really beyond stupid, because we both know nothing happened except that I bested you. Goodness—wait a moment—that *could* be embarrassing to you, couldn't it, if it were to be repeated in your clubs and such? Anyway—sorry," Callie ended shortly, not sounding at all sincere as she stood up, looking toward the doorway. "Well, that's done. Come on, Lester. Let's be on our way."

"Sit . . . *down*," Simon warned tightly, feeling a headache beginning to pound behind his eyes.

"Simon, honestly," the viscountess scolded as both Callie and Lester collapsed into their chairs once more. "Don't you know you'll land many more flies with honey than with vinegar? Be nice to the gel."

"Nice. *Nice*? I'd rather try to pet a wild lion," Simon bit out, then shook his head, knowing he was getting matters nowhere by being so prickly. "Miss Johnston, do you think it would it be at all possible for you to tell me, tell *us*, exactly why it is that you've taken it into your head to murder the earl of Filton?"

"See? I told you, Callie," Lester Plum said happily, nudging her in the ribs with his elbow. "Told you it looked like murder."

Simon looked to Lester, belatedly wondering why the man's lips were black, but then remembered that the young man was also dressed up to look like a woman, so that it probably didn't much matter what color he'd painted his mouth. "What *was* it supposed to look like, Mr. Plum?" he asked, thinking maybe the fellow could be of some help in the interview after all.

Lester wriggled himself forward on the cushions, eager to speak. It wasn't often anyone really listened to him, asked his opinion, or thought it remotely possible that he had anything important to say. "Well, as it happens, Callie thought his knee would be the best place to shoot him. Nothing fatal, you understand. Just maim him—so he'd suffer in bad weather and couldn't dance all night."

"Oh! I *do* like that!" the viscountess exclaimed happily. "Bloodthirsty, but not necessarily lethal. Really, Simon, it seems to me you might have been rather poor-spirited in not allowing the gel her revenge. It *is* revenge you're seeking, isn't it? Never say he ruined you, for that would certainly deflate me."

"Ruined me?" Callie repeated, looking to the viscountess questioningly for a moment before stiffening her spine as the realization of what the older woman meant was brought home to her. "Certainly not!"

"Oh, good," Imogene said, smiling sunnily. "That's all right then, isn't it, Simon?"

"Mother," Simon began, then just shook his head, believing he had enough on his plate at the moment without engaging his parent in a discussion of her harebrained scheme to have him bracketed to the brazen infant with the atrocious haircut and quite lovely legs.

He closed his eyes, counting swiftly to ten, reminding himself that he didn't really care about Caledonia Johnston's legs, lovely or not. Or about her wide, clear green eyes, or her high cheekbones, or that particularly attractive husky voice she employed to say so many outrageous, incomprehensible things. He'd much rather console himself with the knowledge that she was flat-chested as any ten-year-old. "All right then, Miss Caledonia Johnston, we'll try again. *Why* did you want to shoot Filton in the knee, crippling him?"

"Wouldn't keep calling her Caledonia if I was you," Lester interjected helpfully, so that Simon belatedly noticed that Miss Johnston's hands had been drawn up into fists in her lap. "She shoved Rupert Almstead into the pond last summer for calling her that, and it was his birthday."

"It's your name, isn't it?" Simon asked, secretly agreeing that it was atrocious. But, then, Callie didn't seem to be much of an improvement. "I assume, as it's the Latin name for Scotland, that your forebears came from there?"

"One might assume that," Callie answered with an expressive shrug of her slim shoulders, "except that it's not true. My father simply liked the name, as he greatly enjoys salmon fishing in Scotland. I'm only relieved he wasn't fond of the hunting fields of Melton. I've learned to forgive him, but not those who'd dare to address me as Caledonia once they're aware of my feelings on the subject. Rupert Almstead had been warned, and foolishly chose to ignore the warning. You're many things, my lord, but I have yet to believe you are foolish. But, then," she ended, smiling quite evilly for an innocent young girl, "it's early days yet, isn't it?"

She then slapped her hands on her knees and rose to her feet once more, walking across the floor to stand in front of the drinks table, lifting the decanter of sherry and splashing some of its contents into a glass. Taking a small sip after raising the glass in a mocking salute to Simon, she then said, "As you can't seem to bring yourself to the point, my lord, how about you just sit down like a nice London gentleman and allow me to tell you what I believe you want to know? Things will go much more quickly, and your servants can then stop hiding behind the archway, their pointy noses visible from here, and get back to work. Besides, there are two horses tied up near the Green Man, and I worry about them."

Simon had never seen such arrogance directed at him, such—as his mother had termed it—*cheek* from a young woman. From a young man. From anyone of his acquaintance. Surprisingly, he found himself amused by Caledonia Johnston's confident swagger, even by the small shiver of distaste she nearly hid as her palate reacted to what he was sure had been her very first sip of sherry.

He gave in to Callie's suggestion, sitting himself down and gesturing for her to explain what, to him, seemed to have become the unexplainable.

Still holding the glass in her long, thin fingers—although she did not take another sip of its contents—Callie began pacing the carpet, one foot very deliberately brought forth after the other, heel rolling to toe for the space of ten steps before she executed a sharp about-face and came to a halt, just in time to see Simon ogling her long, straight legs, unfortunately.

"If I might have your attention?" she prompted, letting him

know that she had caught him looking at her, the impudent, brattish infant! "Now, I imagine I shall have to begin at the beginning, yes?"

"As that is the first logical statement you've uttered since I was so unfortunate as to make your acquaintance, Miss Johnston," Simon drawled, "I'd have to agree."

"The gel's right, son," Imogene broke in. "You do talk too much. Now dub your mummer and let her get on with it. I'm getting peckish and it's hours until dinner."

"Kathleen will be well served to be given a fortifying snack as well, Mother," Simon said meanly, knowing he was behaving badly, "as she'll need all her strength to pour you into your gown this evening."

"Wretch," Imogene countered, but she slid the dish of sugarplums back onto the table beside her. "I should just die, and then haunt you."

"And this, you're saying, would constitute a change of plan?" Simon quipped, smiling at his mother, whom he really did love most dearly especially because she instantly knew he was teasing her and rewarded him by batting her darkened lashes a time or two and then blowing a kiss in his direction.

"Come on, Lester, let's just leave," Callie said, calling Simon back to attention. "We can rent a wagon or something and go fetch the horses before they starve."

"I'll send someone after them," Simon said quickly, and did just that, summoning a servant and allowing Callie to give him the general whereabouts of the two horses she had most probably tied up in the trees near the Green Man, planning to use them to make her escape after shooting the kidnapped Noel Kinsey. It bothered him, only for a moment, that he was beginning to understand the workings of Caledonia Johnston's decidedly bizarre mind.

"Now," he said tiredly, once the servant was off on his rescue mission, "I think we're all more than ready to hear your story."

Callie was looking mulish, an emotion he found lamentably easy to read in her expressive green eyes. "I don't think I want to anymore. You'll probably think you are honor-bound to write to our fathers, for one thing, and I doubt you'd appreciate the beauty of my plan anyway. Unlike your mother, who seems to be the best of creatures, and who loves you even though you treat her shamelessly."

"How very sweet. I've always wanted a daughter, now that I think on it," the viscountess declared, sighing happily as she popped another sugarplum into her rouged mouth. "I can't imagine why I've been so upset at the prospect. Although I still do need that earl, I believe."

"Oh, good grief!" Simon exploded, running a hand through his hair, mussing it, so that his mother was forced to comment gushingly, "Doesn't he look *sweet* like that, my dear? Really, once you have him broken to the saddle, as I did with his father, you shouldn't have a whit of trouble with him."

"That tears it!" Simon walked over to his mother—stomped over to his mother—and put his hand under her elbow, all but forcing her to her feet. "Good-bye, Mother, have a pleasant life. Plum—you, too. *Out!*"

Lester stood up, awkwardly smoothing down his skirts. "Where are we to go?" he asked, looking to Callie for an answer, as he probably looked to her before he thought to allow himself to take a deep breath.

"Go to the conservatory and pick a few oranges," Simon suggested, steering his mother to the doorway. "Go to the kitchens where each of you can gobble down a chicken. Go to the devil if you've a mind to. Just *go!*"

"Masterful, ain't he?" the viscountess inquired of Lester, companionably putting her arm through his. "Ah well, I know when I've gone too far, even if it is jolly good fun getting there. Simon, don't paw the gel, as I still consider myself to be chaperoning, even if I'm not in the room. Now come along, Mr. Plum. We'll see if Emery can find you some proper clothing, unless you're more comfortable in gowns, which I can't imagine, unless you're leaving off your stays? You can tell me the truth. I'll understand, really, as Simon had this uncle—a great-uncle, actually—who seemed inordinately fond of trying on his wife's underclothes. Are you wearing this gown just for today, or is it your usual practice to—"

The double doors slammed shut with some violence, cutting off his mother's questions, and Simon turned sharply on his heels, his hot gaze penetrating Caledonia Johnston to the marrow as he gritted out from between clenched teeth, "*Talk*, little girl! Talk to me now!"

"Isn't that what I've been *trying* to do?" Callie shot back accusingly, as if he had single-handedly been keeping her from explaining herself. Then she grinned, an unexpected action that somehow seemed to instantly drain all his anger out of him. "You really do have your hands full, don't you, my lord?" she asked. "Are you quite sure I wouldn't be doing you a greater service by simply gathering up Lester and being on my way?"

Simon's gut tightened at her words, which rekindled his anger, for he knew—did not understand why, precisely, but just *knew*—that the last thing he wanted was to see the back of this absurd creature as she walked out of his life. At least not just yet, not when he was caught between believing her to be an incorrigible infant and a unique, fascinating young woman. He also, thinking entirely selfishly, didn't much enjoy contemplating the thought that he might then be spending all his time saving Caledonia Johnston from her own folly instead of doing what it was he had set himself to do. "Allow you to leave? That depends. If I were to set you and Mr. Plum loose, would you toddle off home, wherever that is, or would you still persist in your inane, insane attempts to blow a hole in the earl of Filton?"

"Of course I'd still be after him," Callie answered frankly, and quite unknowingly sealing her fate—or at least her residence—for the next few weeks. "I only fib about unimportant things. This is important. I want to see the man suffer. He deserves it."

"I thought as much." Motioning her to a chair, Simon also sat down, crossing his legs at the knee. He'd have to take this slowly, one small step at a time. Smiling in what he hoped was an accommodating manner, he said, "However, as I'm somewhat in agreement with your sentiments about the man, although not with your method of punishment, I'm willing to listen to you. I'm also willing to tell you right here and right now that I have no intention of turning you and Mr. Plum over to the authorities."

She snorted. Yes, it was definitely a snort. "I know that, my lord. If you were going to do anything so shabby, I'd be sitting in a gaolhouse somewhere even now. Which doesn't mean that I trust you," she added quickly. "Just that I'm not especially afraid of you."

Not for the first time in the space of the past half hour, Simon felt thankful that he had sent Armand and Bartholomew packing. He'd rather not have Caledonia Johnston's low opinion of his power to menace reach their ears. "Go on," he urged for what felt like the tenth time. "Tell me everything.

Please," he added with an ingratiating smile, remembering his mother's warning about flies and honey.

"I live in Dorset, on the North Downs, rather near Sturminster Newton," she began, sliding her spine halfway down the back of the chair, obviously feeling at her ease as she settled in to tell her story. "Lester is our nearest neighbor and my very dearest friend. He's completely innocent in all of this, as you've probably already deduced. He's only come along to London to please me. Neither of our fathers knows where we are, and we'd really enjoy keeping them happy in their ignorance until we can return home on the mail coach at the end of the week or whenever our mission is accomplished. Have you ever ridden as an outside passenger? It's invigorating, unless the weather turns damp. Now, tell me you won't write to our fathers."

"Agreed," Simon said, trying to picture Caledonia Johnston riding atop a speeding mail coach, clinging to the rails as it careened wildly around tight curves in the roadway, loving every moment of her grand adventure. The image was entirely too clear. "Go on. How does Noel Kinsey have anything to do with a young lady from somewhere near Sturminster Newton?"

"He doesn't. But he very much had something to do with my brother, Justyn, when Justyn came up to town last Season," Callie explained, her eyes going cloudy with remembered pain. She leaned forward, eyeing Simon intensely. "You do know that the earl of Filton cheats at cards, don't you? Ruins young men for their money, and sometimes simply for the sport of the thing, or so it's said."

"It has never been proven," Simon pointed out, careful to appear only mildly interested in Callie's declaration even as his thoughts shot forward, imagining he knew what she would say next.

She didn't disappoint him. "Justyn was so young, so green," she said, shaking her head. "He lost every penny, then became desperate enough to scribble out his vowels for another small fortune that our Papa, because he is an honorable man, felt it necessary to pay to Filton. He-he was so ashamed, Justyn was, that he ran away to India, promising to come back with a fortune—which is above everything silly, as he doesn't have half my genius for invention, poor thing. I may never see him again. Papa is crushed with debt, so that I worry for his health and well-being. We had to dismiss most of the servants and raise the rents on the cottagers. With the loss of all that money, and the wet spring and all—we're in terrible straits. And it's all Noel Kinsey's fault!"

"Which, in your tiny but loyal mind, is much easier than blaming the absent and well-loved Justyn for any of your troubles. Of course."

She immediately bristled. "It was *not* Justyn's fault!" Then she subsided, sighing into her cravat. "Oh, very well. So I'm angry with Justyn as well. I was furious at first, actually. But I love him and have forgiven him. He is, after all, my only brother. I *don't* love Noel Kinsey."

"So, not loving Filton, you decided to shoot him. How very, um, logical," Simon concluded, wearily rubbing at his forehead. "And just what, pray tell, would that solve?"

Callie lifted her legs straight in front of her, about four inches off the floor, and began slowly slapping her boots together—a childish expression of impatience and frustration that seemed somehow understandable—which worried Simon not a little. "It wouldn't really *solve* anything," she said, lowering her legs once more, only to cross them at the ankle and begin her boot-slapping again as she looked down at her feet, then smiled up at Simon. "But it would make me feel so *good* to know that he's suffering for what he did."

And then, as if she had suddenly gotten the bit between her teeth and felt ready for a run, she uncrossed her legs and leaned forward, placing her elbows on her knees as she looked to Simon, her green eyes once more shining, alive with quite charming mischief. "I thought and thought, you see, planning my revenge. First, I considered dressing myself up like this and coming to London to play at cards with the bas—er, the man. But I didn't have enough money for that. I also don't know the first thing about playing cards other than what tricks Justyn taught me—and I already knew how much good those did *him*—so I had to rethink my plans. And then, last winter, when it was so damp, I watched my father limping about on his bad leg—the one he'd taken a ball in some years ago in that first trouble with Bonaparte—and inspiration struck. I'd shoot him!"

She sat back against the cushions once more, her smile, and the last of her bravado leaving her. "And it would have worked, too, if I hadn't crawled into the wrong coach."

That was true enough, Simon thought. She had crawled into the wrong coach. Into his coach. Which had been standing outside that particular gaming hell that particular night because he had been inside, taking the first steps in his own plan to bring Noel Kinsey low.

If there was such a thing as fate, he might begin believing that his and Caledonia Johnston's lives were cosmically intertwined. Which was ridiculous.

"You'll stay here until returning to Dorset," he said before he could examine his motives, or his temporary insanity, in more than a cursory manner. "You and Plum both. Give me the address of your lodgings, and I'll have someone fetch your belongings."

"No."

Well, Simon thought, *at least she hasn't gone immediately hysterical on me.* Just *no.* "The subject is not open to debate, Miss Caledonia Johnston," he said, smiling as she shot daggers at him with those lively green eyes at his deliberate use of her given name. "It's either that or the guardhouse for you and Mr. Plum. He'll cause quite a stir in that pink horror, don't you think?"

"Bounder! You said you wouldn't do that!" she exclaimed, leaping to her feet, her cheeks paling.

"I lied," he answered smoothly. "It's a small thing, tricking you with a lie, but it satisfies me in some strange way. You deserve nothing more after kidnapping me last night."

"You'd sink to petty revenge?" Her full upper lip curled into a sneer. "And your mother thinks you're such a grand prize. Ha! A lot she knows, poor woman!"

Simon walked to the doors to the foyer and flung them wide, so that Emery and Roberts, who had both had their ears pressed to the painted wood, nearly tumbled to the floor inside the drawing room. "Escort Miss Johnston back to her chamber, Emery, if you please," he ordered, as the butler flushed and busied himself in straightening the lapels of his coat. "And lock the door behind her. Now, where is the pink horror? I want him in my study within five minutes, or I'll know the reason why."

He turned back to Callie. "Your father's first name, if you please, Caledonia. Come on, don't dawdle. Or should I simply ask Mr. Plum? I merely have to dangle a chicken leg under his nose, I have a feeling, and I'll have your entire life story in a twinkling."

"Camber," Callie bit out angrily as she sat down with a thump. "Sir Camber Johnston. But you can't really mean to tell him what I've done? Even you wouldn't be that mean to an old man."

"No, I wouldn't be that hard-hearted," Simon admitted, the wheels inside his agile brainbox still turning at such a wild pace that he was considerably impressed at his own quick brilliance. "I am merely, with your permission, going to have my mother the viscountess pen him a note explaining your presence here at Portland Place for the remainder of the Season. Yours, and that of Mr. Plum, once I have gotten his father's direction as well. She has a fertile mind for mischief, my mother, she'll come up with some reasonable explanation. You see, *Caledonia*," he ended, knowing his smile bordered on evil, "now that you at last appear willing to listen, and understand just who is in charge here, I am about to make you the happiest of women."

"I wouldn't marry you if you threatened to shoot me in *both* knees!" she exclaimed, obviously remembering his mother's dotty conclusions.

"Now there's a piece of good news to gladden my day," Simon sniped, again aware of some disappointment in learning of her continued low opinion of him. Was he really such an ogre? "No, I had quite another treat in mind, if you will trust me to be your coconspirator?"

Callie tipped her head to one side, clearly reluctant, yet definitely interested, just as he'd hoped. "My coconspirator? In what way?"

"Why, in bringing Noel Kinsey to ruin, of course. It may seem a happy coincidence, but you and I were both in Curzon Street last night on the same mission, that of bringing the earl of Filton to his knees—in my case, only figuratively speaking. I have, for reasons you need not know, recently decided that he has abused his run of luck against callow youths like your brother and should be punished. Shooting the bounder is only a hit-or-miss affair, if you'll pardon my poor joke. However, I very much like the idea of making the fellow suffer. Suffering, for instance, the way he would if you, Caledonia Johnston, were to find yourself betrothed to marry him."

"*Betrothed* to him?"

Simon nodded, now the one with the bit firmly between his teeth and his mind galloping along quite nicely, thank you. "*After* you have been presented at a ball my mother shall hostess, and after he has been made to understand that you are a considerable heiress. *After* you have led him on a merry chase as I am convinced only you could do, pushing him near to distraction as you run hot and cold concerning your receptiveness to his affections, so that he is constantly at sixes and sevens. You could do that, Miss Johnston. If I know nothing else, I know that you have the capacity to drive even the sanest of men into stumbling insensibility."

She rose to her feet once more and stood stock-still, like a doe surprised in a clearing, obviously intrigued, obviously becoming excited with his ideas. "Thank you. Um, at least I *think* that was a compliment. You really already have been planning to punish Filton? How can that be?"

"Another time, Miss Johnston," he said, waving off her questions as he continued to pace, as the ideas kept percolating in his brain. "We'll wave you and your dowry beneath the greedy Filton nose, and you'll lead him on a merry dance. Which will make it even easier for me to relieve him of most of his fortune at the card table, so that he is prompted to scribble his vowels, as your brother did, all the while believing he can repay his debt to me out of your immense dowry once you two are married. Unlike your brother, you see, I am *very* good at cards. The more you lead him on, the deeper he'll gamble."

She passed over his compliment to his own prowess to ask, "What dowry?"

"The one we'll invent, of course, Caledonia," he said slowly, as if speaking to a faintly backward child. "Really, I thought you prided yourself on your resourceful turn of mind. Don't disabuse me now, just at the gate, with the entire race yet to be run. Pay attention. Now, as I was saying, Kinsey will expect you to marry him and, by marrying him, save him from ruin when I call in his debts. Which you won't do, jilting him most publicly—at Almack's, perhaps?—so that the remainder of his creditors get wind of his ill fortune quickly and he ends, if we're very, very fortunate, locked up for debt alongside many of his victims. Or he might flee to the Continent. Either result is acceptable."

He stopped pacing, yet still feeling invigorated by his flashes of brilliance, and turned to look at Callie. "But you'll have to be brought up to snuff, of course, which will take weeks of cooperation on my mother's part. Wardrobe, hair, manners, the whole lot. You and dear Imogene will be very busy. Hard work, all of it, Miss Johnston, but all of it necessary. Now, what do you have to say to that?"

"Go to Almack's? *Me*? Well, I suppose I could. I'm nearly nineteen, certainly old enough for Almack's. Papa's social position would allow it, and as your mother's guest, an invitation probably could be arranged. Well, if that doesn't beat the Dutch. But *me*—at Almack's!" Callie's eyes grew wide as saucers, and she sat down with a thump, nearly missing the chair and landing rump down on the floor. "I-I don't know what to say."

"Ah, you've been struck mute. Another piece of good news to gladden my heart," Simon quipped, really beginning to feel quite extraordinarily good. "Now, go away upstairs with Emery like a brave little conspirator. We'll meet again tomorrow morning, when I'll expect you in my study at nine. Not a second later. We have considerable work to do."

He went to leave the room, then turned about to look at her assessingly. "We'll start with the hair, I believe." *And some deceptive, creative use of cotton padding to increase that nonexistent chest*, he added silently.

"What's wrong with my hair?" Callie asked, reaching up a hand to the poorly trimmed chestnut mass.

"If you don't know that, Caledonia Johnston, I can see that this new plan of mine will be more work than my mother and I will be able to wade through on our own. Expect Mr. Gauthier and Mr. Boothe also to be in my study when you arrive. And perhaps a small army of nuns hired on to pray for us all."

"What—what if we do all this work and Noel Kinsey still doesn't want to marry me, you insufferable prig? Have you thought of that?" she called after Simon, who halted in the doorway, looking to Emery, who only shook his head and grinned.

"If the dowry were large enough, Noel Kinsey would agree to bracket himself to your friend Lester," he explained patiently. "You see, the mamas of most young girls with large dowries won't let Kinsey within a mile of their daughters. In that, you will be different."

"Oh," Callie said, deflated, as if that statement made perfect sense to her. But then she rallied, calling after him, "But I warn you, Brockton, stop calling me Caledonia!"

Simon hesitated for a moment, considered answering her, then only smiled and walked on toward his study. He had been right the first time. Caledonia Johnston was little more than a child, for all of her nearly nineteen years. An inordinately appealing child. Mischievous. Adventuresome. Easily led. She'd fallen for his outlandish lies as fast as he could conjure them up and then push them past his lips.

Let his mother entertain herself in bringing the young heathen up to snuff, believing she could first parade her protégé through Society, and then marry her off to her only son. It might take her mind off this damnable idea of turning herself from an oak into a willow and then snagging herself an earl.

Let Miss Johnston believe herself to be an integral part of a grand scheme to bring Filton down, so that she'd allow herself to become Imogene's willing little doll.

Let them both, two very similar-thinking, interfering females, enjoy themselves to the top of their bents while they remained safely out from under his feet and away from the action.

Leaving him free to destroy Noel Kinsey, just as he'd been planning all along.

Book Two
Kindred Spirits?

"Contrariwise," continued Tweedledee,
"if it was so, it might be;
and if it were so, it would be;
but as it isn't, it ain't. That's logic."

—Charles Lutwidge Dodgson

If you are in Rome live in the Roman style;
if you are elsewhere live as they live elsewhere.
                                                —Saint Ambrose

Chapter Six

Contrary to her son's oft-repeated wishes concerning the
matter—even his demands, backed by his remarkably well-
articulated threats alluding to lonely dower houses and diets
of stale bread and ditch water—the determined viscountess
did *not* allow the planned meeting in Simon's study to take
place the next morning.

In fact, she did not permit him within earshot let alone
within sight of Caledonia Johnston for the remainder of the
week and half of the next. What Imogene did do was to keep
the girl locked up in the best guest bedchamber, secreted behind a door that was opened only to admit Imogene, her maid,
Kathleen, and a small army of Roxbury servants summoned
for one reason or another.

Also privileged to enter were a small battalion of milliners,
dressmakers, and other grinning tradespeople. The latter then
bowed themselves out of the Portland Place mansion with

thanks dripping from their lips, grateful tears in their eyes, and their heads whirling at the thought of their anticipated profits.

Roberts, as a matter of fact, had told Callie that he'd heard one of the tradesmen whisper to his rather comely, giggling assistant that the Tunbridge Wells cottage he'd had an eye on to rent for the space of a month after the Season ended and his wife had gone off to visit her mother in Liverpool was now within their reach. Callie, fairly gently bred, but by no means stupid or starchy, had felt this news to be quite the funniest thing she had heard in days, then went back to sulking because she was stuck staring at the four walls of the guest chamber while the rest of the world were free to come and go as they pleased.

Not that her prison was all that uncomfortable. It certainly was a far cry from her modest chamber at home, boasting a high tester bed that cradled her like an infant at night, so that she slept dreamlessly and awoke each day eager to discover what lay in store for her next.

Her windows looked out over Portland Place, and, although she was not allowed to set a single foot out onto the balcony during the day, she had several times cracked open the floor-to-ceiling windows at night. She would then sneak outside to sit with her nightgown-covered legs tucked up beneath her chin, gazing up at the stars that shone over London, and down at the world she had stumbled into willy-nilly, landing on her head when she could just as easily have ended up in gaol, or worse.

The true stupidity of her now-discarded plan to revenge Justyn's ill fortune on the earl of Filton had come home to roost with a vengeance. The luxury of time to reflect on just how harebrained her scheme had been showed her how cavalierly she had gone about this business of vengeance. She'd acted with not a thought to her own safety or, more importantly, to Lester's well-being. Her thoughts shamed her, shamed her deeply.

She'd also had time to consider, and mull over, and begin to like very much indeed, the viscount's plan to bring Filton low. It had been her wonderful new friend, Emery, who had told her of Brockton's finesse with the cards. Apparently he had honed his skills courtesy of Armand Gauthier, who over the years had been, also according to Emery, both a card shark and a privateer of some note. Why, according to the admiring Emery, Gauthier had even sailed with Jean Lafitte, the pirate who had once been the terror and pride of New Orleans, in America.

At least those were the tales Gauthier wove for people who dared to inquire about his background, Emery told her, not that the butler believed the half of it himself. Although he was convinced that the man's considerable wealth had been the result of ill-gotten gains in some way.

Callie could barely wait to see Armand Gauthier again.

And then there was Bartholomew Boothe, the man Emery said was called Bones. Emery was not quite as enamored of him, for the man was not at all spectacular. He did not press a coin into the butler's palm each time he fetched him his hat and gloves, the way Gauthier did.

But Emery also said that the painfully thin Bartholomew Bones could down a full two ribs of beef in less time than it took to cook it, and still find a moment between bites to lecture everyone else at the table on the ills of eating red meat. And that, Emery said, was *very* impressive! Mr. Boothe would expound on those ills, such as gout and rheumatism, and all sorts of ailments he would then explain in such lurid detail that the viscountess had, more than once, found it necessary to aim a hot, crusty roll at his head to shut him up.

Oh, yes. Dinner with Bartholomew Bones was definitely on the list of entertainments Callie looked forward to—if she was ever let out of this pampered prison!

One reason for her discontent was that Lester, unlike the carefully incarcerated Callie, had been left free to run tame throughout the mansion once his clothing had been rescued from Horsemonger Lane. Not that he appeared downstairs other than for his thrice-daily meals in the ornate ground-floor dining room, for which he would have risked death itself, let alone Simon's piercing stares and pointed questions about how on earth any man of sense had allowed himself to be talked into the most infantile, ludicrous scheme in history.

And so, for the most part, Lester became one of the small party that seemed to be constantly in progress inside Callie's wondrously opulent cell, the single Portland Place male besides Emery and Roberts who had permission to enter this new, private sanctuary.

Callie knew she would be let out of the bedchamber once the viscountess was satisfied with her appearance: with her dress, her hair, her deportment. And as Callie had not, contrary to her last governess's opinion, been reared in a stables, she already felt confident that she would not disappoint the viscountess when it came time to be introduced to a peer of the realm or pick up the correct spoon at a formal dinner.

She could also reach down from the saddle and pick up a handkerchief while riding at a full gallop, shoot the pips from a playing card at ten paces—Justyn could shoot them out from twenty—climb a tree faster than Lester, and beat her father at chess nine times out of each ten games played.

But she hadn't thought the viscountess needed to know

those things, believing that the astute woman might already have guessed at them anyway.

And so, after ten days spent in the guest chamber, being scrubbed and buffed and measured and pinned, Callie would have to say that, for the most part, she was happy enough—and fairly willing to be a good girl and behave herself.

Callie's main source of discontent had been from the beginning and remained that of the existence of one Simon Roxbury, Viscount Brockton. She didn't like him. Liked his mother. Liked his servants. Like his friends. Liked his house. She simply didn't like *him*. Not a jot. Not a jigger. Not a whisker.

He was arrogant, for one thing. She knew, because she was herself arrogant, and could recognize the condition.

He was also domineering, verbose—if verbose meant that he could talk a person to death overweening, dictatorial, rude to his loving if rather unique mother, and maybe just plain mean into the bargain. He certainly had not, Callie knew, shown a single qualm in kidnapping her straight off the street, then locking her up in his house just as if he had the right.

The fact that he was handsome only added to her irritation with the man. She was convinced he knew how very ingratiating he looked when he ran his fingers through his hair, deliberately mussing it as he attempted to look innocent, and flustered, and sickeningly adorable.

He knew how his sun-kissed skin arranged itself into attractive crinkles around his sherry-colored eyes when he smiled, so that he deliberately smiled often, just to annoy her.

And he knew that he was tall, so that he could tower over her, look down on her from his great height, show his well-tailored clothes to good advantage. Why, he probably impressed any number of idiotic young misses who looked up at him worshipfully as he strolled by, tipping his curly-brimmed beaver and twirling his whitethorn cane.

In all, the man was a menace. No, she didn't like him. Didn't like him at all. Definitely. She'd use him, allow him to use her to a certain extent as, together, they worked to destroy Noel Kinsey. Yes, he was giving her a Season—in a way. Yes, she would be going to Almack's. But that was all part of the viscount's plan, not some sort of gift for which she should be grateful.

And she wouldn't be. Grateful, that was. She would just do what she had to do: punish Noel Kinsey. And then she would walk away without a backward glance, without a qualm, without a single regret that Viscount Brockton had looked upon her as an opportunity, and not as a person at all.

She smiled at a sudden thought. No. He didn't look upon her as a person at all. Except when he was exasperated with her, that was.

With luck, she might be able to exasperate him any number of times in an infinite variety of ways.

If she wanted to. Which she didn't.

Did she?

She did not! And with good reason, too. Very good reason!

"Sheila Lloyd," Callie grumbled under her breath, the woman's name, mentioned only once, days earlier, still stuck annoyingly inside her head.

"Did you say something, Callie?" Lester asked as he sat crossed-legged on the floor of the bedchamber, a bowl of ripe plums on his lap.

"Nothing worth repeating," she said quickly, mentally slapping herself for the twists and turns her mind had taken, leading her to thinking about Sheila Lloyd—the *married* Sheila

Lloyd, if she had understood the viscountess correctly. After all, it wasn't as if she cared a fig about Simon Roxbury's life or the people who filled it.

"Will you be having your face all painted like that for much longer, Callie?" Lester asked, comically wrinkling his nose at his friend's appearance, so that she let out her breath in a sigh, grateful for her friend's interruption of her disturbing thoughts. "Turns me off my food, it does, and no lie."

Callie, wiggling her nose, which had begun to itch as the pinkish white paste of cream and crushed strawberries began to dry on her skin, spoke without moving her lips. "Imogene swears the freckles are fading," she said, looking down at the backs of her hands, also liberally slathered with the sweet-smelling but sticky concoction. She had yet to understand all this trouble to rid her of a few freckles she'd gathered while walking about town without her parasol—which would have looked dashed strange with her inexpressibles. But if Imogene wanted them gone, then she'd cooperate and get them gone. "Do you have a knife with you, Lester?"

Lester raised his eyebrows in question, and mock terror. He did have a sense for the ridiculous, which was one of the reasons she so adored him. "That would depend, I suppose. Whom are you planning to kill?"

"Nobody, you blockhead. I haven't wanted to kill anybody in absolute ages," she told him, giving in to the nearly overriding need to scratch at a spot just above her left eyebrow. "Ahhh, that's better. I just thought you could slice me a bit of plum, then slide it into my mouth. I can't open my lips more than an inch until this mess dries or else Imogene will tear a strip off my hide when she comes in here."

Lester nodded, signaling his understanding. "Sorry. No knife. I guess you'll just have to wait. Abstinence is good for the soul, though. The viscountess said so only this morning—right as Roberts was ladling out another whopping serving of eggs onto her plate. I find that queer, don't you? Just as I find it queer that you should call Her Ladyship Imogene. It don't seem right somehow."

"I agree," Callie said honestly, padding over to the mirror in her bare feet as the hem of the considerably taller, larger Imogene's old dressing gown dragged along behind her, as if examining her reflection would help in drying the cream on her face and hands. "But, as she pelted me with a half dozen pieces of sugared apricot the last time I dared to address her by her title, I've grown more accustomed to the familiarity. As long as I'm careful to call her *my lady* when we're out and about, of course."

Another few minutes, and she'd be able to rid herself of her final beauty treatment, thank the good Lord. And if the Viscount Brockton and Noel Kinsey didn't appreciate all her efforts, she might just shoot the pair of them!

She turned away from the mirror and looked at Lester. "Don't you just *love* Imogene, Lester? Isn't she simply the most *famous* person? I'm considering her for Papa, you understand. She can't be more than a half head taller and a half dozen years or so his senior and, since they're both ancient anyway, I don't see how that should matter. Do you?"

"Her Ladyship and Sir Camber?" Lester shivered. "Oh, I don't think so, Callie. If she's able to trick him—and my papa—with whatever farradiddle she wrote in her letters to them? Well, once they were wed he'd probably spend the remainder of his declining years hiding out in the stables, drinking himself senseless after realizing he'd gotten himself bracketed to a crafty, conniving old—whoops!"

"Oh, do go on, Lester," the viscountess purred as she stood

just inside the room, one hand still on the door latch. "A crafty, conniving old what—? Biddy? Or worse?"

Lester colored, his complexion only a few shades lighter than the half-eaten plum he held in his hand. "Callie?" he begged, looking at her as if she was the only hope left to him in this world.

"Biddy, probably, Imogene," Callie answered matter-of-factly, daring to smile at the viscountess, which served to crack the dry, itchy paste on her face, sending a shower of fine pink-and-white powder down the front of her dressing gown. "But he loves you, truly he does. Don't you, Lester?"

Lester scrambled to his feet, the bowl of plums tipping over so that its contents scattered across the carpet. "Oh, yes, *yes*! Adore you as if you was m'own mother, I swear it!" He reached down to rescue a single plum, rubbed it against his waistcoat, and offered it to the Viscountess. "They're delicious. Truly."

"Idiot!" Imogene barked, snatching up the plum, taking a healthy bite out of it before ordering Callie to wash her face and hands in the basin behind the Chinese screen that stood in the corner. "I can't tell you, children, how much younger I feel now that the pair of you are underfoot. Busy, busy, all the day long. It's wonderful. Callie—you do remember that Madame Yolanda will be arriving within the hour?"

Callie splashed more cold water on her face, then groped on the table for a towel, fighting back tears as some of the cream-and-strawberry concoction got into her eyes. Scrubbing at her face as she poked her head and shoulders out from behind the screen, she lowered the towel and squinted across the room at the viscountess. "Madame Yolanda?"

"The hairdresser, dear," Imogene clarified, licking at one finger after the other, ridding herself of the last of the sticky plum juice deposited there as she had sucked on the pit, then extracted it from her mouth and tossed it in the direction of the cold fireplace.

It hit squarely in the center of the dead ashes. Lester, inspired by this action, grinned and immediately sent his own plum pit sailing in the same general vicinity. His aim proved to be less sure than that of the viscountess, so that the pit clanged solidly against the andirons.

"Dolt," Imogene chided affectionately, then turned to Callie once more. "She comes highly recommended."

Callie dried her hands on the towel, turning away to place it back on the table as she asked, her face carefully hidden, "This Madame Yolanda, Imogene. Does she care for your hair as well?"

"Oh, no, no—Kathleen serves me well enough. Why?"

Her face carefully blank, Callie came out from behind the screen and looked at the viscountess once more, at the mass of brassy yellow curls more suited to a much younger—and less wellborn—female. "No reason, Imogene. But I am nervous about anyone touching my hair. Do you suppose we could *both* avail ourselves of Madame Yolanda's services this afternoon, with you taking your turn first? That way I shouldn't be so, um, so apprehensive."

"Lies no better than you, Lester, for all she prides herself on her supposed vices," the viscountess said, subsiding into a chair, her purple-and-white-striped day gown billowing out around her considerable bulk like a hot-air balloon ready to lift off from Hyde Park Corner. "Simon hates the color, you know. I suppose Kathleen wouldn't be too upset if I were to let Madame Yolanda have a whack or two at it. I was thinking red this time—something to pull a gentleman's eyes higher, away from my figure. What do you think, Lester? Would that do the trick? Would that help snag me an earl?"

Lester searched the carpet, possibly on the lookout for a convenient trapdoor through which he might successfully disappear. "Well . . . I really don't . . . that is, I'm not so well up on such—*red*, you say, ma'am?"

"Congratulations, Lester," Imogene said, pushing at her girlish curls. "You have more tact than my son, who says I resemble nothing less than an overgrown canary in the midst of a bad molt." She sighed, looking to Callie. "If Madame Yolanda can't get it back to the mousy brown I sported until the white started creeping in—galloping in, actually—what do you think about the notion of turbans? They're all the crack, I understand, for miserable old ladies past any hope of matrimony. Well, the devil I will! Not while there's a dye pot left on this earth!"

Callie bent to pick up the remainder of the plums that still littered the carpet, rubbing one against her hip before taking a lusty bite of the sweet fruit. She chewed for a moment, considering the viscountess's words, and the mulish expression on the woman's face. "I still don't understand why you should be so afraid of the title of dowager, Imogene."

"You wouldn't, gel, as you are young, and still believe you'll remain young forever. I look at you—" The viscountess sighed and shook her head. "It was only yesterday that Simon's father and I spent our days laughing at life. Now I'm a dried-up old prune of a widow, forced to sit on the edge of the dance floor and watch the fun pass me by, watch life pass me by. Stick dowager in front of my title, gel, and I might as well go into the home wood and fall on my sword—or start collecting cats who climb the draperies with their nasty claws and cough up horrid-looking clumps in the middle of my best satin coverlet. I want a *man* in my bed, gel, not a hairball!"

"I don't think I should be hearing this." Lester bent his head, to hide his flushed cheeks, and headed for the door. "Oh, no, Papa would say I *definitely* shouldn't be hearing this."

"Oh, sit down," Imogene ordered with a wave of one beringed hand. "Nothing's being said here that isn't true. What I'm talking about here is life, my young friends, *life*. Men and women have been pleasing each other under the sheets since the beginning of time. Or did you think your mamas found you both in a cabbage patch?"

Lester collapsed into the striped satin slipper chair and stared up at the ceiling. "I'd rather not think about where she found me, if that's all right with you, ma'am. Or picture the event in my mind, now that I think on it. The whole notion is unconscious."

"Unconscionable, Lester," Callie corrected, trying not to giggle at the sight of her friend in such embarrassed agitation, "although I believe unconscionable to be too strong a word. Imogene—you've been telling a fib, haven't you? You don't care about being a dowager, not really. You don't care that your son might marry—and are even pushing me at his head. All of that dowager business is no more than a pack of lies. In truth, you just care that you might have missed your last chance to—how did you say that?—be pleased under the sheets?"

"Oh, God, make them stop," Lester groaned, dropping his head into his hands, covering his ears. "Please!"

"I knew you were a sharp one, Callie," the viscountess said, slapping the flat of her hands against her legs. "Not that I could tell Simon the whole of it, of course, as sons don't seem able to see their mamas as anything more than sweet tabbies who embroider slippers and wait until there are a dozen people within earshot before inquiring if their offspring are wearing fresh linen."

Lester let out with a strangled cough, even though he'd hadn't had a bite of plum in a good five minutes.

"Buck up, son—I'm almost done," Imogene said bracingly. "I have some reason to be fearful, you know. Suppose Simon marries before I can find myself a willing mate and bring him up to the sticking point. What then, eh? I'm too old to be ogling the stablehands the way I could a few years ago, and too proud to beg. So, with dowager added to my title, I'll end up on the shelf forever. A *dowager*, Callie. Think on it! Might as well hang a sign over my head saying 'too old to bed, too young to die.'"

"That tears it!" Lester exclaimed, jumping to his feet and racing to the door, flinging it open so hard that it banged back against the wall before swinging shut behind him.

Imogene grinned. "I don't know about you, but I thought he'd never leave," she said, sitting back against the cushions. "Now, I suppose your next question, as we're being so wonderfully blunt, would have to do with why I think you and Simon will be making a match of it before the Season is out—and why that particular development doesn't bother me."

Callie picked up the ends of the sash she'd tied tightly about her waist and began picking at the fringe attached to each end. "Since you haven't said a word about any such association since that first day I met you, I had rather hoped you'd forgotten the notion, actually."

"Well, I haven't," Imogene chirped happily, putting her hands on the arms of the chair and boosting herself to her feet. "You're the one. Definitely. He doesn't plan to marry, you know. Has said it so often he believes it, not that I do. And then when I read that Austen woman last winter—well, that has nothing to do with this, except to say that it concentrated my mind on the inevitability of Simon's fate, and made me take a good long look at the stablehands. Pitiful lot! Anyway, one way or the other, I suddenly realized that I was rapidly running out of time to find my own happiness again. I'm no milk-and-water puss, Caledonia Johnston, and neither are you. We may not need a man in our lives, but we damn full well would *enjoy* one."

Callie tipped her head to one side inquiringly. "Why?"

Imogene took hold of Callie's hands and led her over to the bed, pushing her down on the edge of the mattress and sitting down beside her. "Caledonia, how old were you when your mother died?"

"Twelve," Callie said, turning her head and looking at the viscountess out of the corners of her eyes. "What has that to do with anything?"

"A precious lot, I'd say, if I know men and their stammering, stumbling ways with young daughters," Imogene answered. "Your governess—did she tell you about, about the more *intimate* goings-on between a man and his wife?"

Callie believed her cheeks had now turned as fully red as Lester's had earlier done. "Miss Haverly taught me my sums, geography, proper posture, and how to sip soup. My education, however, was not limited to Miss Haverly's view of the world, if that's what you're asking. I have seen animals in the fields. I understand nature. And I've heard more than one of the maids giggling from behind my father's bedchamber door late at night when I was sneaking out to meet Lester and take a moonlight ride to the pond to catch frogs. That *is* what you're asking, isn't it?"

"It is, indeed. Although I do not believe there are any women in existence who are incapable of enjoying the wonders of *nature*, as you've termed it, I do believe there are those of us who are more *disposed*, as it were, to seek the mystery and adventure of the thing." She squeezed Callie's hands. "*You*, gel, are one of those lucky creatures. You grab at life with both hands, the way I have always done. You *enjoy* life, enjoy adventure. You're willing to take risks. You have courage and fire and spirit. Why, if it weren't for the fact that you're a pretty little thing and I'm as homely as a mud fence, I'd swear I had given birth to you, truly I would. And I *will* swear that you're just what Simon needs, which is why I'm willing to see him married to you even before I snag a body for myself. I'm even happy about it."

She squeezed Callie's hands again, then stood up, turning away as she added, "Not that he'll see what's in front of his face, of course, no more than his father did." She turned back to lean her face close to Callie's. "Which is why you're locked up here, gel, until I can gild the lily. Simon thinks he is embarking on this adventure solely to best that Filton fellow, and we'll allow him to stumble along in his ignorance, at least for a while. But we know better, don't we, gel?"

"I know nothing of the sort!" Callie exclaimed, rolling onto the bed so that she could escape the sight of Imogene's grinning face. She rolled over twice more, until she was able to put her feet down on the opposite side of the bed, which she did, standing up as straight and tall as she could with the too-large dressing gown now wrapped around her, cocoonlike. "And if I did, I would be out of this house this instant, and on my way to find myself another pistol!"

Imogene only shrugged. "Have it your own way, gel," she acquiesced, doing her best to look downpin, but losing her battle as she reached into her pocket and drew out a paper she then unfolded and held out to Callie. "I had the servant wait for an answer. Here—read your father's letter."

Callie eyed the paper as if it might bite her, and wrapped her arms around her stomach. "You read it to me," she said, her heart beginning to race as she imagined just what the viscountess could have written to her father, and her father's answer.

Imogene refolded the paper and put it back in her pocket. "There's no need to read it, as I've committed the lines to memory. Let's see, how does it go? Oh, yes. 'My dear Viscountess Brockton'—so formal, yet vaguely intimate, don't you agree? 'I have just now returned from my trip to find Caledonia missing and your servant waiting to ease my worried heart as to her whereabouts. How can I ever thank you for rescuing my dearest Caledonia and that brainless Lester Plum from their predicament, brought about by their own pigheadedness in attempting to cross a rain-swollen stream in a poor wagon on their way back from their ill-advised jaunt to her aunt's estate. Caledonia has ever been one for mad adventures, which is undoubtedly what she thought this small journey would be when Lester suggested it. And to have brought them both to London, so that Lester could be treated by your personal physician, is beyond kind. I thank you again for your generosity.' There. I may have added a word or two, but I think that's about right."

"You told him Lester and I had an accident, and that you rescued us?" Callie asked, walking around to the bottom of the bed, her hand on the post. "How inventive. And tell me, how bad is Lester's injury? Will he live?"

The viscountess only shrugged again. "A broken arm. Just the one wing, nothing worse. But, as I was on my way to London, with no time to lose, and Lester's arm was well enough in the sling I fashioned from one of my very own petticoats, it seemed easier to continue our journey than to backtrack to return you two truants to your homes. After all, you'd already inconvenienced me enough. I am quite the hero, actually, as my servant also brought me a second missive, written by Lester's father, lauding me as a near saint. Either that, or Lester's papa and yours are the two most gullible gentlemen in all of England."

"Yes, that. The second thing. Gullible," Callie remarked absently as she let go of the post and began to pace. "Papa was already gone from home when I left, so he finds it reasonable to believe I had run off to be with Lester. Lester was already on his way to London, so *his* papa sees nothing remarkable about Lester's staying away. Although he is probably grinning from ear to ear to think that his son has landed on his feet so well, finding himself in Portland Place. Yes. Yes. I can see that both Lester's papa and my own were more than willing to accept any explanation that came to them with a crest pressed into the sealing wax."

She looked up at the viscountess. "I would be lying if I said I wanted to leave here. I'm having the time of my life, being measured for fine gowns and looking forward to going to the dance at Almack's. Then there's the prospect of teasing the earl of Filton with the supposed dowry your son says will besot the earl so that he doesn't see himself being ruined until it is too late. I am and will be enjoying every moment of all of that. But any notions you might have of marrying me off to your son are fair and far-out, Imogene, do you understand?"

"Oh, yes. Of course. I understand perfectly," the viscountess agreed with obvious insincerity, cocking her head to one side as they both heard a faint scratching at the door. "It will be enough if squiring you about in society brings me to the notice of a few gentlemen of my own age. I mean, if you don't have the wit to make the most of Simon's plans, I'm certainly not such a slowtop as to miss *my* opportunity. Now, as that is probably Madame Yolanda, I suggest that we put this subject to rest. I simply wanted you to know that this is not your adventure alone and that you owe me your cooperation. Understood?"

"Absolutely, Imogene," Callie agreed, wrapping the dressing gown more fully around herself, knowing she hadn't made her point but also knowing she never would. Not with Imogene. "And I'm sure Lester will likewise agree to forget what he has heard. In fact, he is probably on his knees at this very moment, praying for blessed forgetfulness."

"Poor spineless creature," Imogene said, clucking her tongue. "But I am growing oddly attached to the boy. It took all of my considerable personal discipline not to have Roberts run a note round to Weston's after Lester was fitted for his new wardrobe, asking that he make up a lovely big blue bow we could tie around the boy's throat."

"Shame on you, Imogene. Lester is not a pet," Callie protested.

But she could not help but smile in embarrassed agreement when, before she flung open the door to admit Madame Yolanda, the viscountess quipped, "Of course he is, gel. He's your pet. And now he's mine, too. And we are both half in love with the silly creature. Oh, just look, gel—it's not Madame Yolanda at all. It's Roberts, carrying boxes that must contain the first of your new wardrobe. Marvelous! You'll be able to come down to dinner tonight. Won't Simon be pleased!"

Callie didn't have the heart to tell her benefactress that

she doubted Simon Roxbury would be at all pleased, no matter if she were dressed in breeches or gossamer—or if she came to him stark naked, with a rose between her teeth. He couldn't care about her one way or the other. If he did, he would have found some way to talk to her in these past days, and he hadn't. He had simply been content to allow his mother to handle the "creation" of the "instrument" he planned to use against Noel Kinsey.

And that suited Callie straight down to the ground!

At least that's what she kept telling herself whenever she stood behind the curtains, peering out at Simon as, elegantly clad and looking supremely confident, he strode across the flagway and leapt up into his curricle or his carriage, heading out for a day or evening of pleasure without a thought to her.

Sure, I rose the wrong way to-day,
I have had such damn'd luck every way.

—Mrs. Alpha Behn

Chapter Seven

What England didn't need at the moment was rain, which was precisely what it was getting, by the bucketful. Simon felt as if he had spent the better part of the year running between raindrops, leaping over puddles. The remainder of his time he'd spent listening to Silsby lament the poor state of his master's boots, his master's evening slippers, his master's hose, his master's cloaks and capes, which invariably returned home with damp shoulders and muddy hems.

Of all of it, Silsby's whining dirges were the worst, which was probably why, as Simon carefully crossed the street heading for White's, his ears only faintly registered the sound of approaching hoofbeats and carriage wheels. He instead concentrated his gaze on the puddles left over from the morning's deluge and his mind on wondering why in the name of Heaven anyone would pick up bits of the street and run off with them. What possible use could anyone have for cobblestones?

Then he heard it, the sound of heavy, dull thuds, of voices raised in anger. He hastened to reach the flagway so that he could turn about and look back across the street, and saw the answer to his wonderings as he watched a hail of cobblestones winging their way through the air, to smash against the side of a canary yellow coach.

"Prinny," Simon muttered beneath his breath as the Prince Regent's coach went flashing by, a half dozen outriders doing their best to control their startled horses, the coachman employing his whip to urge his team forward as he yelled for everyone to clear the way. "You'd think the man would have the good sense to stay bolted safe inside Carlton House, where his loyal subjects can't reach him with their small tokens of affection."

Before the outriders made up from the Prince's own guard could react, the four or five attackers—displaced mill workers by the looks of them—had dropped the remainder of the cobblestones they had appropriated for the purpose of pelting His Majesty's coach and were already halfway toward a nearby alleyway, and escape.

"Damn and blast!" Simon shouted as one of the mounted guards wheeled his horse close by him, sending a shower of muddy water over his new pantaloons. "I've half a mind to toss a few bloody cobblestones of my own, damn me if I don't!"

"Experiencing some sort of difficulty, are you, old friend?" Armand Gauthier inquired from behind Simon just as he had raised his fist, shaking it at the last horseman as he followed after the escaping coach. "Prinny ought to give good warning before he goes out and about. That way we could all stay indoors, and avoid being caught in the cross fire. That, or he might rethink spending all his subject's monies on fripperies like that outlandish carriage. Yellow? Surely an unfortunate choice, wouldn't you say? Altogether too recognizable."

Simon, who had been occupied in employing his fine lawn handkerchief in an effort to clean himself of the worst of his muddy insult, looked at his exquisitely clad—and *clean*—friend, and grumbled, "How did he miss *you*, that's what I want to know? You couldn't have been more than a few feet from where I'm standing. I tell you, Armand, I've been cursed with the worst luck today."

The two men proceeded into White's, greeting acquaintances as they moved toward the bow window, where Bartholomew Boothe waited. "You know, Simon, now that you mention it, I have noticed that, and not just today," Armand said as he walked in front of him, leading the way. "And it all seems to have begun that night in Curzon Street, with your abduction at the hands of our dear Miss Johnston."

Simon didn't growl, for gentlemen did not do such things, but he came close, glaring at the back of Armand's coal black head. "She did *not* abduct me," he gritted out from between clenched teeth as they took up their seats, nodding to Bartholomew. "I allowed myself to be taken."

"Of course you did," Armand purred soothingly, so that Simon suddenly understood why there were many of their acquaintance who longed to climb into the ring with his friend at Gentleman Jackson's Boxing Saloon and pelt the living daylights out of the fellow. Not that anyone dared, save Simon himself, who had once landed Gauthier on his back during an exceptionally good sparring contest.

"Oh, never mind," Simon said, smiling as he regained some of his good humor, knowing that he was probably making a cake of himself. "I admit it. She was holding a pistol aimed at my nose, and I had no choice but to do as I was told.

Although I probably could have bested her, given a few more miles and a glass or two less of champagne dulling my senses. So, Bones," he went on, smiling at his friend, "how are you today?"

"Drier than you, Simon," Bartholomew quipped, winking at Armand. "I was watching you from here. Couldn't believe you didn't hear Prinny's coach coming, then watched you vault into the air when you was splashed all over. What say you, Armand? How high did our friend jump? Could we enter him in a contest, lay down odds on how high he could leap against, say, a frog we'd catch in the park? I can think of at least three men who would be willing to take on such a wager."

"Three? I can think of a dozen!" Armand countered, waggling his expressive eyebrows at Simon. "Two dozen, if you'll agree to make it three out of five jumps."

"There are times I believe that you, my loyal and pathetically amusing friends, are all who sustain me," Simon said with a smile as he accepted a glass of champagne from one of the servants, tipping back his head as he took a deep sip of the cool, bubbly liquid. "Otherwise, I should think I have gone stark, staring mad these past ten days. But, listening to the pair of you, I also realize that I may well be the last remaining sane person in all of England. Or, at the very least, the only person of any sense residing in a certain address in Portland Place," he added glumly.

"Haven't seen her yet then, have you?" Bartholomew said, cupping his chin in his hands as he propped his elbows on the tabletop and leaned forward. He was hoping he was right as, true to his nature, he had already wagered fifty pounds with Armand over how long it would take for their friend to break down the door to Caledonia Johnston's bedchamber, climbing over his mother's battered and broken body if necessary.

Bartholomew was holding out for Sunday. Armand had picked today as the one that would bring an end to the battle of wills between Simon and his formidable mother. Another twelve hours, and the fifty pounds were as good as Bartholomew's, and he already had his eye on a fine mare at Tatt's that he'd buy with his winnings. "Good man, Simon. Good man. I admire your patience. Truly."

Simon, who had not been privy to any private wagers, but who knew his friends as well as they knew him, looked at each of the two men in turn, his eyelids slitted, and believed he had deduced the truth. "You're both pathetic," he stated firmly, finishing off his champagne in a single swallow. "Anyone would think that neither of you has anything better to do with himself than make silly wagers on *my* life."

"We don't, Simon," Armand pointed out, adjusting his lace-trimmed cuffs. "And that's the pity of it. We're both here, waiting, champing at the bit, actually, for you to begin your little scheme against Filton. Not that he's here, of course, but we have to begin sometime, introduce the chit to Society and all of that before the Season runs down. Have I mentioned that I am willing to sacrifice myself by leading her out for her first dance?"

"I may be tricking her into thinking she's got some real part in my plan to bring Filton down," Simon said, taking exception to the joking gleam in his friend's eye and not really understanding why, "but that doesn't mean I'll set you loose on her, Armand. She's years too young and green for you. So you won't be leading her out for any dances, unless it's over *my* dead body. Understand?"

"Can you leap that far, Armand?" Bartholomew inquired as

he waved a servant over to refill his glass. "Not that Simon here is all that huge or anything like that. Certainly not as round as Alvanley, for one, or as prodigiously stout as our own Prinny. But only consider the thing. Whether approaching from Simon's side or his toes, it would still be a considerable leap from a standing start, if you take into consideration the fact that—"

"Shut up, Bones," Armand and Simon said at the same time, and Bartholomew subsided into his chair in defeat, his chin colliding with his neckcloth although he was still smiling quite broadly at his own wit.

Simon felt Armand's assessing gaze on him. "She's gotten to you, hasn't she?" he asked quietly. "The pistol-wielding little minx has gotten to you."

"Gotten to me? *Gotten* to me?" Simon shook his head. "Don't be an idiot, Armand. She's little more than a child, and a fractious child at that. I'm a good dozen years her senior, for another thing. And, for another, I don't much like the chit. Add to that the fact that my mother likes her entirely too much, and I'd just as soon I'd never started this whole mad scheme. I should have just sent her packing for her home, let her witless father handle her."

"She just would have come sneaking back, blown a hole in Filton, and ended up in some terrible cell, fending off rats," Bartholomew said. Pronounced, actually. "You did the right thing, Simon. You really did. The safe thing. The prudent thing. Even though it is horribly devious of you, of course. Have you considered what will happen when she figures out what you've done, how you've duped her?"

"I don't prefer to think she ever will find out, Bones, frankly." Simon closed his eyes, sighed. "She'll be coming down to dinner this evening. It was to have been four nights ago, but this time I told Imogene I'd brook no more delays."

He opened his eyes once more, to find Bartholomew glaring at a suddenly smiling Armand. Simon glared at him, too, then realized what was going on between the two men. They *had* been wagering again. Well, he knew who had won this particular bet. Not that it mattered to him, not in the slightest. "My mother wanted to wait until something could be done with the brat's badly chopped hair, or some such thing," he went on just as if anyone was still listening, "then insisted on other female beautifications I did and do not even wish to contemplate."

He picked up his newly refilled glass—it was amazing, the fine service one could secure simply by remembering to monetarily reward excellence—pausing with the rim just an inch from his lips until he was sure both men were attending him again. "I firmly cautioned our dearest Imogene against the dye pots, of course."

"Of course," Armand agreed vaguely as all three nodded their heads in silence, considering the viscountess's own outlandish tresses. "Are we invited to dine tonight? I have to admit that I'm rather curious as to what your dear mother wished to accomplish that it took her a full ten days to work her miracle."

"I'll send you the bills for the phenomenon as they are rendered. That should put your questions to rest," Simon commented dryly, then changed the subject. "Has there been any word on Filton's ailing aunt? Bones? You've spoken to his friends, as you said you would? I'm not wishing the woman underground, but I would like Filton back in town soon, one way or the other."

"She's lingering with some determination as last I heard the thing two days ago," Bartholomew reported, sighing. "But there *is* good news. Seems Filton's aunt wasn't—er, isn't—quite as well off as everyone, including Filton, had believed. With any luck, he'll be cut off without a penny." He picked up his glass, offering it as a silent toast to wise old ladies. "I do love a good gossip, don't you, Simon? Armand?"

"We'll all put on our caps at least once a fortnight then, and play biddies in the parlor, exchanging whispers about the lurid goings-on in Society," Simon suggested, tongue-in-cheek. "Anything to make you happy, Bones."

Bartholomew flushed to the roots of his hair. "As if I'd wear a cap!" he shot back, sniffing.

"This is good news about Filton, though, isn't it, Simon?" Armand inquired even as he grinned at the flummoxed Bartholomew. "Filton was already spending that money, I'll wager, living off his expectations."

"Knowing the man, I'd say you're dead-on, Armand. Making him twice as hungry for a new infusion of funds," Simon said consideringly. "The man is rich enough, but he spends with a free hand, while often forgetting to pay his creditors. I carefully felt out my vintner about Filton just last month, after I learned that the earl also uses him. Suffice it to say the man doesn't hold Noel Kinsey in very high esteem, not that he dares to refuse to sell to him, for then he'd lose his custom entirely. And that's the dilemma of it. Tradesmen are caught between delivering goods for which they may never see payment or refusing to sell to those same people and forgoing any hope of ever seeing so much as a bent penny of what is already owed them."

Bartholomew sat forward, nodding. "As long as Filton and those like him have the appearance of being deep in the pocket, the tradesmen bide their time. Isn't that right, Armand?"

"Correct, Bones," Armand agreed. "But let there be a sniff, a whiff, a *hint* that their pockets are to let, and the tradesmen come down on these same gentlemen like flies drawn to fresh manure. Poor Sheridan had been living with duns in his drawing room for so long he had begun serving them dinner. That, and his embarrassment—for all his grace in concealing it—are probably what's going to kill him in the end."

"Well, we've become rather maudlin," Simon said after silence fell over the table for some minutes. "Not only that, but the mud has dried on my pantaloons, leaving me less than comfortable. I believe I'll head back to Portland Place, to prepare for the great unveiling this evening. Unless there is other news—"

"Just that I've decided against buying that spanking-fine bay mare I saw at Tatt's," Bartholomew grumbled unhappily. He glared at Armand until, as his friends chortled with laughter, he at last allowed himself to smile at his own small joke.

Callie was dressed and ready to go down to dinner as soon as the gong rang, pacing the length of her bedchamber—this lovely room she had grown to detest—and worrying over her appearance.

Did she look fine as ninepence, as Imogene had declared before rushing off with Kathleen, to complete her own toilette? Or did she look "silly," as Lester had flatly declared around a mouthful of cucumber sandwich, a late-afternoon snack meant to keep him from starvation before dinner?

Lester had never seen her as more than a beloved sister, which might account for his reaction at viewing her in anything other than her simple, modest, and definitely youthful gowns. She had noticed that Lester's initial reaction upon seeing her clad in London fashions for the first time had been to swallow hard and croak, "You'll be putting a shawl or something over you, won't you, Callie? A person could take a chill, with her chest all bare like that."

Remembering his words, Callie walked over to the mirror and examined her reflection, raising her hands to the scoop-neck bodice of her simple white gown and giving it an upward tug, wriggling her upper body in an effort to raise the neckline an inch or two.

Or three, she thought, grimacing as she laid the flat of one hand against her throat, looking with some fascination at the swell of her bosom, the rather well-defined and embarrassingly visible shadowy cleft between her breasts. She *did* feel naked, even though her shoulders, back, and arms were covered, straight to her wrists, and her gown—unlike some of her older ones left at home in Dorset—reached modestly to just below her anklebones.

"All this fine material," she mused aloud, "and none of it where it most probably belongs."

But she did like the gown. Liked it very much. It was so soft, for one thing, and clung to her lovingly when she walked. She admired the broad white-on-white band of fairly intricate embroidery around the flounced hem—indeed, she had spent the past ten minutes of her pacing delighting in the movement of those flounces, seeing the glimpse of yellow kid slippers that peeked out with each step.

She also delighted in the narrow yellow ribbon that tied so snugly just beneath her breasts and the almost-straight fall of fabric beneath that ribbon, the material skimming over her flat stomach and flare of hip, making her feel almost as free as she did in her breeches.

She most especially felt some small affection for the sleeves which, although snugly fitted, were capped at the shoulder by small, loose ruffles into which were tucked tiny bunches of artificial flowers—exquisite yellow-silk rosebuds in the form of tiny bouquets. And, just to add the finishing touch, the modiste had fashioned a narrow, fairly tight yellow ribbon that was now tied around Callie's throat, its ends looped to one side in a simple bow in which nestled yet another small silk rosebud.

In short, she believed her gown to be quite wonderful, even if those yards and yards of material began an inch or two lower on her body than allowed for her complete comfort.

She leaned forward and peered into the mirror again, running a fingertip across her cheeks, over the bridge of her nose. The freckles hadn't all disappeared, much to Imogene's frustration, but Callie believed she looked passably good with the few spots that remained, sprinkled as they were in a dusting that added character—yes, that was it, character—to her rather unexceptional features.

Her cheekbones were too high, for one thing, or at least that was what Miss Haverly had declared, tsk-tsking in that lowering way of hers, saying that anything less than rosy red, apple-round English cheeks were "unseemly" in a proper young miss. Her chin, Callie knew, was also too sharp, having—again, according to Miss Haverly—"none of the softness, the roundness, of the proper English female chin, and it's too forward-looking by half."

And it was true, Callie supposed, for her jaw was not only slightly square, it was marred by a small dent at the very center of it. Still, she concluded as she raised her chin, mimicking Miss Haverly's haughty pose, it was also true that she had been blessed with only the one chin, while her former governess owned *two* of them!

The remainder of her face Callie believed to be truly unremarkable. Green eyes certainly were not all that rare or exotic. She much preferred Simon Roxbury's eyes. Although brown eyes were common, blue even more so, the particular sherry color of Brockton's appealed to her very much. Or perhaps it was just the way they seemed to sparkle and dance when he was amused . . .

Callie tilted her head to the left, looking at her right ear, which, thanks to Madame Yolanda, was now almost completely visible beneath her short cap of hair. Ears were funny things. Lester's, certainly, were adorably laughable—standing out from his head so that they fairly waved in strong breezes, and turning an intense red both in the cold of winter and the heat of embarrassment.

Justyn, she remembered, had flat ears, as did she, hugging tightly to their heads. Although Justyn's were rather large, so that he was always careful to keep them covered straight down to the lobe. He said that he wouldn't want to be mistaken for a wild elephant and shot down by some eager hunter before he could explain that he owed this particular disfigurement to his sire's side of the family.

Callie sighed, her breath hitching in a small, dry sob. How she missed Justyn! She and her father had not received more than two widely spaced letters from him. One had been posted from Spain and the other from Italy. There hadn't been much in the way of new information in either of them. He'd taken ship for India, swearing not to return until he could do so in triumph, until he was a nabob and could repay Sir Camber for all the trouble he had brought him. He was in good health. They shouldn't worry about him. And that was all.

How would Justyn feel, she wondered, if he could see her now? He'd always called her his "brat," as Simon Roxbury also did. But Justyn had done so affectionately, rubbing at the top of her head as he passed by her in the dining room on the way to his own chair. He'd also called her his brat when she routinely bested him at chess during long winter evenings when the weather kept them both inside, bored with their own company, so that they stayed up into the wee hours. How she missed him, and those long nights spent talking and laughing and planning wonderful adventures they would have "someday."

Well, Justyn was certainly off on a grand adventure now, having barely survived his first adventure, that of coming to London to double the small inheritance he'd had from their mother. All those long evenings playing at cards had been for naught. He had not been in town for more than a fortnight when he'd met Noel Kinsey, who had picked him clean of every cent, every dream, and then urged him into scribbling his vowels, promising him that his luck was sure to turn sooner or later.

Callie hadn't expected Justyn to make much of a fortune in London, seeing as how he didn't appear to have a head for strategy—obviously, as she bested him time and again at chess. She had even begun to win against him at whist with some regularity, even though he had taught her the game.

But Justyn had been determined, just as he was now resolved to find his fortune in India. If he hadn't chanced upon someone else like Noel Kinsey, and now was locked up in some squalid gaol, subsisting on moldy rice and beetle bugs. She had spent weeks and weeks so angry with Justyn she could barely see straight, but now all she could do was to worry about him, long to see him again. Pray she would see him again.

Callie turned away from her reflection, blinking as tears stung at her eyes. She wouldn't think of any of that now. Justyn was fine. He had to be! He'd write again soon, tell her father and her of his grand adventure and how he was already planning his return to Dorset, having realized that running away from his home was no real answer.

And, when he did return, he would find that she, Caledonia Johnston, had taken revenge for his ill treatment at the hands of the card-sharping earl of Filton. He would be able to hold up his head and not worry that he might run into the earl somewhere and be forced to call the man out.

For, if Justyn was not a premier card player, he was miles better at whist than he ever would be at swordplay, or pistols at ten paces. While his aim was excellent, extraordinary actually, she had never seen him kill so much as a spider without feeling remorse about the thing. Aiming a pistol at a living, breathing person—even someone so evil as Noel Kinsey—was something Callie felt to be completely beyond her romantic, softhearted brother's powers.

Which had left it up to Callie—who considered herself to be much more bloodthirsty and resolute—to rid London, perhaps all of England, of one Noel Kinsey before Justyn returned.

Which had made Simon Roxbury's offer of assistance so irresistible.

Which explained Callie's presence in Portland Place, her willingness to dress herself up, trot herself out, and work her wiles on the earl of Filton, distracting him while Simon slowly, methodically, depleted the bounder's pocketbook.

Which also accounted for her being willing to listen to, and overlook, Imogene's silly prattlings about marriages decreed by destiny and the like.

But none of that explained away why Callie was not at all worried about how she looked for her own sake, but only prayed that she looked pleasing to this same Simon Roxbury. Simon Roxbury, who had not bothered, since she had first come under his roof, his protection, to so much as knock on her door and inquire as to whether or not she had just simply and quietly expired on her bed and her rotting carcass might begin to throw off an unpleasant odor anytime soon.

Callie's pacing became more of an unladylike stomping as she allowed the anger, the frustration of the past days to come to a boil inside her. She balled her newly soft, freckle-free hands into fists and turned to glare at the door to the hallway, thinking that possibly, no, probably—*definitely*—she and the insufferable Viscount Brockton could benefit from a private interview before Imogene could show her off like a pet goose tonight at the dinner table.

Simon stood stock-still as Silsby employed his brush to sweep away invisible threads only those with the sharp eyes of a dedicated valet could see clinging to the bottle green frock coat his master had chosen for the evening. He had taken more care with his appearance this evening than was usual for him, and he reconciled this dedication to fashion with the reasonableness of doing his utmost to appear well dressed for his planned evening, which included dropping in at no less than three routs, with a possible visit to his mistress capping off the evening.

He had not seen Lady Sheila Lloyd for several weeks, as she had been out of the city for some time, visiting with a friend who had just gone through her third lying-in. But she had been back in town for five days now and had sent round as many notes, all of them requesting his appearance at her side at any number of evening entertainments.

Simon told himself that he had not responded to Her Ladyship's invitations because they had, to him, been couched more in the language of demands. He would be damned if he'd become someone's tame lapdog, no matter how delectable his mistress could appear when lying back against ivory-satin sheets, her long black hair tumbling over her magnificent bare breasts, an inviting, fairly decadent smile curving her full red lips.

There had been a time when he'd thought it a terrible waste for Sheila to be chained to Lord Lloyd, who was at least seven years older than dirt. But he had come to realize that Lloyd was also richer than Croesus, and that Sheila had been more than happy to have wed him, hoping to bury him within six months. But, like so many fond hopes, this one had been fated to fail, as Lloyd had lingered on for nearly a decade now, so that Sheila's beauty, although still dazzling, was beginning to blur as the years crept on, moving her closer to thirty, and then beyond. The lines around her mouth, once thought to be delicious crinkles, had etched themselves into ever-deepening grooves of dissatisfaction with her lot.

Not that Simon was the sort to consider only physical beauty. But, when it came to a man's mistress, it wasn't as if he was on the hunt for intellectual compatibility. His requirements did not include someone to curl up in front of the fire with on a long winter's evening, a chessboard between them, perhaps. They'd had an arrangement for the past six months, Sheila and Simon, a mutually beneficial physical association with no promises given, no expectations of making theirs into a more permanent arrangement.

Except that Sheila was showing hints of becoming proprietorial. Demands for his appearance? Hardly! Simon had better things to do with his life than spend it kowtowing to a female, and that female not even his wife. It was time for Lady Sheila Lloyd to be on her way, he decided somewhere between choosing pearl studs to go with his bottle green coat and chasing a fretting Silsby out of the dressing room entirely when the valet had suggested his master remove that same coat for a more thorough brushing.

He would concentrate on the project he had so lately undertaken, Simon decided as he picked up one of the pair of silver-backed brushes that sat atop his dressing table and made another stab at pushing back under control the one unruly lock of hair that persisted in falling onto his forehead.

He would inspect Caledonia Johnston this evening at dinner, praying that his mother had not taken leave of all of her senses and dressed the girl up like some Christmas pudding.

He would put the chit through her paces while Filton was still perched atop his poor great-aunt's bedstead like a hungry, grinning vulture.

He would take her for an early-morning ride in the park, so that she didn't gawk like a country bumpkin when he first drove her out in the Promenade.

He would show her some of the sights and point out that having one's mouth agape while passing by some of the more interesting buildings in London was really not "done."

He would give her instruction on such things as the rudiments of protocol, the strict rules of Almack's, and—he sincerely hoped not—even oversee lessons in table manners if the need arose.

In short, he would now take over where his mother had left off, smoothing out the edges on this admittedly young, undoubtedly naive child he had—in some mad moment he could not now quite remember with any real clarity—somehow thought to hoodwink with a foolish plot meant to serve up to the earl of Filton a whopping helping of his just deserts.

He owed the chit some fun after lying to her so thoroughly. Once Filton had been dealt with, he had to be sure Caledonia was up to snuff so that he could placate her by giving her just a bit of the Season he'd promised. He owed her that much as a reward for keeping his dearest mother occupied for a few weeks, and off the subject of stays and earls.

The diversion meant to keep Caledonia safe, his mother occupied, and his own plan on course was, however, also sure to prove expensive. He supposed he deserved that, and he was getting it, in spades. His mother had been flinging orders about willy-nilly, and the parade of tradesmen in and out of Portland Place had been unrelenting. The cautious Emery even had been pushed to take his employer to one side and suggest that the possibility of both a tighter rein on Her Ladyship's flights of fancy and a swift snapping shut of His Lordship's deep pocketbook would not be beyond the realm of reasonableness.

What Simon had not bothered to explain to his most loyal retainer was the fact that, since the advent of Caledonia Johnston into the mansion in Portland Place, his dear mother had not once broached the subjects of corsets or dower houses. She had kept silent on her entirely mad notion of landing herself an earl before her son could utterly destroy her life by up and marrying the first female to fall into his lap during the Season. Whatever the bills, whatever inconveniences he and the servants might have to endure, they were as nothing compared to watching his mother diet herself into starvation, dye her hair the same hue as a buttercup, tart up her face with rouges and creams, drown herself in scent, then set off for an evening's "hunt."

Yes, having Caledonia in the house, having his mother's idea of the "ideal wife" in the house, had already shown to be more profitable than any niggling economies Emery could think up—and the man had been born to pinch pennies.

Not that Simon thought his mother *really* believed that Caledonia Johnston had been sent to them by some quirk of providence, to become the daughter-in-law she had always dreaded but now welcomed as one did the flowers in May. However, knowing his mother—and, God help him, he did— she might also have already drawn up an agreement with Caledonia, stating that she would not allow Simon to drag her to the altar until such time as Imogene grew more accustomed to the idea of being termed the Dowager Viscountess Brockton.

But it was all of no matter, no importance. Caledonia would keep his mother occupied for the remainder of the Season. Imogene would keep Caledonia busy with shopping and dress fittings and lessons in deportment. And he, Simon, would be left free in his pursuit of Noel Kinsey's social and economic demise and banishment.

It wasn't really all that shabby a plan, actually.

And then Caledonia Johnston could have a few weeks of fun traipsing about in Society. Why, she'd be so thrilled to be dancing at Almack's, flirting with half-pay officers, that she wouldn't even be angry that Filton had been punished before she could excite him into besotted stupidity and rash behavior.

And then he, Simon Roxbury, would forget that same Caledonia Johnston the moment he waved his last good-bye as her coach rounded the corner at the end of the street.

Simon gave his cuffs one last inspection, feeling quite pleased with both his appearance and his brilliant, flawless plan, then frowned into the mirror as he heard a scratching at the door leading to the hallway.

"Silsby!" he called out impatiently, sure his valet had returned, begging to have one last inspection of his employer's attire for the evening. "If you don't understand the word *retire* when placed in the context of departing a room when your presence is no longer requested, perhaps you are anxious to *retire* in earnest, from my employ!"

The door opened a crack even as he glared at it, willing it shut. A moment later, he involuntarily drew in his breath as Caledonia Johnston's head appeared in the opening. Or at least he *thought* it was Caledonia Johnston. She certainly didn't *look* like the half-grown girl he had last seen in his drawing room, dressed up like a young man and appearing, for the most part, as if she had been dragged through a hedge, backwards.

"You're in your usual good humor, I see," Caledonia said as she pushed at the door and eased the rest of her body into the dressing room. "I thought we might have a small talk before we go down to dinner, my lord," she explained.

Simon's brain only registered every second word. He was much too occupied in biting his tongue, that longed to say such things as: "My God, can that glowing chestnut halo really be your hair?" and "I knew your eyes were large, but they now seem to fill your entire beautiful angel face," and, most damning of all if he had been so much of a nodcock as to allow his mouth to open, "You have *breasts*?"

Not being a nodcock, and drawing on years of self-control, Simon scolded instead, his tone cool and detached. "You possess the social sense of a flea, don't you, brat? Whatever makes you believe it is even vaguely permissible for you to enter a gentleman's dressing room?"

She only shrugged, clearly not cowed by his tone. Her movement immediately drew his gaze most automatically to the slight shadow between her breasts—just as his mother had planned, damn her for knowing her son so well. Callie then replied reasonably, if maddeningly, "As you weren't in your bedchamber, I just looked in the next most obvious place. Surely you don't think we need a chaperone, my lord. Or do you harbor plans to ravish me?"

"I heard voices, my lord," Silsby said, popping into the room through the open door to the hall to stand behind Caledonia, and earning himself his employer's undying gratitude by dint of this intrusion. "Is something amiss? Did Miss Johnston become confused on her way to the drawing room?"

Simon pointed at Silsby with his index finger. "That— *that's* it, Silsby," he agreed with more enthusiasm than probably necessary, agreeing that his valet had put his own finger on precisely the problem. "Having seen so little of the mansion, Miss Johnston became understandably confused. If you'd be good enough to direct her, I shall be down shortly myself, as I believe I've just heard the final gong."

"Very good, milord," Silsby said, his smile knowing. "I'll just do that, then be back to give that coat of yours a final brush-up?"

Bowing to blackmail was never comfortable, but Simon took his defeat with good grace. Nodding his agreement to Silsby's plan, he then avoided Caledonia's gorgeous, glorious, aggravated green glare until she at last turned on her heels and exited the dressing room.

At which time Simon Roxbury, Viscount Brockton, a man who considered himself toughened by war and forged hard as iron by his years in society, allowed himself to lean heavily against his dressing table, his knees having somehow lost most of their starch.

"And beneath it all, and for my sins," he breathed quietly, "I already know that she possesses a most magnificent pair of long, straight legs." He closed his eyes and shook his head, dreading the next few hours of this altogether-depressing, bewildering day. And all the days that stretched between this moment and the one where he would wave Miss Caledonia Johnston out of his life.

"My God," he groaned, wiping a hand across his mouth as he thought about those coming days, thought about possibly introducing the maddening, maddeningly beautiful but naive, green-as-grass Caledonia to society, to Armand Gauthier. "What have I done?"

Love is blind; friendship closes its eyes.

—French Saying

Chapter Eight

If one did not enter purgatory until after death, Simon had to wonder what name to give to the near eternity he'd spent having dinner in Portland Square the previous evening.

That his mother had wrought a near miracle—in keeping with the religious theme Simon found himself drawn to when thinking of the evening—was not to overstate her success. But having to spend the entire evening listening to his mother's glee at having performed this marvelous feat would, Simon was sure, have tested the patience of Job.

"Now, watch, Simon," she'd commanded. "Watch her walk. Floats, don't she? You would think she'd clump across the room, like most horsewomen, but she don't. Had her walking with a book on her head all the week long. Two books, near the end of the thing, then the whole set. You might think me to be rough-and-tumble, Simon, and I am, but that don't mean I don't know what's right and proper."

Simon had smiled, and nodded, and averted his gaze from Caledonia Johnston's angry glare.

"See? See, Simon?" his mother had continued once they were all at table. "See how she holds a fork? I taught her that. Not that she came to me a total loss, but I rounded off the edges, put the patina on her. I may not see the point to all this playacting and fancy manners, but I'm not blind to them, either, or their importance in this namby-pamby world that honors such nonsense."

Simon and Roberts had exchanged pained glances.

"Won't embarrass you either, I promise. There—there, did you see that? Chews with her mouth nicely closed. Not like that Bones fellow of yours. Thank the good Lord I had the sense to send round notes this afternoon to the pair of those boys, warning them away from here this evening, as I wanted us to be private, more like family. Nice enough and all that, the two of them are, but Gauthier is much too easily amused, and that man Bones sucks up food like a pig swallowing down slops. Expect him to snort soup up his snout any moment, I do. Roberts, I want another serving of the—damn, boy, but you're good at this anticipating stuff, ain't you? Knew I wanted the beets almost before I did. But raise his wages again, Simon, and he'll soon own us. You pay them so much now, the servants would probably chew for you if you asked them!"

Simon had been forced to glare at the painting over the sideboard, because Roberts was already diligently studying the ceiling.

"And the hair, Simon. What do you think of the hair? It's too short for my liking, but short is all the crack now, Madame Yolanda says. What did she say? Oh, yes. She's to look like an urchin, that's what. But a clean one, of course. Do you think her neck's too long? I don't. That ought to please you, Simon. Oh, *smile*, son, why don't you—or are you going to frown like that the whole of the night? If you was to get hit hard on the back of your head, if I was, for instance, to tell Roberts here to give you a good stiff swipe, why, your face could *stay* that way, do you know that? Think on it, Simon, that's all I ask."

Roberts, Simon remembered with a small chuckle, going against every rule of proper service he had been taught, had then groaned aloud and perforce dared to sit himself down at one of the side chairs placed against the wall, dropping his head into his hands.

But Simon *had* thought on what his mother had said, on all of it, as he had excused himself directly after the last plate was removed. He thought on it as he escaped the dining room, and the house entirely, giving his round of evening social engagements not a single thought before heading off to a long night of solitary drinking, and thinking some more, at his club.

And he had reached a few conclusions. One of them, that of sending his mother to America on the first ship leaving the docks, he'd discarded as mere wishful thinking brought on by too many glasses of champagne.

But early the next morning he had summoned Caledonia to his private study. They had things to discuss before Caledonia murdered him in his bed or he took the coward's way out and deliberately went stark, staring mad.

There was a sharp knock at the door, and Simon turned as Caledonia entered, looking just as ladylike as she had the previous evening, dressed now in a simple day gown of sprigged muslin, a narrow emerald ribbon somehow tied up—most fetchingly, dammit—in her short, cropped hair.

"You summoned me, my lord?" she asked, her faintly husky voice edged with steel.

She was also achingly beautiful again this morning, perhaps even more beautiful than she had appeared last night, if such a thing were possible. "I didn't *summon* you, Miss Johnston," he corrected, hoping to show her that he was willing to be friendly—just not too friendly. "I merely requested Roberts to ask if you could attend me for a moment or two, if it was convenient."

"Attend you?" She closed the door and stood very still just inside the room. "Or *entertain* you? Perhaps you wished for me to walk for you again, or even chew for you? I chew prodigiously well, you know. Or would you rather I discuss the sad state of the English weather? I have been coached in all sorts of empty-headed prattling, although I had no chance to show off my expertise in inanities last night, as your mother refused to shut her own mouth long enough for me to get a word in edgewise. Oh, yes—I've murdered her, in case you're wondering about her absence this morning, and have ordered the most obedient Roberts to bury her body somewhere in the mews. Emery, who came as near to blushing as his starchiness allowed when Imogene asked him to comment on the fetchingly clever cut of my bodice last night, has gone to locate a second shovel. There was a most remarkable spring in his step as he went off on his hunt, even with him being fairly aged and all."

Simon looked at her for a long time, seeing the hard anger in the set of her full, pink mouth, the determination in her stiffly straight spine—and the light of wicked humor dancing in her glorious green eyes. God. Why did he suddenly, inexplicably, find himself longing to soundly kiss the incorrigible brat? "Poor old Imogene," he pronounced sadly, whipping his errant thought back behind a then firmly closed door in his mind, barely able to keep his lips from twitching in his own sudden good humor. "I will miss her."

And then, in a most remarkable moment that would forever live in Simon's memory, he and Caledonia Johnston fell into each other's arms like the best of chums, laughing like naughty children.

"This is nice," Callie said as she opened her mouth, allowing Simon to feed her another grape. She lay on her back as she spoke, her head on Simon's knee as the two of them reclined on the blanket he had spread on the grass in a secluded corner of Richmond Park. "I believe I should probably be very good at *decadent*, don't you?"

"Decadent isn't precisely what we've been striving for, brat, but yes, I do think you'd be rather good at it," Simon said, peeling her another grape as she gave out with a delighted giggle.

How strange that they had started off so very much on the wrong foot—the incident of the pistol, and the clog, still embarrassed Callie when she thought of it—only to end up crying friends. How they had laughed in his study that morning, Callie doing a more than passable imitation of Imogene's behavior at table the previous evening, with Simon playing the role of Roberts with all the pained grimaces and eye rollings of a premier tragedy queen.

It was only when they'd heard the viscountess in the hallway, bellowing out Callie's name, that Simon had sobered, putting a finger to his lips to warn her to silence until his mother turned into the morning room, lured more by the scent of fresh-cooked ham than by any desire to see her protégé.

Simon had then taken Callie's hand, still warning her to silence, and the two of them had sneaked down the hallway toward the kitchens, and the servant stairs.

Within ten minutes, Callie had raced off upstairs to fetch her bonnet and a thin shawl and Simon had convinced the cook to pack up a basket with stuffs he'd located in a speedy ransacking of the larder and cupboards.

Within fifteen minutes they had been in Simon's curricle, on their way to a picnic in Richmond Park, giggling like two mischievous children who had escaped the nursery for a bit of a frolic.

"We're lucky that the weather cooperated," Simon told her as he fed her yet another grape while she smiled up at him, thinking him to be immeasurably more human than she had heretofore believed. She felt quite at her ease with him, as if he were another older brother, much like her beloved Justyn. He popped an unpeeled grape into his own mouth. "Comfortable, brat?"

Callie still wasn't quite sure how she had come to be lying with her head in the viscount's lap, looking up into his handsome, unreadable face but, as he had told her to make herself comfortable as they sat on the grass, it had seemed a good idea at the time. After all, she and Lester had always been this informal, and Simon Roxbury *was* a very good friend.

That was it. She had always felt comfortable with male companionship. Simon Roxbury was like Lester. Like Justyn. There was really no harm in it, surely there wasn't.

She wiggled her stocking-clad toes now as they peeked out from beneath the hem of her gown, then wriggled her entire body a time or two, repositioning her head on his thigh. "Imogene's list of rules—she presented me with one, you know, which I immediately tore into pieces when she left the room—included occasionally being allowed an unchaperoned walk to church with a gentleman, or an early-morning excursion to a park," she told him, grinning. "However, I can recall no mention of an unchaperoned picnic in that park. In short, I'm thinking that we're in breach of one of Imogene's rules, just as I was last night, daring to come to see you in your dressing room."

"And you're correct in your thinking on both counts, brat," Simon said affably, but she sensed that he was at least momentarily unnerved by her remark. And so, to lighten the suddenly tense mood, and as words seemed to fail her, she gifted him with a bright smile.

"What is it?" he asked. "I'm not sure I should be happy with that smile."

"Nothing," she answered quickly. "It's just that I like it when you call me brat. You have my permission to call me your brat any time you wish."

"How wonderful for both of us, I'm sure," Simon purred, shaking his head. Then he positioned his hands under her shoulders and raised her up so that she drew her legs under her for balance and sat there, looking at him, wondering why she suddenly felt a chill in the air, as she had only been teasing him. Hadn't she?

"However," he went on, his tone still lazy as he reclined almost prone against a tree trunk, so that she felt happy again, "as we're friends now, as well as cohorts in our planned escapade, I suppose we'll both be forgiven a few small, harmless lapses in propriety. From now on, in private, I will be Simon and you will be Callie. All right? Now, are you ready for the chicken, or will you have me feeding you grapes all the afternoon long?"

To answer him, Callie reached for the basket, opening it and giving a small squeal of delight as she saw the whole roasted chicken the cook had wrapped inside a checkered cloth. "I'll have a leg, if you don't mind, and I'll eat it with my fingers, too, the way I do at home. Oh," she said, sighing as she ripped one leg free, "you cannot know how I've longed to put off this pretense of being a lady!"

Simon watched as she took a healthy bite of crisp brown skin and dark meat, then he personally dabbed at her greasy chin with one of the linen serviettes he'd pulled from the basket. He then leaned back once more, seemingly content to watch her eat. "You *are* a lady, Callie," he said, so that she smiled around a mouthful of chicken, pleased that he had dropped his insistence on calling her Caledonia. "Tell me, and this is just out of my own curiosity— is your father a baronet or a knight? Having that Sir stuck in front of his name has eased our problems mightily, getting you into society. But I remain curious."

"Papa's only a lowly knight, I'm afraid," she answered easily, ripping off the other chicken leg and handing it to Simon, who began devouring it with as much enthusiasm as she had shown. "And for the silliest of reasons."

"How so?" Simon asked, sitting up again, the better to gnaw on the chicken bone.

Callie told the story in between taking small nibbles at the chicken leg. "Well, you see, Papa just happened to be sitting nearby when one of Her Royal Majesty's maids began choking on a fish bone during a banquet at some local estate party a dozen years or so ago. The knighthood was his reward for saving her—not that he'd meant to do any such thing."

"He hadn't?"

"Oh, no," Callie explained, laughing. "Papa, more the worse for wear after several rounds of toasting His Royal Majesty's health, saw the poor woman choking and bolted to his feet in a panic, planning to race off to get her some assistance. But he drunkenly tripped over the hem of the lady's gown as he turned to run, causing the two of them to pitch forward over the edge of the table—at which point the fish bone shot straight out her mouth and everyone declared Papa to be a hero. Only think," she said happily as Simon began to chuckle, repeating something Justyn had said more than once, "if Papa had only had the foresight to fall on Her Royal Majesty herself, we'd all be peers today."

At that last statement, Simon rolled onto his back, holding his sides as he laughed so hard tears formed in the corners of his eyes. "What—what was your father before his fortunate stumble?" he asked at last, wiping at his streaming eyes with one edge of his serviette.

"A gentleman farmer," Callie told him, trying to hide her own giggles. "Nicely well-off, actually, but becoming Sir Camber seemed to effect a profound change in him and— with Mama no longer about to keep him from such flights of fancy—he concentrated on raising both my brother and myself as if we would someday move in London society. We were both already more than half-grown, and fairly wild, motherless children, but none of that served to dampen Papa's enthusiasm. Justyn found himself inundated with tutors, and I, sadly, a progression of governesses, each one worse than the last. Thank goodness Justyn let me sit in with his tutors, so it wasn't all terrible. Would you like me to say something in Greek? I can, you know."

He looked up at her rather quizzically. "I see. That explains you better to me, I believe."

Callie shrugged off his comment, not sure if she liked it. "The knighthood means nothing to either of us, you understand, especially as the honor expires with Papa, but he was determined," she said, frowning. "I also think it's one reason Justyn went off to London once he reached his majority—to hunt up his fortune, as there seemed precious little hope of another providential fish bone."

"And Lester?"

Callie smiled, picturing her good friend in her mind's eye. "Oh, Lester. His papa is the local squire, and the man spent some years with his nose fairly out of joint after my papa's noble feat raised him a notch higher in what passes for society in Sturminster Newton. But that's all settled now. I think he had wished for a match between Lester and me, actually, until he realized that I quite routinely lead poor Lester around by his nose, which proved that we'd never be more than very good friends. And he is, you know. My very dearest friend."

"Poor Lester, if you're saying that this deep friendship you feel for him explains why he allowed you to dress him up in that pink horror," Simon said, his sherry eyes twinkling, so that she knew he was funning her.

"Lester—Lester is somewhat *malleable*," Callie said carefully, drawing on her lessons with Miss Haverly. And then she sobered, deciding it was time for some home truths. "Just as you believe *me* to be, my lord. But I'm not, not really. I wouldn't be here, wouldn't have allowed myself to become a part of your plan, if I couldn't see the sense, the simple beauty of the thing."

His gaze, that had been so concentrated on her, shifted to the horizon. "Really?"

"Oh, yes. I'm very impressed with it, you know, which is also why I have been so diligent at my lessons. I still can't believe I've allowed strawberries and cream to be rubbed on my face, or spent an hour a day pacing my cell with a three-volume copy of *Pride and Prejudice* on my head. I had to be very careful with the books, as your mother seems to consider Miss Austen to be on a par with Shakespeare."

Simon, still lying at his ease as if he had nothing better to do than sprawl on the blanket, asking her questions, tossed his denuded chicken leg in the general direction of the basket, then wiped his fingers on the serviette. "Your *cell*, Callie? Isn't that a bit harsh?"

Callie raised herself onto her knees, threw back her head, using the chicken leg to cross her heart dramatically before holding it high into the sky, like a sword. " 'Oh! give me liberty, for were ev'n Paradise my prison, still I should long to leap the crystal walls.' " Without relaxing her Boadicea-like pose, she then looked at Simon down the length of her nose and pronounced proudly, "John Dryden."

"The impudent little brat wants a spanking," Simon shot back at her without hesitation as he tossed the serviette after the chicken leg. "Simon Roxbury, Viscount Brockton."

Callie collapsed on the blanket in amusement, her head just inches from Simon's, and the sun shone down on the pair of them, adding its warm glow to the budding friendship that had replaced any animosity that might have remained between them. At least that's how Callie saw the thing. How she hoped she saw the thing . . .

Maintaining their relaxed poses, their faces only inches apart, they spent the next half hour or more discussing philosophy, the late war, the problems of the poor, and—for the last five minutes or so—the relative merits of chocolate over beef if one were to be stranded on a desert island for a year with only one or the other to eat. Callie's reasoning, that of beef turning rank and chocolate remaining good almost forever, won that argument for her, at which time Simon asked if he could possibly trade the beef for smoked ham, and the argument was back on again.

It was such good fun to have someone to talk to again—really *talk* to—now that Justyn had left England, Callie decided as both she and Simon sat up at the same time and attacked the picnic basket once more, all this talk of food making them both hungry again. Lester was a good sort, a wonderful friend, but he did not possess the quick wit of someone like Justyn, someone like Simon Roxbury. She was always the leader with Lester and, much as she liked being in that position, there was something about matching wits with her brother, with the viscount, that challenged Callie in a way that made her feel *alive*. So very alive.

"We're going to do this, aren't we, Simon?" she asked after a bit, once the remainder of the chicken, neatly dismembered, had been devoured. She was holding out her glass at the moment, frowning as Simon refused to fill it more than half-full of rich white wine. "We're going to rout Noel Kinsey so thoroughly he won't be able to figure out the reason behind his fall until he is lying facedown in the gutter, his life in tiny little pieces and raining down on his broken body."

"Bloodthirsty creature, aren't you?" Simon asked with a smile. He then became serious, although she quickly noticed he wasn't really answering her question, or even agreeing with her. "Still, Callie, Imogene's done a fine job so far, even if she only finished what your governesses began—not that I'm so uncaring of my health as to repeat any of the above in the woman's presence, either the praise or the mention of the governesses."

"I should think not!" Callie agreed enthusiastically. "Imogene didn't hold out much hope when she first saw me in my breeches, then went to work with a will. I hadn't the heart to tell her I didn't eat with my fingers or walk as if my feet were stuck ankle-deep in mud, and just allowed her to believe she had wrought a miracle."

"And I thank you for that." Simon picked up a long blade of seed-topped grass and desultorily began to twirl it between his right thumb and index finger. "But there's still work to be done, you know, before you can enter Society enough to take dead aim at Filton. Not that there isn't time for more lessons. At last word, our quarry remains in the country, and I don't know when he'll return to London."

"That's all true enough." Still feeling this niggling itch at the back of her neck—as if there were something going on that she might not like if only she knew what it was—Callie took refuge in a bit of bantering. Imitating Imogene's speech, she said, "There is one small remaining problem, curse it all. She can walk, she can talk, she can even eat—but the dratted gel simply don't dance."

Simon had been about to stick the blade of grass in his mouth, but hesitated, the blade a mere inch from his open mouth. He looked, curse him, almost relieved to hear of her sad lack. "She don't—you *don't?*"

Wrinkling her nose and shaking her head, Callie admitted, "Not a step. Miss Haverly was going to hire a dancing master for me just before Justyn came home in disgrace and Papa could no longer afford to keep her on. Papa had plans to bring me Out in the Small Season last fall, you see—it being shorter, and less expensive. But that's neither here nor there, and I wasn't that dreadfully disappointed, truly. But this matters, doesn't it? That I can't dance?"

Simon tossed the grass away with a flick of his wrist. "Oh, yes, Callie, it matters. Although, not it would seem, to my mother. Imogene, helpful dear that she is, and without consulting me first, announced early this morning that she has already sent out invitations for a small ball in your honor. I believe she wants to show you off to her friends or some such thing. That was one of the reasons I wished to speak with you today, Callie. I wanted to make sure you were up to being displayed like a prized pet pony. Because, you know, we can easily cancel the thing. Especially as you don't know how to dance, if you're the least bit concerned about your lack of social—"

Callie leaned forward eagerly, waving her hands to ward off his words, her niggling suspicions melting in her eagerness to hear more about her debut. "A small *ball*? I'll get to have a taste of Society perhaps even *before* Filton returns? Have myself some *fun*? You know, until this moment I didn't really believe any of this was actually going to happen. Oh, we *talked* about it, and I've let Imogene fuss over me and all—but I never *believed* it. Not really. Oh, Simon, how wonderful!"

He looked toward the horizon again, his throat working as he took a deep swallow of wine. The niggle started up again, but Callie ruthlessly pushed it down, much happier to be happy.

She pressed her hands to her cheeks and shook her head. "Me, Caledonia Johnston, having her very own ball. It's beyond wonderful! And such a pity that Miss Haverly was sent away before we could get beyond globes and sums and water painting, and on to the things that really matter."

Simon looked at her curiously. "I don't understand. The things that really matter?"

Callie nodded, still caught up in the idea of having her first waltz. "Yes, of course. Dancing, the proper use of a fan, the rules of flirtation—there are rules, aren't there? Heaven knows there are rules for everything else in London Society. One of them," she said firmly, coming back to earth just as Simon pulled a cheroot from his pocket and stuck it in the corner of his mouth, "pertains to never lighting up a cigar in the presence of a lady."

"Is that right?" Simon commented with easily discernible indifference while making short, neat work out of lighting the tip of the cheroot. "Never?"

"Never!" Was he testing her? How far should she take this obvious trampling of London manners as per the social commandments according to Imogene? "I remember distinctly. It was on your mother's list. Number three, as I recall."

"And there can be no exceptions?" Simon asked, his head now wreathed in smoke and with him clearly enjoying himself at her expense.

"Oh, never. Definitely never," Callie repeated, drawing in the smell of smoke, the aroma reminding her of Justyn, and pleasing her very much, although she wasn't about to let Simon know that. "I should take immediate umbrage, and insist that you discard the smelly thing at once."

"Insist, is it?"

She ignored Simon's twinkling sherry eyes, which had such a strange, unsettling effect on her, and concentrated on the game she believed they were playing. "Yes. Insist."

He held the cheroot between his fine white teeth, and smiled. "This is interesting. And if I didn't comply?"

Callie looked to the curricle that stood nearby, the horses munching at the grass at their feet. She sighed theatrically. "Hmmm . . . this does present a problem, doesn't it? I can't complain to my chaperone, for we are quite alone here, aren't we? I can't, in this silly gown, outrace you to the curricle so that I can ride off in high dudgeon, because that would mean driving alone through the streets of London. I am quite sure that also is not done."

"Definitely not done. Leading you back to not going on a picnic unchaperoned in the first place, yes?" Simon put forth helpfully—or it would have been helpfully, if he hadn't been still grinning. "Perhaps you should have committed Imogene's entire list to memory before tearing it to shreds?"

All right. He had proved his point, delivered his lesson. Quite well, in fact. Now it was *her* turn! "Perhaps," she said, agreeing with him. "However, as chance would have it, I am not totally without alternatives." Callie lifted her wineglass, eyeing it in speculation, then looking pointedly at the lit tip of Simon's cheroot.

"You wouldn't!" Simon exclaimed, quickly holding the cheroot behind his back.

With her mouth deliberately closed so that she could both smile and raise her eyebrows speculatively at the same time, Callie watched him, the wineglass still poised for use as a weapon. Simon eyed her questioningly for some moments before he said with the ease of understanding that had thus far served to endear him to her, "You're threatening me for a reason, aren't you, brat?"

She lowered the glass. "Yes, I am, actually," she admitted, then spoke quickly, so that he couldn't interrupt. "Your mother has been a dear, truly, but I can't imagine myself dutifully taking lessons from her in how to capture a man's attention. And this is important, isn't it? It isn't enough to look the part of the debutante, not if we wish to entice Noel Kinsey—who couldn't possibly be overly interested in milk-and-water pusses in their first Season. I have to be unique, different. Perhaps a bit forward? Do you understand what I mean, Simon? How do I trick him into thinking I am interested in him and still behave like a lady? And you want me to more than interest him—you want me to *stagger* him, yes?"

"Your supposed dowry will stagger him sufficiently," Simon told her, once more placing the cheroot in the corner of his mouth, his guard relaxed—which is precisely how Callie wanted it to be. Poor man, for all he thought he understood her, he just didn't know her all that well, did he? Why, she almost pitied him, Callie decided silently. And he did look so very handsome with a cheroot. Very handsome, indeed. She could quite easily bring herself to flirt with him—just for practice, of course.

So thinking, and striking while the proverbial iron was still hot from the stove, she waved off his answer. "Yes, yes, the supposed fortune I've inherited from my great-aunt, who passed away only a year ago, so that I am just out of mourning and come to London to be popped off by that same aunt's bosom chum, the Viscountess Brockton. Imogene told me all about that silliness. But heiresses must be knee-deep all over London during the Season. It will take more than deep pockets to make me unique, bring me to Noel Kinsey's particular attention."

"You could always tackle him in the gardens, I suppose," Simon suggested, his mouth smiling even as his sherry eyes became somehow shuttered, as if he had just thought of something distasteful.

Callie shook her head, dismissing his words even as she rejected the recurring and increasingly unsettling thought that Simon might be rethinking his plans for her, and rushing on, "You're deliberately not understanding me, aren't you, Simon? I suppose I shall just have to say this baldly, without wrapping it up in fine linen, as I suppose I should. I want you to teach me how to flirt, my lord Brockton. I want you to teach me how to attract a man. How to, if needs must, even *kiss* him. I've never done that, you see. Kissed anyone."

Simon, who had been drawing on his cheroot at the precise moment Callie made her final request, seemed to have swallowed a mouthful of smoke. He began choking, throwing the cheroot out onto the grass as his eyes began to tear and he coughed into his hand.

"Oh, poor, dear, Simon!" Callie chirped, testing her proficiency in the realm of demonstrating convincing feminine inanity. "Are you all right?"

Simon rewarded her with a killing glare. "You," he said accusingly, slowly recovering his breath, and his voice, "you want me to *what*?"

Callie, bored with tiptoeing around the thing, finally lost all patience with subterfuge. "Oh, stop acting as if I'd just asked you to burn down Parliament! I thought you said we were friends."

"Friends?" Simon repeated, glaring at her again. Really, the man had refined glaring to an art! "I see I'll have to rush home to my study and find old Samuel Johnson's dictionary, to refresh myself with the nuances of his definition."

"Don't be so deliberately thick, for goodness sake, for you can't fool me!" Callie rolled her eyes in disgust. Really, Lester had never given her one-tenth the problem his lordship was presenting when faced with one of her very simple, reasonable requests. "I only said that I want you to teach me to flirt, how to capture a man like Noel Kinsey. Is that so difficult to understand? Or do you want your mother to instruct me? And concentrate your mind for a moment on the notion of Lester giving me lessons. Imagine it, Simon, if you will. Your mother?" she pulled a face. "*Lester*?"

Simon held up his hands in front of him, signaling surrender. "All right, all right. I'll do it. Dear God, help me. I'll do it."

"Good!" Callie exclaimed, feeling supremely satisfied. "When shall we begin?"

Simon sighed, looking at her as she rather childishly wriggled where she sat, smiling triumphantly, wonderfully, alluringly unaware of her exceedingly formidable beauty. "I think we already have, brat," he said dully, so that she frowned in confusion. "For my sins, I think we already have."

And then, believing a light had dawned somewhere inside of her, taking her closer to womanhood than she had thought herself to be, Callie blushed to the roots of her hair. "Was I flirting, Simon?" she asked quietly, nervously lowering her eyes to the blanket.

"You're flirting now, Callie, and quite well," he grumbled back at her, reaching over to take her hand in his. "But let's get started with the more formal, structured aspects of the preliminaries to the mating ritual as they are played out by Society, shall we? Let's concentrate for the nonce on the male contributions to the game."

Her fingers tingled under his touch, sending heat all the way up her arm, into her face. This couldn't be good. This couldn't be good at all. But she had begun this course, and she'd finish it! "That—that seems a proper place, yes. Go ahead."

"Thank you," Simon said, humor evident in his tone, even as Callie's second thoughts about this entire conversation served to melt her knees, so that she was immensely glad she was sitting down. "Now, to begin." He lifted her hand to his mouth, placing a perfunctory kiss on the back of it. "That, Callie, is acceptable. All right?"

Callie fought the shiver that had begun to run up her once-burning arm, the slight queasiness that turned her stomach to jelly. "Acceptable. All right," she said as calmly as possible, nodding her understanding.

He kissed her hand again, this time her fingertips, then raised his eyebrows as he looked at her. She wondered if he noticed that she was fast dissolving into a puddle of insensibility. He probably did, damn him! "That, you may have noticed, is rather more intimate, and not to be allowed unless the man in question is the prancing French dancing master I will employ for you the moment we return to Portland Place."

Callie cleared her throat, which had become most alarmingly clogged. She blinked twice, trying to concentrate her mind on the subject at hand. "Too intimate. And what should I do about that?"

"You are to withdraw your hand at once and stare the miscreant into stunned apology, at which point he will beg your forgiveness and probably ask to lead you into the dance. You will then be wonderfully polite and agree, because if you refuse to dance with one gentleman, you are forced either to retire or sit the whole evening long, turning down all offers. If you are disposed to like the gentleman, you have won a slave for life. If, however, you take him in dislike, especially after having been fairly well *forced* into giving up a dance to him, well, then I suggest you make it a point to tread on his toes a time or two, just so that he knows he may be forgiven his forward behavior, but the insult has not been forgotten."

"You're teasing me, aren't you, Simon?" Callie asked, still very much aware that he had not let go of her hand. She'd give him another hour, then insist he release her. "Because I have to tell you, that's above everything silly!"

"Society is silly, Callie," Simon pointed out, mentor to pupil, then raised her hand to his lips once more, his eyes on her face. "And now, your final lesson for today, as we must be getting back to Portland Place."

This time he turned her hand at the last moment and pressed a kiss squarely in her palm, the tip of his tongue tracing a faint, tormenting circle against her skin before he allowed her to withdraw from his grasp. "There. Now, my dear student, my little country miss who wishes to play the role of *une femme fatale*, how do you respond to that?"

"Like this?" Callie answered shakily. And then—feeling as if her entire world had somehow suddenly shifted on its axis—she slapped him flat across his wickedly grinning face.

*I am not at all the sort of person
you and I took me for.*

—Jane Welsh Carlyle

Chapter Nine

"Explain it to me again, Armand," Bartholomew Boothe
said as he sat in Simon's study later that same afternoon, a
glass in his hand and a perplexed frown on his face. "You're
saying that my new bay both is *and* isn't the same one I saw
at Tatt's? Just what is that supposed to mean? Throckmorton
promised me he had just bought her. And at Tatt's—he even
showed me his bill of sale! That's why I took her off his
hands, to help him over his gambling debt. He's dipped badly,
Throckmorton is, he told me, and had no choice but to sell
her. Which didn't keep me from getting myself a smacking
great bargain, as I only paid half what I would have if I'd
picked her up at Tatt's."

He looked from Simon to Armand Gauthier as he patted
down his elaborate and too-large cravat, his confusion giving
him the appearance of a perplexed pigeon—an *underfed* perplexed pigeon with his oversize breast feathers all a-ruffle.

"Are you saying that Throckmorton wasn't being honest with me? Is that what you're saying, the both of you?"

"Face the truth, Bones. Throckmorton put one over on you, and that's all there's to it," Armand told him, slyly smiling at Simon, who only nodded his agreement.

Bartholomew glared at Armand. "He isn't dipped? Feeling the bailiff's pinch?" Then he shifted his increasingly anxious gaze to Simon, obviously fighting against believing either of them. "Not drowning in the River Tick? Pockets to let? Run aground?"

"He's flush as he ever was, Bones," Simon concurred, taking a sip of champagne. It was nice, relaxing this way before dinner in his own house, surrounded by his friends, his mind free of thoughts of the infuriating young girl upstairs. Well, as free as it could be, he supposed, absently rubbing at his recently abused cheek. "He's also probably off somewhere doing a jig, happy to be rid of his mistake and having recouped half of his money."

Bones shook his head furiously. "No! No, you're wrong. The horse just must be sickening for something. So bright and lively she was at Tatt's last week, and again when I first bought her—so bright and lively! And now she just stands there. Stands there! Not a bit of spirit—and I had thought to race her!"

Armand spoke into his brandy snifter. "Drop another live eel down her gullet and she'll show you spirit again," he suggested, winking at Simon over the rim.

Simon laughed into his fist, knowing that their gullible friend Bones, Throckmorton, and even the most creditable Tattersall's had been taken in by the most elementary of ruses. A sluggish horse invariably turned wonderfully brisk and lively with an eel in its belly—until the squiggly thing was digested, that was. Just as a fractious horse made stupid on ale could be sold as a calm, lady's mount—until he became sober once more and kicked down the rails in his stall.

"Give it up, Bones," Simon advised as Bartholomew continued to glare at Armand, "and have the poor mare sent to your estate to snore out her declining years. Either that, or make an early-morning visit to Fish Monger Lane tomorrow."

"The perfidies of man," Bartholomew grumbled at last, shaking his head as if his disappointment outstripped his anger at being duped—then had expanded itself to include not only the perfidious Throckmorton, but all of mankind, for Bartholomew's judgments were often as sweeping as they were tardy. "Takes the heart out of a person of conscience such as myself, truly it does."

"Poor Bones," Armand commiserated as the obviously crushed man rose as if he had suddenly gone old and jaded and toddled over to the drinks table to refill his glass. "How it pains me to see the bright light of love for your fellow man extinguished. I am devastated for you, completely and unequivocally, and I must tell you how much sympathy I have for your deep pain." He winked at the viscount. "So, Simon, do you think you could talk your cook into a serving of eel in parsley sauce for our friend this evening?"

Simon bit back a laugh, watching Bartholomew's spine stiffen as the man filled his glass until it splashed over the rim. "You're a cruel man, Armand," Simon said with as much censure as he could muster, which wasn't much. "I've always admired that in you."

Armand nodded his handsome dark head, acknowledging Simon's words as a compliment. "As I have always admired your expertise with the clever twisting of the sharp, bloodless knife of nefarious invention, my friend. Speaking of which, how goes our protégé? Is she champing at the bit to assist you in bringing Filton to his knees? That is, if you've been at long last allowed to examine the extent of your dear mother's progress with the chit? Although I shouldn't complain, I suppose, as my revoked dinner invitation has now been reinstated."

Simon resisted the impulse to touch his fingers to his cheek. "She's passable enough, I suppose," he said, dismissing Callie's beauty, wit, and intelligence by means of the unrevealing damning of faint praise. "There's still a prodigious amount of work to be done before Imogene can launch her, that's for certain. Thank God it's too late in the Season to have to deal with presenting her at Court, even if that will limit her invitations. But I still refuse to involve her in my plans for Kinsey, not that she knows that. Or *will*," he ended, glaring at Bartholomew as if to brand that thought to the man's brainbox.

Bartholomew returned to his seat, his glass already half-empty. "What sort of work, Simon?" he asked, winking at Armand, and clearly out for a bit of revenge on at least one of his friends for having pointed out his gullibility in getting himself stuck with a worthless slug of a horse. "Lessons on horseback? No, didn't sound as if she needed those. Perhaps in how to best aim a bit of footwear at a peer's head? Again, it seems the young lady is already proficient. Oh, but have you given her a rendering of your family crest to study, to commit to memory as it were, so that she doesn't end up riding home from Almack's in the wrong coach?"

Simon laughed along with his friends, although his heart wasn't really in the joke. "I've half a mind to turn Callie over to you for the remainder of her tutoring, Bones," he then threatened, "as she tells me she can't dance."

"Callie?" Armand repeated questioningly, his voice a soft purr. "How charmingly informal, I'm sure."

Simon shot him a look, kicking himself mentally for his careless verbal blunder. There was no room for lapses with Armand Gauthier and, if he knew his man at all, he'd probably pay for this one within the hour.

Bartholomew also lost his smile as he quickly sat forward in his chair, aghast. "Can't dance?"

"Not a step, or so she says, and I am forced to believe her. So, Bones, will you volunteer to teach her?"

"Not me!" Bartholomew vigorously shook his head in denial. "Haven't set foot on a dance floor in three years, and I'm not about to change my ways now. It's the waltz, you know," he announced with conviction meant to impress his companions. "The waltz was the very death knell for dancing."

"Which is the same as to say Bones has an unfortunate habit of treading all over his partner's instep in any dance more intimate than a quadrille," Armand slipped in. "Isn't that right, Bones?"

"Miss Millson had to retire from the Season, no thanks to me," Bartholomew gritted out, retelling a three-year-old story they all already knew. "It was either that or try to clomp around with a crutch stuck up under her arm, which couldn't have helped her prospects any, considering she already had that unfortunate squint." He sighed deeply, as if proving that he was, as always, the victim of a cruel world. "Her papa still cuts me each time we happen to pass each other in the clubs. It was my fault, I know, but that don't mean I also was responsible for the silly chit ending up eloping with her penniless country doctor, does it? Well?" he asked, looking at Armand and Simon searchingly. "Does it?"

"No, no, definitely not," both men answered in unison, for to disagree would only mean a rehashing of the entire laughable sequence of events, which would get them nowhere and only upset Bones more than he was at that moment.

"Which brings us back to Miss Johnston and her sad lack of skill at the dance," Armand pointed out, looking to Simon. "I take it you'll be hiring a dancing master and arranging for a few lessons?"

"Done and done, as Imogene has one Odo Pinabel even now tippy-toeing across my carpets," Simon told him, cocking his head toward the front of the house, in the direction of the music room. "If you listen closely, you can hear my dear mother pounding out the very first off-key notes of a—why, that's a waltz, I believe. Hadn't you heard her before this? Ah well, perhaps my ears are more finely attuned to discordant sounds. I don't hold out much hope for success with Imogene insisting upon hammering out the rhythms, do you?"

They all listened for a few more moments, Bartholomew wincing as the viscountess picked her way through a rather difficult passage, hitting two incorrect notes for every one that rang true. "I'd heard the racket, Simon, but thought the dear lady was simply practicing her scales. But to ask Miss Johnston to learn to dance to that? Well, it won't do. It won't do at all!" he announced, putting down his wineglass as he rose to his feet, smartly pulling down his waistcoat over his nonexistent belly. "At least I can remedy one problem. Besides, I think I want a look at Simon's new responsibility, just out of curiosity, you understand."

Simon rose as well. "She is *not* my responsibility, Bones," he corrected, allowing Armand and Bartholomew to precede him to the doorway. "I am merely being prudent, keeping her out of harm's way until I can deal with Kinsey, then rewarding her with a bit of a Season for her trouble—and to thank her for keeping Imogene occupied. No more, no less."

Armand halted in the doorway after Bartholomew had already passed through, turning to look at his friend. "Do you really mean that, Simon?" he asked, looking at him closely.

"I do," he answered, gathering up every ounce of conviction he could find inside him. He was shocked to realize that, after spending several hours with Callie that afternoon, crying friends as it were, that conviction made for a pitifully small bundle.

Armand smiled, his flash of white teeth nearly as mischievous as the glint in his dark eyes. "Then I wouldn't, using poor Bones as an example, be treading on any toes if I were to decide—upon further acquaintance, of course—that our dear Miss Johnston might possibly become more to me than your responsibility?"

"She is not at all in your style, Armand," Simon pointed out, aware that his jaw muscles had grown uncomfortably tight. What the devil was the matter with him? "For all her daring, her breeches, her outrageous behavior, she is gently bred and reared. As her guardian, I—"

"Her *guardian*?" Armand asked, cutting him off. "Oh-ho, I scent a contradiction here. I believe you just told me that she is not even your responsibility, much less your ward. Or is it only me that you have found necessary to warn off the tasty little morsel?"

"Callie is—" Simon stopped, took a deep breath, and deliberately ended, aware that his friend was intentionally baiting him, "Miss Johnston is not a tasty little morsel, Armand."

"But, my friend, even from my quite short association with her, I believe I can safely conclude she's also a long chalk from, say, a Miss Millson," Armand pointed out with maddening certitude. "She needs, deserves, a man of intelligence, of spirit. She'd be entirely wasted on a country doctor or the like. Don't you agree?"

Simon's next words were drawn from desperation, but they sounded impressive enough, for all he knew that Callie would laugh in delight if she were to hear them. "Her father is Sir Camber Johnston, a man knighted for his invaluable service to the Queen herself. Banish the sight of her in breeches from your mind, Armand. If she was for a moment outrageous, she remains as untouchable as any debutante."

"Which makes my conclusions all the more true, and all the more sad," Armand said, his tone and his expression equally noncommittal. "You and your mother are both going to do your best to take that enchanting little minx and turn her into a patterncard of all the most boring virtues exhibited by the endless parade of insipid debutantes cluttering up the ballrooms this and every Season, aren't you? Which would be a damnable pity, in my opinion. A small wager, if you will, Simon? The price Bones paid for his slug of a horse seems fair, with the winnings going to one of the local charities. You cannot make a sow's ear of our little silk purse. Not to entertain Imogene, not to turn me away from the memory of the sight of her in breeches, not to convince yourself that you are immune to her rather, as you yourself termed it, *outrageous* charms. Are we on?"

"You're out for some private mischief, aren't you?" He stared at Gauthier as that man coolly averted his eyes, holding out his hand and inspecting his cuticles. "My God, Armand—you are, aren't you?" Simon asked, for once unable to read his friend's motives. "Why?"

"Because I like this little Callie of yours, old fellow," Armand said, his American drawl now faintly tinged with the accents of France. The man was deliberately employing the voice that Simon had heard him use to such great advantage as he laid down his winning hand at cards. "And because," he continued, "as much as it pains me to admit it, of the love I bear you. There is, you see, more than one way to ruin a woman. And a man. In short, I believe you might just have your eyes on the wrong prize, Simon."

Simon threw back his head, laughing aloud. "You're out of your mind!" he exclaimed, walking back to pick up his glass of champagne. "Now go on, follow Bones into the music room, rescue Miss Johnston from her dancing master, and do your best to beguile her with your handsome presence. I'll be along in a moment. I just remembered something I have to do, a few papers I promised to sign."

"You're opening the field then, Simon? You don't really want her for yourself?" Armand asked, addressing the viscount's back as he stood at the drinks table, pouring himself another glass. "Are you sure?"

Simon turned around, nonchalantly resting his hip against one corner of the small table. "Positive, Armand. Have at it with my blessings, if you're so eager to catch your neck in the parson's mousetrap. Just be careful, as Miss Johnston has evinced an interest in learning how to flirt," he said, returning drawl for deliberate lazy drawl, for the first time not seeing the man as his beloved comrade but as his possible adversary.

It was also, he realized as Armand smiled, saluted smartly, and quit the room, the first time he might have lied to his best friend.

What worried him was the thought that he might also be lying to himself, a thought he immediately banished as ridiculous.

* * *

Callie hadn't realized how much she had been counting on Simon to become her dancing master until her real instructor had shown up, out of breath and perspiring quite heavily. He had doubtless run all the way to Portland Place—perhaps even leapfrogging over the knocked-prone body of his hapless current pupil in his haste to pocket the exorbitant amount of money Simon seemed compelled to pay anyone who so much as pointed him in the correct direction as he searched out the dining room in his own house.

Not that she wasn't pleased with Mr. Odo Pinabel. He was certainly a nice enough man, if one didn't mind his affected lisp, or the fact that his hands seemed perpetually cold and clammy. Or that his breath smelled of onions.

And then there was his eyebrow. The poor man only possessed one of the things—stretching straight across the bridge between his eyes and as thick and black as a woolly, creeping bug. She couldn't seem to keep her gaze off it.

Although the eyebrow did come in rather handy, seeing as how Callie was already learning to count "one-two-twree" by its movements. She was entranced by its jerky climb up Mister Odo Pinabel's tall forehead, moving hitch-hitch-*hitch*! with each beat, the last one signaling that, yes indeed, it was now time to dip and turn and begin to count again.

So there were the clammy hands, and the onions, the deliberate lisp, and the eyebrow—added to the Viscountess Brockton's inexorable attack on the pianoforte—none of which made waltzing quite the romantic adventure Callie had pictured in her mind's eye.

"One-two-*twree*, one-two-*twree*. Fasther, Mith Johnston, fasther!" Mr. Odo Pinabel commanded, his eyebrow climbing higher and higher, threatening to disappear into the thick black thatch of hair that seemed so out of place on his head—

almost as if it had landed there by mistake and might actually belong to someone else. "Mith Johnston, cro-operate, pul-eeze! It would be twerrible to twrip in public, and shimply *cruth-ing* for my conseth-ah-quence."

"Yes, Mr. Pinabel," Callie said, averting her head, for it seemed that the dancing master not only lisped, his speech was as damp as his palms. She'd nearly drowned when he'd talked of crushing and consequences. "I'll try."

"It'h shimply the mushic, that'th all," Mr. Pinabel assured her as the viscountess hit another chord, one that should be heard only the once and then lost for all time. This, however, was Callie's second thought, the first being that there had been four unfortunately moist esses in Mr. Pinabel's explana-tion. If there had been an even half dozen, she decided, pru-dently ducking her head and rolling her eyes as he whirled her into another turn, she'd have to learn to waltz with an um-brella guarding her face.

When the door to the hallway opened and Bartholomew Boothe walked in, Callie looked at the newcomer with enough smiling enthusiasm to make the clearly uncomfort-able man blush above his high shirtpoints.

"I've come to rescue you from that jangle of well-meant noise I heard as I passed by the door just now, Miss John-ston," he hastily announced, bowing to her, his gaze raking her from head to foot as he did so, the light of appreciation in his eyes doing wonders for her mood. "And may I say," he continued as he straightened once more, "that I have never been so honored as I will be to play your accompaniment for the remainder of your lesson."

"Hah! Over my broken and bruised body," the viscountess declared flatly, banging both her heavily beringed hands down on the keyboard and discovering yet another chord best lost to the ages. "I'm getting the hang of it, Bones, and I'll thank you to stop leering at the gel and go away. You aren't needed. Aren't wanted. Haven't been asked, either, now that I think on it. Or am I wrong? Did that interfering son of mine send you?"

"Well, um, well—" Bartholomew stammered, still inspecting Callie, who—feeling rather proud of her appearance and more than willing to show herself off a little bit—deliberately stepped away from Mr. Pinabel, took hold of her skirts at either side, and then turned herself in a full circle so that he could see all of her new splendor. She then grinned at Bartholomew again and wrinkled her nose in a playful move that let him know she had been deliberately baiting him. Or was that flirting with him? She'd have to ask Simon, if he ever deigned to give her another lesson.

"Bones! I'm talking to you!" Imogene pressed, giving the keys another hard bang. "Did my son send you?"

Bartholomew looked at Callie solemnly, grinned quickly in what more closely resembled a pained grimace, then sobered once more. It was as if he knew he shouldn't smile and by that smile condone her forward behavior, yet at the same time felt he might be insulting her if he didn't at least acknowledge her own happy smile. He was so sweet, so adorable—so clearly confused and put out of kilter—that Callie longed to kiss his cheek.

With her back to Imogene—who talked a lot about being outrageous but strangely didn't advocate any such behavior for Callie—she blew him one instead.

Bartholomew's eyes very nearly popped out of his skull, and he quickly turned to Imogene. "Ma'am, you were asking? Did Simon—*did* he—did *I*? Um, that is, um—*what* was the question again, please?"

"Thought you had more to say for yourself, Bartholomew Boothe," Imogene said, tsk-tsking a time or two before she gave in to a triumphant smile. "Struck you dumb, hasn't she? Did it all m'self, you know, with no help from Simon. A miracle, don't you think?"

Bartholomew let out his breath in a rush, visibly relaxing now that he had been given permission to say what was on his mind. "Oh, yes, ma'am," he declared feelingly. "A true miracle. Hard to believe Simon thinks there's still a prodigious amount of work to be done until she's up to snuff and ready to set loose on the town."

Callie turned her head away, as if reacting to a physical blow. "He—he said that, Mr. Boothe?"

"You were doing well enough with your cow-eyed looks and stupid stammering, Bones," the viscountess grumbled, rising from the padded bench to walk toward Bartholomew in what greatly resembled a militant stomp. "Should have kept to it rather than trying to string a single silly sentence together using someone else's words."

She sailed past Bartholomew—who nearly fainted in gratitude at having been dismissed with only a scolding and not a cuff on the ear—and poked her head out into the hallway to bellow: "*Simon*! I'll have a word with you! *Now*! Oh—hullo, there, Armand. Come to ogle, like that idiot Bones? Well, don't just stand there—come in, come in! We give performances each day at two and four, tuppence a ticket. So sorry that the trained monkey doesn't arrive until tomorrow, but we do the best we can. *Si-mon*!"

Callie stuffed a knuckle into her mouth to keep from giggling at the viscountess's tirade, then gazed at Armand Gauthier rather quizzically as he pressed an impudent kiss against Imogene's powdery cheek. He clearly wasn't in the least bit afraid of the woman—unlike Mr. Boothe, who looked as near to tears as the belowstairs maid, Letty, had been just this morning when the viscountess had dared to look at her crooked for having arrived with a breakfast tray lacking a teapot.

"Excuse me, miss," Mr. Gauthier said now, strolling into the music room as if he owned it and crossing to take up Callie's hand, pressing a kiss against her suddenly heated skin, then stroking the back of her fingers with his thumb. "I was told Miss Caledonia Johnston was somewhere about, but I cannot see hide nor hair of the young woman. Perhaps I am simply too dazzled by your beauty? Where is the little ragamuffin, do you know?" he asked, making a great business out of peering about the room, as if the missing Miss Johnston was stuck behind a chair in one of the corners. "Ah, well, we won't miss her, will we? Come, my most enchanting creature, let us be away from here—a watery English sun and my carriage both await."

Callie, who knew the devastatingly attractive man was teasing her but had no idea how to respond to his careless bantering, looked to Bartholomew Boothe in mute appeal.

She might just as well have applied to the bust of Mark Antony on the mantel, for all the good that did her. Bartholomew, fully occupied in staying out of Imogene's way as that good lady reentered the room, only ducked her imploring glance and hurried over to the bench the viscountess had so recently vacated. He sat himself down and proceeded to do his best to pretend he was invisible.

Callie's head was spinning with the knowledge that Armand's Gauthier's hand-kissing, the intimate squeeze he had given her fingers, fell into some dangerous gray area between impersonally polite and downright provocative. She took a deep breath, looked the man square in the eye, and mumbled, "It is a distinct pleasure to see you again, Mr. Gauthier, I'm sure." Then she rolled her eyes heavenward, believing that to be the most inane, stupid response she could possibly have made—other than to make some comment on *his* comment on the weather.

So thinking, and not much caring for being put so much on the spot by the man, she then added, smiling, "But I really must remain here, I'm afraid, as dinner is to be served within the hour. However, if we were to locate a small round hat and a tambourine, Mr. Gauthier, would you be willing to play the part of the performing monkey the viscountess mentioned? You seem to have the requisite love of mischief, if not the tail. Oh, and you might return my hand to me anytime you feel it convenient to do so, as I've lately realized that I have developed a most overpowering attachment to it."

"Now, that's more like it!" Mr. Gauthier said laughing, releasing her hand, then turning to Mr. Boothe. "Bones, remember this extraordinary day. I think I'm in love!"

"And that's a bleeding pity, that's what that is, Armand Gauthier," Imogene declared flatly from the doorway, "because the gel's already spoken for. *Si-mon!—NOW!*"

"Really? Your hopes still lie in that direction, do they, Imogene? How exceedingly interesting," Mr. Gauthier drawled, turning curiously to Simon, who had just entered the room, looking handsome, yes, but very definitely oppressed.

Callie decided she liked him oppressed, considering the fact that he had so thoroughly confused and upset her this morning with his light bantering, followed by his seemingly innocent offer of friendship, followed by his horribly embarrassing lesson in hand-kissing—followed by her slap to his cheek and an uncomfortable silence that had lasted through the repacking of the picnic basket, the long ride back to Portland Place, and his hasty desertion of her in the foyer.

"You bellowed, Mother?" Simon quipped, tight-lipped. "What's wrong now?" He then turned his steely gaze on the decidedly *de trop* and almost comically mortified Odo Pinabel. "You," he said almost amicably, "go away."

The dancing master gathered up his papers and his cloak in the space of a heartbeat, departing the room with all the ungraceful haste of a man clothed in lamb chops desperate to escape a den of hungry lions.

"Now there goes a flap-mouthed creature who will cost you an arm and half a leg for a mere quarter hour's service," Imogene remarked rather happily, watching the dancing master's flight. "And you think the gel's gowns cost you a fortune? Hah! The sum's a trifle compared to what you'll end up dealing out to keep the servants working in this madhouse without feeling the need to spill all our family secrets in those gossipy pubs they patronize. Either that, Simon, or our private business will be served up for dinner all over Mayfair."

"And you'd love it," Simon bit out, clearly unhappy. "Now, what the devil's going on in here? Can't you even control something as elementary as a simple dancing lesson, Mother, without my assistance?"

"Why, you miserable puppy! As if this was *my* fault!" Imogene exploded, drawing herself up to her full, and definitely impressive, height. "You're not too old for a good caning, Simon, I warn you."

Callie opened her mouth to defend the viscountess, then noticed that Armand Gauthier, rather than appearing embarrassed by this family contretemps, was smiling as he delicately took snuff, his gaze shifting from mother to son as if he were watching a play. "You're *enjoying* this, aren't you?" she demanded of the man who still stood beside her. "Don't you find that to be the least bit strange?"

"Imogene loves nothing better than a good argument, so that Simon, being a dutiful son, indulges her from time to time," he explained. "Keeps her blood flowing, or so she says. A real tartar, that's our Imogene. I'd marry her in a minute if she'd have me—and if she didn't outweigh me."

Callie's upper lip curled into a sneer. "So much for your great love of me, Mr. Gauthier," she shot at him. She had to speak loudly to be heard over the viscountess, who was just then complaining about Lester's recent discovery of delicious chocolate tarts in a small stall near Piccadilly, and biting stays, and the ignominy of becoming a—curse it all!—*dowager*.

Bartholomew ran a finger down the length of the keys, the unexpected sound calling everyone to attention. "Allow me, please, Simon," he said importantly. He uncoiled his painfully thin form from the bench with the air of one who delights most in issuing prophecies of doom—and doing it with the air of someone whose sentences invariably end with "I told you so!"

"I think not, Bones," Simon growled, pinning a stunned Callie to the floor with a single dark look. His expression told her that Armand Gauthier had been fair and far out this time. The viscount wasn't playing any sort of game with his mother, but was truly incensed. And not at his mother, either, but at *her*.

His next words proved her right. "Callie? There seems to be a problem, as we appear to be minus one dancing master. Now why am I so sure this is your doing? And I thought you understood there was a time limit to these lessons in deportment. Explain yourself, if you please. Explain yourself now."

Incensed? *He* was incensed? And he wanted *her* to explain? How dare he! He knew what he'd done just this morning—trying to both tease and frighten her, keeping her off guard and off-balance and at his mercy (when she had been planning to do the same to him, which had *nothing*, less than nothing to do with the matter at hand!).

Oh, yes, he *knew*. Just as he knew that he was the one who had been so maddeningly pernicious as to have Imogene hire a dancing master rather than take the time to demonstrate a few simple steps to her himself. And then he sent the man away—all of which just went to show how much he wanted his plan to work, and how very little of himself he expected to expend in the process.

Oh, no. It wasn't Simon Roxbury who was being poked and prodded and measured and pinned. It wasn't Simon Roxbury who had been locked up for nearly a fortnight, being forced to practice how to be insipid and boring, and being treated as if he had been reared by wild wolves and was only just now learning how to walk upright. And then—and then!—for him to act as if it were she, not he, who was delaying their plans to set her loose in society to entrance Noel Kinsey?

How *dare* he!

Well, if he wanted to know what was going on, she imagined she could be coaxed, not *ordered*, to oblige him—and in spades!

So thinking, and with the smile on her face hiding—she hoped—the extreme dislike in which she took him at this moment, Callie dipped into a creditable curtsy.

Then, with a graceful sweep of her hand meant to include the company, the room, the mansion, the entirety of London itself, she began, "It's really all quite simple, my lord, if you think you can follow along. Listen carefully. I came here to shoot Noel Kinsey. You stuck your nose in where it didn't belong and wasn't wanted, thwarted my very good plan, then enlisted, nay, *blackmailed* me into going along with your own convoluted scheme to bring Filton down. You have me lying to my father—not that this is an unheard-of occurrence, but you shouldn't have encouraged me. You've got poor Lester wandering about London alone, which can't be good for him, or for London for that matter. And Noel Kinsey isn't even in the city! And I let you talk me into all of it, which is my fault. The rest of the fault, however, is yours, Viscount Brockton, and I'll never forgive you for so underestimating me and so overestimating yourself!"

"Yes, definitely. I adore this child," the wealthy, handsome, debonair, highly desirable object of feminine affections and aspirations, Armand Gauthier, announced to nobody in particular.

"Oh, stubble it," Callie warned him halfheartedly, then continued, barely taking time for a breath. Her eyes never left Simon's face as her words came faster, her voice rising as she built to a crescendo of anger and frustration. "You then turned me over to your sweet if outrageous mother, who believes she is grooming me as her daughter-in-law. You two really should have a small talk about that, I think, for I wouldn't have you if you were served up to me on a silver platter with an apple stuffed in your mouth."

"You'd think she was my own dear child, wouldn't you, Simon?" the viscountess chirped, looking at Callie, her expression near to beatific.

Callie rolled her eyes at the interruption. "Imogene, *please!*" She made another sweeping gesture with her outflung arm, this time aiming toward the pianoforte. "Bones here—you don't mind if I call you Bones, do you? No, I didn't think so. Well, Bones here has cast himself in the role of helpful if pessimistic observer." She turned to glare at the second man. "And Mr. Gauthier—and I *will* continue to call you Mr. Gauthier—has been ogling me this past ten minutes, even going so far as to say he now loves me, although he did not *chew* on my hand, as you did this morning, my lord."

"*Chew*?" Armand mouthed the word silently, smiling at Simon all the while, so that Callie longed to box his ears.

"And now to *you*, Simon Roxbury!" she continued, the bit firmly between her teeth as she glared at the viscount. "Among your other failings that are far too numerous to mention, and with this supposed ball your mother is hosting for me looming heavily on the horizon, you have—*all* of you— conspired to frighten away my lisping, spitting, wet-palmed dancing master just as he was teaching me to count to one-two-*twree*. Not that any of this matters a whit, you understand, because this plan of yours simply isn't going to work. I'm *leaving*!"

And with that—with Bones's mouth at half cock, with the maddening Armand Gauthier applauding softly, with the viscountess looking unexpectedly docile, even crushed, and with Simon glaring at her as if he wanted either to spank her or kiss her (she'd examine that later, once she was safely in a coach heading to Sturminster Newton), and with Lester somehow appearing in the doorway, a chocolate tart stuffed halfway into his mouth—Callie lifted her skirts a good three inches above her ankles and quite inelegantly stomped past her friend and out of the music room.

"You went and made her mad, didn't you?" she heard Lester scold as she stopped a few feet down the hall, trying to catch her breath while swallowing hard in an attempt to push her heart back down her throat. "And just when I brought Scarlet home with me, too. Now what am I supposed to do with her?"

Scarlet? Who or what was a Scarlet? Callie poked her head around the corner, looking toward the ground-floor foyer. She saw a fairly pretty street vendor standing there beside a clearly flummoxed Roberts—who was pinching what looked to be a dead rat between his thumb and forefinger—a wooden tray piled high with pastries hung around her neck.

Leave it to Lester Plum to ruin her fine, dramatic exit! "Lester?" she asked carefully, backing up a few paces, until the rather vacantly smiling creature was once more out of her sight. She turned to her friend, her teeth clenched, murder in her eyes. "What in bloody hell have you done to us now?"

And then, in a move that surprised her as much as it must have shocked her good friend, Callie burst into tears and ran straight up the stairs, to fling herself on her bed and sob.

Strange! that such high dispute shou'd be
'Twist Tweedledum and Tweedledee.

—John Byrom

Chapter Ten

If there were a more unpleasant way to spend an hour, Simon couldn't recall it as he sat in his study listening to his bosom chums and his beloved mother rail at him over his callous, hard-hearted, obnoxious, cavalier, selfish, close-to-criminal behavior toward that sweet young girl, Caledonia Johnston.

"There's nothing else for it, Simon," Bartholomew Boothe proclaimed at last, clearly having decided the thing for them all. "You'll have to send her home."

That statement brought the only smile to Simon's face that he had been able to muster since the contretemps began, as his mother, Armand—even Lester, who had trouble speaking with his mouth stuffed full of chocolate tart—all turned to Bartholomew and spoke as one, even if their statements were very revealingly dissimilar.

"Oh, I don't think so, Bones. She'll just pick up her pistol and go Filton-hunting again, if you'll remember the reasons behind this entire exercise," Armand said, inclining his head toward the still in-the-dark viscountess who had no idea how Simon was using Callie's presence to entertain his mother.

"Send her home? Are you daft, man? With everything going so splendidly?" the viscountess sputtered.

Simon's right eyebrow climbed his forehead. "Splendidly, Mother? A moment ago you said this entire affair had taken on all the hallmarks of a disaster of biblical proportions. And blamed me for it all, as I remember."

Imogene gave a dismissing toss of her head. "I sometimes exaggerate. You know that. Don't rub my nose in my failings now, Simon."

"Would I have to go, too?" Lester Plum bleated, shaking his head sorrowfully. "Never say so, now that I'm folded so nicely in the flap of luxury."

"That's sitting in the lap of luxury, Lester," Simon corrected smoothly as he stood up to signal an end to the discussion. He leaned forward to plant the palms of his hands on the desk. "This is getting us nowhere," he then told them, looking most intensely at his beloved mother, who had already opened her mouth, clearly ready to continue her harangue against her only son. "I'm going upstairs to talk reason to the brat."

Bartholomew nodded sagely. "Going to apologize, eat a little humble pie, wear a bit of sackcloth and ashes. That ought to do it. Though I wouldn't call her brat, Simon. Seems a mite contradictory."

"I'll try to keep that in mind, Bones," Simon said, walking around the desk, stopping in front of Armand Gauthier. "Well? Out with it man. I know you have something to add."

"You'll go into her bedchamber?" Armand only asked, picking up a pair of dice and closing his fist around it so that his knuckles showed white. "Unchaperoned?"

"Don't be an idiot, Armand!" Simon said, his temper sparked once more. "There's nothing between Miss Johnston and me but a mutual desire to destroy Noel Kinsey."

Armand looked at him levelly. "So you say, my friend, so you say—and Lord knows you never lie, even to yourself." He also stood up, neatly pulling at his jacket cuffs. "I'll be leaving now, if you don't mind, as I have just recalled an appointment with my confessor. Just send round a note, Simon, if you find yourself desiring his address. Bones—are you coming with me?"

"To your confessor?" Bones asked, confused. "Why would I want to do that?"

"Because his confessor is probably an innkeeper at some low dive at the bottom end of Bond Street," Simon bit out testily. His mother looked at him with a beaming smile that made him long to plant the clever-tongued Armand a facer. Just one good, solid punch, meant to rearrange his friend's knowing expression which had so encouraged his already-ambitious mother into believing that, yes indeed, there was a very good chance of a match between her son and Caledonia Johnston.

"I'll give you a quarter hour with her, son, no more," the viscountess declared, taking hold of Simon's arm as he made to brush past her. "I'll play Cupid, but I'll be damned if I'll have you make me into a procuress!"

Simon took a deep breath, looking at each occupant of the room in turn. "I begin to wonder if Noel Kinsey's downfall is worth it," he said, then stomped out of the room, wishing he might be leaving on the next tide, as was Byron, who had wisely decided that he'd had enough of London for the nonce.

"My lord? You should know this, I suppose," Lester called after him by way of a friendly warning. "She throws things sometimes."

"I'll keep that in mind," Simon replied, never breaking stride as he walked into the foyer, where Roberts was still standing in front of the round table in its center, looking down at a black splotch on its highly polished surface.

"What do I do with it, milord?" he asked, pointing a finger at the offending article. "Emery says to give it to Silsby, but as he was laughing to split his sides as he said it, I don't think I should."

Simon eyed the item in question owlishly for a moment, then picked it up and stuffed it into his pocket. "There, Roberts, that's one problem solved. Now, what has Emery done with the young woman?"

"Scarlet?" Roberts asked, his face splitting into a grin. "He took her to the kitchens, milord, just as the viscountess ordered and I'd already said m'self, seeing as how I know how her ladyship dotes on fine pastries and the like. She said as how you wouldn't mind, as you delight in emptying your pockets for servants, and females cost a full two pounds less in tax a year than men." He frowned as a sudden thought hit him. "You wouldn't think of replacing us all with females, would you, milord? That is to say, if you was squeezed for pennies or anything?"

"Only if you discover a great need to give me advice on how to handle Miss Johnston, Roberts," Simon warned, turning for the staircase.

"Oh, not me, milord!" Roberts averred feelingly. "But I did hear Emery saying to Silsby that we wouldn't be at such sixes and sevens if the vola . . . vowel-a—"

"Volatile, Roberts," Simon supplied helpfully, amazed at his own forbearance.

"Yes, milord, that's it. That's what Emery said. He said we wouldn't be at such sixes and sevens if the *vol-a-tile* young miss was to be out and about with other young misses, seeing the sights and picking up ribbons and laces and such, seeing as how she has nothing to do all the day but twiddle her thumbs. Does that help, milord?"

"I'll keep it in mind, Roberts," Simon promised dully, not surprised to know that the goings-on of the master of the household had become a point of common discussion belowstairs. "I'll keep it in mind." Then, suddenly impatient to have this ridiculousness settled once and for all, he bounded up the stairs two at a time, heading for Callie's bedchamber. He knocked his knuckles against the wood with all the charm and subtlety of an army storming the gates of an enemy city.

"Oh, just go away, Lester!" Callie called from behind the door. "There aren't enough chocolate tarts in all of England to make me forgive you this latest silliness."

"I agree, brat," Simon said, not enjoying having been put in the position of cooling his heels in his own hallway. "All that remains is whether to shoot him or hang him. Let me in and we'll discuss his punishment."

"Simon—Lord Brockton?" Callie's usually attractively husky voice held a faint squeak. "*You're* knocking on my door?"

"I refuse to answer the obvious. Now open the door before I have to resort to the mutually embarrassing prospect of asking Emery to fetch me the key."

He heard a slight rustling on the other side of the wood before the handle turned and Callie's head appeared in the resulting crack as she pulled the door open. "Mutually embarrassing for whom, my lord? You and Emery? For I certainly am not the least bit embarrassed. I'm *angry!* Mostly with *you!*"

"You've been crying," Simon said, taking in the slight puffiness around her large green eyes, and suddenly feeling as if the only thing he, as a gentleman, could do was to go off to slit his throat. He'd had no idea her unhappiness could affect him this deeply. "I never meant to make you cry, Callie," he said honestly, entering the guest chamber as she let go of the door and walked away from him.

"I never meant to cry, and it has most certainly served to ruin my day," she countered, hoisting herself up so that she was sitting on the edge of the bed, her toes dangling a good foot above the floor. "I meant to punish you for treating me like a child and expecting me to behave like a woman, ring a mighty peal over your head, then walk away the victor." She cocked her head to one side, looking at him inquiringly. "Does that make the least bit of sense, my lord?"

"Simon," he corrected, longing to sit down beside her and knowing that it was the last place he should be. That this chamber was the last place he should be. That being alone with Callie Johnston was not only foolhardy, it was dangerous. "And I apologize."

"For what?" she prompted meaningfully, a small light of mischief dawning in her eyes. She might have been brought down by the events of this day, the events of these past days, but she was by no means out, and Simon was beginning to wonder why the damnable chit only lived under his roof and did not yet own it. She certainly was intelligent enough, courageous enough, daring enough, to have already conquered most of England, not just taken command of Number Forty-nine Portland Place.

Giving in to his inclinations and banishing his conscience to perdition for the moment, Simon crossed the room and sat down beside her on the satin coverlet. After all, they were friends now, weren't they?

"Where should I begin?" he asked, remembering their ill-fated interlude in Richmond Park that morning, the interlude that never should have happened, just as his entire scheme to ruin the earl of Filton should have remained his own project and not been fudged about to figuratively include this innocent yet *volatile* young girl.

She looked at him for a long moment—during which time he realized, yet again, how extraordinarily beautiful she was in her most individual way—then shook her head. "Never mind," she said, "I suppose I'll forgive you in any case. I think we were both equally guilty, the two of us having momentarily forgotten why we have formed this alliance, as it were. It's just that it's taking so *long* to put our plan into action. Do you think we can perhaps convince Mr. Pinabel to return?"

"Oh, he'll be back," Simon said confidently, reaching into his pocket to withdraw the dead black lump he'd picked up in the foyer, "if only to retrieve this. He left in such a hurry that he completely ran out from underneath it."

Callie reached out her hand, gingerly touching a single finger to the clump of what Simon privately believed to be horsehair. "What—what is that? Oh my dear Lord, I've seen this before! It's Mr. Pinabel's *hair*!"

Simon balanced the toupee on the end of his finger, holding it up so that Callie could get a better look at the thing. "He must have been devastated when powdered wigs were taxed out of fashion," he mused, beginning to chuckle in spite of the presumed seriousness of the discussion he was supposed to be having with Callie.

"Let me see that!" She snatched the hairpiece from him and hopped down from the bed, going over to stand in front of her dressing table. She plopped the toupee down on top of her head and bent from the waist to admire her reflection in the low mirror, saying, "One-two-*twree*! One-two-*twree*! No, Mith, that'th *twerrible*!" Making comical faces, she tilted her head this way and that before removing the false hair and turning about to look at Simon. "Oh, this is delicious! Do you suppose his eyebrow is horsehair as well? Do you suppose he's really bald as a melon?"

"One can only speculate, if one has a desire to do so. I find that I do not," Simon said with as much seriousness as he could muster, but finding himself unable to keep from smiling. "However, this settles it, brat. The man can't return. I'd never be able to look at him without seeing how you looked in his hair. I do have my reputation to consider, and falling to the floor, clutching my stomach and howling like a mad dog would do my consequence no good whatsoever."

She grinned as she came back to the bed, returning the toupee to him before once more sitting herself. "Which leaves me with no dancing master, I'm afraid," she said, peering up at him out of the corners of her eyes. "Perhaps Mr. Gauthier could be induced to volunteer to be my tutor? Will you ask him?"

"When the devil goes ice-skating," Simon muttered under his breath as he roughly shoved the ridiculous toupee back into his pocket, a pronouncement that brought another giggle to Callie's lips. "You're flirting again, brat. You do know that, don't you?"

"Oh, most definitely, *Simon*," she told him, causing him to realize just how much he enjoyed hearing his name on her lips. "I wanted to see your reaction to my mention of Mr. Gauthier. I find him to be rather appealing, in an irritating sort of way. It's as if he has his own reasons for everything he does, and looks at the rest of the world as if it has been formed for his own personal amusement. And he seems rather secretive, as if he knows some sort of joke nobody else does."

"That's a fairly good description of the man, actually," Simon told her. "And he uses all his tricks to great advantage with the ladies, however, so be careful."

Callie sobered. "You can't mean that anyone would take him seriously," she said, shaking her head. "Why, as if I'd believe a man who said he was in love with me after only meeting me for the second time."

"He said that?" Simon asked, looking at her intently, secretly pleased that this inexperienced woman-child could see through Armand's banterings when many more sophisticated females could not. "When?"

She waved away his question. "It doesn't matter, because he was only teasing me, you know. Just as you were this morning, in the park."

Simon studied the rose pattern of the carpet at his feet, knowing that his lessons in flirting, the intimate kiss he had pressed in Callie's palm, had not been entirely the actions of an impersonal tutor. Yet, where she had seen through Armand's flirting, she also had chosen to not look deeper into his own motives. Unfortunately, he had. And he was suddenly even more uncomfortable than he had been—and growing less sure of his plans for Callie by the moment.

"Mr. Gauthier has a most interesting accent," Callie said, swinging her feet back and forth as Simon watched, so that he belatedly realized that, for all her new air of sophistication, she wasn't wearing shoes. "At times I think he is French, then English, then perhaps even American. Emery has told me a few things about him, although I find most of it difficult to believe."

"Armand was reared in New Orleans, in America," Simon told her absently, his mind more fully occupied in appreciating the vision of Callie's stocking-clad toes, the fragility of her ankles, the memory of how long and shapely her legs had appeared when she had been playing the part of a young man. "Or so he says."

"Or so he says?" Callie repeated. "Don't you believe him?"

"I'd be a blockheaded fool if I did," Simon said, "seeing as how Armand delights in telling wild stories. The most empty-headed ladies of the *ton* find this litany of lies to be highly attractive, which amuses Armand, I believe."

"And Mr. Gauthier does all this fibbing on purpose?"

"Armand does enjoy exploiting the foibles of his fellow man," Simon agreed, "but he is usually content to be an observer of society rather than a participant. Usually."

"But not right now?" Callie asked, showing again her quick intelligence. "He isn't just standing back and observing our plans for Noel Kinsey. He doesn't approve, does he?"

"I've seen him more pleased," Simon admitted, looking down to see that Callie had impulsively placed her hand on his arm. "I believe he sees you being hurt in some way."

"Well, that's just above everything silly!" Callie protested, obviously not seeing any danger in Simon's plan, or in their close proximity in this, her virgin bedchamber. "I'm going to go to balls and routs and plays. I'm going to dance and flirt and dangle my nonexistent dowry in the earl's face so that he is so lovestruck you can fleece him at cards and rid him of his fortune. Nothing could be simpler or less dangerous. How could I possibly be hurt?"

"You could fall in love with Armand," Simon suggested, watching her carefully.

"Fall in love with—is that why you've come up here? To warn me away from Mr. Gauthier as if *I* was one of those absurd society misses who would believe a man so obviously insincere as your deliberately secretive friend? Well, if that isn't above everything silly!"

"He's wealthy, handsome, intelligent, agreeable—an extremely good catch, Callie."

She rolled her eyes. "And insincere and full of himself, and entirely too *smooth* for my liking. Anything else? Or have I put your mind to rest on that head?"

"Or you could, in your gratitude, fall in love with me," Simon continued, desperately aware of their proximity on the bed, of the way her thigh was brushing up against his, aware of the scent of her, the innocent beauty of her, his attraction to her. An attraction he had been fighting since first discovering the impudent creature in his coach. And if she now compared him to Armand, or her brother Justyn, or even to her good and comfortable friend Lester, he might, he realized with a sinking heart, go into a sad decline.

He watched her press her lips together, moistening them with the tip of her tongue. "That's Imogene's hope, not mine," she said, averting her eyes as Simon took her hand in his, stroking his thumb across the back of her knuckles—doing his best to ignore the fact that his heart had just done a small flip in his chest. "You don't really believe I'd talk myself into doing any such thing, even to please your mother, whom I definitely adore?"

"I don't know," Simon said honestly, his hopes still most ridiculously on the ascendant. "My mother has had her share of outlandish ideas."

"Her yellow hair," Callie said, trying to smile, and failing.

"Her stays," Simon added helpfully, still stroking his thumb across Callie's knuckles, his fingers wrapped around her wrist, feeling the sudden leap of her pulse as his own responded in kind.

"Believing those chocolate tarts Lester discovered don't matter if she hides them in her bedchamber and only eats them when nobody else is looking." She looked down at their joined hands. "Would you please stop that?"

"No. Believing the title of Dowager Viscountess to be a fate worse than death."

"Believing she could stand to live with that title if you were to marry me." She looked up at him again, her green eyes wide and appealing, and only slightly apprehensive. "Why not?"

"Because you like it," Simon told her, his voice dropping to a low whisper. "Because I like it. Because I'm a bloody fool."

She continued looking at him. "Oh."

"Yes. *Oh*," he said softly, gently tugging on her captured hand, drawing her closer to him, closer, looking deeply into her eyes even as she looked questioningly into his.

"Bloody hell," he groaned, giving in to the moment and consigning the future to where it belonged, which was far, far away from this mad, glorious Now. He carefully slanted his mouth across hers, finding her lips to be a perfect fit against his own, just as her body fit him so well, her softness folding into his arms as he gently drew her closer, closer, his arms reaching so completely around her it was as if he had brought her entirely into his world, making her a part of him.

But Now didn't last long, and the truth of the future all too quickly intruded on his thoughts again. The truth that there was no room for Caledonia Johnston in his life, no possible end to this madness but disaster. Especially once she found out how he was tricking her into believing he was actually going to expose her innocence to Noel Kinsey.

He tore his mouth away from hers, burying her head against his shoulder, trying to recapture his breath, his sanity. "This is madness," he told her gruffly, closing his eyes tightly as he heard the unsteadiness in his voice, realized that he was having significant trouble remembering precisely how to breathe.

"You don't have to sound so angry about it, my lord," Callie said, attempting to put the flat of her hands between them, push him away. "Or are you simply afraid that Imogene will come walking in here at any moment and begin prattling about bridal clothes? I'm not entirely stupid, you know, and what you've just done has gone miles beyond anything permissible."

She gave him another push, this time escaping because his arms had gone slack at her words. "Well," she said, looking up at him as if measuring him for his coffin and delighting in being in charge of his execution, "that certainly served to cool your ardor, didn't it, my fine mentor? I begin to think Armand Gauthier is the safer of the two of you. Clearly any young woman going into Society should first be given lessons not in proper curtsies and how to leave calling cards, but in pistols and swordplay."

Simon roughly rubbed a hand across his forehead, attempting to coax his brain into locating some coherent thought that he could then force past his lips. It wasn't working. For the first time in a very long, long time, he found himself non-plussed, entirely at a loss—and he had been brought low by a mere girl!

"I beg your forgiveness, Caledonia," he said at last, rising from the bed—he'd been sitting beside her on the bed! Well, that, obviously, had been his first mistake. No. Coming to her bedchamber had been his first mistake. No! Thinking up this mad scheme had been his initial error. He should have sent her packing to her father with instructions to tie her to her bedpost the moment he'd got her in his clutches. *That's* what he should have done.

And why hadn't he done it? Armand had warned him. Bones had warned him. Not that Bones didn't warn against everything from sleeping with the windows open to eating any undoubtedly inferior meat his dinner hostess had ordered dipped in bread crumbs or buried in concealing sauces. Bread crumbs? Sauces? What was he thinking? Why was he still here? Why wasn't he downstairs, gulping poison? "Callie, I—"

"You want my forgiveness? Well, you can't have it! I won't give it to you!" Callie said, also jumping down from the bed. "What do you have to say to that?"

Simon looked at her standing there, her arms akimbo, her stocking-clad toes peeking out from beneath her hem, her cap of burnished curls tangled against her cheeks, her green eyes flashing somewhere between righteous indignation and unholy glee at having put him in such an untenable position, and he suddenly threw back his head and laughed out loud.

"My God, Callie!" he then blurted out honestly, feeling extremely lighthearted, and young, and most definitely alive. "If I were Armand, I'd be saying that I think I'm in love!"

Callie eyed him narrowly for the space of three heartbeats. Then, with a dismissive toss of her beautiful head, she declared flatly: "Ha!"

"Ha?" Simon repeated, more than slightly taken aback.

"Yes, Simon—ha! Ha, ha, *ha!*" she said, already walking toward the door. "You'd say anything to keep me here, so that Armand Gauthier isn't proved right and so that Bartholomew Boothe can keep telling you you're wrong. You'd do anything to keep Imogene happy, and occupied, and out of your way while you go about your business—whatever that is. And you still want to destroy Noel Kinsey and need me to help you. That's why you said what you said. Why you did what you did is equally obvious—you're a cad and a rotter and probably despicable! And I'll give you five seconds to remove yourself from my *boudoir*, my lord Brockton, or else I'm going to tell your mama on you. I mean it!"

Simon felt both his ardor and confusion fading, to be replaced with a mounting anger. "You may lead Lester around by the ring you've put through his nose," he gritted out angrily. "You may have my mother dancing to your tune, all of my servants singing your praises and telling me how best to please you, but I'll be *damned* if you'll tell *me* what to think! No wonder your father was so eager to swallow my mother's absurd lies and leave you here in London—it's probably the only peace he's had since the day you were born!"

"Get out!" Callie ordered again, reaching for a small statue of a milkmaid carrying a pail. "I can't stand the sight of you. And if you think, for one single moment, that I felt the least bit kindly toward you when you kissed me—well, you're fair and far-out!"

"Oh, no, you don't," Simon warned as she raised the statue, taking hold of her arm and pulling her hard against him, almost knocking the breath straight out of her. "Now, little brat—tell me you're indifferent to *this*!" he growled, then crushed his mouth against hers again.

The immediate explosion inside his skull could not have been more powerful if Callie had succeeded in braining him with the statue rather than letting it fall to the floor, where it landed with a dull *thunk* against the carpet.

His reaction to their first kiss had been tame in comparison to what he felt now, this sudden hunger, this most immediate need to have her, possess her, never let her go. And when she slipped her hands through his arms, pressing them against the back of his waist, he was lost.

She wasn't soft and yielding, as she had been before, but gave back as good as she got, pressing against him almost angrily, fitting herself to him—did any two people ever fit so well?—allowing him to penetrate her mouth with his tongue.

He skimmed his hands across her waist, then slid them upward, over her flat rib cage, to the tantalizing firmness of her small, perfect breasts. His thumbs grazed her nipples beneath the thin fabric of her gown. She sighed into his mouth and began using her tongue in a duel with him, shattering the last of his common sense, his lifelong dedication to Sweet Reason.

He didn't know how long someone had been knocking on the door to the bedchamber before he heard it. Callie must have heard it at the same time. They both suddenly, mutually separated, Callie looking at the floor, Simon raising his eyes to the ceiling as if to ask a Higher Guidance just what in bloody hell had just happened.

"What is it?" he called out when he could just as easily have inquired as to the day, the month, the year—for he felt as if he knew nothing, had forgotten everything in the world except the feel and smell and taste of Caledonia Johnston.

"It's your mother the viscountess, milord," he heard Emery call from the other side of the thick wooden door. "She said for me to tell you that she has always been one to turn a blind eye when the situation suits but that she won't be going to hell for you, sir, begging your pardon."

Simon looked to Callie, who had gone over to her dressing table and was now sitting on the edge of the bench, looking as if she had just suffered a tremendous shock. "I'd better go," he said quietly.

She only nodded, avoiding his eyes.

"We'll have to talk about this, you know."

She nodded once more.

"Some other time."

Only another nod.

"I'm—"

Her head shot up, and she looked at him with tear-filled eyes. "If you say you're sorry, Simon Roxbury, I'll skin you with a butter knife!"

It was his turn to nod, and he did so, then turned and left the room, quietly closing the door behind him.

"Is everything all right now, milord?" Emery asked as Simon paused outside the door, belatedly realizing that his cravat was all but undone and remembering that, at some point, Callie's fingers had been tangled in its folds. "The viscountess said that the young miss was feeling homesick, and that you had gone to talk to her. She won't be leaving us, will she, milord? We've all grown rather fond of her belowstairs, and Mr. Plum as well."

"Really?" Simon commented, finding it difficult to believe that Emery could be so informal.

"Oh, yes, milord, it's true. Brings a bit of life to the place, Miss Callie does, if you don't mind my saying so, and keeps her ladyship from mucking about too much in all our business. Roberts is especially fond of Miss Callie now that Her Ladyship's time is more taken with fittings and the like and less with trying to outfox him at every turn. It truly would be a pity if they were to go."

Simon looked at Emery quizzically. "How long have you been with me, Emery?" he asked, both shocked and enlightened by the man's long speech.

"I was a footman to your father, rest his soul, my lord, and watched you grow from a boy."

"Yes, I thought so. And yet, in all this time, this is the first I can remember you being quite this, well, this *familiar*."

"Yes, sir," the butler returned, lifting himself up very straight, returning to his usual formality. "Shall I pack my bags, milord?" he asked sorrowfully.

Simon turned, looking at the closed door to Callie's bedchamber. He remembered their kiss. He remembered the lie that hung between them. He could visualize Callie's reaction when she learned he'd taken Filton down by himself, cutting her out of the action. He then turned back to the butler, a rueful smile curving his lips. "Only if I can go with you, Emery," he said, walking off toward his own chamber. "Only if I can go with you."

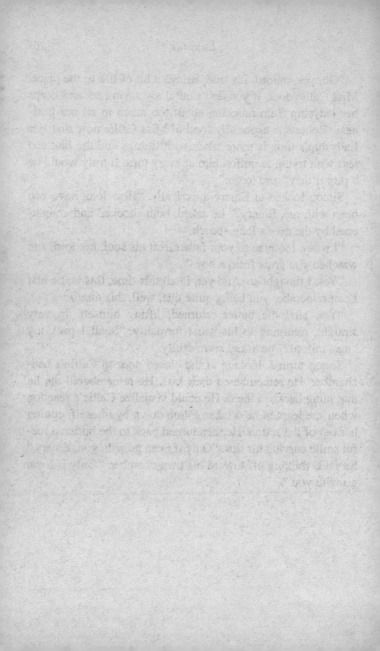

Book Three
Friends and
Accomplices

Just then flew down a monstrous crow,
As black as a tar-barrel;
which frightened both the heroes so,
They quite forgot their quarrel.

—Charles Lutwidge Dodgson

These widows, Sir, are the most perverse creatures in the world.

—Joseph Addison

Chapter Eleven

For the length of two entire days and nights, Callie seriously considered going home. What was she doing in London in the first place? She had come here for one reason, and one reason only, that of shooting Noel Kinsey, Earl of Filton.

A simple enough thing, if one thought like Caledonia Johnston, that is.

But, no. She had to crawl into the wrong coach. She had to come smack up against Simon Roxbury, Viscount Brockton. He, in his turn, had to be the most insufferable, annoying, infuriating, interfering creature ever to walk upright on God's green earth. Not only had he wheedled her mission out of her, but he had stuck his sleek aristocratic nose into her business and then—which was probably the most humiliating of all—taken charge of her, her plans, everything!

How had she let this happen? She wasn't a follower, she was a leader. Anyone who thought differently could just apply to Lester Plum, who could probably be found sitting in the Viscountess Brockton's boudoir right then, discussing the finer points of French pastry, the delights of cream sauces, and this evening's menu, all while munching on the illustrious Scarlet Upwode's chocolate tarts.

Noel Kinsey, the object of Callie's thoughts of revenge, was nowhere to be found. The curst fellow had been out of the city for more than a fortnight. That was a long time. Long enough for Callie to be gifted with a new wardrobe, cursed with enough lessons in deportment to stun an ox into submission, saddled with the viscountess's hopes for her son's matrimonial future, and smitten to the marrow by that same odious, insufferable Simon Roxbury, who was no better than he should be—and probably worse.

How had her anger turned to interest, and her interest to what she most firmly believed to be a transitory infatuation generously mixed with exasperation? She'd somehow succumbed to a temporary muddle of her heart and brain that had left her—*her!*—hiding in her bedchamber like some dieaway miss. Why, she had even confided in the viscountess, in a most blatant lie, that her monthly flux had come upon her with a vengeance and she simply couldn't leave her rooms.

She wasn't a coward! She wasn't anything of the sort! So why was she still hiding here, locked away from the comparative freedom of the remainder of the Portland Place mansion? Why was she cooling her heels by lying in her bed reading foolish magazines or standing at the window like some lost soul, staring out over the street below, wishing herself outside in the watery sun that had broken over London since she had first taken to her bed?

She ought to murder Simon. No, murder was too good for him! She ought to take a page out of their plans for Noel Kinsey, that's what she should do. She ought to marry him, actually marry Simon Insufferable Roxbury, that's what she ought to do. Marry him and take very, very good care of him so that he lived to be one hundred or more, suffering her retribution every day.

For he had gotten to her. He had gotten deep inside of her. He'd touched a spot she hadn't known existed, a soft, squishy part of her that thought less of the vindication of her beloved brother, Justyn, or of revenge against the hated Noel Kinsey than it did of honeyed kisses and sweet embraces and long nights spent indulging in ecstasies Simon's kisses, his touch, had promised.

Which was, of course, why she hated him.

Oh, how she wanted to be able to hate him!

"Good news!" Bartholomew said, bursting in on Simon's solitude, his self-imposed exile from his family and friends that had lasted two long days and two very nearly sleepless nights spent sharing the hours with a decanter of brandy.

Simon eyed his friend curiously, then looked past him to see Armand enter the study, the satisfied smile on his friend's face nearly compelling him to hoist his weary body up and out of his chair just so that he could march across the room and knock the man down.

"Good news?" Simon then repeated, wondering how his tongue had grown fur overnight, then rubbing a hand across his still-unshaven cheek. Lord—how low could one man sink?

He didn't know what had done more to drive him into the bottom of a bottle. His disastrous interlude with Callie? The sight of Silsby as he had stumbled into Simon's bedchamber last night to see the rapidly balding man trying on Odo Pinabel's toupee? Being forced to listen to the valet explain that someone named Scarlet had come to live in Portland Place, and he longed above everything to impress her?

Had his formerly bachelor household always been this bizarre? How had he never noticed?

Bartholomew, clearly upset at being ignored, proceeded to wave a folded newspaper in front of Simon's face. "I was right, Armand, he didn't see it. I told you so. Probably hasn't seen a newspaper in days, poor old sot, ever since he made poor Miss Johnston so upset and sent us all away. She hasn't forgiven you yet, has she, old friend? Well, she will now, by God!" he ended, slamming the newspaper down on the desk, setting off a thunderclap of pain behind Simon's eyes that made him wince.

"What is it?" Simon asked, drawing the newspaper to him. Lifting it up, he scanned the words in front of him, silently questioning when it was that he had forgotten how to read. In fact, the only thing he could remember was that he only drank champagne, and that he limited himself for a reason. Brandy, if he indulged in more than a single glass, had always made him sick. Wretchedly sick. Sick unto death. He felt a belch rising and turned it into a cough. "Christ on a crutch," he grumbled, looking to Armand. "Are you going to help me, or just stand there, grinning like a bear?"

Armand took up a chair in front of the desk, folding his long length into it and crossing his legs at the knee. "It's like Bones said, Simon. Good news. Just what you've been waiting for, or so you've told us, told yourself. I've been seeing the thing differently of late. Miss Johnston, however, is probably only slowly coming around to my same conclusion in these past two days, realizing your perfidy even as you continue to fight it. Did she spurn you? Is she even still here?

Have you had her locked in her rooms, thrown a bar across the door? Because you can't let her go, Simon. Not now when you're discovering that Imogene was right all along."

"Go to blazes, Armand," Simon said dully, dropping his head into his hands. "And don't go running to Imogene, if you bear me any affection at all. Because you're wrong. Dead wrong. On all counts."

"Still fighting the inevitable, I see. Too bad," Armand said, sighing theatrically. "Pity."

"Fighting what inevitable? What's a pity? What are the two of you talking about?" Bartholomew asked, snatching up the newspaper once more. "Doesn't anyone want to hear the good news? Filton's aunt has gone and stuck her spoon in the wall! Last week, as a matter of fact. She's all tucked up in the family vault by now, the way I figure the thing."

Simon looked to Armand, who only nodded at him, winked, and said, "A woman is dead, Bones. And you consider this to be *good* news?"

"Well, not for the aunt, certainly, Armand," Bones agreed, at last dropping into a chair, so that Simon no longer had to watch the man flying around the room like an agitated bird caught indoors. "But she *was* old, Armand. Dead old. Old people die, that's the way of things—have to make room for the younger ones, you understand?"

"I believe I do, Bones," Simon said, beginning to feel some of his good humor returning. "Although I've never heard the natural order of things described in just that way—as a necessary resettling of real estate. So, the aunt is dead. And where is the so-estimable Filton, I wonder? Will he come back to London, as he promised, do you think, or go into mourning?"

"Go into mourning? Only if his aunt didn't leave him her fortune. Except that, without a fresh infusion of funds, he'd need to be back in London more than ever, wouldn't he? Still, let us hope, for the sake of your plan, that she didn't line his pockets for him," Armand supplied silkily as Roberts entered, two glasses of wine balanced on a silver tray. "Ah, thank you, my good man. This is just what our small party needed. I didn't request a glass for you, Simon," he explained as Roberts left the room. "Would you care for some champagne, or would a bucket of cold water over your head suffice?"

Simon eyed him narrowly. "Miss Johnston says you're rather appealing, in an irritating sort of way. You know, I'll be damned if I don't agree with her, at least partly."

"And I'd probably be damned if I could know half of what the two of you say to each other," Bartholomew complained, shaking his head as he glowered at his friends. "So? Now what do we do?"

Simon also shook his head, in his case hopefully to clear it—relieved that, as easily could have happened, his eyeballs had *not* tumbled out of their sockets. He squinted at the mantel clock. "What do we do? As it has already gone noon, I would say that the two of you sit here while I go upstairs and let Silsby reconstruct me, then the three of us will take a drive past Filton's residence. If the knocker is back on the door, we'll know that I can set my plan in motion. Agreed?"

"Then she dances now?" Bartholomew asked, obviously believing Callie was to be a part of that plan—which, it had been explained to him a dozen or more times, she was not. Bones was a good sort, but he did have some difficulty with details. "Good. I was worried about that."

"Damn!" Simon said. He banged his fist against the desk top, then winced as his teeth did a small jig in his skull. He rose from his chair and started toward the door. "You brought me your copy of this morning's newspaper, Bones, I take it?

I'll have to have my own copy burned before Cal—er, Miss Johnston sees it. Once she learns Filton is back in town there'll be no holding her. She'll want to be out in Society as of tonight, and probably insist the blasted man be invited to her ball."

"You can't launch Miss Johnston into the social whirl tonight if you wanted to, Simon. It's Sunday, remember," Armand reminded him, tipping back his chair so that he could look up at Simon as he stormed past. "The lovely Lady Lloyd will be expecting you, as she does each Sunday. As you already disappointed her last week, you might want to rethink another insult. She could prove to be troublesome if she were to take it into her head that you'd thrown her over for some young country miss your mother is sponsoring. I doubt Miss Johnston needs that sort of problem as she enters Society as—what was it?—oh, yes, as her *reward* for entertaining your mother."

Mention of his mistress had stopped Simon in his tracks, and he wheeled about to look down at Armand. "You're right. Miss Johnston doesn't need that complication. I'd forgotten all about the woman. Dammit, she will be expecting me tonight, and I'll want to be running Filton to ground, start emptying his pockets."

He thought for a moment, pleased that his head had begun to clear. "Sheila has always found you attractive, Armand," he then said, his tone deliberately conversational. "I mean, there *is* our plan for Filton to consider?"

"*Our* plan, Simon?" Armand smiled. "When did my few lessons to you on the art of card sharping turn this adventure into *our* plan?"

"You taught Simon how to *cheat*?" Bartholomew exclaimed, clearly upset. "You really did? Oh, I don't think that's quite fair. Do you?"

"Not cheating, or at least not precisely. Only how to recognize how it is being done, and when, Bones," Simon corrected, longing to be upstairs and soaking in a hot tub. "I have no doubts as to my ability to best Filton in a fair game, but Armand decided I needed a bit of an *edge* if I wanted to bring the man down while he was fuzzing the cards."

"And *we*—as this is now *our* plan—want Filton fleeced, disgraced, and out of the city before our dear Miss Johnston's advent into society, yes?" Armand asked, shooing Simon toward the door. "Now, let's be on with it. The sooner Noel Kinsey is out of the way the sooner I can watch the real fun. And no amount of tutoring, my good friend, is going to save you in that coming contest."

"Armand, I'm warning you—"

"Oh, and I'll keep the estimable Lady Lloyd amused for you," Armand interrupted, then looked to Bartholomew. "Next week, Bones can take his turn with the dear woman. Right, Bones?"

They both looked to Bartholomew—who was sitting in his chair, his mouth agape.

"Bones?" Simon asked facetiously. "Aren't you going to say anything?"

Bartholomew closed his jaws with a snap, opened his mouth again, held up a finger as if about to make a point, then just shook his head and swallowed down the last of his wine.

"Now, *that's* refreshing," Armand drawled as the last of Simon's headache drained away.

*   *   *

Roberts handed the viscountess her fan just as she was saying, "You know, with that fire going it's deuced hot in here, and—" Clearly happy at having once more anticipated Her Ladyship's needs before she could voice them, he bowed his head in Callie's direction, acknowledging her silent applause at his quick thinking.

"He's getting much too good at that, and entirely too pleased with himself because of it," Imogene groused as Roberts, a sprightly spring in his step, exited the drawing room, leaving the viscountess, Callie, and Lester gathered intimately around the tea tray. Lester had opted out of remaining downstairs in the dining room with the viscount and his two male guests, who had spent the majority of the day in Portland Place.

Callie was still nervous. She'd been nervous all through dinner, especially as Armand Gauthier kept looking at her quizzically even as Bartholomew Boothe had simply *looked* at her—barely taking his eyes off her throughout the entire soup course. It was as if Bones either expected her to pick up the bowl and drink from it or if, between taking a last look at herself before leaving her chamber and coming down to dinner, unbeknownst to herself, she had somehow managed to grow a second head.

It was all very mysterious, but did serve to keep her occupied, so that she had little time to look down the table to where Simon sat at its head. He ate sparingly, sipped plain water, spoke seldom, and fairly well looked as if he had spent the last two days being just as confused and miserable as she had been herself.

Which thought, so far, had turned out to be the highlight of her day.

"His Lordship doesn't look well, does he?" she asked as the viscountess handed her a teacup. "He barely touched his red mullet with Cardinal sauce, which was delicious. And he was very quiet during all of dinner which, although a welcome change from his pontificating, became almost disconcerting once it became noticeable. Perhaps a tonic is in order?"

"Hah!" the viscountess snorted, touching a hand to her bright yellow tresses—she had balked at the last moment when Madame Yolanda had suggested a lovely soft brown more suited to Her Ladyship's advancing years. "It's not a tonic that boy needs, but a good clap upside his head. As if diving into a bottle ever did a man any good at all, and so I told his father the day after he learned that I'd discovered he'd been sending posies to a little dancer in Covent Garden. Cheeky little thing, with two of her front teeth still sticking out when she clamped her jaws shut. Never did understand the attraction, frankly. But you remember that, dear—a good boxing of the ears never fails to get their attention. Lester— would you be so good as to open a window? There's a dear."

The viscountess snapped open her fan and began waving it beneath her chin. "Of course, the little dancer was *before* I gave the dear man that good clap on his ear. We were married two weeks later and he never looked anywhere else until the day he died, rest his soul," she ended, winking at Callie, who sensed another bit of matchmaking hints about to be headed in her direction.

But Lester, bless him, saved her. "How would one do that, my lady?" he inquired, obviously with genuine interest. "Close one's mouth and still have her teeth showing? You mean like *fangs*? Callie, what has fangs? Lions? Tigers? My God—*snakes*! Is her ladyship funning again, Callie? She has to be funning, doesn't she?"

The viscountess rolled her eyes at Callie, then looked at Lester in some affection as she retrieved a lace-edged handkerchief from between her prodigious breasts and began pressing it lightly to her temples. Her liking for Lester was obvious as well as understandable. After all, she and he were kindred spirits—at least gastronomically. Why, she had even gifted him with another new suit of clothes, to thank him for bringing Scarlet home to her.

"Don't think about it, Lester, dear," Imogene advised kindly, still fanning her flushed face. "Such deep thoughts will only hurt your head. Think instead to our upcoming battle of beggar my neighbor. I've won the past three nights, you know, so it should be your turn to have some luck with the cards. Either that, or it's time for a new game. I do so love playing games."

Mention of card-playing sent Callie's mind winging back to Noel Kinsey—the still-absent Noel Kinsey—and her plans for the bounder, which had already been too long delayed.

"Will Mr. Pinabel be returning tomorrow, Imogene?" she asked, remembering the upcoming ball and the fact that she had yet to master the waltz. Not that she would be allowed to waltz in any case, until she had been to Almack's and received permission from the patronesses. But they were rapidly running out of time, as her voucher to Almack's had arrived this afternoon—a coup Imogene had pulled off somehow and had not been shy to crow about for nearly an hour, barely taking time out to breathe.

Not that the woman could take a single deep breath in those stays she continued to wear, even as she continued to eat and eat and eat. Callie bit her bottom lip as she looked at the viscountess, who was sitting very straight in her chair, unable to bend because of the whalebone that was sewn into the corset Kathleen had laced so tightly around her midsection.

At the moment, the viscountess was sitting with a prune pastry halfway to her lips, looking at it as if it might have worms and begin moving at any time. She looked rather pale all of a sudden, a considerable change from her earlier, more robust color, so that her rouge stood out vividly against her ashen cheeks. There was a thin sheen of perspiration beginning to appear across her forehead, along her upper lip.

"Imogene? Are you all right?" Callie asked nervously, fatalistically, and fairly sure she knew what was coming. She motioned for Lester to move over to the couch and sit close beside the older lady. It was probably the second prune pastry. Lord knew one was enough for anyone after the meal they'd just ingested. "Imogene?"

"Warmer and warmer," the viscountess remarked in a singsong voice, blinking as she smiled at Callie. "And all the pretty colors . . ."

"Hard to port! Catch her, Lester!" Callie ordered, hopping up from her own chair as Imogene's smile faded and her eyes rolled up into her head. Picking up her skirts, she then ran to the hallway, and the head of the stairs, to see Simon and his friends climbing toward her. "Simon—Imogene's fainted!" she called out, then turned on her heels and raced back into the drawing room to see Lester pinned between the raised arm of the couch and an unconscious viscountess.

"Undo her stays," Simon ordered as he ran into the room, obviously taking in the problem at a glance but unwilling to do the deed himself as long as there was a female present who could manage such a personal chore for him.

"With all of you standing here?" Callie sniped, glaring at him. "Oh, she'd like that, I'm sure. For pity's sake, Simon, rescue Lester and then send everyone away. And have someone fetch Kathleen."

Things happened very quickly after that. Imogene was hauled back into a sitting position by her loving son while Armand and Bartholomew rescued a gasping Lester from being crushed under the woman's deadweight, which was considerable. The three men then left the room, or escaped it—that depended, Callie supposed, on who was doing the describing of their actions. Simon knelt on the floor in front of his mother, balancing her bulk against him so that Callie could reach over the back of the couch and begin undoing buttons and laces.

"This is the second time in two days, as I heard how she fainted in your rooms yesterday," Simon complained, as one of the viscountess's headdress feathers poked him in the eye. "Why in God's name she persists with this nonsense—"

"We both know why she's doing it," Callie interrupted, grumbling under her breath as her fingers encountered a large knot in the corset strings. Then, realizing she couldn't tell the truth, revealing Imogene's rather earthy reasons for the stays—how could she possibly tell the son that the mother longed to be bedded?—she took refuge in some quick half-truths. "She doesn't want to be a dowager and think she needs to look young and lovely to catch herself a husband. For a while, she thought she'd be happy enough with the title if you married me—she likes me, you understand, and believes I wouldn't banish her to the dower house—and the stays came off. But they're back now, and with a vengeance."

She stopped to glare at him for a moment. "Can't you at least hold her steady? I'm having the devil's own trouble with these laces."

"We can always exchange places," Simon offered from between clenched teeth as his mother's considerable upper body, clad in its yolk yellow satin gown, folded over him like a viscount omelet. "So then you're saying she isn't still dreaming her dreams about making a match between the two of us? I don't believe that," he ended flatly.

"Neither do I," Callie bit out as she returned her attention to the laces. "She still sees the two of us as fated for each other. And, much as I adore her, I can't seem to shake her from the notion. However," she said, remembering to tell embarrassing lies Simon would easily believe in order to protect Imogene, "with the two of us being so silly as to not yet see what she finds to be so clear, she says she'll once again settle for nothing less than a marriage of her own that saves her from being labeled an old woman. Not that I believe that, either. I think she wants to *shame* us into marrying, saving her from a life spent swooning face first into the pudding or fainting dead away while taking the air in the park."

"Can you both talk *and* work?" Simon asked tightly, trying his best to keep his mother from sliding to the floor. "This satin is slippery, and the very devil to work with, trying to keep her from falling."

"Certainly," Callie bit out as she felt an unreasonable anger growing inside her, digging her index finger underneath yet another taut ribbon. They hadn't spoken in two days, and now they were talking about Imogene? How dare he! Men! They were totally without feeling! "Besides, I'm almost finished with both. Now, as I was saying—*and*, while all of that aforementioned silliness does everything to explain her hair . . . and her corsets . . . and her ridiculous feathers . . . and her *slippery* gowns," Callie said, breathing heavily as she worked the long row of tight laces free one by one, "it does less than nothing to explain her prodigious consumption of red mullet . . . and oyster pâté . . . and green goose . . . and sugared

fruit . . . and mounds and mounds of Scarlet's chocolate—
there! I've got them all! You can lay her back now."

Callie, now nearly breathless herself, leaned heavily over
the back of the couch, her forearms resting on the carved
wooden back, looking down at the viscountess as she lay
propped on the pillows, a faint hint of color appearing in the
older woman's cheeks once more as she slowly came back to
consciousness.

Imogene began moving her head from side to side, moan-
ing softly. Then her eyelids fluttered open.

"Simon," she said, smiling at her son, who was still on his
knees beside her, then reaching out one beringed hand to run
her fingers through the lock of dark hair that had fallen forward onto his forehead—or been knocked there by one of the
feather plumes. "Aren't you just adorable? You are, you
know. Just altogether adorable."

Callie's involuntary and quickly smothered giggle brought
her to the viscountess's attention, so that she lifted her hand
to her head, further dislodging her plumes. "Why, hullo,
Callie. What are you doing here?" Then Imogene frowned,
looking up at the ceiling. "And what am I doing here?
Where am I?"

"Somewhere between being sent to the country with a keeper
and being hauled off to Bedlam, Mother," Simon supplied dryly,
slowly getting to his feet. "You fainted. *Again.*"

"I did? Oh, dear, I suppose I did."

"Yes, Imogene—oh dear," Callie scolded, righting the di-
sheveled plumes, which actually only made the matter worse,
as Simon had been in the process of leaning over to kiss his
mother's cheek and ended up with another feather stuck in his
eye. Callie chose to ignore his low curse. "Imogene, this has
to stop, do you hear me? For one thing, you're much too sub-

stantial to be swooning. You look silly, rather like a Great Dane attempting to make himself into a nervous lapdog, if you don't mind the comparison. And you almost smothered Lester this time. For another, you'll never catch yourself a husband by *falling* over on him, now will you?"

The viscountess pulled a face and began to laugh, a deep rumbling laugh that came from her belly and served to make her shoulders shake. "You're right, Callie. A Great Dane. Or a great hulking tree trying to play at being a delicate rosebush. I like that comparison better, although I understand what you're trying to say. Marry Simon here, and I'll stop. Truly I will. I'll make do being both a dowager and a grandmother, I suppose, and perhaps even grow posies or some such silliness, and give up any thoughts of having myself a fine—"

"Imogene!" Callie broke in quickly, knowing the woman, still slightly woozy from her faint, was about to say the sort of thing that routinely sent Lester scampering, red-faced, from her presence.

"Mother . . ." Simon echoed, not understanding Callie's nervousness, she was sure, but merely trying to avoid another lecture on the subject of marriage.

"No? You won't do this one small thing for me? Then the stays *stay*," Imogene said, shrugging again as she winked up at Callie as if to say she was better, had herself back under control. She allowed her son to haul her up to a sitting position as Callie hastily threw a shawl over the woman's shoulders to preserve her modesty. "I've heard that the earl of Mitcham has come up to town, and I invited him to your ball, Callie. I've known Freddy for forever, even if I haven't seen him in dog's years. His wife died two seasons back, not that he ever liked her above half. It was money he wanted, you see, not the gel. I've got plenty of money, loads and loads of it. He might have me. Of course, he hasn't seen me since I've gone to fat. So handsome, Freddy is, and *thin*. Not that I ever liked him above half, but needs must, you know."

She looked at Simon again, her complexion about four shades above stubborn. "You hear me, Simon? The stays stay. That's all there is to it."

Simon threw up his hands, both physically and figuratively. "All right, Mother, if that's what you want. I'll just have Roberts follow you around with a chair, so that you can fall into it whenever you feel faint. That ought to make for a pretty picture at Callie's ball."

"He called you Callie again," the viscountess said, smiling up at her as Simon stomped from the room, obviously in high dudgeon, and good riddance to bad rubbish, Callie thought meanly. She could hear him call for his friends so that they could be off for a night of gambling until dawn, or so Roberts had earlier told her. "I think we're making progress, don't you? A few more fainting spells and we'll have him."

"I think you've squeezed all the blood out of your brain-box, Imogene, that's what I think," Callie told her as she walked around to the front of the couch and sat down beside the woman. "Please, Imogene, if you feel any affection for me, any small affection at all, stop this silliness about Simon and me making a match of it. Because it simply isn't going to happen, Imogene. Why, I sometimes think I don't even very much *like* your son."

"Miss Johnston," Simon imperiously called to her from the doorway as a flustered Kathleen rushed into the room to minister to her mistress. "I returned to make certain that my mother is in good hands before excusing myself for the rest of the evening. However, now that she does appear to be feeling more the thing, perhaps you could get on with your instructions in deportment in preparation for your debut? Among your other failings when it comes to the social graces, I see that learning to be sure of the number of your audience when you speak is one lesson that needs to be brought home to you."

That said, and looking smugly superior, Simon turned and quit the room.

"I take that back, Imogene," Callie said as she collapsed against the cushions. "I *know* I don't like your son. I don't like him so much as a little bit!"

Alas, how love can trifle with itself!
—William Shakespeare

Chapter Twelve

Simon might have been deluding himself but, as his reality had become something that confused him mightily and was, at times, dashed uncomfortable to contemplate, he had decided to believe that a second dancing lesson was in order. A day apart following their harsh words to each other during Imogene's badly timed swoon should, he hoped, have both smoothed the waters and reminded Callie that she still needs must learn to dance before Simon would allow her out and about to entice and then destroy Noel Kinsey.

After all, she wasn't to know that he had already put his plan into action the previous evening after storming out of the house. She also didn't know that Kinsey was already feeling the pinch in his pocket after gaming against him until dawn at White's, so that Simon had decided to give the man a good four and twenty hours to recover his breath, and to begin to champ at the bit, longing for another go at recouping his losses.

And so, Simon would spend the entire evening at home, bolstered by his friends throughout dinner and afterward. It was a good plan, a safe plan, a workable plan.

As it turned out, Callie, achingly lovely in mint green, spent the entire hour before dinner and dinner itself chattering with everyone, but him. Smiling at everyone, except him. Asking the opinion of everyone, excluding him.

But that was all right. He could forgive her some small, female fit of pettiness. He was a man, after all, a gentleman. He could be magnanimous. Even if he had longed to climb up onto the dinner table, march down its length, careful not to tip over the immense silver saltcellar or bang his head on the chandelier, and throttle the impudent chit!

After dinner, with Imogene safely barricaded upstairs with Kathleen and the dye pots, and Bartholomew picking out the tunes in the music room, Armand graciously took over Odo Pinabel's role. He put Callie through her paces in the quadrille and the few country dances she did know, before moving on to the waltz.

Simon, not trusting himself to come within ten feet of Callie without either shaking her or kissing her, remained on the sidelines, trying to appear as avuncular as possible. It was unsettling for a time, seeing the appreciative look in Armand's eyes as the man held Callie's hand, his right palm resting lightly against her dainty waist. It was decidedly unnerving watching Armand as he watched Callie watch her feet as they practiced the steps.

But then, after tipping up her chin so that she was forced to look at him, converse with him as they dipped and swirled, Armand's appreciation seemed to be replaced by an unaccustomedly youthful gleam in his eye and a broad smile on his handsome face.

Simon, intrigued, left his seat and walked forward a few paces, careful to keep out of the dancers' way, but coming close enough to hear what they were saying as they whirled past. After all, Callie was supposed to be practicing her social graces as well as her dancing. He was certainly justified in checking to see if she had learned anything in the way of polite, harmless, unprovocative conversation.

"Have you ever had anyone walk the plank, Mr. Gauthier?" he heard Callie ask, and had to cover his unexpected smile with his hand. Because, clearly, Callie was not practicing polite conversation. She was practicing her flirting. And, by the look on Armand's face, she was gaining high marks for her efforts.

The minx. The brat. The incorrigible, maddening, infuriating brat! It was all Simon could do not to laugh out loud.

"Only on Tuesdays," Armand replied in mock seriousness, neatly executing another turn. "And only, as I believe we're supposed to be chatting about the weather as we dance, if it was sunny."

"Of course," Callie answered logically, and without missing a step even as she caught out Simon as he was belatedly trying his best to play the chaperon, glaring at her in dark warning. "After all, it would already have been a rather *damp* occasion, wouldn't it? Now, tell me more about *booty*, if you don't mind?"

By their third turn around the small floor, Simon could hear Armand calling her Callie and she was responding with his Christian name, and it was obvious that a warm friendship had been struck between them.

Which was a good thing, Simon concluded much to his own shock, as he suddenly knew he would give Armand Gauthier half his fortune if the man asked, and with no explanations necessary, but he'd be damned if he'd let the man near Callie again if he thought, for even a moment, that Armand might decide to make a run at her.

After a while, with Callie clasping her waist and protesting that she was breathless and more than a little dizzy, Armand coaxed Bartholomew from the bench and took over for him. Callie dragged the reluctant man to the floor for a second practice of the quadrille, the dance that would open her ball. Bartholomew had protested mightily at first, prophesying smashed toes and bruised insteps. But, in the end, he performed quite well—he, too, put at his ease by Callie's light banter, her friendliness.

Why, she even deigned to smile a time or two at Simon himself, which he considered to be eminently preferable to the expression he had seen on her face when last she'd looked at him directly during dinner—the word *mulish* most easily coming to mind.

It was all very convivial. Relaxed. Friendly. Comfortable. Even *safe*—a word that, when Simon thought of it, brought on his only real frown of the evening. Because if he had learned nothing else, knew nothing else, wished to investigate his feelings at all, he knew that "Callie" and "safe" had no business occupying the same sentence. Not where he was concerned.

Still, the evening was a success, and then ended fairly early—with everyone saying their good nights and going off on their own pursuits as Callie, who had begun to yawn into her hand before eleven, excused herself and went up to bed.

Yes, a most convivial evening all in all, an unexpected pleasure that had gone a long way to ease the strain between Callie and him. So cheered was he that he rashly had promised to take her out for an early-morning drive through the city and countryside the following morning.

And, if Simon had been the sort to believe in omens, he might have canceled that small excursion the moment he walked into his dressing room, already pulling at his neckcloth, to see Silsby ducking behind the modesty screen in the corner, his head wrapped in a towel.

"Silsby?" he ventured, hopeful of coaxing the man out again. "What's that on your head? Do I smell something? Yes. Yes, I do. What *is* that foul odor?"

"I-I thought you'd be gone until at least midnight, milord," the valet put forth almost accusingly as he inched out from his hidey-hole, his feet dragging, his gaze firmly on his reluctant toes.

"I can imagine that you did, as that's what I'd told you when I went down to dinner. Forgive me for disappointing you. And now that I've found myself in the strange position of having apologized to my own valet—what the devil is on your head that is smelling up the room?"

"You don't want to know, milord," Silsby mumbled tragically, his voice barely above a whisper. "Truly, sir, you don't."

Simon finished untying his neckcloth and slid the long linen piece from his throat. "On the contrary, Silsby, I believe I would perish of disappointment if you were to deny me. Now, take off that towel, if you don't mind."

Silsby's hands flew to his head, as if the viscount's very words were enough to remove the coiled towel if he didn't clamp it firmly to his skull. "I can't, milord!" he exclaimed, clearly horrified at the suggestion. "Not for another hour. Lord knows what will happen if I don't do just as she said."

Simon considered this for a moment, wondering if it might be best if he tamped down his curiosity. He decided not. "Just as *who* said, Silsby?"

"Kathleen, milord," the valet answered sorrowfully, taking a single step closer to the light, and toward Simon, who immediately backed up two paces, his eyes beginning to sting from the foul odor assaulting his nostrils. "It—it's to help grow new hair, milord," he continued, each word leaving his lips slowly, as if he had to force them out. "For Scarlet, milord."

"You're *that* smitten, Silsby?" Pursing his lips as if considering the valet's words—but in reality trying to keep from laughing out loud—Simon nodded sagely a time or two, then said, "I see. And, to help you in this quest to, um"—he struggled to find just the correct word—"*improve* your hair, you naturally applied to the woman who turned my mother into a fourteen-stone *canary*?"

Silsby pulled the makeshift turban from his head then, so that the brace of candles standing on a table behind him made a sort of halo around his head. This halo highlighted the four-inch-long, greasy, tangled spikes of thinning hair the valet usually combed straight back from his forehead in the hope of camouflaging his fairly shiny pate. And the stench intensified, which was probably a good thing, as Simon's eyes were now watering, both from the smell and his barely suppressed hilarity.

"God, Silsby, you must love your chocolate-tart goddess very much!" he at last choked out, holding his folded neckcloth to his nose and mouth, to keep away some of the smell.

"Yes, milord, so much that I'd do anything for her to notice me, as I was struck by her the moment she came into the house," the valet concurred solemnly, nodding his head. The motion sent another wave of something that smelled like camphor and onions in Simon's direction. "But, then, milord, you'd know how I feel, wouldn't you?"

Simon's good humor evaporated as he eyed Silsby through narrowed lids. "Now just what is that supposed to mean? And for God's sake, man, put that towel back on. You look like you've just had a horrible fright."

Silsby did as he was ordered, then looked to his employer again. "I spoke out of turn, milord," he said apologetically and perhaps a bit frantically, looking past Simon to the door, and escape.

"Why should you be any different from the rest of the staff, Silsby?" Simon remarked. "Go on—say what you were going to say."

"Well, sir," the valet began, clearing his throat, "it's not like it's no great secret or anything, is it, sir? What with you buying Miss Johnston everything under the sun, and having this ball for her and everything—and letting her friend, Mr. Plum, live here and all? The old dear is happy, Roberts is over the moon, and even Emery is saying nothing could suit us all more. We're all most pleased for you, milord," he ended, smiling brightly, as if he had just said something wonderfully brilliant. "Most pleased."

"I see," Simon said, nodding, "Well, thank you, Silsby, but I believe that you and the rest of the staff are laboring under a misapprehension. Miss Johnston is here to entertain my mother and for a . . . for a . . . well, for reasons that don't concern you. There's little that smells of April and May in this house—most especially in this room. However, in order to save me from my mother, you will, as a good servant to your master, keep that piece of information between ourselves?"

"Oh, yes, milord! It wouldn't do to upset her ladyship when she thinks she's getting her own way," the valet averred sincerely, then pointed to his towel-draped head. "And this, my lord? We'll keep mum about this as well?"

Simon rolled his eyes heavenward. "Oh, indubitably, Silsby. You may rely on my discretion."

"Thank you, sir," the valet said quickly, then bowed himself out of the room after Simon assured him he could competently undress himself this one evening.

However, once alone in the room, Simon sat down on a straight-back chair he used when Silsby was helping him on with his boots, and only stared into space for a long time, realizing that, just perhaps—as he had admitted to Silsby—everything was not quite so splendid as he had just this evening tried to make himself believe.

Callie could think of nothing more pleasant than riding through London up beside Simon Roxbury—unless he would hand over the reins to her, which would make her happiness complete.

He was being the perfect gentleman this morning. He'd complimented her on her choice of gown. He'd personally assisted her as she climbed onto the seat of his curricle—which was smack up to the echo and had two of the finest horses in the traces that she had ever seen. He had taken on the role of guide as he drove her through Mayfair, past Hyde Park, and then westward, out of the city and into the rolling countryside.

And all the while that they drove, his hands light on the reins, he kept up an easy banter meant to amuse and enlighten her. He spoke not a word about Noel Kinsey or their plan or, worst of all, what would happen to her once they had accomplished their mission.

He also did not speak of those moments in her chamber, when they had both lost their tempers, and their heads, and done something best left unremarked-upon, and then forgotten. Or at least that's how she believed Simon saw the thing, so that, if he did dare to mention any of it, she would lose all of her good humor and burst into tears—or hit him.

It was only as the scenery changed from houses and public buildings and turned to fields and green trees that the silence between them became charged, uncomfortable, and Callie's earlier happiness began to fade.

Only to disappear entirely when Simon turned to her after one particularly lengthy silence and, reaching into his waistcoat, pulled out a single, folded sheet of paper. "Here," he said, holding it toward her even as his eyes remained on the road ahead. "I've taken the trouble of writing down a few more bits of elementary information for you."

Callie eyed the paper suspiciously. "I should have known," she said, surprised at the sudden, nearly overwhelming urge to smack his hand, and the paper, away. "I try and try, but I'll never please you, will I?"

"Don't be—"

"Silly?" she interrupted hotly, snatching the paper from his hand and tearing it into small strips, flinging those strips over her shoulder so that they wafted away in the breeze. "Stupid? Simpleminded?"

"Stubborn," Simon responded, "if you wish to be at all lyrical, and stay with the letter 's.' " With the reins transferred to his left hand and the horses still entirely under his control— damn him for his easy expertise—he reached into his waistcoat once more, extracting another folded sheet. "Shall we try again?"

"Yes, why don't we!" Callie exclaimed hotly, taking the second paper and, again, tearing it into shreds, then tossing the pieces into the air. "Are we quite done now?"

He turned to her, smiling in that wonderfully indulgent way of his—curse his eyes!—and reached into his waistcoat once more. "I can go on as long as you can, Miss Johnston. Remembering the fate of my mother's list of rules, I took the precaution of having my secretary write up a number of copies. Shall we go for three, or perhaps an even half dozen— or will you realize that learning the names of Almack's patronesses may be of some importance?"

Callie snatched the paper from his hand and unfolded it, quickly reading down the list of names. "That's what it is," she announced, as if he had been no more sure of the contents of the note than she had been. "I don't think I understand."

He shifted the reins so that he was once more holding them with both hands. "My God," he said, turning to smile at her, so that her stomach did another one of those small flips that had become almost the norm whenever he smiled at her, "now there's something I never thought to hear from you—an admission that, just perhaps, you don't know everything. But, then, I suppose this is my fault. I imagine I should have first told you that you'll be going to Almack's tonight."

Her jaw, and her stomach, dropped. "I'm going *where*? I thought that wouldn't be until—but I'm not ready! Am I ready? I couldn't be ready, could I? And what about the ball? Am I still to have my ball?"

He returned his gaze to the all-but-deserted road, as if expecting a huge mail coach to come bounding over the hill at them at any moment, startling the horses, and wished to be prepared for any emergency. "Actually, as Imogene planned the timing rather badly, the ball has been postponed for three weeks," he told her as calmly as if he were pointing out another site of architectural interest. He turned and smiled at her once more, looking young, and handsome, and rather endearingly childlike. Oh, yes, she really could punch him!

"Ordinarily," he went on as a strange buzzing began in her ears, "this sort of reshuffling would be disastrous, but I'm Viscount Brockton, and I can do things others cannot. Are you impressed? Bones was impressed."

"Postponed," Callie repeated, realizing her lips had gone numb—was this how Imogene felt just before she fainted? "Or do you mean that it's been *canceled*? That's it, isn't it? You've canceled my ball. Why?"

"There's a lovely, tall tree to our immediate left, Miss Johnston," Simon pointed out in a drawl that made her long to choke him—there were so very many ways to kill him, and she had a sudden desire to explore at least a dozen of them. "Perhaps you'd like to fly up into its boughs so that you can be as high as your temper?"

"I am *not* losing my temper, Simon Roxbury!" she shot back at him. "I *refuse* to lose my temper, for you would say it just proves that I cannot be trusted to play out our plan the way it is supposed to be done and cancel Almack's as well. But that doesn't mean that I don't think you're the most evil, pernicious, *back-stabbing*—"

"Her Royal Highness, Princess Charlotte, is to be married at Carlton House the night Imogene selected for your ball," Simon interrupted just as a drop of rain splashed against Callie's nose—she was surprised it didn't sizzle, so hot was her anger. "It is to be a small, intimate ceremony, but it seems that many private parties and balls already had been thrown together at the last moment, to celebrate the nuptials. Your ball would have been one too many, that's all. We want to make sure Filton chooses ours, don't we?"

Callie subsided against the seat, glaring at him, only slightly mollified. "Oh, I suppose that's all right, then."

"How magnanimous of you. Prinny will be so pleased not to have Imogene set up as competition for the favor of his guests."

She wrinkled her nose. "Don't be snide. But this does set us back, doesn't it? I mean, Almack's is splendid, and will make for wonderful practice, but Bones told me he doesn't think Filton has set foot in Almack's for these past five or more Seasons."

Simon smiled at her. "Bones is correct, Callie. However, as word also came to me—never mind how—that Filton's great-aunt has now died, and didn't leave her nephew a groat, I'm convinced the man will be dowry-hunting with a vengeance in London's premier marriage mart within the next two weeks."

"Two weeks? So long?"

"Patience, my dear. Filton's been living fairly high on his expectations this past year or more, since his great-aunt first took ill, as a matter of fact. But even he must show some sign of mourning, of being respectful to his aunt's memory, before kicking up his heels in London. You just consider this evening at Almack's as part of your necessary preparation, for both the ball Imogene has conjured up and your meeting with the dear earl. Filton will come to both you and London all in good time, to be enraptured and spurned and left to lie, as I believe you've said it, facedown in the gutter, his life in tiny little pieces and raining down on his body. You just have to be patient. Now, are there any more questions?"

"His *broken* body, actually," she corrected, then held out her hand, watching raindrops hit her palm. "And now I only have two more questions, my lord," she said as sweetly as she could. "One—as I will be given permission tonight by one of the patronesses on this list, this also will mean that I may waltz at my ball, yes? And, two—do you think we should be looking for somewhere dry where we can wait out this shower? Straw wilts when damp, you know, and I am most heartily fond of this bonnet."

"There's a small inn just ahead, beyond the next curve in the roadway," Simon told her, urging the horses into a trot, then turning to smile at her. "Nervous?"

"About Almack's?" she asked, wishing his smile didn't affect her so much. "No, I don't think so. I haven't had time to be nervous, which is probably a good thing."

"I didn't mean Almack's. You'll be splendid," he said, his expression serious. "I meant, are you nervous about going with me now, unchaperoned, to a small country inn?"

She froze him with her glare. He had yet to say a word about what had occurred in her bedchamber. Was this how he was going to treat what had happened between them— as a joke? Did he think she was a child, to be infatuated with him over a silly kiss or two? That she'd be frightened of being alone with him, fearing she might well leap onto his body and beg for yet another kiss? To have him touch her again?

Well, she wasn't, and she wouldn't. In fact, she didn't give a snap of her fingers for him, the rotter, and it was about time he knew it. "Ha!" she said with a flip of her head, turning away from him. "Don't be ridiculous. Why on earth should I be nervous?"

"No reason," he replied silkily, so that she wished she'd had the foresight to secrete a large brick in her reticule, a brick with which she could pound on him.

The rain remained a slow drizzle until they reached the inn yard, then showed signs of turning into a deluge. Simon tossed the reins to the ostler who ran out to greet them, then made short work out of grabbing Callie at her waist and hauling her down from her perch. He all but carried her inside the door to what—it had appeared from the roadside and now was proven—was little more than a rude country tavern.

She blinked raindrops from her lashes as she walked forward a few paces to peer into the common room. "Oh, this is nice," she said as she saw a half dozen men sitting around tables, sipping ale and eating what looked and smelled to be bowls filled with fragrant rabbit stew.

She turned to Simon, noticing his frown but not much caring what he thought. "We have an inn much like this near my home. Justyn would take me there every once in a while, whenever he was at home. We'd sit with the farmers and talk to the coach passengers and sometimes even play darts. I'm rather accomplished at darts, Simon. Do you think we might be able to—"

"No, brat, I don't!" Simon grabbed hold of her elbow, pulling her close against his side. "I agree that the occupants look safe enough. If anything, I should be worried about protecting them from association with you. That being the case, Callie, there will be no conversing. There will definitely be no dart playing. The last thing I need right now is more trouble. Understand?"

He then ushered her into the common room and, pulling out a chair at the table closest to the door by the simple expedient of hooking one of its legs with his booted foot, rather roughly pushed her down onto it. "Now, just sit here and behave yourself. I'm off to find the innkeeper and secure us a private dining room. I won't be longer than five minutes."

Another young woman—most young women—would have looked up at Viscount Brockton adoringly, impressed by his masterfulness, and said, "Yes, my lord. Anything you say, my lord."

But Callie had never really much cared for being like other young women. She glared up at Simon, realizing that she was definitely still angry with him—and for any number of reasons. How dare he think she would get him into trouble? How dare he believe she didn't know how to behave?

And, worst of all—how dare he kiss her, then act as if it meant nothing to him, that it was nothing more than something to *tease* her with! "Go to the devil, Simon Roxbury," she told him, pulling her elbow free of his grip. "You just go to the devil!"

He took off his curly-brimmed beaver, shaking water from it as he looked around the taproom, then sighed. "Make that four minutes."

"There's no need to hurry on my account," Callie bit out, stripping off her gloves and flinging them onto the table as he turned and walked back into the hallway. He was probably ready to burst into the kitchen itself in search of the innkeeper or some female he could then sit down beside Callie—who was already looking longingly at the dartboard hung on the far wall.

Her fingers itched to feel a dart balanced between them.

She cocked her head to one side, smiling at an exceedingly harmless-looking young lad dressed in a farmer's smock and loose trousers.

It was almost too simple.

By the time Simon returned, Callie had removed her bonnet and abandoned her reticule—prudently hiding it beneath Simon's hat. She stood with her toe on the chalk line drawn on the floor, a dart poised between her thumb and index finger, her gaze intent on the target as two of the farmers placed small bets as to whether or not the "young miss" could score a second bull's-eye.

She did.

"You're incorrigible," Simon said quietly as he walked up behind her. She stood her ground, letting him know she was not in the least afraid of his anger, and watched the young farmer try, and fail, to duplicate her feat. "And you're only doing this to punish me, aren't you?"

She smiled at him so sweetly she marveled that treacle didn't run out of the corners of her mouth, to dribble down her chin. "That thought did occur to me, yes, although it isn't the only reason. Will you now box my ears, *brother*?"

"Brother?" Simon repeated, looking to the men who were now urging Callie into another game. "Well, at least you have some sense. And you're enjoying yourself, brat, aren't you?"

"Oh, yes!" she said, her smile now quite genuine. "I've been so *good*, Simon—even you have to acknowledge that. I've stayed in my lovely cell and never once climbed its crystal walls. But now I have to have a little fun. I may even deserve it. Is that all right?"

Simon looked to the doorway, then back to the men sitting at the tables. "Oh, bloody hell," he said, stripping off his coat.

"Two out of three, Callie, and then we'll have ourselves some stew in the room I've reserved for us."

Then he turned away from her and held out his hand for the darts. "Bets, gentlemen?" he inquired. "Remembering, of course, that I taught m'sister here everything that she knows."

The rabbit stew was delicious, so tasty that Callie—remembering that she was away from Imogene's ever-watchful eye—dared to use bits of crusty bread to sop up the last of the gravy and onions, then lick her fingers when she was done.

Simon sat across from her in the small private dining room, his elbows propped on the heavy oak, his chin in his hands, his empty plate shoved to the center of the table. "In the societies of some countries," he drawled as she pulled her smallest finger out of her mouth, sucking on it with pursed lips, "what you're doing would be considered a most provocative act. England being one of them, I believe."

She bit down on the tip of her finger, and spoke around it. "I don't understand," she told him, sucking on her fingertip once more before removing it, then blushed to the roots of her hair as she saw his involuntary wince. "Oh."

"Yes, quite. *Oh*." Draining the last of his ale—champagne being beyond the scope of the bill of fare at the Duck and Drake—he rose and walked to the small window overlooking the inn yard, standing with his face averted from her, his hands clasped behind his back. "The rain has nearly stopped," he remarked, rather tightly. "We'll be on our way in another ten minutes."

Callie wiped her hands on her serviette, then neatly folded it and replaced it on the table as she looked to Simon. He was so handsome in his white shirtsleeves, with only his buff-colored waistcoat covering his fine, broad chest, and the slimness of his waist and hips visible beneath his close-fitting breeches. He was so handsome she could cry.

"Imogene will be frantic," she said, also rising. "I doubt she believes an acceptable toilette for Almack's can possibly be completed in less than four hours. And are you quite certain Noel Kinsey won't be in attendance? How do you know that, how can you be so sure? I know you said I should be patient, but I really wish to be on with it. I've been good, you have to admit that. But now I want to have the man back in London where I can help you destroy him. Armand says you're certainly able to do that, being very proficient at card-playing himself."

Simon turned around, smiling at her, although that smile didn't seem capable of reaching his eyes. "It's easier to speak of the absent Noel Kinsey, and our plans for him, than to talk about what's really on both our minds? Isn't it?"

"What's really on our minds? What else could there be?" Callie tipped her head to one side, pretending not to understand what Simon meant. She spared only a moment to consider the why and how of what had happened, precisely when she—Caledonia Johnston—had become such a craven coward. Another quick look at Simon gave her the answer. She hadn't been the Caledonia Johnston she remembered ever since this dratted man had first kissed her, and possibly even before that.

He looked at her intently for a moment, then at the closed door to the hallway. "Let me find a servant and have him tell someone to have my curricle around front in ten minutes—then we'll talk, all right?"

He waved her back to her chair as he exited the room and she sat down, willingly. After all, it was preferable to falling down, and her knees were showing signs of buckling at any moment. She'd been having fun, playing at darts, teasing Simon by calling him "brother," going so far as to companionably clap him on the back after a good throw. And then she had been happily engaged with the rabbit stew—for losing at darts seemed to have given her a prodigious appetite.

But now she was very much aware of how alone the two of them were—just like that day in her bedchamber—and she was finding it difficult to think, to breathe. She only wondered if Simon had escaped the private dining room for the same reason—to collect himself, to keep from giving in to the temptation to investigate whether or not kisses were just as sweet the second time as the first.

"There, that didn't take a moment," he said briskly as he reentered the room. "Now, where were we? Oh, yes. How I know so much about the comings and goings of one Noel Kinsey. It's simple enough to explain," he began, taking up his own seat once more. "In a word, brat—servants."

"Servants?" Callie shook her head. Really, it was impossible to follow Simon as he jumped from one conversation to the next. One moment she'd thought he'd wanted to discuss them—the two of them—and the next he was back to Noel Kinsey. "But how—?"

"There are levels and levels of society, Callie," he continued, "one of the most interesting being that of the servant halls both in London and in the countryside. Here, in the city, there exist several taverns devoted entirely to the servant class, all broken down as to the hierarchy peculiar to such individuals. Butlers and majordomos frequent one, footmen another, valets a third. The talk there revolves around their own lives and that of their masters—with each one trying to outdo the other as to how important those employers are, where they have been, who they're gambling with, dancing with, marrying. And, of course, there is the usual litany of complaints. For instance—did you know that just a month ago Filton turned off both of his footmen and his undercook, cheating all three of them out of their last quarter's wages? Just one of the many reasons I'm looking forward to bringing him low."

Callie wriggled in her seat, her eyes gleaming, her smile wide. "No! And you really know all of this? What else do you know?"

Simon pulled his watch from his pocket, levered it open and checked the time, then snapped it shut once more, sliding it back into his pocket. "Would you care to know what the earl of Filton had for dinner last night?" he asked, clearly delighted with himself.

Callie slapped her palms against the tabletop, totally relaxed once more. Because Simon was right. Here, alone together at this inn, was no proper place to discuss improper kisses. She didn't need any of Imogene's strictures to tell her that. "Oh, this is delicious!"

"Not really," Simon quipped, laughing out loud. "I don't much care for stuffed tripe, myself. Now, shall we go? I'm having visions of an hysterical Imogene sending Lester out by way of a search party which, I'm quite certain, would mean losing our dear Mr. Plum forever."

Callie stood, pulling on her gloves as she watched Simon shrug back into his jacket, then picked up her bonnet and headed for the door. And then she stopped, halted in her tracks, and narrowed her eyelids. "Something isn't right here, Simon."

He turned to her slowly, one eyebrow arched. "Really?"

She nodded furiously. "Yes. Really. When we were driving,

I believe you spoke as if Filton were not in London yet. Hinted that he most certainly would not be at Almack's tonight, although he would attend one of the assemblies within the next few weeks. But now you've told me what he had for dinner last night."

"I did?"

"Yes. Yes, you did. You couldn't know what he'd eaten for dinner if he was still in the country. Gossip doesn't travel that fast." Her bonnet flew in the direction of the tabletop. She pulled off her gloves, one after the other, and tossed them in the same general direction, then sat herself down once more. "Noel Kinsey is in London, isn't he? Now. Today. Yesterday. Tell me, my lord. Is it possible that he never left the city at all?"

Simon stood very tall, very still. "As you've said, Callie, as my mother has agreed—there are times I simply talk too much."

Callie was barely listening to him. She was too busy thinking about walking the floor with books piled on her head, and strawberry-and-cream potions, and long days locked inside Portland Place contemplating a revenge she now knew Simon Roxbury had never planned for her to share. "He's here. *Here*, in London. And you're probably already halfway to ruining him. Aren't you? Oh, how could you?" she asked, her voice low, husky, full of hatred, hurt, real physical pain at his betrayal. "How *could* you!"

He walked over and perched himself on one edge of the table. "Now, Callie, let me—"

"Explain? Let you explain? You don't have to, Simon. I already understand. It's all clear as crystal!" She popped out of her chair like a jack-in-the-box, pushing her chin into his face even as she repeatedly poked a finger into his chest to punctuate her next words. "You couldn't lock me up. You couldn't send me back to my father with any degree of surety that I'd stay put," she said, her words all but tumbling over themselves.

"But then there was Imogene," she went on quickly. "Ah, yes. Imogene. With her stays and her silly dieting, and her insistence on starving herself into becoming a countess, at the very least. She took a liking to me, thought up a pleasurable fantasy of matching the two of us together, marrying me off to her dear, only son. Ha! Is that when you first glimpsed an answer to your dilemma—to all of your problems? You knew what you could do with Caledonia Johnston—how to keep the interfering chit occupied and out of the way. Oh, yes, I see it—I see it all. Imogene was a bother to you. *I* was a bother to you. But put two bothers together, send them off in circles, chasing their own tails, believing their own plans, your own *lies*—and you would be left free to play out your own game."

He tried to take hold of her finger, but she pulled herself free, slapping at his hand. "But then Imogene arranged for a ball. Did it behind your back, I'm sure. That must have given you quite a nasty turn, Simon. That, and you probably began to feel sorry for the poor country girl you'd duped so badly. So you got me a voucher to Almack's, the one place Filton would never go. You'd *reward* me with a little fun because I'd amused Imogene for a few weeks, throw me a small bone to keep me happy, keep me from asking too many questions. You even *kissed* me, made me feel as if I might actually be desirable. Anything, anything at all you could do to keep me content to cool my heels in Portland Place. Anything you could do to keep me out of your way. Bastard! Am I still right? Well? Am I? Feel free to stop me anytime I say something that isn't right."

He didn't have to stop her however, as Callie found she had run out of breath, and she was closer to bursting into tears than she wanted him to know. With a small cry of exasperation, she whirled on her heels and stomped off to look out the window at the stable yard below her.

"I was desperate that first day, grabbed at the first idea that seemed the least bit plausible. Because you wouldn't have gone home if I'd asked you, would you?" Simon said from somewhere behind her.

She shook her head, quickly, and without turning to look at him. She didn't want to answer him at all but knew he'd push at her and push at her until he got some sort of response.

"You would have kept chasing after Noel Kinsey, dragging poor Lester behind you, ruining my chances of completing my own carefully thought-out plans for the man. And probably getting yourself thrown into the guardhouse and Lester transported for your trouble."

"I would not!" Callie exclaimed, her anger overtaking her to the point where she had to look at him, had to stare him down for his arrogance, his condescending view of her abilities. "Besides, Filton ruined my brother, nearly ruined our whole family. I had every right to exact revenge on him. You're only going after him because you don't like him on general principles. You've said so yourself. *Mine* is the more pressing mission. You're only playing a grown man's game, and you just couldn't stand it that I might succeed and you fail."

Simon was quiet for a long time. A long time during which Callie tried to regain her breath. Even as she watched a tic begin in his left cheek, even as she swallowed down hard as his sherry eyes went nearly black.

When he spoke, it was quietly, and with his hands drawn up into fists at his sides. "A game, Callie? Is that what you think? My solicitor's son blew his own head off two months ago, after Filton tricked him into gambling away every penny of his inheritance from his mother. Robert was nineteen, Callie. Nineteen. The only child of a widowed father. And there was no recourse, nothing anyone could have done to bring Filton to justice. James, my solicitor, hanged himself a week later."

"Oh, God," Callie breathed, groping for a chair and sitting down, her eyes stinging with tears. "I didn't know. I didn't know."

"Out of respect for my old friend and his son, I made certain the circumstances of their deaths didn't get out. So nobody *knows*, Callie, not even Armand," Simon said quietly. "But, then, he didn't ask. He, unlike you, simply trusted me to have a good reason for what I wanted to do."

"Yer 'quippage be ready in the yard, Guv'nor!" a male voice called out from the other side of the door at the same time there were three hard knocks against the stout wood.

Simon picked up Callie's bonnet and handed it to her, then stepped back, his hot gaze never leaving her face as he said in a clear voice, "Thank you. We'll be right there."

Then, when she didn't move, he took the bonnet from her nerveless fingers and placed it on her head, tying the bow to the left of her chin. "We have to go," he said, helping her to her feet, running his hand along her cheek, trailing his fingers down the side of her throat. "You've said a lot that's true, Callie, and much that isn't. For one, you're wrong about why I kissed you. That kiss wasn't for your benefit, but for mine.

And it was a mistake, one that won't be repeated. You don't have to worry about that, I promise."

"A mistake." Callie repeated, nodding, secretly amazed she could still talk, still stand upright. "I see. Well, that's a relief. Shall we go?"

They were halfway back to Portland Place when Callie spoke again. "Does Filton have any idea why you're after him, do you think? I mean, if he were to make the connection between you and your solicitor's son—"

"Filton fuzzes cards, Callie," Simon told her as he feathered a corner with an expertise she would have admired if she weren't so miserable, so worried about a man who'd just said he'd made a "mistake" in kissing her. "At the heart of it, he's a coward."

"Still," Callie went on quickly, "I think the plan you made up in order to keep me out of the way is better than yours to just empty his pockets. Safer, and with a more public humiliation. I want to help, Simon. I want to be part of the plan, this time for real. Because it was a good plan, it really was. His disgrace *should* be a public one."

"No."

Callie's sympathy died as her back went up. "You tricked me, Simon. Remember the books. Remember Imogene parading me like a prize pig at the fair. You owe me this chance to be part of the plan, now more than ever—now that I know how truly evil Filton is. I've *earned* that chance! Simon. Simon?"

He sent his whip out over the heads of his matched grays. "I said, no. I meant, no. I will say no, and mean no, forever. Do you understand me, Callie?"

"Oh, yes, of course. I understand you, my lord." Callie answered tightly, the wheels inside her brain turning at a furious rate. "I understand you perfectly."

No matter that Simon's were known as the fastest bits of horseflesh in all of London, it was still an unbearably long, quiet, and immeasurably tense ride back to Portland Place.

Ay, now the plot thickens very much upon us.
      —George Villiers, Second Duke of Buckingham

Chapter Thirteen

Simon had begun to think he'd be an old, old man before Lady Sarah Sophia Jersey—known to her intimates as Silence—stopped talking at him and let go of her death grip on his sleeve, so delighted she was to have the Viscount Brockton and his two friends at Almack's. Although he'd never seriously planned to accompany the ladies to the Assembly, any thoughts he'd had of seeking out Filton and continuing his plan to empty the man's pockets had been postponed after his forced confession to Callie.

Because Filton might show his face at Almack's, just as Callie had suggested, damn the man. And he'd be damned himself, Simon would, if he'd let her get within twenty yards of the villain.

Not now. Not ever.

"Again, Sally," he told Lady Jersey when she paused in her never-ending monologue of *ton* gossip and other inanities to take a breath, "I cannot tell you how grateful I am that you've condescended to allow my mother's young companion for the Season entrance to these hallowed rooms. I promise you, Miss Johnston is as refined and conformable as she appears, and highly cognizant of your notice. Yes, sweet and well-mannered—and with quite a handsome dowry through her great-aunt," he added confidingly, knowing he could count on Lady Jersey to keep that small, deliberately shared secret to herself for no more time than it took for her to waylay a half dozen male guests and start wagging her tongue—reported to be hinged at both ends—at them.

After all, what better way to keep Filton away than to have Callie surrounded by no less than two dozen impecunious younger sons and middle-aged fortune hunters? In that way, at least, his plan that never had been a plan could still work to his advantage.

"How much?" Lady Jersey asked quickly and concisely— for once not saying in twenty words what could be said in two. Her eyelids were slitted, her expression one of avid, if carefully concealed, genteel interest. It would not, after all, be prudent to behave like a common shopkeeper in these affairs, but business was business, and marriage between peers and well-cushioned young heiresses was the most serious business of all.

"Now, Sally," Simon warned laughingly, then bent low to whisper in her ear. The patroness let out a small squeal of delight and deserted him where he stood, taking straight aim at a small clutch of bored and eligible bachelors propping up pillars at the edge of the dance floor.

"Good, that should keep Callie occupied and safe enough," he said quietly, satisfied with himself as he turned in quite the opposite direction and headed for his mother. She was sitting with but not quite among the other older ladies and hired companions, her bilious yellow hair concealed beneath a gold-gilt turban, fanning herself with a vengeance as the heat of the room—and, doubtless, her tight stays—played havoc with her usually sturdy constitution.

"It's all going as planned, darling," he told her in an easy lie that was nearly the truth, bending down to speak quietly into her ear. He hoped his words penetrated the yards of cloth swathed around her head. "Callie will be the belle of the ball within a heartbeat, her dance card filled even before Filton arrives, if he does come at all."

"Well, if that isn't above everything stupid," his mother responded, the speed of her fan accelerating, the pitch of her voice a shade or two too loud not to attract unwanted attention if anyone had been sitting closer to her which, thankfully, was not the case. "I thought you wanted him panting after the gel now that I've brought her up to scratch. I vow, I haven't slept in a week, worrying and worrying, and now I see I was right to worry. You're not doing this at all right, Simon. Not at all right."

"Thank you for your confidence in me, Mother," Simon responded, catching Bartholomew's wave to him out of the corner of his eye. "Now, you move yourself closer to the biddies and say just what it is we've rehearsed—about how you're bringing Callie out as a favor to your dear old friend—and leave everything else to me, if you please. I promise you, if you do as I say we'll be able to stumble through well enough tonight without Filton so much as talking to Callie. I merely wish to dangle the bait tonight," he lied quickly, "not toss her straight into his lap at first sight."

"Impudent, arrogant puppy!" his mother responded, then broke into a wide smile that threatened to split her face. "Strip me naked if that isn't Freddy! Look, Simon—over there! Isn't that the earl of Mitcham? Good God, it is! Fetch him to me—fetch him to me at once!" She grabbed on to Simon's arm as he made to do her bidding—happy enough to have Imogene occupied with a little husband-hunting—holding him in place. "No! Wait! Simon—how do I look? This demmed turban—is it on straight? And what do I do? What do I say? Simon?"

Simon bent and kissed his mother's cheek. "You're the most handsome woman here, Imogene," he told her earnestly. His too-tall, too-large mother might no longer be young, and never had been anyone's vision of pink-and-white English prettiness, but she was definitely still the most impressive, imposing-looking and, yes, *handsome* female he'd ever encountered. "Now smile, my love. I believe the earl is coming this way. Shall I trip him for you?"

"Don't mock me, son, I'm a desperate woman," his mother warned, then gave him a small shove as the earl of Mitcham neared, sending Simon straight into the man's path.

"You're here to pop off a *granddaughter*, Freddy?" Imogene was saying within ten minutes, Simon staying around to enjoy some of the fun. "God, Freddy—never say you're *that* ancient? Can you still be up to riding—er—riding to hounds? No, you can't be, can you?"

"And you're as bright and lively and full of vinegar as ever, Imogene," the earl chuckled, not seeming to take umbrage at the viscountess's plain speech as he creakily lowered himself into a chair beside her, leaning his cane against his knee. Simon gave his mother a small wave, bowed in the earl's direction, and made good his escape, pretending not to notice that the woman was looking suddenly oppressed.

"There she is, Simon, getting ready to go down the dance with Werley," Bartholomew told him as he joined him on the side of the dance floor. "That will keep her bored senseless for the next half hour, poor thing. He prates of nothing but his horses, then misses every third movement of the dance, so that he ends up standing just where he shouldn't, still blithely talking stud fees. Armand's got her after that, for the second waltz, and the rest of her card is already full unless I miss my guess and all those young bucks that made a beeline toward her a few minutes ago were asking directions to the dinner room. They're buzzing like hungry wasps all around the dance floor, Simon, talking of her beauty—her *dowry*. By noon tomorrow you'll have every fortune hunter and half-pay officer from here to John o'Groat's leaving cards, sending posies, and cluttering up your drawing room. But there's still no sign of Filton, so that's all right."

"I still think he might attend tonight," Simon told his unusually loquacious, always fretful friend confidently. "I'm looking forward to seeing him here, actually. Callie was right. The plan that was never a plan still can work—as long as I keep her safely out of it. I can hear myself now, telling Filton all about Callie and the whacking-great fortune she's just inherited from her great-aunt—then inquiring of him if he hasn't just had the same sort of splendid good luck with a great aunt of his own. I'm so glad we didn't invent an uncle, or a rich cousin—as the great-aunt connection is so very apt, so fitting."

"And mean," Bartholomew said, shaking his head.

"Yes. And mean. Anyway, I'll let him simmer with that for a moment, then complain to him about how Imogene and I are now faced with popping the fortunate girl off—and ask him if he might possibly know of someone who might be interested in a simple country miss with more money than she knows what to do with." He lifted his handkerchief to touch the corners of his mouth. "Tell me, Bones, do you think he'll drool?"

"You've a nasty streak in you I hadn't noticed until now, Simon," Bartholomew said, looking at him consideringly. "Do you know that?"

"Thank you, Bones," Simon said, watching as another of the patronesses, Countess Lieven, approached Lester Plum— who had just stuck a fat knot of licorice whip between his jaws. The countess had a spotty-faced debutante in tow, obviously intent on having the two of them introduced, as the main purpose for Almack's existence was the pairing off of male and female, with marriage as the object. "Uh-oh. Over there, Bones—watch our Mr. Plum. This has all the hallmarks of being delightful."

And it was. Lester, his left cheek now bulging suspiciously, bobbed his head a half dozen times—his version of a bow, Simon could only assume—then stared at the debutante's extended hand as if it might be poisonous.

When it became obvious that the young lady was not about to withdraw her hand, Lester rolled his eyes like a panicked stallion ready to bolt and bowed over it. He placed a smacking kiss on the nearly dead white flesh, then hastily withdrew his handkerchief and rubbed it fiercely across her skin, removing what, Simon was sure, had to be a telltale trace of licorice spittle.

Lester then stood up very straight—like a brave soldier brought to the wall to be shot—and swallowed down hard, wincing as he did so, the knot of licorice nearly visible as it made its way down his gullet. He then reached into his pocket, pulled out another licorice whip, and handed it to the young woman.

"Oh, poor puppy," Bartholomew groaned commiseratingly, as if he knew just how Lester felt, having made his own share of faux pas at Almack's before he'd refused to step inside the front doors these past three years. "The countess will bounce him now, for certain. And probably us as well, for having brought him."

"Oh, you of the faint heart, Bones," Simon said, laughing as the spotty-faced debutante, wearing a smile that came within a whisker of beatific, slid her arm through Lester's and allowed him to lead her onto the floor to join the set just forming. "Perhaps we London gentlemen have been going about this courting business all wrong—posies, drives through the park, odes to my lady's eyebrows. Have you any sugarplums on your person, Bones, or have you decided not to dance tonight?"

"I don't believe it!" Bartholomew exclaimed, shaking his head as Lester and his female companion danced by. "And I've never seen the like before. Um, about those sugarplums? Do you really think—uh, oh! Filton at four of the clock, Simon. Stap me if you weren't right. And he's looking fine as nine pence, too, just as if he didn't owe his oppressed tailor close to three hundred pounds. Are you going to take straight aim at him, or wait until he comes to you?"

Simon turned in the direction Bartholomew had indicated and watched as Noel Kinsey—resplendent in his knee breeches, if a tad paunchy beneath his long-tailed coat (Simon really, *really* didn't like the man)—lifted a quizzing glass to his eye and surveyed the dancers. Obviously on the hunt for heiresses, he scanned the line of young ladies about to begin the quadrille and stopped as his gaze alighted on Callie, who was, Simon knew, both unknown to the earl and the most beautiful woman in the room.

"Where's Armand?" he asked tersely, wanting to know the positions of all the players before he began the game.

"Just rounding the corner at the far end of the dance floor with Callie now returned in his arms," Bartholomew supplied quickly as the movements of the dance brought Callie and Armand together, really outdoing himself in his role of "spotter" for the evening, "and taking dead aim at Filton." He took a deep breath and let it out slowly. "Here we go, Simon, for better or worse."

"It's not a marriage we're after, Bones," Simon growled, finding that he did not at all like the way Noel Kinsey was looking at Callie—and what would everyone think if he raced to the middle of the floor and threw a shawl over her lovely, exposed shoulders? "Now, come on. First we talk with him, then we leave him alone for a space, to ruminate over what we've said, and then we lure him off to White's for a night of cards. He'll go easily enough, once he hears a bit of what we have to tell him about Callie, then finds that she has no space on her dance card for him."

Callie was within the hallowed walls of Almack's, the dream of every young woman in England. She was wearing a lovely white gown that shimmered in the candlelight and whose skirts whispered when she walked. Her hair had been styled with care, to look artlessly informal while still faintly regal, a narrow white-satin ribbon tied through it and stuck with pearls. Her dancing slippers didn't pinch at her toes. Her dance card was full, she'd had eight invitations to go down to dinner, and she was, even in her own humble assessment, the belle of the ball, the success of the evening, the cynosure of all eyes, the most talked-about, gawked-at, popular young woman in all of London Society.

And she was miserable.

How many of these men would be paying the slightest bit of attention to her if Simon and Bones and Armand—even Imogene and Lester—weren't running from ear to ear, whispering hints of her tremendous dowry?

Why, she could probably slide to the floor in a swoon, sing a hymn at the top of her lungs—and totally off-key—strip down to her petticoat and do a jig in front of the fiddlers, even walk to the middle of the dance floor and fling herself down and throw a foam-at-the-mouth fit, all without a flicker of notice . . . if it weren't for those whispers.

But that wasn't what had Callie feeling miserable.

She was miserable because of the things Simon had told her that afternoon, because she had goaded him into an explanation she never should have heard. Simon had his reasons for wanting to destroy Noel Kinsey. Good reasons. Private reasons. Terrible reasons.

That he'd had reasons had been enough for Armand, for Bones, for Imogene.

But it hadn't been enough for her. No. Not for Caledonia Johnston. She'd had to push, and push, until he was forced to relive a sorrow best revenged, then forgotten.

And now he hated her. Despised her. With every good reason.

Not that her own reason for wanting to punish Kinsey was no longer valid, but it paled beneath Simon's story of his solicitor and that man's son. At least Justyn had escaped with his life, if not his pride, intact. He would come home again someday, sadder but wiser. Young Robert was dead.

Oh, yes, Simon had every reason to be angry with her, disgusted with her. What was equally terrible was that she couldn't even bring herself to feel the least angry with him for having tricked her.

Because he'd been right all along. She'd been silly, juvenile. Impetuous. If she had been allowed to keep to her half-thought-out schemes she and Lester would eventually have failed, been caught out, arrested, punished.

And she wouldn't have gone home after Simon had found her out, carried her off to Portland Place. Simon had been correct there as well. She would have stubbornly stayed in London, searching out Kinsey, trying to shoot him. Shoot him! How could she have thought such a thing? Planned such a thing?

Those hours of walking with books on her head, of listening to Imogene's endless lessons on deportment—everything—had been no less penance than she'd deserved. In fact, her weeks with Simon and his mother had been more in the way of a reward than a punishment. Even she was insufficiently thickheaded to see that.

And, over the course of time, Simon had come to care for her, at least a little bit. As she had come to care for him. Very much.

How much growing up she had done in these past few weeks. In so many ways.

Still, Simon hated her now. She'd known it that afternoon at the inn, the moment the light in his eyes had died. Whatever it was that they'd shared, it was over now. All that was left was for her to come to Almack's, to behave herself, and to please Imogene by being the "well-dowered" belle of the ball while the woman desperately hunted out prospective lovers to enliven her old age.

It was the least she could do for the dear lady.

And yet, now that they were actually at Almack's, now that

the music was playing and she felt herself being caught up in all the same romantic notions of every other young woman present tonight, Callie wanted, longed, to dance with Simon.

She never had.

She had, however, watched his every move as he'd walked around the perimeter of the dance floor, talking to an older, yet still-lovely woman whom Callie believed to be one of the patronesses. The woman earlier had made a great fuss out of introducing her to Armand as if she hadn't already known him, then told him he could lead her out for her first waltz.

She had continued to watch as Simon spoke with his mother, then with Bones, and still watched as he stood with Noel Kinsey, laughing and talking and acting as if they were the best of good friends.

She was watching so intently, in fact, that she missed a step and trod heavily on Armand Gauthier's instep as he led her into another sweeping turn of their second waltz of the evening. Waltzing twice in the same evening with Gauthier, she had been told—by Gauthier—virtually ensured her social success. "Oh!" she exclaimed, flustered. "I'm so sorry, Armand!"

"As well you should be," Armand told her, somehow keeping from missing a beat of the music, so that no one save the two of them knew of her misstep. "I was just most fulsomely complimenting your emerald-bright eyes—and you weren't paying me the least attention. And you're not smiling, Callie. People are watching. It's very lowering to both my consequence and my high opinion of my own charms if you're to look as if you aren't in alt over being honored by my attention. But this is Simon's fault, isn't it? You're in love with him."

Callie missed another step. "I believe you're left with two

choices, Armand," she told him as he tried not to wince—for this time she'd really come down hard on his toes. "Either talk about something innocuous, like the beastly weather we've been having, or lead me off this dance floor so that I might save you further injury."

"As soon done as said," he drawled. As they were already dancing near the edge of the floor, he guided her to a fairly isolated pair of straight-back chairs, snagging a glass of warm, watery lemonade for her as he passed by a young hussar who clearly had been in the act of taking the refreshment to quite another young lady entirely.

"That wasn't nice," Callie said, taking a sip of the liquid for she was, indeed, rather thirsty.

"No, it wasn't," Armand agreed smoothly, "but it's also one of the privileges of my checkered, and perhaps nefarious past. I'm allowed a license given few others, as no one is quite sure whether it's true that I have shot down six men in duels, killing four and seriously injuring the others. Such a dreadfully *lethal* man, I am, to be sure. No one is willing to challenge my prowess."

"And you've made up that tale and all those other fantastic stories out of whole cloth, haven't you?" Callie asked, more than willing to leave the subject of her love for Simon behind them. Had Simon seen them leaving the dance floor? Was he even now watching them, wondering what they were talking about?

"Only two or three of them," Armand told her, removing the glass from her hand and taking a sip himself before pulling a face and pouring the remainder of the contents into a nearby potted palm. "My God, how can you drink this? How can they *serve* this? Now, what were we saying? Oh, yes. I only laid the foundations of my reputation, Callie. The remainder of the construction was left to the wholly gullible, wonderfully inventive minds of those darlings of Society who have nothing better to do with their time than speculate on my lurid past."

"You were a card player," Callie said, eyeing him closely, wishing she could ask him to kiss her hand, just so that Simon could see him do it.

"I played cards," he said, smiling.

"You were a privateer."

"I may have shared a ship or two *with* pirates."

Callie giggled, just in case Simon was watching. She felt fairly certain Simon wouldn't want her tumbling into love with Armand Gauthier. Why, he might even feel it his duty to come join them. Lord! Was she that desperate? Yes. Yes, she was. "And," she said, throwing out a story of her own making, "you're really the bastard son of a Turkish emir."

"That was last week, I believe," he told her, winking. "This week I am the bastard son of an American cotton planter again, or so Bones heard at White's. Which brings us back to Simon, who has just left for that place, Noel Kinsey following along behind like a good little piggy."

Callie shot a look toward the doorway, her heart dropping to her toes. She had been so sure he was watching her. "Simon's leaving? And Filton with him? But he didn't even *see* me!"

"Oh yes he did, my dear. And rest assured Simon will spend the evening singing your praises, and of the depth of your purse. Simon will also tell him that he will be the one who says yea or nay to any plea for marriage brought to him on your behalf. That should be enough of a lure to keep Filton stuck to Simon's side until our dear friend can fleece the man down to his hose. So you see, my dear? You are being a help. Truly. You're also completely and totally out of harm's way, which is just where Simon wants you."

Callie allowed her posture to slump, just a hair, but if Imogene saw her there'd be hell to pay when they got back to Portland Place. She didn't think she could stand another balancing session with that three-volume set of *Pride and Prejudice*. "I've made such a mess of everything, Armand. Right from the beginning."

"Well, yes, I suppose you could see it that way, Callie. I, on the other hand, am enjoying myself most heartily. Now, if we've evaded the subject long enough, may we return to it now? Are you in love with my good friend, the Viscount Brockton?"

Callie blinked back sudden tears. "You shouldn't ask me a question like that."

"Again, true enough. We're all just chock-full of truth tonight, aren't we? But I have asked the question, haven't I? Do you have an answer?"

Callie smiled wanly, remembering the events of earlier that afternoon, and Simon's rejection of her. "Yes. I love him. I love him with all my heart and soul. For all the good that does me."

There was a slight pause, with Armand not speaking quite so quickly as he had before, so that she turned to look at him, to assure him if he was concerned for her. "I know he doesn't love me, Armand. Really, it's quite all right. I'm quite all right."

"Of course you're all right, Callie," Armand said, patting her hand. "And Simon is an ass."

"He is not!" Callie exclaimed. "He's the best of men. The very best."

Armand's eyes became hooded as he yawned into his hand. "I know, I know. Simon is the greatest of good fellows. Honest, upstanding, moral—all those things I am not. You were probably drawn to him by his exemplary behavior toward his mother, his dedication to the poor, his many charities, his very real concern for his fellow man."

"Well, yes," Callie admitted, confused. "I suppose those things are important."

Armand stood and offered her his arm, smiling down at her, pretending not to see the tears standing in her eyes. "Strange. You don't sound overly impressed with Simon's more stellar attributes. Is there something else?"

She rose, slipping her arm through Armand's, allowing him to lead her around the perimeter of the ballroom still littered with waltzing couples, toward a waiting, and wilting, Imogene. And Callie remembered something that wonderful, lovable lady had said the other night. "Yes, Armand, there is something else, something that stands head and shoulders above all his other wonderful qualities. He's adorable," she told her friend sadly, looking up into his openly surprised expression as a single tear ran down her cheek unheeded. "Simon is altogether *adorable*."

She didn't know it, but she had left Armand Gauthier speechless for the very first time in his life. She didn't know it for two reasons, the first being that Armand recovered quickly enough, saying something about having to toddle off to White's himself to lend Simon moral support as he continued his fleecing of Noel Kinsey. And because Imogene, when they got within earshot, began talking fast and furiously, her feathers waving, her fan flapping, her expression bordering between harassed and thoroughly disgusted.

"He's *ancient*, Callie," she said, grabbing the younger woman's arm and pulling her down into the chair beside her own. "Dead old—and shorter than me, shriveled up, as it were, from his great age. Popping off a *granddaughter*, gel, for the love of heaven! No fight left in that grizzled dog, I tell you. I nearly feigned a swoon, just to be rid of the creaky old thing."

"Who *are* you talking about, Imogene?" Callie asked, barely able to say good-bye to Armand before he politely excused himself and deserted the ballroom as Lady Jersey, who was losing eligible bachelors the way a leaky bucket loses water, stood by and wrung her hands.

"Why, Freddy, of course. He was here, Callie, just as I'd hoped. Ha! If I'd only known, I'd have hoped for him to bring a stepladder with him, so that he could reach m'nose! And he's *fat*, Callie. Short, and . . . and—*stubby*! All in all, I'd rather keep sleeping alone, thank you. Oh, I've never been so disappointed since I got my last good look at Prinny now that he's run to fat and squiring ladies old enough to be his mother. Well, we might as well leave, I suppose. You've danced twice with Gauthier, which will have the gossips bracketing you to him by tomorrow—I don't like that above half, let me tell you—and now that I've crossed Freddy off my list, there's no one here who interests either of us. And Simon has bolted, ungrateful son that he is. See if you can catch Lester's eye, as he has been put in charge of escorting us back to Portland Place. I haven't seen the boy above twice all night long. Do you suppose he's in the supper rooms? Horrible food, Callie, as I remember, and not worth the trip down the stairs."

"Lester isn't very particular when it comes to food, Imogene. Hot, cold, tough, stringy—it really makes no never mind to him," Callie said, then motioned to her friend to come to her as she spied him cowering behind a pillar across the room as if he was hiding from someone, for she, too, was more than ready to leave Almack's behind her. "I'm so sorry your evening's hunt wasn't more successful."

"As well you should be," the viscountess answered with a sniff. "I worry myself into a frazzle, fretting over you, not sleeping more than a wink these past days—do you think Kathleen covered these bruises under my eyes well enough? Well, never mind. I'm old now, and worthless, so it doesn't matter if I perish from lack of sleep. And now here I am, well after midnight, a bloody turban stuck on my head, propping up the wall at Almack's just like some white-haired dowager, with no hope of ever getting a man back into my bed. You should be feeling sorry for me. I can't face raising a herd of those homely pug dogs, Callie, truly I can't."

"Imogene, you're becoming overset," Callie warned, worried that the dear lady's threat of a swoon might become fact. She winced as the viscountess grabbed hold of her forearm, the woman's strong fingers digging through her long gloves and into her skin. "What? Is something wrong?"

"Wrong? No, not wrong, precisely—just disgusting, that's what! See, over there—it's Lady Lloyd, the shameless creature. Look at that lusty-looking fellow just *dripping* off her arm. If she dares to come this way I'll have no choice but to deal her a crushing setdown, Callie, I swear I will, I'm that jealous. And she can't be more than twenty years my junior. Oh, all right, maybe a little more. Thirty, perhaps."

"*Lady* Lloyd?" Callie repeated, her blood running cold. "Would that be *Sheila* Lloyd, Imogene?"

The feathered plumes waved drunkenly with the viscountess's energetic nod. "One and the same. No dearth of men in *her* bed, even if her husband is past anything more than a few memories of what once had been." She sighed audibly. "How I wish I could be like her, and not have to worry about this marriage business! Takes herself a new lover every few months, and still she's welcome everywhere. I dislike her, but the woman has flair, don't you think?"

Callie looked where Imogene was discreetly—thank heavens she was being discreet!—pointing, and saw a beautiful, black-haired woman of about thirty. She was tall, and sleek as a cat, with flawless skin, a dazzling smile—and a bosom that was, to say the least, impressive.

Callie glanced down at her own more modest bosom, then echoed the viscountess's mournful sigh. "Imogene," she said quietly, "isn't Simon among Lady Lloyd's admirers? I remember hearing her name, that first day I came to Portland Place."

Imogene choked and coughed, as if she had tried to speak and swallow at the same time. "You remember that? No, surely you don't remember anything of the kind. Because I didn't say any such thing. Did I, gel? I wouldn't have said anything—would I?"

"I think you did, Imogene," Callie pressed on, for some reason needing to hear what she was sure she already knew. "In fact, I'm sure of it, spoken when you were telling Simon that he should make a match of it with me. I believe your words were something on the order of warning Simon that marriage meant he would then have to shed himself of 'that cat, Sheila Lloyd.'"

Imogene kept her head averted, although Callie could see a dull red flush stealing up the older woman's throat, a throat the viscountess then cleared with a mighty *harrumph*. "Well, that certainly does sound like me, doesn't it? I spoke out of turn, Callie, I'm sure, and without really knowing what I was saying. Simon hasn't the least interest in the woman, never has. How could he—with you in the house?"

"You have desires, Imogene," Callie said dully. "You said as much, several times. It is not unreasonable to believe that men have the same desires."

The viscountess laid a hand on Callie's arm just as Lester collapsed into the chair beside his friend. "Women like that are a convenience, love, nothing more. My own dear husband availed himself of a *convenience* or two before we were wed, but none after, I assure you, as I kept him much too busy. Now, there are those women who believe that lovemaking is only for the lower orders, that there is no enjoyment in the act, and *their* husbands undoubtedly seek out more receptive partners."

"Lovemaking? She's at it again, Callie? I can't listen to this. I'll be with our cloaks, stuffing up my ears with them, most likely," Lester squeaked, jumping up and all but tripping to the floor in his haste to run away from this new embarrassment.

"Lady Lloyd is Simon's mistress, Imogene," Callie said flatly, ignoring Lester's hasty escape to the vestibule. "It's as simple as that."

"I shouldn't have bothered trying to cover myself with a fib, not with you being such a bright gel—and demmed pushy, now that I think on it," the viscountess said, shaking her head. "Well then, there's no sense wrapping up the rest of this in fine linen, is there? All right, Callie—Sheila Lloyd *was* my son's mistress. But that unfortunate liaison is over. Done. Dead and gone."

"And how would you know that?" Callie asked, deciding that, if she had already been called "demmed forward," she might as well ask whatever she wanted. Because it certainly was interesting that Simon had stopped seeing Lady Lloyd. When could that have been? Before, or *after* she, Caledonia Johnston, had barged willy-nilly into his life?

"That's simple enough. Roberts has assured me that Silsby has assured him that the Lady Lloyd is now firmly in my son's past, and has been from the moment you arrived in Portland Place. He sent off her *congé*—that's her dismissal, my dear— wrapped in a diamond necklace. Probably the one she's got strung around her neck tonight. That's one more reason I took off my stays—which would have remained off if Simon weren't such a slowtop in figuring out what I already know. I intend to shame him into recognizing his feelings for you if he can't see them for himself."

She patted Callie's arm a second time, thankfully not noticing that Callie's eyes had become suspiciously moist once more. "Now, let's find that ninnyhammer Lester and go on home. Not that I'll sleep again tonight, more's the pity."

Callie followed along meekly, taking only a moment to peek at Lady Lloyd and her necklace one last time as they walked to the vestibule. Not that it mattered that Simon had given the woman the necklace, or that he had once bedded her, once desired her. He was free to do as he wanted.

If only he wanted her. . . .

Once they had made their way into the vestibule, and with Lester staying at a safe distance—deliberately standing out of earshot—they allowed servants to retrieve their wraps.

"You really haven't been sleeping, Imogene?" Callie asked as they left the building. "Shouldn't you have Kathleen give you a small glass of laudanum? It can't be healthy for you to be so tired."

"Laudanum? I think not! Laudanum's for dieaway misses and old ladies. Once you and Simon have this Filton fellow routed and settle things between yourselves—well, I'll sleep well enough then, I suppose. Although I have to say that Freddy was a sad disappointment." She allowed Lester to take her arm as they walked down the stairs to the flagway and the waiting coach. "Ah, well, there's still your ball, Callie. Perhaps the pickings there will be better."

Callie smiled encouragingly. "I'm sure there will be many gentlemen at the ball who will be more than happy to court you, Imogene," she said as the groom hopped down to open the coach doors and lower the steps.

"One can only hope, I suppose," Imogene said, winking at Callie in the light of the torches on either side of the doorway behind them. "I only know I want a warm body in my bed before winter, Callie. So maybe I'll just have to be a little brazen myself."

Lester, hearing this, gave out a small yelp and backed off down the flagway, appearing ready to hire a hack to take him back to Portland Place.

"Oh, don't be such a namby-pamby, Lester," the viscountess scolded, motioning for him to come back. "I very much used to *like* being brazen. Why, I remember the time—"

"Callie! Caledonia Johnston!"

Callie, who had been laughing at the flummoxed Lester, turned around at the sound of her name being called out and let out a scream of her own before launching herself at the young man who had seemingly appeared out of nowhere.

"*Justyn!*" she cried, wrapping her arms tightly around his neck as he lifted her clear off the ground, swinging her around in circles as she rained kisses on his cheeks and hair. "Justyn, I don't believe it! You're home, you're home! How did you know? How did you find me?"

"If you stop choking me, I'll tell you," her brother said, disentangling himself from her tight embrace and leading her back to where the viscountess and a grinning Lester were waiting.

Callie, laughing, and crying, and not caring a whit that she was probably making a cake of herself, grabbed on to Justyn again, holding him tightly, afraid he was a figment of her imagination and might disappear again if she so much as blinked.

She rushed through the introductions, never taking her eyes off her brother, who looked older, taller, and even more handsome than she remembered—his clothes fitting him like a second skin, his hair longer than it had been when he'd left, his entire air one that exuded confidence, a belief in himself she had never seen before as he bowed so elegantly over Imogene's hand.

They had both grown up so much since last they'd seen each other. Except that Justyn seemed happy, while she knew herself to be sunk deep in despair. Not that she'd allow Justyn to see her unhappiness!

"So you're the one who started all of this, are you?" the viscountess said, eyeing Justyn assessingly even as Callie swiftly lifted a finger to her own lips and shook her head, silently pleading for Imogene to remain silent on that particular subject. "Don't look much like your sister," the older woman went on brightly, with only a small acknowledging nod to Callie, "what with that blond hair and all. Well, let's not stand here giving the tongue-bangers more to talk about—send your coach away and ride back to Portland Place with us."

"Done and done, my lady," Justyn agreed, squeezing Callie's hand, then smiling at Lester. "Talked you into another grand mess, did she, Lester, old fellow? Your papa and ours think not, but I can always smell Callie's mad starts at ten paces. Yet this time you seem to have landed on your feet, the pair of you. That's certainly refreshing—and very different from the usual consequences of one of her wild schemes."

"Hah! You'd think so," Imogene said as she allowed Justyn to boost her up into the coach. "But that's just because you didn't see the boy after she'd dressed him up in a horrid pink gown and marched him up and down in front of White's—not that I'm supposed to be saying anything of the sort, so I'll shut my jaws right now before Callie pokes my ribs a third time. You can stop now, gel, I get the point. Come along, son. I can see we're going to be talking half the night. What fun!"

Callie climbed in behind Imogene, still smiling, still excited almost beyond words, but also realizing that, now that her brother was home, she'd have to tell him why she was in London, and what dangerous mischief she had planned.

Justyn probably wasn't going to be pleased.

Madame, if a thing is possible, consider it done; the impossible? that will be done.
                                    —Charles Alexandre De Calonne

Chapter Fourteen

The coach had traveled halfway back to Portland Place before Justyn—who had been explaining that Emery had sent him running off to King Street to find his sister when he could no longer bear to watch him pacing the drawing room, impatiently waiting for her to come home—mentioned in passing that he had not come alone to London.

"You've hired a valet?" Lester promptly asked, clearly impressed with his country neighbor's dashing turnout, as he had already said several times, declaring that he'd never seen Justyn look so prime.

"I have, yes, and he's with me," Justyn told him, proudly tugging at his shirt cuffs, "but that's not who I meant." He turned to Callie, who once more took hold of his hand, feeling unable to resist the impulse to keep touching him, assuring herself that this happiness she felt was not the result of a cruel dream. "Papa's come with me," he said, smiling. "And we stopped off in Ockham, seeing as how he'd gotten it into his head that you couldn't possibly go on here in London without Miss Haverly by your side to make sure you behaved as a young miss ought."

"Horrible Haverly?" Callie exploded, aghast. "Oh, Justyn— how could you let him do that?"

"You're not pleased?" Justyn asked, as if he'd just presented her with a wonderful present, just to have her reject it out of hand.

"Pleased? *Pleased!* The dratted woman will have me saying *prunes* and *prisms* until I'm cross-eyed, then read me a lengthy sermon on how I'm to go on at a formal dinner, and how I'm to walk, and stand, and *eat* and—Justyn, you *rotter!* You're *laughing* at me!" She gave him a mighty shove with both hands, pushing him into the corner of the coach, then slapping at his forearms as he lifted them to protect himself. "Miss Haverly isn't here at all, is she? *Is she?*"

"Call her off, Lester, call her off!" Justyn appealed, laughing as Callie continued her attack. "All right, all right, I made it all up! I give over, brat—now stop pummeling me. Is this any way for a young lady to act?"

"Who opened the door to the nursery and let the infants out?" the viscountess grumbled, then began to chuckle herself. "You got her good with that one, young man, I'll give you that. And there's no question that you're her brother, for the pair of you are as smart and sassy as can be. Lester—look at you, poor boy, still not understanding that these two monsters have been teasing. You've been outgunned and outclassed all your life around these two, haven't you?" She patted his hand. "Well, you just never mind, all right? I'll protect you."

"Ha!" Callie collapsed against the squabs, fairly breathless. "And who's to protect Lester from you, Imogene, when you start in to talking about your *brazen* days?"

"Who—who *did* you bring with you then, Justyn?" Lester asked, clearly not wishing to listen to the viscountess in case Callie's words might set her off again, with more talk of bed warmers and the like. "Did you really bring Sir Camber?"

Callie winced at hearing her father's name, remembering that Justyn had mentioned their papa quickly before dangling Miss Haverly's name in front of her, knowing how glad she had been to be shed of her last governess. "Papa's really here?"

Justyn nodded. "And Lester's papa as well. They're waiting for us now, at the viscount's residence." The coach pulled to a stop in front of Number Forty-nine Portland Place. "Ah, and we're here. Come along, brat. Sir C is champing at the bit, waiting to blubber all over his littlest chick."

"Oh, my God—wait!" Callie put a restraining hand on Justyn's elbow as her brother went to open the coach door. "We can't go in yet. Lester has to have a broken arm first."

Justyn slowly turned his head, looking across the way at Lester Plum, who had turned chalk white as he cowered, shrunk against the seat. He then transferred his gaze to his sister, nodding as if he understood completely, and—having lived with the girl for more than eighteen years—he probably did. "A broken arm? Of course he does," he said smoothly. "You hold him, brat, and I'll give him a good whack with my cane."

"Callie!" Lester squeaked, nearly diving into the viscountess's magnificent bosom.

"Justyn, don't tease," Callie scolded, giggling.

Imogene patted Lester's back, murmuring, "There, there,

boy, there, there. I won't let the bad man hurt you," as she screwed up her face in an attempt not to laugh. "But we have to do something, Lester. Some time has passed since your supposed accident, but your father will still expect to see your wing in a sling."

"Sorry, Lester," Justyn apologized. "I couldn't resist. But, as Her Ladyship says, you'll need a sling of some sort. I'll ask the reason for it later. Much later, if I'm smart. Something to do with some sort of accident, as I recall. Well, never mind. Needs must when Callie drives. Would you care to sacrifice one of your petticoats, sister mine?"

Callie gave Justyn a smacking kiss on the cheek to thank him for being so good-natured about another of her "mad starts," then bent down to tear a strip off her petticoat—unfortunately one trimmed in lace.

"You're the best of good brothers, Justyn," she declared as she worked quickly, folding the strip of cloth so that the lace was fairly well hidden, then motioning for Lester to lean closer so that she could tie the makeshift sling behind his head. "And I'll tell you everything tomorrow morning, if you'll just help us get through tonight. Lester, stop squirming; it's too dark in here for me to tie a good knot with you moving about like this. Now—which arm was broken? Imogene, do you remember if you happened to say which arm was broken? Oh, it doesn't matter. Justyn—I promise, I'll tell you every last detail tomorrow, when the viscount meets you. But for tonight, dear brother, if you love me, you'll just smile and keep your questions to yourself, all right?"

"Happily," he promised, as the groom held the door open and he jauntily hopped down before the steps were dropped, then reached up a hand to assist the viscountess to the flagway.

"Oh, certainly, you're happy enough now," Imogene said to him as she took his arm, then lifted her skirts a dainty inch and headed for the steps leading up to the brightly lit front door of the mansion. "Tomorrow you may be singing a different tune. Now, tell me about this Sir Camber and Squire Plum. They're both widowers, is that right? There's a real dearth of widowers in London this Season, and now I've got a pair of them in my own drawing room. Guess that makes me happy, too. All that remains is to see if this is a curse or an unexpected stroke of good fortune. Tell me—how tall are they? Are they *old*? Do they mind a woman with more heft to her than a feather? And tell me this—do you think they might . . ."

Callie rolled her eyes as she listened to Imogene until the woman's questions faded into the distance, then skewered her childhood friend with a look. "We're going to have to lie like Trojans, Lester, at least until tomorrow, when Simon will be here to help us. Can you do it? Are you up to it? Lester? *Talk* to me."

"Papa? *Here*? Oh, God," Lester mumbled, his eyes wide and blank as they stared straight ahead without seeing her, his jaw rather slack as his tongue tripped over his words. He lifted his right arm, sling and all, to rub at his forehead. "I think I'm going to be sick."

Callie slapped down his "broken" arm and grabbed hold of his shoulders, giving him a bracing shake. "Don't you dare, Lester Plum, don't you dare. Listen to me," she commanded, taking charge, just as she had since she was four and he was seven, and she had taught him how to climb a tree—forgetting that she had not yet learned how to climb back down again.

In desperation, and knowing one sure way to reach him, she reached into the pocket of his waistcoat and pulled out a licorice whip, slowly waving it back and forth in front of his nose, as she would have waved a vinaigrette or some burnt feathers in front of Imogene's if the woman looked ready to swoon. "We are going to be fine, Lester, dear, just fine. We've been fine so far, haven't we? Lester? Are you listening to me? We're fine. We're just *fine*."

Lester blinked twice, nodded, then held out his left hand and took the licorice whip.

Simon rose at nine after coming home at ten minutes past four in the morning, so that he was definitely tired. He was not, however, so exhausted that he couldn't appreciate the ridiculousness of the turmoil he had been in since first meeting Callie at the point of a pistol—a situation that was now bordering on the absurd.

He had gone from being intrigued, to being more intrigued. From exasperation to infatuation. From anger, to pleasure, to confusion. He had traveled all the way to the end of his wits and back again. More than once.

At times, he'd longed to see the back of her, even as, daily, he'd pulled her deeper and deeper into his life. He'd wanted her gone, wanted her never to leave. Longed to be free of her, yearned to hold her so close she couldn't go if she tried.

In short, in long, and regardless of any way he tried to deny it—and, oh, how he had tried!—he quite possibly could be falling in love with Caledonia Johnston.

She believed he hated her, of course. She couldn't know that he had feigned disgust at her persistence in order to keep her from trying to help him. Telling her about Robert, about James, had not been easy, but she had deserved to know the truth. After all, he had allowed her to believe she was going to have a hand in bringing Noel Kinsey down. The truth was the least she deserved. Damning her with that truth had been cowardly, yet necessary.

He knew Callie now, knew her straight down to her toes. And she had proved him right. It had taken her no more than a few minutes to go from sorrow at his explanation, embarrassment over his abrupt confession about Robert and James, to offering, yet again, to help him rout Filton.

The girl was a menace. A treasure.

And now, after all they had gone round and round in circles these past weeks, for all the arguments, the teasing, the lessons in flirting, their shared kisses and confusion, she was asking for his help. Needed his help. Felt able, after all they'd been through, to ask for his help.

It was rather lovely, actually. It showed him there was hope for them yet, if they ever got disentangled from this business of Noel Kinsey—which he planned to do, and with a dispatch that would make the man dizzy.

"Simon? Are you still listening to me?" Callie asked as he stood at the mantel in the drawing room and looked off into the distance, thinking his thoughts. "I know you have no reason to help me, and probably are wishing I'd just go away, drown myself in some ditch. I don't blame you. Truly I don't. I've been nothing but a bother to you from the beginning, one way or the other."

"Yes, you have disturbed me mightily, Callie. One way or the other," Simon repeated, wondering how he had ever believed Callie to be little more than a child. This was a woman who stood before him now. A beautiful, disturbing, desirable woman. And she *knew* what she'd put him through. She probably even knew he'd barely been able to sleep since the first time he'd kissed her. They really did have to sit down together and have a long talk. Or possibly just a short talk, followed by a long kiss.

"Please, don't interrupt me, Simon," she said, rolling her eyes. "We don't have time for that now. Papa and Justyn and the Squire will be here from the Pulteney at any moment. I fobbed them off well enough last night, but now we have to meet with them again, and somehow brush through what happened these past weeks without landing Lester and me in the basket. If you can't find it in yourself to care about me, think of Lester. Do this for poor Lester, Simon, and I'll go away, never to ask anything of you again. I promise. But I just know my family won't take me away without first meeting with you, thanking you for taking care of me. As they've already planned to stay a week in town, we *must* all be telling the same lies. You can see that, can't you?"

Simon looked at her, dressed in a fetching lavender morning gown, and did his best not to let his affection for her show in his eyes. She was telling the truth. She was more concerned for Lester Plum than she was for herself. He rather liked her like this, unsure, a little nervous, slightly off-balance. It made for an interesting change. He was, he decided, a rather mean man for thinking this way.

"You have my complete attention, Miss Johnston, I assure you, and Lester my entire compassion," he said formally, inclining his head in her direction. "So far, I am to remember that Lester's arm is healing quite nicely. As it turns out, it was a bad sprain and not a break at all, which is, I'm sure, a highly acceptable turn of events for the poor boy, as otherwise he'd be forced to keep his wing in a sling for another two or three weeks. What else?"

"What else? Simon, there is a plethora of *else*!" Callie gave an exasperated sigh that had Simon biting the inside of his cheek. "Papa and the Squire know *nothing* about why we're really here, for one. Justyn can't *possibly* find out why we're really here—he wouldn't like to be told of me taking the reins into my own hands, as it were. And I've received a note from Noel Kinsey, asking me to go driving with him this afternoon at five. I sent back an answer with his servant, saying I'd be delighted, seeing as how I had seen you with him at Almack's, so I know he's acceptable."

Simon eyed her coldly, all his good humor gone. "You couldn't have said that last bit before, Callie. I would have remembered. Oh, and by the way—you're *not* going."

He watched as she jutted out her adorably stubborn chin and shot back very predictably: "Oh, and by the way—I most certainly *am* going. I have to protect Justyn."

"Protect Justyn?" A red haze had formed in front of Simon's eyes. He was rather growing used to this phenomenon when Callie was about. "Protecting Lester makes sense, as the boy is helpless on his own. But now you're back to protecting that damned brother of yours? My God, how I long to meet this paragon, this short-sighted, dramatic-acting, easily gulled, *runaway* of a brother who can inspire his adoring sibling to repeated flights of raging stupidity. I can barely wait to blacken both his eyes for him."

Callie's hands balled into fists. "Justyn has never asked me to defend him. I only want to protect him because I love him."

"Ah, yes," Simon said, understanding—and knowing Callie's words were precisely those he would have put into her mouth for her, had he the power to do so. Callie was the sort of girl—no, the sort of *woman*—who would dare anything for those she loved. Face any danger, and welcome it. Hadn't that been why he'd been allowing her to believe he disliked her?

So that, loving him as he hoped, prayed, she did, she would not feel the need to *protect him*?

"Callie—" he warned, prudently breaking off as his mother strode into the room, looking about quickly and then inquiring where the gentlemen were. She was all dressed and painted and primped and, clearly, somebody had better show up soon and be mightily impressed before she exhaled too deeply and her stays kept her from ever inhaling again.

Callie, obviously seeing the viscountess as an ally, immediately ran to her and demanded that she agree that a ride in the Promenade with the earl of Filton was exactly the sort of thing their excursion to Almack's had been for—hadn't it?

Imogene, as yet not privy to anything but the first, sham plan her son had conjured up, gingerly sat her tightly laced self down on the striped satin couch in the center of the room and looked to her son. "What's the matter, Simon? Having second thoughts about throwing Callie at Filton's head? Now, why is that, I wonder?" Then she smiled, looking very much like a satisfied cat with canary feathers sticking out of her mouth.

"Mother—" Simon began warningly—hadn't he been warning Callie when his mother entered? Was he destined to spend the morning doing nothing more than calling out names, knowing he would be cut off at any moment, before he could say anything else?

And, sure enough, he had barely gotten that single word past his lips before Callie interrupted him, saying, "It's not fair, Imogene. It was my idea to bring Filton down—*mine*! And now, just as things are progressing so nicely—oh, I admit it might have been better if Justyn had waited another week or two before coming home to muddle the business—Simon is cutting up stiff over exactly what he'd wanted in the first place. All your hard work, Imogene—all your care of me, your lessons—will you let them go all for nothing, just because Simon is balking at the first fence?"

Little minx! How dared she use his own mother against him? Just because he'd used his mother against her—well, he wouldn't think about that right then.

"Let me hasten to correct you on one point if I might, brat," Simon said, stepping forward, putting himself between Callie and his mother. "It was your idea—much as I can understand your reluctance to own to it—to *shoot* the blackguard. Everything since has been *my* idea. And, because it is my plan, it is up to me to adjust it if I see problems now that didn't at first present themselves. Mother," he said, bowing to the woman, "I have decided to keep Callie as far away from Noel Kinsey as possible. You agree, of course?"

Imogene merely smiled. Evilly.

"Problems, is it?" Callie slammed her fists against her hips, leaning forward belligerently, deliberately goading him. "Such as?"

"The gel has a point," Imogene said, nearly gloating, she appeared so happy. And still slightly evil, bless her and curse her. "And every right to an explanation of this change of plans. What problems, dear boy? Tell me. Tell us. Please. Did I say please? No! We demand it, actually."

A man shouldn't even consider strangling his beloved mother, but Simon felt the thought nudge at his brain for just a moment. He couldn't say that the mere thought of Noel Kinsey being alone with Callie in the park was enough to bring his blood to a rapid boil. Not if he didn't want his mother jumping up to run through Mayfair, crying the banns within the hour. He and Callie had some serious talking to do before he could allow his mother to get the bit between her teeth. Some very serious talking.

So, being an intelligent human being, and a gentleman, and a man who treasured his own skin, Simon opened his mouth again—and lied through his teeth.

"Armand has already planned to invite Filton to a small gaming party at White's, scheduled, as it happens, for two o'clock this afternoon. A limited group, high stakes, and the probability of gambling until the wee hours. As I've already made a rather serious incursion into Filton's pocketbook—not that you've bothered to ask—he is doubtless more than eager to sit down with me again, in the hope of redeeming a few of his markers. In other words, be prepared to receive a second note from our friend Noel Kinsey once Armand's arrives on his doorstep, begging off until tomorrow. And now, if you'll excuse me, I've just remembered something I forgot to tell my secretary."

Callie stepped to her left, blocking his passage. "You mean to have him write up a note, to send it round to Armand, arranging all of this nonsense you've just made up out of whole cloth," she accused quietly, so that the viscountess—busily rummaging through a dish of comfits, searching for her favorite flavor—didn't hear her. "Oh, Simon, you should be ashamed of yourself."

"I'm mortified, brat," Simon told her honestly, then exited the room through the rear archway. He was on his way to the servant stairs when he heard the door knocker go on the ground floor. "I'll be right back, to meet your family," he called to Callie.

"You'd better be," Callie replied. "Lester's hiding in his room, his head stuck under his pillows, and I need someone here to help me knit another row in our blanket of lies without dropping a stitch."

Simon turned, smiling at her. "That's very good, Callie," he said, complimenting her. "But I'm relying on your vast experience in this area of fibbing and truth-bending to carry us through."

She cocked her head to one side, measuring him with a narrowed-eye look. "You're not angry with me anymore, are you, Simon, as you were at the inn? You're trying to be, especially about my having agreed to ride out with Noel Kinsey, but you're not. You understand why I did it."

"Angry with you? Why, Callie, I don't know what you're talking about. I've never been angry with you. But understand you? Oh no. Never, brat. Not in a million years."

"Now who knows how to tell whopping great lies?" she asked. "I'm as transparent as window glass to you, and I'm not quite sure I like it," she ended, then ran to the top of the stairs, to greet her family—but not before Simon saw the leap of happiness in her eyes.

If only they could get through these next few hours, these next few days, these next few lies, without killing each other . . .

Once he had scrawled a note to Armand and sent Roberts off with it, Simon returned to the drawing room, to see three unknown men variously positioned around the room.

One, the youngest one—blond and considerably handsome—he decided had to be Justyn. That left Sir Camber and the squire, and he quickly decided that Lester's father had to be the rather large man sitting on the chair closest to Imogene, wearing much the same happily bemused expression that was his son's hallmark.

Which left the tall, thin gentleman standing next to the mantel—and wearing last year's fashions—to be none other than Sir Camber Johnston, Hero of the Fish Bone.

So thinking, Simon walked briskly into the room, introducing himself and learning that, yes, he had been correct, for the gentleman he'd decided must be Sir Camber immediately took his hand in both of his and began pumping it furiously, thanking him effusively for having taken in his dear daughter and giving her the Season she so richly deserved. His effusiveness explained away the man's gullibility in believing Imogene's note to him—the man was too grateful to have looked beneath the surface of the lie.

It was then the beefy squire's turn to wring the blood from Simon's fingers. Without allowing more than a smile and a nod from Simon, the man then went on at some length about how honored he was to know that his only son—"a good boy; a good, good boy, for all he's only sparsely furnished in his upper stories"—had been befriended by the viscountess. Smartest thing his boy ever did, the squire said, getting himself stuck in the mud so that the viscountess could pull him out again.

"My turn now, I believe," Justyn said smoothly. He extended his hand to Simon, saving him from possible permanent injury as the squire proved with his grip that he was a man who worked his own fields and possessed the vigor and strength of a prizefighter half his age. Indeed, Simon had already noticed his mother measuring the man from head to toe. She was about as subtle as a racetrack tout sizing up a fleet-footed mount. This thought Simon rejected as soon as he had it but, unfortunately, too late to completely banish the image, and the connotations, from his mind.

"Delighted, Mr. Johnston," Simon said, trying to concentrate on Callie's brother, assess him without prejudice.

"It's a pleasure to make your acquaintance, my lord. Please allow me to add my thanks for your kind care of my sister. I only hope the brat hasn't given you too much trouble."

Simon smiled at Justyn's easy use of the word brat. It would appear that he and Callie's brother already agreed on at least one subject. He decided to learn to know the young man better, and draw his own conclusions, ignoring Callie's assertion that her only brother couldn't so much as choose his own cravat without her assistance. "The credit belongs mostly to my mother, gentlemen," he said, bowing in Imogene's direction. "And the pleasure has been both hers and mine."

"Well, I'll tell you, my lord, you've both worked a miracle, that's what," Sir Camber said, splitting his coattails with some flair and seating himself in a chair near the fireplace. "I hardly knew the child when I saw her last night. You've done wonders with her—although I'm not quite sure about the hair, you understand. It used to be much longer."

"Really?" Simon commented, looking to Callie, who had moved to stand beside Justyn, the pair of them looking very much alike in their features, if not their coloring. "I could have sworn it was about this same length when I met her."

"Tell us about India, Justyn, now that we're all here to listen," Callie commanded quickly, sending a look toward Simon that told him she didn't think he was being quite as helpful as he could be. "We didn't get to talk more than a minute last night before the squire started nodding off, so that you went back to your hotel. You look wonderful—did you make your fortune?"

"Well, here comes a story I've already heard," the squire said, slapping his beefy hands on his knees before standing up and turning to look down at Imogene. "Would you care for a turn around the block in the boy's fine rented carriage, my lady? I'd like to see a bit of London whilst I'm here, and I'd be honored to have your company. Besides, it's not good to have the horses standing too long, the way I see it."

Simon covered a laugh with a cough as he watched his mother do her best imitation of a maidenly simper—and a woman built less for simpering he'd yet to encounter. "Why, I'd be delighted, kind sir," she said, hopping to her feet with such alacrity she nearly stepped on the man's toes before he could move away and offer her his arm. "We'll just have Roberts run off upstairs and get Kathleen to fetch my shawl and bonnet."

Tall, Imogene then mouthed silently to Callie and Lester as she turned her head back over her shoulder on her way out of the room, her grin wide and pleased—but not half as wide and satisfied as was Roberts's own grin as he stood just in the hallway, a bonnet already in one hand, a paisley shawl in the other.

"Could I interest you in a glass of claret, Sir Camber? Anyone else?" Simon asked, then said that he hoped they could dispense with formalities while the four of them talked, an offer of friendship and camaraderie with which both gentlemen readily agreed.

"I never made it to India, actually," Justyn said a few minutes later, once all of them were seated in comfortable chairs in the center of the room. "My last post to you was from Italy, wasn't it, brat? Yes, I thought so. I wrote that letter while still aboard ship, then went ashore, posted it, and met my destiny—all within a day."

"Your destiny, Justyn?" Callie asked, sitting forward, on the edge of her seat both physically and with her obvious eagerness to hear everything he had to say. Simon watched her face, believing the love for her brother he saw there made her even more beautiful than she had been before. If he had ever wondered why a young girl would go to such lengths to avenge her brother, he would wonder no more. There was a very special love between this brother and sister, and Simon felt suddenly excluded, and rather slighted in not having been blessed with a sibling or two of his own.

Justyn took a sip of claret before answering. "Yes, Callie, my destiny, melodramatic as that may sound. It was on the docks that it happened—and I'll do my best to keep this short and simple, as Papa has already heard the story. The ship was being unloaded and a young boy had broken away from his nurse and wandered onto the docks. There was a shout and I turned to see the boy in danger of being knocked into the water by a whacking great load of swinging cargo. Without really giving it much thought, I ran over to him, snatched him up—and met my destiny. Actually, I didn't meet her until I'd been unconscious for a few days, as the cargo that missed the boy gave me a glancing blow on the head that rattled my brains for a while."

"You could have been killed!" Callie exclaimed, then frowned. "Justyn, did you say *her*?"

He nodded, smiling. "Signorina Bianca Alessandra di Giulia, daughter of Conte Alessandro Antonio Giacomo di Giulia, the most sweet, beautiful, wondrous creature in the entire world—and my wife. She's waiting for us in our father's house, for she's increasing, and the trip from Rome was marred by more than one storm, so that she told me she couldn't face any more travel right now."

"I—I—you have a—and there's going to be a—oh, Justyn!" Callie exclaimed, throwing herself into his arms. "I can't believe it. Why didn't you say anything last night? You must have been dying to tell me. That's above everything wonderful."

"Yes, it is, isn't it?" he said, smiling at Simon over an armful of Callie. "Unless you choke me to death, brat, leaving my poor Bianca a widow."

"Oh! Oh, I'm sorry," Callie said, retaking her seat and smiling her thanks to Simon, whose only function thus far had been to offer her his handkerchief so that she might wipe her moist eyes. "There's more, isn't there, Justyn? I can see it in your eyes. Tell me the rest of it."

"Like my friend, the squire, I've heard all this before. And, happy as I am, I think I'll get myself another drink, if nobody minds, and take m'self off to that corner over there," Sir Camber said, rising. "Didn't sleep a wink all night, I didn't, on that lumpy mattress at the Pulteney. Might just take you up on your offer to stay here in Portland Place, Your Ladyship, just for the good night's sleep it might gain me."

Imogene, who had returned to the room to fetch her reticule, appeared ready to drool at this dose of good fortune. "That would be wonderful, I'm sure. The three of you, all sharing our humble roof? Yes, yes indeed. Above all things wonderful. I'll just go tell Emery before the squire and I are off."

"Justyn?" Callie prompted, as Imogene minced away again, doing her best not to look at the sight of the woman in a feminine simper.

Her brother spread his hands almost apologetically as he looked to Simon. "What else? Well, I'm waist deep in money, as luck would have it. For one thing, Bianca's father settled a ridiculously large fortune on me for having saved her little brother," he said. "I thought to turn him down, as I wasn't planning on being a hero or anything like that, but he made me see the sense of the money, as Bianca is accustomed to wealth. Bianca's papa is a great believer in not standing in the way of true love, but he wasn't about to see his only daughter living in poverty. And so I've come home, the prodigal returned as it were. To have you all meet my dearest Bianca, to have our first child born in England, to pay back Papa for all the heartache I have caused him—and to get some of my own back from one Noel Kinsey, Earl of Filton. Do you know him, my lord?"

"Oh, dear," Callie breathed, also looking at Simon, her eyes more filled with apprehension than interest. Apprehension, and warning.

"I'm vaguely acquainted with the man, yes, and a more unlovely fellow would be difficult to find," Simon answered carefully. Then he asked, "What do you have planned for him?"

Justyn smiled at his sister. "I met a man aboard ship, brat, a most wonderful old fellow. You would have adored him. We spent all of our time talking together and playing at cards, weeks and weeks of playing at cards. Oh, the things that clever man taught me! And do you know something?" he went on, his eyes narrowed. "Filton *cheats*."

"Imagine that," Simon breathed quietly, earning himself a swift, killing look from Callie.

"Yes, my lord," Justyn said feelingly, "imagine that. I don't know how I could have been so green, so easily duped. But I'm the wiser for it, let me tell you, and now I'm going to seek Filton out and win back every penny I lost to him, and then some. I want to bring him low, destroy him if that's possible."

Simon looked to Callie again. "Imagine that," he repeated. "You know, the more I look at the two of you, the more I can see the resemblance between you and your sister," he then added, wondering how long it would be before Callie threw something at him.

Just then there was a commotion in the hallway and Roberts ran in to say that her ladyship had made it down the stairs well enough, then sat down on a bench in the foyer, waiting for the carriage to be brought round—and fainted dead away into the squire's arms . . . and would Miss Johnston please come right away, as the squire is starting to open her ladyship's buttons and that couldn't be at all proper, could it?

"We ought just to leave her," Callie complained, hopping to her feet. "Fainting's the only rest she's been getting this past week or more, to hear her tell it. Now, not a another word until I return, you hear me," she warned tightly. Then she followed after Roberts, who was telling her that two of the other footmen were supporting Her Ladyship and all that was needed until the poor dear roused was a woman present, to make things "proper."

"Of course," Simon promised. Then, waiting until he heard Callie's heels clicking on the marble staircase, he leaned forward and began quietly, so that a near-to-dozing Sir Camber didn't overhear, "I think, Justyn, my very new but soon to be very good friend, that you and I should meet privately at White's at, say, one o'clock today, to join with two other friends of mine, and to have ourselves a small talk . . ."

This is a pretty flim-flam.

—Francis Beaumont

Chapter Fifteen

Callie was yawning into her hand as she heard the door to Simon's chamber opening, signaling his return from his long day and evening spent gambling with Noel Kinsey. She sat up straighter where she sat, cross-legged and at her ease, which happened to be in the very center of Simon's high, wide bed.

"It's about time you found your way home," she announced baldly, arranging her white-muslin dressing gown, which covered her from throat to toe and was, she believed, about as alluring, and seductive, as an empty grain sack.

Simon stopped where he was, lifted the small brace of candles he carried, and peered in the direction of the bed. "I must be slipping. I should have known she'd be here," he said quietly, and to nobody in particular, or so it seemed as he then approached the bed and set down the candlestick. "Just champing at the bit to know everything that's going on with Filton, aren't you, brat?"

"On the contrary," Callie responded, stung. As if she'd stoop to *begging* to find out what she wanted to know! "Tomorrow will be soon enough for me, at which time I'll quite easily pry it all out of Justyn. Unless you want to tell me first?" she added, for that was the reason she was there. She wanted to hear everything about their encounter with Noel Kinsey. About Justyn's behavior when confronted with the man.

Not that she'd admit that to Simon. Especially after he was so correct in knowing why she had dared to invade his bedchamber.

"I'm only here to report to *you* about my day since you spirited my only brother out of Portland Place and left me here to fend for myself," she continued firmly, her chin held high, when he remained silent to her suggestion.

He arched one eyebrow at her, provocatively, maddeningly. "Really?"

"Yes, *really*." How strange it was to care for somebody so much, and yet want to box his ears at the same time. "You may have taken me out of the plans for Noel Kinsey, but that doesn't mean I've got nothing to do but sit here and twiddle my fingers while you play at conspirator and Imogene makes a cake of herself with the squire. Your lies have set me up as an heiress, remember? You've introduced me to Society, *foisted* me on Society, as it were. Ah, you look surprised. As well you might, sir. Noel Kinsey is not your only problem at the moment, and mine, for once, aren't the only fibs that must be maintained, perhaps confessed. However, even though this does present a problem—for *you*—I must admit I've had a vastly entertaining day, to say the least."

"How gratifying for you. Entertaining, you say? In what

way? Pardon my informality, but I've felt I've had my neck in a noose all night."

She watched Simon lift his chin so that he could begin untying his intricate cravat, then slide the snowy white muslin from his throat. It amazed her, how at ease she felt here in his bedchamber, how at ease he himself seemed to be, with her sitting in the middle of his bed. There was something to be said for first crying friends with the man you loved. And she did love him. Madly. Not that she'd tell him. Oh no. That admission was going to have to come first from him. He owed her that much after tricking her about his plans for Filton, for making her feel the gullible fool.

"Are you going to tell me about your day, or make me guess? In what way was it so entertaining?" Simon prodded when she didn't answer. He sat down on the edge of the coverlet Silsby had turned back hours ago, before Callie had given the valet permission to retire early—or go chase Scarlet around the carving table in the kitchens, whichever suited him best.

Callie stretched out her legs on the bed, allowing her bare feet to poke out from the hem of her dressing gown, and leaned back against the mound of full, soft pillows. "Well," she began, then took a deep breath and went on quickly, "it would appear that I am a smashing success, if you must know. The drawing room, the music room, the breakfast room, and my chamber—all are filled to the brim with flowers from my devoted admirers. Nosegays, bouquets, even a potted palm— why on earth would anyone send someone else a potted palm?—began arriving almost the moment you and Justyn did your flit."

"We did not do a *flit*, brat. We left. Men do that. Women entertain callers, and men go to their clubs."

"Whatever," Callie said, shrugging, then peered up at him from beneath her lashes.

"Ah, the flirt is back! You can't wait for tomorrow, can you? You can't wait for Justyn to feed you everything you want to know. Is Filton pockets-to-let yet? Was he devastated to have missed his chance to meet the great Johnston heiress, crushed to discover that her brother Justyn, also demmed deep in the pockets, has finally learned his way around a fuzzed card? Is the man destroyed, broken? Have I, just to please you, then gone and shot him in the knee, to bring home our lesson? Oh, the questions that must be buzzing around in that inventive head of yours!"

Callie bit her lip, refusing to be baited. "Wrong, wrong, *and wrong*. I couldn't care less. Truly. The world doesn't revolve around you, you know. Now, if I might continue with *my* story? *Thank* you. Where was I? Oh yes. Imogene was highly put out that only five gentlemen chose to bring me candy, but she's manfully making do with one particularly large box crammed with chocolates she had sent up to her rooms. We then learned that the squire cannot come within ten paces of a room holding roses or else go into a fit of sneezing likely to blow out the windows. He and Papa took themselves back to the Pulteney dining room, leaving your mama to lament the loss of 'dear Bertram' all the afternoon long—*that* was mightily depressing, I can tell you, much as I adore your mama. It's very lowering, watching a strong woman go all soft and mooning and simpleminded. I mean, all he did was undo her buttons."

"Imogene's in love? Well, that could be depressing, couldn't it? She'll doubtless now have Kathleen pulling in her stays until they both turn blue."

"Yes, that's true. But it may have been for the best that the squire left, because Lester came down to tea with his sling on entirely the *wrong* arm, which undoubtedly would have been remarked upon by either Papa or the squire. Lester became so flustered he ripped off the sling and stomped on it, saying that he didn't want to lie anymore and end up going to hell in a handkerchief—he meant handbasket, of course—and stomped off to help Scarlet roll out dough."

"God bless the boy," Simon said, shaking his head.

"Yes, God bless him. Oh, and I've had several dozen invitations hand-delivered, six offers to ride in the park tomorrow, four requests for my company at the theater, and three personal notes from ladies of the *ton* who are quite convinced they attended the same young ladies' seminary as my dearest mother and wish for me to come to tea and meet their sons."

"Society has clasped you to her bosom. Congratulations, Callie."

"It's not all that wonderful, Simon. I had to listen while two of my many gentlemen callers read odes they had written to my eyes and my dainty toes—did you know that after *rose* and *bows*, there is virtually *nothing* that rhymes with *toes*? That did present a problem to young Baron Darton, but he overcame it with a will, somehow working the words *highs* and *lows* into his masterpiece. Oh—and I received one proposal of marriage, but Imogene said that really doesn't count, as Sir Reggie is seventy if he's a day and proposes to every debutante worth more than half a crown."

Simon smiled, then stood up, beginning to shrug out of his jacket. "Dear Sir Reggie."

Callie sighed theatrically. "*Deaf* Sir Reggie, you mean. I had to yell my very polite refusal into his ear horn, which gave me such a fit of the giggles that Imogene quit the room, saying she has washed her hands of me and refuses to be my chaperone anymore. She also has vowed that she'll never sleep again, not because of me, but because of her affection for Squire Plum and his robust good health and, she hopes, *stamina*—discounting that misfortune with the roses, of course—and for fear you might not approve of the match."

She crossed her hands behind her head and grinned up at him as he stood very still, one arm half out of his sleeve, clearly stunned at this mention of his mother's ambitions. He'd talk to her now, she was sure of it. "There's more, but it can wait. So. How was *your* day?"

She watched, delighted, as Simon threw back his head and laughed out loud, finally sobering to say, "Not half as exciting as yours, unfortunately, but it went tolerably well. I talked your brother out of spanking you, for one thing. I should be rewarded for that, don't you think?"

Callie reached beside her and picked up the bowl of green grapes she had been munching on earlier. "Here," she said, offering it to him. "Unless you'd like me to shower you with rose petals. That could be arranged—unless you sneeze like the squire? What did you tell Justyn—just so that we keep our lies similar."

"I told him the truth," Simon said, taking the bowl and putting it on the table beside the candles—which was probably a good thing, or else she might have pummeled him over the head with it.

Callie sat bolt upright on the bed. "The *truth*! Oh, Simon— how could you?"

"There was nothing else for it, Callie," he explained as she maneuvered herself to the edge of the mattress and aimed her bare feet at the floor. "Your brother is no fool, and he knows you well."

She sighed, pulling her dressing gown snugly around her body, very much aware of how close she was standing to Simon, how close he was standing to her. "No, he's not a fool, is he?"

"I like him, Callie. Immensely. And you'll be happy to know that he thinks I'm sterling—simply sterling. I saved his sister from a certain meeting with the gallows, and have even been so obliging—and simpleminded—as to find myself rather inordinately enamored with the chit, much to my dismay. All in all, I'd say Justyn is most pleased."

Callie shook her head, rattling her brains back into line, for surely she hadn't heard Simon correctly. "Say that again, please," she asked, aware that her voice was wobbling.

"Say what again?" he asked, his smile telling her he knew exactly what she was asking.

"That last part, of course. That part where you said you're enamored of me. Or is that enamored *with* me? Oh, never mind that. Are you? Are you really?"

"Enamored?" He ran the back of his hand along the curve of her cheek, a move that turned her knees to water. "Did I say that? I must be more tired than I thought. I always talk too much, you've said so yourself. It's even worse when I've had less than five hours' sleep in two days. Still, I couldn't have said that."

She could see the devil dancing in his sherry eyes, and her heart began a small, joyful jig. "Yes, Simon, you said that. I heard you most distinctly. And you're right. Your tongue runs on wheels, you talk so much. I've heard you as you've all but cursed me. I've heard you joke about your feelings for me in the meanest possible way. I've heard you tease me, fling insults at me for being a silly, headstrong child. I don't always find it convenient to obey you, but I do listen. I listen to you very well, so I know I heard you correctly just now. Say it again, all right?"

He reached out a hand and cupped her chin, so that she swallowed down hard, feeling this new, exciting tension that had suddenly sprung up between them, reveling in it even as it frightened her. "This isn't the time, brat," he said quietly, his voice barely more than a husky whisper. "And it is most certainly not the place. You should be in bed—in your own bed."

She put up her own hand, to capture his, to keep it pressed against her skin. She knew when she was too frightened to be anything else but brave. She also knew when to lie, and she recognized the time for truth. The truth all but burst from her now; she couldn't hold back the words if she tried. "I'm where I belong, Simon, and we both know it. And if you won't say the words, I will. I love you, Simon Roxbury. I love you with all my heart, all my mind. I love you when I'm angry with you, when you make me laugh, when you go behind my back and appropriate all my fine plans, even when you leave me alone to listen to ear-clanging poems from silly little boys who can't hold a candle to you, you smug creature. There," she ended with as much bravado as she could muster, knowing her voice was sounding clogged with her sudden tears, "what do you have to say to that?"

He was silent for some moments, so that she actually began to believe that she had been wrong, that she had mistaken everything, that Simon felt no more for her than he had for his erstwhile mistress—and they hadn't discussed that yet, had they?

"Well, perhaps I overstated myself," she said, trying to fill the silence. "I mean, I am young, aren't I? And terribly impressionable? I mean, just because I find myself going to sleep each night thinking of you, and waking to thoughts of you—well, that's really not important, is it? And just because something deep inside me melts whenever you smile at me, and even when you yell at me—that could just mean I should eat more, or sleep more, or something like that. So maybe I don't love you." She lifted her chin, challengingly. "Yes, definitely. I don't love you, Simon Roxbury. Not a drop. I'm just a silly child, that's all. I'm so sorry to disappoint you, as you've already admitted that you're enamored *with* me, but there it is. I don't love you. So sorry."

He moved closer to her, his smile wide, his thumb tracing over her bottom lip before she could pull herself free of his casual touch. "I adore you, Caledonia Johnston," he said, his voice coming to her from a great distance, even though he was now so close to her she could barely focus her eyes on his. "I adore you and love you with all my heart, all my mind. It's the last thing I wanted, the last thing I expected, but I definitely do love you. How could anyone listen to a speech such as your last one, and not love you? I'm only a man, Callie, and I can only fight for so long. I love you. You love me—that speech to one side, of course, as I didn't believe a word of it. But now, before we both go to hell in Lester's handkerchief, you're going back to your own chamber. Now, this minute. Right after I kiss you."

"Kiss me? You're not teasing? You really do love—oh, Simon, isn't this wonderful?" Callie breathed, as his mouth covered hers, clung to hers, heated hers.

But Simon Roxbury was a man of his word, damn him. She was back in her own bedchamber not five minutes later, her head full of dreams and her body tingling with strange sensations she longed to investigate more fully the moment she got the dratted man alone again. And, she decided with a sinking heart, that time wouldn't come until Noel Kinsey was out of their lives.

If only there were something she could do to help speed him on his way. . . .

"Simon—a moment, if I may," Imogene called out as her son walked past the open doorway of the breakfast room the following morning. "That is, if you still have time for your mother, the woman who brought you into this world, the poor soul who labored for hours—*days*—enduring the rack of pain that is childbed in order to *squeeze* you out of—"

"I believe I'm getting a vague recollection of your identity, madam," Simon said as he turned and entered the room, cutting Imogene off before she could go into further and quite lurid detail, as she was often wont to do. "What have I done wrong this time?"

The tightly laced Imogene sat back against her chair—well, she rather *toppled* back, as she could not really bend at all above the hips, so that she was leaning rather than relaxing against the harden wooden back. "If you don't know, son, I'm certainly not going to tell you!" she announced, glaring at him as if he'd just broken her motherly heart into a million small pieces.

Simon pulled out a chair and sat down, although he had breakfasted an hour earlier. "I see this is going to take some time," he commented, reaching for a breakfast bun someone had left on their plate. "Would it help if I simply apologized, and promised never to do it again?"

His mother made a threatening noise low in her throat.

"No," he said, smiling. "I suppose not. Yes, well, carry on then, Mother. Although why I'd think you'd need my permission is beyond me. Have at it. Flay me alive with all that you're certainly not going to tell me."

"Don't be thick, Simon," the viscountess commanded as she popped a piece of bacon into her mouth. "You talk too much, and entirely too smartly when you consider you're speaking to your beloved and aged mother, but you're hardly ever thick. Still, as I love you, I'll help you along. Give you a hint or two, as it were. Prod your memory. Tell me, Simon—what haven't I been doing these past weeks? Can you tell me that?"

What *hadn't* his mother been doing? She was still complaining about becoming a dowager, about *not* becoming a dowager—her views of the subject shifting back and forth too rapidly for him to keep track of exactly where she stood at any moment. So what *hadn't* she been doing?

A sudden thought hit Simon, and he turned his head away as he raised a hand to scratch at the side of his neck, only barely resisting the urge to slip a finger under his suddenly too-tight collar while he was at it. "Sleeping?" he then asked with a wince.

"Well, there, you see? You're *not* thick! That's right, Simon, I haven't been sleeping. Which is why I was awake very late last night, and found myself to be a bit peckish, which found me making my way to the kitchens—I can't see bothering servants to do what I can do for myself. And do you know who I found in those kitchens, curled up and snoring on a table? *Silsby*! And do you know *why* I found Silsby snoring in the kitchens? You may feel free to interrupt anytime you want to confess, Simon."

"Silsby was in the kitchens because it was more than his life was worth to crawl onto his usual cot in my dressing room and within easy earshot of my chamber once he realized Callie was sitting on my bed, waiting for me?" Simon suggested dully, then added, "I've always said the servant quarters in this pile are much too limited."

"They wouldn't be if you didn't hire every second footman and parlormaid in all of London," Imogene replied reasonably, then grimaced as, with a small windmill whirl of her arms, she propelled herself forward and plopped her elbows on the tabletop. "So, now that I know, and you know that I know—what are you going to *do* about it? I've given you half of this morning to come to me on your own, but you haven't. Shame on you, Simon. Shame!"

"Nothing happened, Imogene," Simon began, then sighed, shaking his head. "Not that I didn't want it to," he admitted with a sheepish grin, for he was speaking with his mother, after all. "Once I'm done with Filton—"

"You've compromised the gel, Simon. You love her, I know you do, have always known it. And the child is dotty for you, for her sins. Now the two of you are flitting back and forth between your bedchambers in the middle of the night. Well, I can't turn a blind eye to that, and don't want to, because I'm tickled to my toes about the whole thing. Just tickled. So why not get on with it? Surely you know this can't wait until you've finished playing your silly little boy's game with the earl of Filton?"

"The game, as you call it, Mother, is already all but over, which was what I was going to say when you interrupted me," Simon told her. "It has almost been *too* easy, as a matter of fact. We finish with him tonight, at White's. As for the rest of it? I've already sent around a note to the Pulteney, inviting all three gentlemen to a small dinner party here tomorrow evening. After dinner I'll take Sir Camber to my study and beg his permission to pay my addresses to his daughter. But that doesn't mean you have to wait that long to discard those damned stays. Unless you've set your sights on the good squire, that is? After all, he is, as you've said, *tall*."

"And robust," Imogene added, giving out with a satisfied sigh. "Healthy." She shook her head, frowning. "As to these stays? I don't think I can keep to them much longer, not even for an *energetic* man." She gave a wave of her hand— the one holding a square of toast heavily laden with strawberry jam. "But that's neither here nor there, is it? I'm much too pleased with how everything is working out between you and Callie, which is precisely how I saw it working out the moment I first heard about the gel. You're your father's son, Simon, and she'll never be able to say *you* aren't, well, *tall* enough!"

Simon pushed back his chair and stood, refusing to believe he was blushing. "We never had this conversation, Mother," he said, shaking his head. "And, if I'm very lucky, I'll be able to forget it." He walked around the table and pressed a kiss against the woman's forehead. "Now, why don't you just go upstairs, have Kathleen take off those stays, and have yourself a long nap. You look exhausted, and we've got a dinner party tomorrow night, remember?"

She took hold of his neckcloth, holding him at eye level. "And an announcement to make?"

"And an announcement to make," Simon agreed, smiling. "Just don't tell Callie, all right? I'd like to be able to tell her something without her first learning it on her own."

"And she's given up on destroying Filton with you, has she? Given you *carte blanche* to handle the thing without her help, even let her brother in on the fun while still keeping her shut out, locked up safely here in Portland Place, being measured for gowns after weeks of having me to contend with, all the time thinking she was going to help you rout Filton? And all for love of you?" Imogene asked, releasing her son's neck-cloth in order to pick up another piece of bacon. "Now why do I find that so difficult to believe?"

His smile faded slowly as he watched his mother's jaws working, munching on the thick strip of bacon.

Simon remembered Callie's determination, how she'd held a pistol on him, how she'd gone after Noel Kinsey in the middle of the street, in the middle of the afternoon.

He knew how passionately she felt about bringing the man down, punishing him.

Simon knew how angry she'd been when she'd found out he had tricked her, had made her think she was a part of his plan when he'd really meant to cut her out, keep her safe.

He'd seen the almost-hungry look in her eyes when she'd asked how Justyn had done last night, now that he was a part of the plan.

And he believed she would be content to sit back while two men she loved took on Filton on their own, without trying to help them, protect them?

Was he bloody insane?

"I'm an idiot, aren't I, Imogene?"

"Oh, most assuredly, darling," his mother answered smoothly as she swallowed the bacon and then liberated a piece of toast from the pile in the middle of the table. "Better not to let this drag out a moment longer. Get Filton gone tonight, son, as you've boasted you will. Or she'll do it for you. Hurry along now, time's a-wasting!"

What Simon didn't hear as he rapidly strode out of the room, a man with a mission, was Imogene's quiet: "There's a good son. Go off to worry and chase your tail, boy, and it serves you right. I'll teach you to try to hoodwink your poor old mother into staying out of your way. Old? *Ha*! Not me!"

Callie believed she was being forced to endure the longest, most depressing day of her life. Hours and hours had been filled with fittings for her ball gown, and another visit from a scissors-wielding Madame Yolanda. She'd had to endure an hour-long quizzing from the viscountess on the life and times of one Squire Plum. She'd been closeted with Lester nearly forever, attempting to convince that badly rattled young man that the lovable but rather volatile Imogene was *not* about, overnight, to become his stepmother.

And all of this was made even worse by Simon's absence. How dared he say he loved her, and kiss her, and then steer her off to bed with nothing more but a single, searing kiss to cling to, to dream about all the night long?

Where was he? What was he doing? Was he even now sitting across a table from Noel Kinsey, slowly draining his purse? Was Justyn with him? How smart was Noel Kinsey? Was he beginning to suspect a plot against him? Were Simon and Justyn in any danger?

Would the clock stay stuck on the hour of two for the remainder of eternity?

Oh, how she loved Simon.

How she worried about him and his grand plan.

Oh, how angry she was with him!

How she continued to worry, to feel helpless, useless.

Which made Caledonia Johnston long to tweak the determined spoilsport by doing a little "downfalling" of her own. If she only could figure out the *how* of it.

Which, of course—as night follows day, as tears come after laughter, as pride goeth before a fall (Callie could have driven to Ockham and applied to Miss Haverly for more trite sayings that foretold of doom and destruction)—meant that, when the earl of Filton unexpectedly showed up on the doorstep, Callie welcomed him with a broad smile and a full quiver of flirting tricks learned at the knee of the master. That would be Imogene, not Simon.

While Imogene was locked upstairs, Madame Yolanda working her miracles with the dye pots, Callie dragged an unwilling Kathleen into a far corner of the drawing room to act as chaperone, then sat down beside the earl of Filton and proceeded to bat her eyelashes, smile her most winning smiles, coo over and compliment his title, and drizzle compliments on the man's vain head like sugar glazing poured over a hot bun.

She learned that the earl, who could turn a sarcastic phrase but nary a single intelligent one, was a slave to his own consequence, a man easily made to believe that he was the fairest of God's creatures. In his own mind he was complete to a shade, totally irresistible, and—by the time he departed Portland Place—believed without question that he was only a single broad hint away from being accepted by Sir Camber. Sir Camber Johnston, who would doubtless fall on the man's neck, eager to give his daughter—and her new fortune—over to this most clever, magnificent, infinitely superb, titled gentleman.

Not that it had been easy. For one thing, Noel Kinsey was not the most attractive man—at least not in Callie's opinion. Although her brother was blond, and she had nothing against fair men, Filton was underbelly-of-a-fish pale, with the look of one who ventured into the sun only on his way home from spending his nights in gaming hells.

At no more than three-and-thirty, he was already going soft around the edges, running to fat, so that she found herself in very real fear for his waistcoat buttons when he bent over her hand (his kiss against her palm, she knew, should have warranted a slap, but she rewarded him with a giggle instead).

And, worst of all, he flushed a very uncomplimentary puce whenever he became earnest, which he did at least a half dozen times during their half-hour-long visit—each time he had to screw himself up to saying something that flattered her, rather than himself.

In fact, the only ease Callie found at all during their time together was when she would bring up the subject of Noel Kinsey. Noel Kinsey was one subject the self-satisfied man could expound upon at length—and did—on any subject from how well his form flattered his tailor to how distinguished had been his ancestors (all of whom were probably spinning like tops in their graves, listening to the pompous, foolish creature).

But, all in all, Callie considered the interview to be a grand success, and Noel Kinsey had gone away with a disgustingly chipper grin on his face and a lilt in his step, probably already composing an announcement of their betrothal to the newspapers. Simon didn't know it yet, but she had sent him a dithering fool to gamble with at White's, with his head most definitely occupied in counting his bride-to-be's money, and it would be mere child's play to empty his pockets to their linings.

She could hardly wait to tell Simon what she had done. Oh, yes, he'd be angry. At first. But it wasn't as if she had gone out driving with the man. He'd come to her. And she'd helped Simon, she really had. She just needed to point this out to him quickly, that's all—before he strangled her.

With that in mind, Callie corralled Simon the moment he reentered Portland Place an hour before dinner.

Simon listened to Callie as she told him what she had done, a small muscle in his left cheek beginning to throb noticeably halfway through her gleeful recitation. She talked faster, smiled more, and the tic doubled and redoubled its speed. And then, once she was done, he ran the rough side of his tongue up one side of her and down the other, calling her foolhardy, pigheaded, stubborn, reckless. And those were the nicest things he said!

"I hate you," she told him, speaking through gritted teeth.

"No, you don't," he contradicted her, smiling for the first time since she'd waylaid him to tell him of her brilliance. "You love me. Why, you might even adore me."

"Of course I do!" she responded—reasonably, she believed. "Why else do you think I hate you? Well, let me tell you, Simon Roxbury—I'll never help you again!"

Simon was still laughing as she raced out of the room, throwing perhaps the first maidenly fit of her life. It was very lowering, this business of being in love, and Callie remained locked in her rooms for the remainder of the evening. She dined on lovely pheasant rather than brackish water and stale crusts and hoped Simon missed her so much he would come crawling to her, begging her forgiveness.

Instead, Lester showed up around eight, bearing a chessboard and the news that Simon, Justyn, Bones, and Armand had all gone out together yet again, on their way to play their own board game, called "Fleece the Filton."

It was all very depressing. And annoying. Just the sort of annoying that, if she were of a mind for mischief, could lead Caledonia Johnston into one of her "mad starts."

*Love is like the rose: so sweet, that one always tries to
gather it in spite of the thorns.*

—Anonymous

Chapter Sixteen

"He's as good as finished, then, isn't he?" Armand commented as he sat at his ease in Simon's study. "I can see why the fellow stuck to low gaming hells and fleecing green-as-grass youths from the country. He's got the skills well enough for sharping, but not the brains. Only a fool would have continued playing last night, when it was obvious that he couldn't possibly recoup his losses. But, then, he was desperate, and the four of us were the only ones willing to allow him to continue punting on tick."

"It didn't hurt that Callie all but threw herself at his head yesterday," Justyn remarked as he stood in front of the mantel, sipping from a glass of claret. "Any time I thought he might be balking at playing another hand, all I had to do was mention her name, and her *fondness* for him, to have him scrawling his vowels for another hundred pounds. Why, he's into me for over a thousand, and twice that to you, isn't that right, Armand?"

"One thousand to you, two thousand to Armand, three thousand to Simon here, and fifty to me," Bartholomew said, reading from a list he'd pulled from his waistcoat pocket. He raised his head and looked at Justyn. "That's fifty pounds, not fifty thousand," he clarified prudently. "I don't gamble deep. Gambling's a curse."

"Here you go, Bones—add this to the lot. I've put the total at the bottom," Simon said, opening the top drawer of his desk, pulling out a closely written sheet of names and amounts and pushing them toward his friend. "I've bought up every gambling marker Filton has had floating around the city for pennies on the pound—as it seems no one had any great hope of collecting on them once they heard what he owes us—and all of his tradesmen's bills as well. Those I paid for outright, in full measure."

Bartholomew gathered up the paper, scanning it, his expression confused. "These must total over ten thousand pounds! Why would you do that, Simon? We have him on the run. It would only take us another week, perhaps two, and we'd have had him on our own, without needing these."

"Because I want it over, Bones," Simon answered tersely as Armand began to chuckle. "Filton ogling Callie, my drawing room knee-deep in impecunious young bucks and aging roués. I simply want it *over*. Which it is, and has been from the moment, scarcely an hour ago, when I told Filton that I've sold all of his debts to a moneylender who deals in such matters. I also told Filton about Robert and James, just so that he'd know why he was being punished. The tradesmen all have their money, which is a good thing. We received a small pittance of winnings for our trouble—all of which has already been sent off to our charities, gentlemen, with my thanks to you. And Filton gets his own personal dun, a rather forceful, industrious fellow who will have him clapped up in the Fleet in a heartbeat—or worse—if the man hasn't the sense to flee to the Continent."

He looked to the clock on the mantel. "By my reckoning, Filton should be on his way out of London by now, first to hide at his estate, licking his wounds, then preparing for his departure to Calais or some such safe foreign port."

"You're wrong there, Simon," Justyn said, stepping forward. "I saw him not a quarter hour ago, as I was walking here from the Pulteney. Right here, in Portland Place as a matter of fact. I teased him, told him only callow youths come mooning around a young lady's address, hoping for a sight of her. I invited him to accompany me here, but he declined. You know, I don't think Filton's being here is quite a good thing now that you've told us he knows he's entirely rolled up, and that you deliberately engineered his downfall. Do you?"

"Was he on foot?" Simon asked, his voice taking on a sharp edge that had Bartholomew frowning, sure there was something wrong but, for once, not able to put his finger on precisely what.

"He was, but I thought I saw his crest on a coach that drove by a few moments later with him in it, just as I was about to knock on your door. Why?"

"Down, but not out, and a cad to the end," Armand drawled silkily. "I wouldn't let her out of your sight, Simon. She's the only chance he's got left to him."

"It's because of the way she led him on yesterday, of course," Simon said, his voice now most definitely edged with steel. "To hear her tell it, she did everything but drool on his neckcloth, the brat."

"He'd want Callie after a single visit with her?" Justyn asked, clearly bemused. "She's a good enough old thing, but she couldn't have bowled him down that easily, could she? No, wait. It's the dowry, isn't it. I keep forgetting the fool thinks Callie is neck deep in money."

"How very right you are," Armand agreed, nodding. "There is love and then there is love of money, Justyn. What better way to recoup his losses than a marriage to the heiress, the heiress with the conveniently wealthy brother—which has to make the idea twice as lovely? Not above a spot of cheating, I doubt the man would find it too difficult to bend to kidnap and compromise. Which also would, upon reflection, serve to discomfit Simon here, as her guardian, more than a little bit. Inventive little devil, isn't he? What now, Simon?"

"What now?" Simon repeated, sitting back in his chair, twirling his glass of champagne between his fingers. "Callie won't be walking out today, not as I've asked Imogene to keep her close all afternoon, supposedly preparing for the ball. So we won't have to worry about that, if you're right, Armand. And Filton wouldn't be so foolhardy as to believe he could snatch her out from under our noses anyway. He'll soon tire of standing about, waiting for her to appear, and eventually realize that his plan is nothing more than a dream born of desperation. That—or I'll have to do what Callie has wanted to do from the beginning."

"And that would be?" Justyn asked.

"I'll have to shoot him."

"Yes, there is that," Bartholomew said, standing up and wagging a finger at Simon.

"Oh, sit down, Bones, I was being facetious. I'm not going to shoot him," Simon said in exasperation.

"No, no," Bartholomew agreed, nodding his head furiously. "That's not what I meant. You talked about Callie shooting him, didn't you? But what if Filton wasn't here to run off with Callie at all—but to shoot *you*, Simon? I mean, you're all only guessing that he's here because of Callie. He can't be liking you above half right now, could he? I know I wouldn't. Putting a hole in you could be the only pleasure the man has before he's forced to leave England. Lord knows, I'd be tempted, if you'd done as much to me."

"Well, congratulations, Bones, you've done it again," Armand drawled from his comfortable corner. "Simon put it to you to worry, and you've done your usual slap up to the echo job of it, coming up with a not-too-implausible possibility for misadventure none of us has thought of. Simon? Filton couldn't have been best pleased by your visit to him this morning?"

"I didn't linger after telling him what I'd done, hoping for an offer of refreshments, if that's what you mean," Simon said, then shook his head. "No, I don't believe it. Filton is many things, two of them being a cheat and a coward. If he came to Portland Place, it wasn't to shoot me or to run off with Callie, compromise her. It was with the idea of throwing himself on my mercy, hoping for some sort of reprieve. Even then he couldn't screw his courage up to the sticking point, and just crawled back into his coach and ran away. He's probably halfway to his entailed and therefore useless to him country estate by now, his tail firmly tucked between his legs."

"If you say so, Simon," Armand said, walking to the drinks table to pour himself another glass. "But I'd still like to see our mounts brought round in, oh, say an hour? We four might take a ride past his house, to see if the knocker has been taken from the door by then. Callie will be safe enough here, with the servants put on the alert."

"Agreed," Simon said, finishing his champagne, then turn-

ing the discussion to the dinner party that evening, hinting
that he would be making an announcement that would keep
poor Bones speechless for a week.

"Lester, don't touch that, I mean it! They were made ex-
pressly for Imogene, and whatever is left over must be thrown
away," Callie scolded, pulling the plate holding a single
chocolate tart out of her friend's reach and then continuing
with what she'd been saying. "Now, having heard all that I
heard, Lester, what do you think?"

Lester eyed the single chocolate tart with the eyes of a man
who hadn't eaten in days—which was ludicrous, as there
were still bits of powdered sugar dusting his waistcoat from
the cakes he'd been munching on his way to answer Callie's
summons to her bedchamber. "I think young ladies aren't supposed to listen at keyholes, that's what I think," he said,
frowning. "How many did she eat, if there's only the one
left?"

"One, Lester. One. Scarlet prepared two as a special breakfast treat, and Imogene ate one not two hours ago. And this
one is not to be eaten. There!" she exclaimed, tipping the plate
so that the tart slid into the wastebasket beside her small writing desk. "All gone, Lester. All gone."

"That breaks my heart, Callie, I swear it does," Lester
lamented, seeming to blink back tears.

Callie rolled her eyes, then took a quick peek at the small
crystal clock on her dressing table. It hadn't gone noon yet,
and still so much had happened. Imogene had come to her, all
a-twitter, hinting of portentous happenings at the small dinner
party planned for that night, already yawning into her hand as
she began nibbling at the chocolate tart Callie had offered her
even as she complained, yet again, that she would never, ever,

sleep another wink. She had gone on and on about biting stays and energetic squires and sons who never disappoint, then allowed Callie to ring for Kathleen, who took her sleepy mistress off for a small lie-down before luncheon.

Small lie-down, indeed, Callie had thought at the time. And so she thought again now, smiling, knowing that Scarlet had, on Callie's orders, lightly dosed Imogene's chocolate tart with laudanum, just enough to nudge the already exhausted woman into slumber. With any luck, the old dear would have her first good sleep in weeks—not waking until it was time to prepare for the dinner party.

With that one good deed behind her, Callie had then tripped off down the stairs to Simon's study. She had decided it was time she apologized for having taken umbrage at the notion that he, the man who said (or at least sort-of said) he loved her, should also take it into his head to protect her. He had her best interests at heart, after all, not wishing for his beloved to be put within spitting distance of Noel Kinsey as that man struggled to maintain a hold on his rapidly dwindling pocketbook.

She might not like that she had been cut out of the plan to bring the earl down even as her brother had been invited into it, but she did understand Simon's reasons. She even considered them, after giving the matter some more thought, to be fairly laudable.

And, if the door to his study had been tightly shut, not left slightly ajar, and if she had not heard her brother speaking about how he'd seen Noel Kinsey skulking about in Portland Place, and if she hadn't prudently stayed behind that slightly ajar door and listened to all that had been said after her brother's statement? Well, then Callie might even now be having a small lie-down of her own, resting on her bed, dreaming maidenly dreams, hoping womanly hopes.

But the door had been ajar, and she had heard all that her brother said . . . all that Simon and Armand said . . . all that Bartholomew Boothe had opined and suggested.

And suddenly she was back in the game—more than ready to hop in with both feet to protect her beloved Simon, dragging Lester along willy-nilly behind her. The possibility that Simon would not appreciate her help today any more than he had yesterday, or had at any other time she'd offered it did cross her mind, but she ruthlessly pushed it aside.

"Well, what do you think?" Callie asked at last, disgusted with Lester for lamenting the loss of one particular chocolate tart when there was doubtless a kitchen stuffed full of them downstairs. "Do you think Simon's right, and Filton came here to grovel, then couldn't bring himself to knock on the door? Or is he waiting outside even now, either to kidnap me—as if he could!—or to shoot Simon? And don't you think we should do something?"

With a last, long look toward the wastebasket, Lester sat back and spread his arms in defeat. "I don't know, Callie. Why do you ask? Why don't you just tell me what I think, like you always do?" the dear man asked fatalistically, cutting short Callie's arguments before she could voice them and, generally, saving her considerable time all around.

"So, after seeing the little brat on the stallion's back, it was either tattle on her to our father, or teach her," Justyn said, finishing up the last of his second glass of claret. "I chose to teach her." He smiled. "And she's quite good, isn't she?"

Simon nodded. "I'd say she's exceptional. In fact, I can't wait until the Season is over and we can go to the country, so that I can watch her ride like that again." He looked at the mantel clock again and stood up. "I suppose we've settled as much as we can and whiled away a pleasant enough hour. Gentlemen? Shall we take that ride now, and assure ourselves that Filton is nothing more than an unlovely memory?"

"You should stay here, and let us ride ahead, just to be careful," Bartholomew said, not for the first time, so that Simon tossed him a searing look meant to say that he was not the sort to hide from trouble—not that he expected any.

"You think he'd shoot me down in broad daylight, Bones? Noel Kinsey? I can't see it. I really can't."

"I can see him being idiot enough to make a desperate try for Callie before he gives up and goes away," Armand slid in smoothly as he also rose, setting down his glass. "But, no. The man doesn't have the bottom for shooting people. You coming, Bones?"

Bartholomew sighed the sigh of a man never taken seriously and also stood, waiting as Justyn passed in front of him, all four men on their way out of the study—only to be halted by Emery's unexpected presence in the doorway.

"A word, sir, if I may," the butler squeaked, addressing Simon.

"What is it, Emery? Is there a problem with the dinner arrangements? I know we're more men than women, but I'm sure you can manage the seating."

The butler shook his head, then twisted his hands together in front of his waist, looking not at all like a stately butler, but more like a person about to say something he very much didn't want to say. "It's not that, my lord, or even the housemaids, who are scraping chairs from here to there across the dining-room floor for some unknown reason, playing havoc with the wax. It's—well, it's Miss Callie, my lord. She, well, um . . . she's at it again, sir."

"She's *at* it, Emery?" Simon asked, tilting his head as he looked at his butler, who grimaced, then nodded fiercely. "*How* is she *at* it?"

Emery took a deep breath as he looked to each of the four men in turn, then allowed his shoulders to slump as he began speaking. "It's not that I'm not one what can keep a secret," he said quickly, his formal English deserting him as he visibly and verbally became more agitated, "but I don't know what she's about, my lord, and that boy just does whatever she says, and—oh, sir, he really does look most dreadful in pink."

"Pink?" Simon's stomach dropped to his toes. "Emery— are you saying that Mr. Plum is wearing a gown again? Why?"

The butler clapped his hands together a single time as if trying to capture an elusive thought, then intertwined his fingers, as if he was now contemplating falling to his knees in prayer. "I don't know, my lord, truly I don't. But he is, and Miss Callie is wearing her breeches, and Mr. Plum is carrying Her Ladyship's muff, and smiling, and calling it a nice doggie, and—"

"Bones, fetch Emery a glass of claret, if you will," Simon said, helping the butler to the closest chair and pushing him into it.

"That would be the price of one eel-fed horse you owe me, Simon," Armand drawled as he took the glass from Bones and handed it to the butler. "I told you it would be impossible to make her into a demure little miss."

"Shut up, Armand, will you? Just shut up," Simon growled, then lowered his voice and asked Emery to please begin at the beginning and not leave anything out. Just what was Miss Callie doing, where was she now—she was upstairs, wasn't she?—and what did he think she would do next?

The claret seemed to have a bracing effect on Emery, who drew back his shoulders and began his explanation again, this time starting at the beginning and leaving nothing out. "I was downstairs, my lord, in the foyer, checking on Roberts's job of work polishing the door latches, when Miss Callie and Mr. Plum came down. Heading out for a walk they were, Miss Callie said. Only Miss Callie was dressed all in her breeches, and Mr. Plum was—well, you know how Mr. Plum looked, my lord. Silly."

"They were going out?" Simon looked to Armand, who was no longer grinning. Nobody was grinning.

"Yes, my lord, they were. Miss Callie was happy enough at first, too, until Mr. Plum picked up that fur muff of the viscountess's and set in to, well, *petting* it, my lord, and calling it a puppy. He was grinning and sort of *swaying*, and Miss Callie gave him a cuff on the shoulder and said she should have known better than to leave him alone with a wastebasket while she got dressed—that's what she said, my lord, I don't know why. And then she winked to me and said, 'It worked once, Emery, it worked once,' and the two of them went tripping out the door."

"She's bolted! Yoicks and away!" Justyn exclaimed with brotherly exuberance, starting for the doorway. "Loose the hounds, and we'll see if they can pick up her scent."

"But they didn't go anywhere, my lord," Emery protested, tugging on Simon's sleeve as he went to follow after Justyn.

Simon was caught between a towering anger and a dizzying elevation of his sense of the ridiculous. "No? Then they're back in the house?"

"Almost," Emery squeaked, shaking his head again. "They, well, they simply haven't gone, that's all. They're still outside, my lord, walking up and down on the flagway, Miss Callie with her hand under Mr. Plum's elbow as he weaves back and forth, back and forth—like they're *waiting* for someone, or *looking* for something, or something like that." He looked at Simon imploringly. "They're not doing any harm, not really, but I was right to tell you, wasn't I, my lord?"

"I'll throttle the brat!" Simon exploded, brushing past Armand on his way to the foyer. "I don't know how she found out what we're thinking—although I can imagine it—and now she's out to see for herself if Filton is still skulking about. She thinks she's saving me, you know. Oh yes, that's what she's thinking. Of all the harebrained, stupid, idiotic—Justyn, what is it?"

Justyn was standing in the open doorway, caught between racing toward Simon or bounding down the steps to the flagway, his mouth open, his hands balled into fists. "It's the queerest thing. I opened the door just in time to see two men pulling Lester into Filton's coach and driving off with him," he declared, then turned on his heels and opted for running out onto the flagway.

"*Lester?* Why would anyone want to run off with Lester?" Bartholomew asked, although no one answered him.

"Callie?" Simon breathed, momentarily unable to move. "Callie!" he bellowed, breaking into a dead run that had him outside on the flagway in mere seconds, to see the love of his life mounting one of the horses that had just been brought round, as he had earlier requested. "Caledonia Johnston!" he bellowed again, pointing to the flagway at his feet and feeling much like an overburdened parent chastising a misbehaving child. "You get down here right *now!*"

"I can't!" she called to him as the gelding reared up and wheeled about smartly. "Bones was wrong. He wasn't going to shoot you. It's me he's after. The fools who snatched him must have thought Lester was me. Come on, Simon—I've got my pistol. We can catch them."

"Ah, she's got her pistol," Armand drawled with a twinkling smile. "There is that, Simon. One could almost call that being prudent, if one chose to ignore the rest of it. No, I think not. The wager was for demure. You still owe me."

Simon spared only a moment to glare at Armand before relieving a gape-mouthed groom of the reins of his own hack, all the while helplessly watching the love of his life ride off up the street in the direction of the maze of construction and overgrown land that made up the north end of Portland Place.

He ground out a few unlovely words that had Armand giving out with a shout of laughter. He then mounted his horse in a single bound and took off after Callie, who had taken off after the coach—followed closely behind by Armand and Justyn and even Bones, who was holding on to the reins of the groom's ancient mount with one hand, his hat with the other, and trying desperately to get his second foot in the stirrups.

To the casual observer out for an early-afternoon stroll, it must have been a rather bizarre scene—a closed coach, its window curtains drawn tightly shut, lumbering along at top speed, followed closely by five gentlemen riders—two of whom were yelling at each other, two of whom were laughing as they rode, and one who was trailing behind, looking rather bilious as he clomped along on a mount with a back as hard as a washboard and a mouth as tough as old shoe leather.

Not that Callie cared a hoot what Mr. and Mrs. Citizen might be thinking. Oh no. She was much too busy cursing herself for a fool and trying to shout down Simon, who kept telling her to turn her horse and head back to Number Forty-nine.

Why had she insisted Lester accompany her? She could have walked the flagway twice as easily without him at her side, the two of them pretending they were out for a casual stroll while she scanned the street and alleyways for any sign of a skulking Filton intent on shooting her beloved, thick-headed Simon.

And once she'd realized that Lester had gobbled down the laudanum-laced tart while she'd stepped behind the screen to change into her breeches? Well, she most certainly should have altered her plan then, when Lester had begun to giggle and sway, and generally act as silly as she'd ever seen him.

But, no. She had to be stubborn. She had to do things her way. She had to strip a near-boneless Lester of his coat and shirt and pull that ridiculous gown over his head, then tie her best straw bonnet beneath his chin. She had to steer him out the door and directly into danger.

How could she be so stupid!

How could Filton have been so stupid? How could the men he'd hired to snatch Miss Caledonia Johnston have mistaken poor Lester for her? And what were they thinking now, now that they had Lester inside the coach? Surely they would have discovered their mistake by now? Not that snatching Lester was their only mistake—they had already passed by Devon-shire, the last possible turnoff from Portland Place, and were heading straight for the construction at the end of the street, cutting off their own avenue of escape.

"They're slowing down," Simon called to her as his mount came abreast of hers near the end of Portland Place and the beginning of the muddle of half-completed buildings and muddy lanes that bordered on the newly named Regent's Park. She looked to him as he pointed to a mansion that was under construction and said, "They're stopping—there! Give me your pistol."

Reigning in her mount to a walk, Callie obediently reached into the pocket of her jacket and pulled out the long-barreled pistol. She then passed it over to Simon with an apologetic smile. "He wasn't going to shoot you, Simon. It was me he wanted, after all. I did tell you I'd impressed him with my attraction to him, didn't I?"

"Yes, he was after you all right, and it was Lester that he got," Simon bit out angrily as he took hold of the reins of Callie's horse and pulled it to a complete stop as the other three riders gathered around them. "I think he's realized that, brat, and that's why he stopped—to toss Lester back to us like a fish not large enough to keep."

"Filton won't hurt him?" Callie asked, truly worried for her friend as she stared at the back of the stopped coach.

"Not unless there's a profit in it for him. I'm about to explain to him that there won't be," Simon bit out, passing her reins back to her and slipping the pistol into his pocket. "Now stay here so that I know where I can find you and kill you." He then urged his mount forward once more as the off door of the coach opened and Noel Kinsey stepped out, probably in hopes of negotiating some sort of settlement in exchange for Lester's safe return.

Callie pulled back on the reins, keeping her horse from following after Simon's, and turned to Justyn, who was grinning at her as if having a jolly good time. "You heard? He didn't mean that, Justyn. Simon loves me. He does."

"He might love you, brat, but that don't mean he still doesn't want to kill you. Lord knows I've felt the same myself, time and again. Let's just hope Lester's all right."

"It is rather silly, isn't it?" she said quietly, caught between tears and a smile. "I mean—*Lester*?"

"Oh, I don't know. He makes quite an armful of woman," Justyn said, winking at her. "Look, Callie—they've pushed him out of the coach. Either that, or he's fallen out. God—he's staggering about like a drunk and likely to fall into that whopping great hole. Come on, Callie, let's go get him out of harm's way."

Callie looked at Lester, to see her friend weaving drunkenly—knees bent, arms flailing—toward a large excavation ditch near the side of the partially completed mansion. *Honestly*, she thought, rolling her eyes. The man might be able to down a whole chicken in a single sitting, but he certainly couldn't hold his laudanum! "Get him? I don't know, Justyn, Simon said—"

"Simon has his hands full enough with Filton, not that I can't help mentioning that you picked a dashed silly time to start listening to the man when he asks you to do something. Armand, Bones—lend Simon a hand while Callie and I do a little trick we learned at a gypsy fair a few summers ago. Callie, do you remember it?"

Lester had seen them and was waving to them now, Callie's bonnet hanging down his back, dangling from its tied strings. He grinned vacantly as he careened wildly, tripping over stones and walking almost sideways, heading straight (well, not precisely *straight*) for the edge of the deep ditch. "I remember," Callie said, pushing her heels into the gelding's flanks, urging the horse into an immediate gallop.

It took only seconds, from beginning to happy ending, but it felt like hours.

They rode down the cobblestones side by side, as they had often ridden the fields in Dorset, hell-bent for leather, laughing into the wind, brother and sister off on a spree. The horses' hooves struck sparks on the stones, then made dull clumping sounds as they ran out of street and hit against the packed dirt of the construction area where Lester now stood rocking in place, a broad, oblivious smile on his face as he lifted his hand in a drunken wave, calling out, "Yoo-hoo! *Yoo*-hoo!"

Callie spared a moment to look to the other side of the coach, watching as three men scrambled off to disappear into the rubble—obviously not having been paid generously enough to stay and fight for their employer. And she smiled, and gave out with an encouraging shout, as she saw Simon, her dear, wonderful Simon, level Noel Kinsey with a single punch, sending that odious man clear off his feet, to land rump first in a huge mud puddle.

"Lester!" Simon called out then, the coach horses having taken exception to being left without a driver and moving off on their own, so that now Simon also had an unobstructed view of Lester's imminent peril.

"We've got him!" Justyn called out as Callie bent to her left and Justyn—bravely putting his mount squarely at the narrow expanse of ground between Lester and the edge of the hole— leaned to his right and, together, they reached down and grabbed Lester under his arms, lifting him from the ground and carrying him safely away from danger.

Callie would have been packing, if she had any clothing of her own other than the shirt, jacket, and breeches now rolled into balls and tossed in a corner of her bedchamber. As it was, even the gown on her back wasn't her own. So, instead of slamming cupboards open and closed, and tossing gowns and undergarments willy-nilly into a portmanteau, she was forced to pace the carpet in front of her bed, calling herself several dozen kinds of fool.

"He doesn't hate you," Lester said around a mouthful of licorice whip.

"Shut up, Lester," Callie responded shortly, then dropped to her knees in front of him. "Oh, darling, I'm so sorry. I didn't mean that, truly I didn't."

"That's all right, Callie," Lester told her, patting her head. "It's not like I'm not used to it. Shut up, Lester. Sit here, Lester. Wear this, Lester. Don't eat that, Lester." He pulled a wry face. "Should have listened to that last one, I suppose. My head still aches, as if I'd drunk a dozen bottles of wine. What dreams I had this afternoon, as I lay on my bed! I thought I'd been dragged off by woolly bears, then flown up to the sky by a pair of Peg's Sorcerers."

"That's a pair of winged horses, Lester. You know—Pegasus?" Callie blinked rapidly, beating back tears. "And that's all my fault as well. Simon has forgiven me a lot, but he won't forgive me this. You didn't see him, Lester, before he left with Justyn and the others to take Noel Kinsey off to the guardhouse. He was incensed."

"Well, I forgive you, Callie," Lester said. "For all of it. Although it would have been nice if you could have found that nice little doggie. I think he got lost somewhere along the way. Oh, hullo, Simon. You're all back from turning Filton over to the authorities then? He'll really be locked up for stealing me? Callie, look. Simon's here. See? I told you he didn't hate you."

Callie clambered to her feet, then turned her back to Simon, walking over to the window that looked out over Portland Place. Her heart was beating so rapidly she could barely breathe. Couldn't think.

"Yes, Lester," she heard Simon tell her untactful friend. "Filton's locked up, and will be for some time, between his crime against you and his mountain of debt. And your father is downstairs, looking for you."

"He is?" Lester grimaced. "He doesn't know about the—well, about the *pink*, does he? I don't think I'd want to see him just now, not if he knows about that."

"Your secret is safe, Lester," Simon told him kindly, so that Callie could hear Lester walking toward the door. Deserting her. Leaving her alone to hear Simon tell her to go away and never darken his door again.

"Thank you, Simon," Lester said, stopping to shake Simon's hand. "Thank you so much, for everything. Well, I guess I'll be off now. I think I'll search out Roberts before I see m'father, ask him if he's seen the dog I had with me earlier. He may have, yes?"

"Anything's possible, Lester," Simon said kindly.

And then the door closed behind the departing young man. And Callie's heart dropped to her toes.

"You were very kind to Lester," she said as the silence in the room threatened to destroy her.

"I like Lester," Simon said, his voice coming to her from across the expanse of carpet.

"You were kind to Justyn as well."

"I like Justyn," Simon told her, his voice sounding closer, nearer.

She didn't turn around, didn't dare to turn around, look at him. "And Imogene. Your mother. For all that you tease each other, you love each other very much."

"Dear Imogene." He was closer now. She could almost feel him touching her. "She's downstairs right now, her stays gone, delighted, she says, that Bertie likes her better upright rather than swooning about like some dieaway miss," he said, his voice tinged with wry humor. "Yes, she calls him Bertie. And he's calling her Daisy. Says she reminds him of his favorite cow. Imogene's flattered, so I didn't pursue it. Are you all right?"

Callie's bottom lip began to quiver. She hated that. Really hated that. "You hate me."

"I love you."

She shook her head, still refusing to turn around, although the scene outside the window had become an unrecognizable blur as viewed through her tears. "Yes, you love me. But you also hate me. That's why I have to go away now, back to Sturminster Newton. You hate the way I go on mad starts, act without thinking. You'd choke me within a week, were we to . . . well, were we to marry."

"Marry? Now when did anyone ever say anything about the two of us marrying?"

Callie's eyes grew wide as she drew a deep breath in through her nose, then whirled about, fists clenched, to confront the most maddening, infuriating—"How *dare* you!"

His smile nearly earned him a boxed ear. "Hullo, darling. I was beginning to forget what you looked like. Except for the fact that you haunt my dreams, my every waking moment."

"You're impossible, do you know that? *Impossible!*"

"But you love me."

She grabbed on to his coat lapels and gave him a mighty shake. "Yes. *Yes!* I love you!"

His hands closed over hers, partly because he might have wanted to touch her, partly because he probably thought it

prudent to defend himself. "And I love you, Caledonia Johnston. I love you and I'm going to marry you, even if I have to
argue with you all night long to get you to agree to the match.
Tell me, do you think we'll spend our entire lives like this?"

Callie pressed her cheek against his chest, her tears running
freely now. Tears of happiness, tasting of love. "I've learned
my lesson these past weeks, Simon. I was a child when I came
to London, but I'm a woman now. I've got no more time for
mischief."

"Oh, I most seriously doubt that, especially as, at this very
moment, actually, I'm planning a little mischief of my own,"
Simon said as he lifted her into his arms. A moment later, Callie found herself being slowly lowered to the mattress, safely
cradled in his arms, ready and willing to enter his world.

For a long while she kept her eyes tightly closed—as
Simon kissed her, as his hands skimmed over her body, as she
accustomed herself to the delicious weight of his lower body
against hers.

But her other senses seemed heightened because she could
not see, refused to see, was, perhaps, a little afraid to see.

She felt the sleek thickness of his hair as she ran her fingers
through it, her skin tingling as she encountered the hot, burning skin of his throat as her sense of touch told her that her
mind had somehow commanded that she work loose the studs
that held his shirt.

She could smell him, that heady mix of tobacco and good
soap and fresh linen.

She could taste him, the salt on his skin as she pressed her
lips against his bare chest, the tang of the champagne he had
drunk when she raised her mouth once more for his kiss.

She could hear him, as he whispered endearments into her
ear, as he soothed her even as he excited her, as he promised

to take care of her, never hurt her, always love her. Always, always love her . . .

She felt the cool of early evening wash over her heated skin as her buttons opened, as her gown and underclothes fell away.

And still she kept her eyes tightly closed, afraid, just this once, to give in to impulse. She was more than content to let Simon take the lead in this, her greatest adventure.

Her head tipped back, her mind awhirl with strange yet wonderful sensations coming to her from her breasts, the pit of her stomach. Callie struggled to understand how anything could be this wonderful and this frightening at the same time. So moving, yet so entirely paralyzing. So longed-for, yet vaguely feared.

It was only when Simon's hand slipped between her thighs that her eyes shot open, opened wide, and she breathed out, "Simon? Simon, I—"

"Hush, darling," he whispered from somewhere very close, his voice somehow humble, awed, as if he, too, was experiencing something very new, very wonderful, yet at the same time frightening—a trip into an unknown they both longed for without knowing how it would end. "I'm here, Callie. I'm here. I'll always be here."

"Hold me," she asked, uncaring that she had somehow begun to whimper. She felt so small, lost inside a cavernous universe, whirling round and round, going higher and higher, feeling a warmth growing deep inside her, growing stronger, higher, wider. "Hold me!"

"Forever, darling. Forever," Simon breathed against her mouth, moving over her more fully as her body turned to liquid, as her muscles dissolved and a sob tore from her throat at the ecstasy that exploded without warning.

And then, while her mind attempted to assimilate her pleasure, Simon rose over her and settled between her legs, entering her with a swiftness that took her breath away on a small, silent protest of pain that was just as swiftly gone.

"I love you, Callie," he told her as he rested against her, giving her a moment to think, to breathe, before he began to move. Slowly. Gently. Then more quickly. Moving in her, with her, as her body, which certainly knew much more than her mind, responded with a will of its own.

And the pleasure began again. And grew. The excitement. The adventure. All the thrill and verve of life wrapped around them, more exciting than any other adventure. With Simon holding her, with her arms tight around him, with her heart and her life in his hands, they rode to the crest together, and tumbled over the edge.

They lay locked together for long moments before Simon levered himself away from her, looking down into her face. "Are you all right, darling?" he asked, tracing the track of one of the tears that had escaped down her cheek. "I didn't hurt you too much?"

Callie looked up at him in the dim golden glow of fading sunlight. "You didn't hurt me at all, Simon," she told him in all honesty, as all she could remember, all that she ever would remember was how wonderful she felt at this moment, how cherished, how loved, how very complete.

I do believe there are those of us who are more disposed, as it were, to seek the mystery and adventure of the thing, Imogene had said when speaking of the act of love between a man and a woman, and the words came back to Callie now. *You, gel, are one of those lucky creatures.*

Imogene was right. She had all the mischief, the excitement, everything she longed for in this world. Right here. In Simon's arms.

She reached up her hand and cupped Simon's cheek. "Oh, darling, your mother is such a brilliant lady," she said, then dissolved into giggles as his mouth opened, his face screwed up in comical dismay.

"Shh, Simon, we don't have to talk now," she told him, pushing him onto his back and burrowing her head against his shoulder—she fit so comfortably into that lovely small dip beneath his shoulder. "I have years and years to explain it to you."

More
Kasey Michaels!

Please turn this page
for a
bonus excerpt from

Come Near Me

available from Warner Books
Winter 2000

It was like a dream, being inside Daventry Court. A fairy tale. Such beauty, such order, such a feeling of stepping from the mundane, everyday world and into a fantasy land where time stood still, where the outside world went away, leaving only those favored creatures allowed inside its portals.

Leaving only Adam Dagenham, Marquess of Daventry.

Sherry had thought of him all that afternoon. How handsome he was. How friendly. How he had looked at her with those dark, brooding eyes that seemed to reach deep inside her, to her heart, her soul.

She'd made a hideous fool of herself, of course, behaving like a hoyden with no sense of who he was, of the respect his station, his very bearing, demanded.

Had she really pushed the Marquess of Daventry into the stream? Oh, she had, she had! And then she'd handed him her petticoat, which had been beyond anything stupid. Childish.

And yet?

And yet he had seemed to enjoy her company, had even invited her father and her silly self to dinner tonight.

How she'd badgered poor old Mary all the afternoon, trying on and discarding a half dozen gowns and finding none of them suitable, and all of them too childish by half. She'd insisted on rosewater for her bath, and she and Mary had taken turns scrubbing her hair with the finest soaps until it squeaked as Sherry pulled her fingers through the long tresses now piled on top of her head, straining to be released from the combs that held the hopefully sophisticated upswept creation in place.

Mary said she looked slap up to the echo, as fine as any London lady, but Sherry wasn't so sure. She wore no lip rouge, no paint on her cheeks, no fine diamonds in her ears. Her ivory gown was provincial in the extreme, with a neckline much too high and a hem that totally hid her ankles. She looked what she was, a country miss who'd never had a Season, a child who was noticeably lacking in town bronze.

So what was she doing here, surrounded by

beautiful furniture, fine portraits, vases filled with roses cut from the marquess's own gardens? She didn't belong here. She'd bore the worldly marquess to flinders inside of a minute.

"Papa—don't do that. Behave yourself," she warned in an almost violent whisper as she turned away from the mirror in the Daventry drawing room, disappointed in her reflection, and saw her father hefting a vase in his hand, as if considering its weight and worth. "The marquess will be joining us any moment."

Stanley Victor pulled a face at his daughter, but dutifully replaced the delicate vase. "Made 'em in China eons ago, make 'em now in some county up north or so," he said, interlacing his fingers, then pushing them away from his body so that Sherry could hear each of his big knuckles crack in turn. "Just wanted to see if it were the genuine article. Your mama taught me that trick, looking for marks and such on the bottom, feeling the weight. Could buy a fine pack of hounds for the price of this useless bit of plaster here. Pity."

As Stanley Victor measured everything in hounds, Sherry only nodded and tried to engage her father in conversation more suited to the evening. "Are you hungry, Papa? I'm sure you'll enjoy your dinner," she said, hoping against hope he wouldn't tuck his serviette into his collar or find it necessary to compliment his host's gastronomic offerings with more than two or three discreet belches. She loved her father dearly, but even her mother had said the man had the table manners of a pig bumped up to the trough.

"Hungry, is it, missy? Starved half to death is more like it. Look at that, gel," he demanded, pointing to the mantel clock. "It's already marched past five-thirty. The marquess can't be a hunt man. Any fellow of sense knows we have to sit down within the minute if I'm to finish in time to get my rest and be up with the boys."

The "boys," Stanley Victor's hounds, rose at four, baying and yapping and generally letting the world know it was time for them either to be fed or gotten ready to chase a poor fox across the countryside. This explained why Sherry, whose rooms overlooked the kennels, usually slept with a pillow clapped over her head. She liked the boys, truly she did, but there were days she wished her father were more devoted to fishing than hunting. Fishing was bound to be quieter.

"I'm sure His Lordship will join us shortly," she said now, then turned as she heard footsteps in the hallway. A moment later, a nervous smile pinned to her face and her hands fully occupied with trying to find a place to put themselves that wouldn't look either gauche or idiotic, she watched as a handsome young man entered the room.

"Adam, I don't see why I should be dragged into this bound to be stultifying din—" the young man began, then stopped dead, staring at Sherry. "Well, hello there, dear lady," he went on quickly, recovering nicely, if she didn't count the embarrassed rush of color in his cheeks.

A moment later her hand was lifted to within an inch of the young man's kiss, then held for a few seconds before he released her. "Dear lady, I am Dagenham, for my sins, and you must be Miss Charlotte Victor. M'brother failed to mention that he'd invited an angel to dine with us, a goddess. Our humble home is more than honored, and I shall have to slay my brother at once, for seeing you first."

He then turned to bow to Stanley Victor, who was looking the stylishly dressed young man up and down with a fairly baleful eye and a slightly curled lip. "Greetings, good sir," he continued, his voice full of fun, of joy and mischief. "You must be my assignment for the evening. How jolly. Would you care for a drink? Lemonade for you, Miss Victor, of course."

"A drink, is it?" Stanley Victor blustered. "Now there speaks a man of sense, even if he does dress like a popinjay. Oh, close your mouth, Sherry, I'm not going to say anything to put you to the blush. Boy knows he looks like a popinjay. He'd have to, stands to reason. Probably even does it on purpose, thinks himself to be right pretty. Don't you, boy?"

"I often find myself to be adorable, yes," His

5

Lordship answered, winking at Sherry, so that she no longer felt as if she had to grab hold of her father, stuff her reticule into his mouth, and drag him back to Frame Cottage.

She watched as the elegant Lord Geoffrey Dagenham strolled to the drinks table, silently marveling at the dangerous height of his shirt points, the intricacy of his cravat. He poured out two glasses of wine and her lemonade, then served them to his guests, his tongue still behaving as if it were hinged at both ends as he prattled on about the weather, his own hounds, the tour of the Daventry kennels he would give her papa after dinner—all seemingly without taking a breath.

He was a handsome young man, almost classically so. His smile was Adam Dagenham's smile, his eyes, although lighter in color, held the same twinkle. His form, tall and muscular, mimicked that of the marquess, and his hair, dark blond to his brother's black, displayed the same tendency to wave, to resist attempts to keep one unruly lock from falling forward onto a smooth forehead.

He was also nearer her age, probably splitting the difference between hers and his brother's. He was still young enough to be silly, to be amused by her unsophisticated ways. Handsome and witty enough to turn any female head, win any female heart. She liked him immediately, was not in the least in awe of him, and felt she could hold her own with him in any conversation. He didn't frighten her, as the marquess frightened her, intrigued her.

And yet Sherry could only see him as a slighter, paler imitation of the marquess. He didn't make her heart skip when he looked at her. Her stomach didn't do a small somersault when he bent over her hand. Her knees didn't turn to jelly at the sight of his smile, the sound of his laugh.

How odd.

Fortunately for Sherry's still-jangled nerves, by the time the marquess entered, apologizing for being late even as he shook hands with her father, Lord Dagenham and Stanley Victor were deep in conversation centering on the "boys," and her father was too busy to disgrace himself further with remarks about the lateness of his dinner.

Unfortunately, also for Sherry's still-jangled nerves, that left her and the marquess quite alone together as they sat near each other on matching couches—she waiting for some kind soul to announce dinner before her heart stopped completely.

The silence in their corner of the drawing room was deafening as Daventry sipped from his wineglass, looked at her over the rim.

She put down her own glass, aware that it was either be rid of the thing or risk spilling lemonade all over her gown. Did he have to look quite so intense? Half so handsome in his dark blue evening dress? So very different from the laughing man

7

who'd just this afternoon sat rump-down in the stream, then used her petticoat to wipe at a smudge on his cheek?

"You're frightened to death, aren't you, Miss Victor?" he said at last. "Why?"

Another young woman might have laughed off his question, or gone racing from the room, crying. Most every other young woman would have dissembled, lied to him, told him he was mistaken, that she wasn't in the least frightened. Frightened? How silly! Why on earth would she be frightened?

"I'm terrified, actually," Sherry answered honestly, dredging up all of her courage so that she looked the marquess straight in the eye. "As to why, my lord, I should think that's obvious. I don't have the slightest idea why I'm here, or what to say. I may even use the wrong fork at dinner." At this embarrassing thought, she leaned forward slightly, anxiously, to add: "There won't be more than three, will there? Mrs. Forrest taught me what to do with three, but beyond that, I'm afraid, I would totally disgrace myself in front of your very proper servants."

The marquess nodded quite solemnly. "Yes, I see your problem, Miss Victor. We can't have that, can we? I know. I'll have the servants shot."

Sherry looked at him for a long moment, then burst into laughter. "Idiot!" she exclaimed, forgetting all over again that this was the important, powerful marquess of Daventry. "We should only have them face the wall, as so not to witness my faux pas. Shooting them is probably unnecessary, although I must thank you for the offer."

"Ah, there we go," Adam Dagenham said, his smile filling her near to bursting with an emotion she found impossible to name, although it was definitely a very nice emotion. "For a moment I thought I'd dreamed our meeting earlier today. Call me a gudgeon, Miss Victor, and I'll be convinced it really did happen."

She picked up the ends of the ribbons tied beneath her bodice and wrapped them around her finger, avoiding his eyes. "I can't do that, my lord," she said, her head bowed as she bit her lip, refusing to giggle at his nonsense. "These surroundings and your title forbid me."

She felt him move closer as he rose from the couch and pulled a low footstool forward, sitting down beside her. "Then I'll burn down these forbidding surroundings," he said, taking her hands in his, rubbing his thumbs across the back of her fingers. "I'll renounce my title and fortune to Geoff over there, although he'd run through every last penny within a fortnight. I'll live beside the stream, and you can come visit me every day, bringing me your smile, your laughter. And perhaps a crust of bread," he added, chuckling, "as I'd probably be starving."

Sherry raised her gaze, unable to look at his

hands on hers any longer, unwilling to think how easy it would be to raise their clasped hands, to lay her cheek against his tanned skin. "I think you may be insane, my lord," she said, whispering the words.

"Oh, Miss Victor, I'm convinced of that," he answered just as quietly. "It's a sudden madness that settled on me just today. Isn't it wonderful?"

Wonderful. A lovely description, if incomplete. Frighteningly wonderful was probably more exact, or at least that was the conclusion Sherry reached during dinner. Her father, never shy, dominated the conversation, as she picked at course after course, until the entire parade of elegant food-stuffs was finished and His Lordship suggested Lord Dagenham and her father go straight to the kennels to inspect a new litter of hounds.

"You could be a little more subtle, brother," Lord Dagenham said as Sherry blushed to the roots of her hair—she really had been doing that a lot today. "However, as I'm finding myself unmanned by your mooncalf ways, I believe it's probably for the best that I take dear Mr. Victor away. You're embarrassing, old son, really you are. Miss Victor," he said, bowing, "my condolences. Don't let him drool on you, all right?"

"Eh?" Stanley Victor grunted. He looked to the marquess, then to his daughter, and shook his head, dismissing whatever thought had tried to enter it. "No. Couldn't be," he said, oblivious to anything but his dogs, just as he ever was, then he shook his head again and followed after Lord Dagenham, asking him how many pups the bitch had birthed.

"Well, that was uncomfortable," the marquess said, waving away a footman and holding the chair for Sherry himself so that she could rise, then offering her his arm. "Shall we take a stroll in the gardens? The roses are particularly fine this year; unusually early, the gardeners tell me, and almost shamefully abundant. Perhaps you noticed a few in the drawing room?"

"A few? There were at least four vases of roses, as I recall," Sherry smiled up at him as he pushed open French windows leading to a wide flagstone patio. They'd have conversation now, she knew, and she'd probably embarrass herself, and him. After all, what did she have to say that could possibly interest a marquess, a gentleman used to London debutantes? She could only hope she didn't say anything *too* silly.

"Oh, my," she said a moment later, forgetting her fears as she let go of his arm and hastened to the stone stairs leading down to the gardens.

She tripped down the stairs, holding her skirts above her ankles, and took a half dozen steps into the rose garden, then turned to gaze up at the marquess. "I can't believe there are so many different roses in the whole world, yet alone in one garden. I've never seen . . . never imagined!"

She raced to her right, cupping an immense yellow bloom in her hands. "Why, it's as big as a dessert plate! And here," she said, her gaze falling on a bush nearly as high as she was, its inky dark leaves fitting frames for several dozen blooms as white as snow, each as perfect as a snowflake. "And over there," she continued, lost in the beauty that surrounded her inside the huge, walled garden, "that pink. I've never seen such a pink as that. This isn't just a garden, my lord. It's *paradise!*"

Adam Dagenham descended the steps slowly, his eyes never leaving Sherry's face, never looking at the flowers. Her heart stood still, waiting for him to take her hand, to lead her along the curved paths of the garden.

"Yes," she heard him agree as the buzzing in her ears grew louder, as her heart pounded not in fear, but in anticipation. "That's just how I would have put it, Miss Victor. Paradise. A veritable Eden. And not a snake in sight. Shall we take that stroll now?"

This is the story of Adam Dagenham and Sherry Victor. A lovely dream. A Paradise in the making. But is this dream too good to be true?